BOOK 3
OF

The River Quintet

YOUNG LIVES IN A CHANGING WORLD

Johannes van der Zee

JOURNEY OF A DUTCH SAILOR TO A TRADING POST IN NEW NETHERLAND

Ray E. Phillips

Quill Publications | USA

QuillPublications.com
Illustration by Arturo Aguirre

ISBN: 979-8-9899063-2-1

Typesetting by C'est Beau Designs

Preface

Can you imagine finding yourself among people with an entirely different culture, unable to understand their ways and unable to explain yours? It must have been like that when a high-spirited, youthful Dutch sailor met his counterpart among the Woodland Indians of North America. The setting is along Hudson's River in the autumn of 1616.

First, in this story, you must make your way across an ocean with all the challenges of hardships and dangers that are inescapable in the 17th century. The story begins on a ship sailing from the province of Holland heading for the New World on a fur-trading mission. Endured are the unbearable boredom of a becalmed ship and the bone-rattling terror of a savage storm. You will get to know some basic tools of maritime navigation: the telescope, the compass, and an instrument for calculating latitude. Finally, by the time you disembark, you will know about sea shanties, tulips, and the mystique of the sea.

In the New World, you will share the young sailor's adventures in the wilderness: spending a winter in an overcrowded trading post notable for quarrelsome shipmates and "cabin fever" and then sharing intense experiences with a Mohawk Indian, Tail Feather (of Book 1). You will also see some astonishing features of the Hudson River and visit a Mohawk village in the Adirondacks Mountains.

Misunderstandings on the part of Johannes are superimposed on long-embedded prejudices and these, together, represent the collision of vastly different cultures. Long-held European attitudes about "civilized" and "savage" behavior become meaningless. At first skeptical of one another, the two principal characters share their understanding of the celestial system and the inviolable roots of their cultural beliefs. The power of a simple magnifying glass, a romantic moment between Johannes and one of Tail Feather's sisters, as well as encounters with dangerous plants and animals all come up in the story.

The book explores the differences in technology, social customs, morality, and spiritual beliefs, all from the perspective of youthful innocence. The technological achievements of one culture contrast with the Stone-Age implements of another. A paradox, however, slowly emerges: the societal misuse and abuse of advanced technologies, inventions, and methods versus the application of ingenious ways to cope with the harsh realities of forest life. The story of Johannes's visit to the New World opens your window to a panoramic view of the intrinsic values of the Indigenous people, collectively referred to as the "First Nations."

—R.E.P.

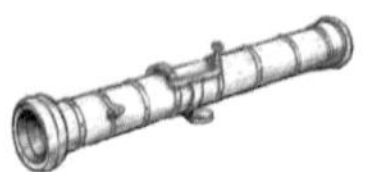

Special Thanks

A note of heartfelt thanks to all those people who have contributed their advice, assistance, and constructive criticism to the creation of The River Quintet:

The late Kenneth Little Hawk, Mi'kmaq-Mohawk storyteller
William "Chip" Reynolds, (formerly) Captain of the *Half Moon* Replica Ship
Janny Venema, author and (formerly) Dutch translator and Associate Director, New Netherland Research Center, Albany, NY
Walter Woodward, Connecticut State Historian
Stefan Nicolescu, Research Scientist and Collections Manager, Yale Peabody Museum of Natural History, New Haven, CT
Barrie Kavasch, author, Institute for American Indian Studies, Washington, CT;
Teachers at the American School for the Deaf, West Hartford, CT
The late Frank Kozelek, Sleepy Hollow, NY
Research staff at various libraries, including those at Kent Lakes, Corinth, and Glens Falls, NY, Windsor, CT and Shepperton, England
Joan G. Sheeran and Wendy Phillips Kahn, editors
Sophie Seypura and Arturo Aguirre, illustrators
and Patrick Seypura, digital publisher and website manager.

—R.E.P.

This reissued and corrected version of Johannes van der Zee *was prepared and published following the death of Ray Phillips in July, 2021. The editors have made minor changes and proofreading corrections and now offer this edition in loving memory of the author. Throughout the writing of The River Quintet Ray Phillips devoted himself during his last decades to bringing history alive with accuracy and compassion.*

—Joan G. Sheeran and Wendy Phillips Kahn

The Dutch Republic

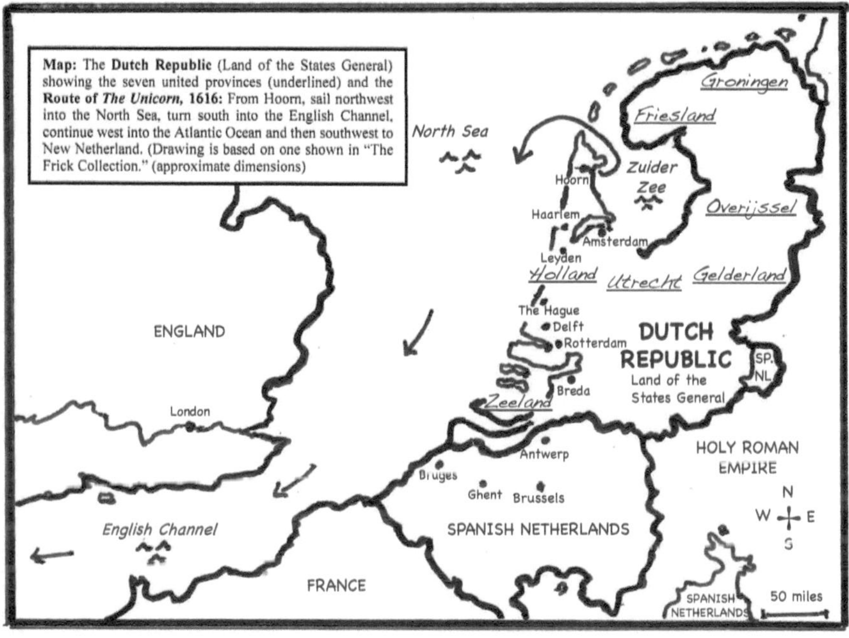

Map: The **Dutch Republic** (Land of the States General) showing the seven united provinces (underlined) and the **Route of *The Unicorn*, 1616:** From Hoorn, sail northwest into the North Sea, turn south into the English Channel, continue west into the Atlantic Ocean and then southwest to New Netherland. (Drawing is based on one shown in "The Frick Collection." (approximate dimensions)

Contents

PART I

The Story of Johannes van der Zee

CHAPTER 1

Outward Bound

High atop the foremast of *De Eenhoorn* (*The Unicorn*), Johannes van der Zee looked down upon a small Dutch universe. All around the harbor, blunt-nosed fishing boats and scows (top-heavy with Norwegian timber) bobbed at their moorings. He watched a sleek yacht under doubled spritsails speed across the bay. In a steady flow back and forth, smaller boats with puffed up sails or oars zig-zagged between ships and shore.[1]

Johannes was but an ordinary seaman and the youngest member of the crew. He knew that he was the least experienced. He fully expected to be given the hardest, the most tedious, and the dirtiest duties of all. Instead, to his astonished delight, the bosun assigned him the lofty station of lookout. There under the sun of early morning, he looked onto the entire village and port of Hoorn sprawled out before him.[2] It was Johannes's first high view of anything, and his head pulsated with excitement.

The wait since dawn on the foretopmast would soon be over. What lay ahead for a young man on a great ship was the thrill of an ocean voyage. He found himself bursting with youthful eagerness and on the top of the world with a breathtaking view.

At one end of Hoorn's long curved beach lay a keel, curved upward at both ends, the backbone of a great ship-to-be. A small army of workmen fitted high-rising ribs along the keel to shape the skeleton. Other workers labored near an oversized black caldron, bending long boards in its spouting steam, boards that would flesh out the ship. Giant tripod cranes lifted the heaviest timber; these would soon become masts.

At the other end of the beach, white bonnets swarmed among the baskets of fish-for-sale like a school of herring trapped in a tidal pool. In between the shipbuilding and the fish market was a broad wood-planked pier crisscrossed by horse-drawn carriages and people in high hats and flowing capes of black and brown. Crates and barrels were stacked up neatly along the edges of the pier.

Just getting high enough to see this view was itself an amazing experience! The young lookout had never climbed a mast before. As a boy, he had never climbed a tree for there were few trees in Holland. But at daybreak he had grasped a long shaky ladder of rope and begun to step higher and higher. Terrified, he had not dared look straight down, placing each foot on the next rung by feel. Instead, he had kept his eyes moving across the distant realm where water and the land come together. Now, once aloft, his feet stood solid on the barrel that made a place for the lookout. He glanced at the deck far below with barely a shudder.

The young sailor drew the floppy brim of his cap down in front for shade. He was careful not to rub against anything where oozing tar would stick to his new duffel breeches or on his new yellow vest. Often, he shifted his weight in the little space to ease his awkward position in the rigging.

Just above him a long orange streamer fluttered, the standard of the Dutch East India Company.[3] Beneath him he heard the gentle flapping of sails slung loosely across the lower yards. Muffled voices of men rang out from the deck. Now and then from far away came the piercing clang of church bells. And above it all, gulls—with graceful, flowing turns as they searched for castaway scraps of fish—kept up their raucous screeching.

With the honor of foremast watch went the close-up glass.[4] Early that morning, the bosun had taken a silver tube from a leather case and solemnly handed it to the new lookout. "Use this well," he cautioned, "and woe be to you should a scratch come to it." It was with pride and a touch of jitters that the youth cradled the precious silver tube as if it were his mother's fine porcelain. Somehow, he had carried it up the rope ladder by tucking it beneath his chin as he shifted his grip from one hold to another.

Johannes took up the long silver tube. Glass on each end glistened. Holding it at one eye, he marveled at the bigness of things that popped into view. For the entire morning, he swept the shore from one end to the other, spying into the private affairs of others under cover of great distance. No one could pass the time aboard a ship with more pleasure.

Glowing in the brilliant mid-day sun the village of Hoorn came into view. The tube showed in detail tiny things that he had not been able to see well before: yellow roofs atop narrow, step-faced houses and tree-lined canals. Rising behind the canal houses was the newly built East Church. Here he had spent many Sundays. Practicing with his "big eye," Johannes found the weathervane, a golden rooster that perched atop the steeple. He smiled to think that the rooster seen in his little round view crowed from a height that was no higher, perhaps, than his own perch on the mast.[5] Towering windmills in the far distance broke up the horizon with whirling white sails. Even beyond them were the greens and browns of cultivated polders, areas of land that had been once under water. And over it all floated a single, scallop-bellied cloud that traced a shadow across the landscape, as a hand might do on passing slowly in front of a well-lit painting.

A pretty view aside, Johannes itched to sail. Already over were his many days of bone-weary labor helping to roll and lift giant kegs of food and water onto the ship and to haul ropes and chains, sails, planks, spare wood, and the thousand-and-one things needed for a long voyage. He had hefted countless bricks and flattened stones for ballast, placing them along the keel as carefully as if setting hen's eggs in a basket. Adding to the cargo were huge bundles of trifles (glass beads and colored cloth) along with hoes, axes, and kettles. These were meant for trading with the *Wilden* in New Netherland for a ship-full of pelts.[6,7,8] Everything else—big or small—had to be squeezed into the overstuffed hold of the ship. Somehow, the crew still had to find a place for dozens of chickens, two sheep, and one squealing pig of enormous proportions.

Here sitting in the harbor was a fully laden ship, readied in every way for a long voyage. Yet it had already strained at anchor for four long days waiting for the blustery wind from the west to let up. On this day, the wind was steady, and it came directly from the south. Even *The Unicorn,* chomping at her anchor bridle, seemed to know that the time for sailing had come at last.

At this moment, however, all that Johannes and his mates could do was to pace idly on deck or fidget in the rigging and listen for a few magical words that would set the whole into motion: words that would free the ship from its underwater grasp of land and send it to New Netherland, an ocean away.

And so, Johannes, like the other sailors, waited. And he waited. After that, he waited some more. As the glaring sun of mid-day beat down on him, he felt beads of perspiration on his forehead. Now and then, he shooed a fly flitting around his head. At times in the heat, waves of giddiness washed over him. "Steady now," he told himself again and again. "Do not faint. Not way up here." It helped to bend his knees from time to time and to wiggle his feet, long numb from endless standing in his little round tub.

As the sun passed well beyond its high of noon, Johannes spotted a small cluster of men at dockside. Fixing his close-up glass on them, he made out the wide-brimmed hats, white ruffled collars, black cloaks and full breeches with tassels at the knees that were the markings of well-to-do merchants. Some sported a long feather in their hats. He knew that the one wearing a red sash for luck was his father. Johannes waved again and again for attention, but, alas, he was too far away to be seen by the plain eye.

The men on the dock conversed with animated gestures or walked nervously in little circles. Suddenly, one of them, in a long flowing robe all black, knelt in prayer. Each of the others gathered round and stood with hands clasped together and head bowed.

A moment later, one of the gentlemen broke away and walked to the edge of the wharf. There, the two men standing on the beach brought him down onto their shoulders and carried him across the debris-strewn beach. They carefully set him dry-footed into the bow of a waiting skiff. The two returned to the wharf for huge sea bags, each one a struggle for two to carry. These, too, went into the skiff. Soon, powerful strokes of oars headed the skiff toward *The Unicorn.*

Johannes tried his best to follow the jouncing skiff through his glass. It was a wobbly view, and the effort made him a bit woozier. Still, he did his best to keep the little boat in sight. He focused on the figure seated at the bow, a figure that held tightly a large roll tucked beneath one arm and something white and wiggling beneath the other.

As the skiff drew closer to the ship, a deckhand announced in hushed voice, "The master!"[9] The words spread quickly across the ship and rose aloft as if carried by an updraft to men standing in the rigging.

The man was tall, lean, and young by all appearances. His beard was short and pointed. Once at shipside, he handed his underarm parcels to the bosun on deck. Then one foot found the hemp steps that dangled from the railing. The shipmaster climbed slowly. At the top, he threw a leg awkwardly over the rail to gain the weather deck. He paused for a moment to preen before the crew, which was wide-eyed with curiosity. His feathered, cone-shaped hat was worn at a jaunty angle. A long and billowing cloak over Spanish sleeves, wide breeches, and knee-high boots loose on top completed his dashing figure. Now it was clear that he carried rolled-up charts. The wiggling, white thing was a dog, small, with curly hair and huge brown eyes.

The shipmaster nodded to the pilot-navigator. No word was exchanged. He ascended the few steps of the stern castle to the hatchway that led into the quarterdeck cabin. In another instant, he vanished through the hatch. The sea bags followed him in the straining arms of others, and they, too, disappeared into the quarterdeck cabin.

Johannes studied the pilot-navigator with more than ordinary curiosity. He wore a black, loose-fitted gown and a necklace of white beads that ran behind his well-trimmed, black beard. The necklace ended in a silver cross that dangled well below. He stood straight as the mast before him. His was a black hat, flat and shapeless, the kind often worn by sea-going men from Iberia. Wing flaps at the sleeves nearly hid his folded hands. Much of the time, the pilot-navigator stood with his hands placed together at the fingertips as if he were praying. His deep-set eyes seemed to pierce into the distance as if looking for some eternal truth. Altogether, his was the air of a sea-disciplined man who wore his fervent religious soul across his face.

The wind blew directly from the south on the ebb tide. All was favorable for *The Unicorn.* Yet, waiting continued while the crew paced aimlessly. "Where are you, shipmaster?" Johannes asked, certain that no one could hear. For him, it was the perfect moment to free a ship from its earthly bondage. "The ship is ready," he added, "all hands yearn to go." With his head queasy, tongue dry, belly empty, and feet gone dead, the eager lookout on the top foremast felt the agony of boredom. "What keeps us here, shipmaster?" he asked again and again. Still, the hatch on the quarterdeck remained tightly shut.

The pail that Johannes had carried up the rope ladder held some biscuits and salted beef. More precious was a tankard of water that he sipped from time to time. The pail had another purpose, and that was for his ordinary relief.

Now and then a gust caused the loosely set mizzen sail suddenly to fill and carry the stern aside. The ship slowly drifted round until it took up the slack of the anchor cable. Then, the sudden strain on the hawser caused *The Unicorn* to shudder. Lines on the rigging became taut with an easy-to-hear snap.

As the day passed, the flagging lookout leaned out from his post with one arm hooked around a shroud, trying to fight the mighty boredom that even his magical, long glass could no longer relieve. He felt the coolness of its smooth, shiny metal on his cheek. He stroked its side with loving caresses as if it were Bello, the little dog he left behind. His fingers lingered over the braided cord around his neck that tethered the long silver tube. Again, and again, he misted the lenses at each end of the silver tube with his warm breath and polished them on his sleeve.

Memories of the summers spent at his grandmother's tiny house by the sea came flooding back. That was where he, as a small boy, heard much about seafaring. Early every morning, he would walk with his grandmother to the sandy coastline to scan the horizon, looking for the return of his grandfather's ship that had left the harbor many years before. Even now, his grandmother held hope that one morning the red sail of Ship-skipper Van der Zee would be there to greet her.

While still reliving those memories, both sweet and sad, the young sailor was suddenly jolted back into the present time by a loud commotion at the pier. He spotted a pair of milk-white horses pulling a flatbed wagon. The horses stopped near the ring of men. From it stepped a stout, hatless, and bespectacled man. Johannes trained his big eye on the gathering. He made out long bows exchanged and brisk hand gestures that brought two workers off the wagon. Each picked up items too small for Johannes to make out, even with his long silver tube. The items were carried one by one from the wagon to a waiting sloop. Whatever they were, each was cradled and placed into the hold with the tenderness befitting the newborn son of a king. The stout man supervised every detail. And the young man on the mast, with life renewed by curiosity, saw it all.

The loaded sloop soon made its way to the side of *The Unicorn*. There, fatherly care brought each object, one-by-one, up the rope step-way. It was only when the coddled things were put in rows on the quarterdeck that Johannes could see what the fuss was about. They were... he squinted through his viewing machine to be sure... they were flowerpots. "Flowerpots!" he whooped in disbelief to no one.

Up to now, Johannes had understood all the complex details that made a ship ready to sail. All the work of securing the rigging and of gathering, loading, and stowing provisions and goods-for-trade had a purpose. Every man on board had a special duty. The chickens, sheep, and pig would serve a need for the outgoing journey. The ship, crew, animals, and cargo all came together as naturally as branches sprout on a tree. But this bewildering sight of flowerpots was too much even for a youthful imagination.

Ordinary seaman Van der Zee counted thirty-six pots in all. In the center of every pot was a small plant. Each plant sat on the quarterdeck, exposed to sunlight but protected from wind by the taffrail. Only when the last pot came onto the ship did the stout man climb aboard. The dangling stairway came up after him, and the sloop drifted astern.

Turning his eyes away from the unusual cargo, the young seaman surveyed the ship once more. Even at anchor, he felt one with it.[10] Weeks before, he was drawn at first sight to its sturdy lines, round at each end, a deep weather deck, and a strong tumblehome. In truth, the ship reminded him of a wooden shoe. As a boy, he had made sailing ships out of many an old shoe. He remembered poking a stick into mid-shoe for a mast and attaching a colored piece of rag for a sail. He launched his toy schooners, many painted with dyes from berries and decorated with a tiny flag, at the shore of the Zuider Zee. How he loved watching his ships pick up the wind and blow across the sea. He always stood watching them until they were out of sight. His little sister sometimes cried at the thought of never seeing the wonderful foot-ships again. He thought, "Would she cry if she could see *The Unicorn* disappear at the edge of the horizon?" He paused for a thoughtful moment, "Yes, I think so."

Now, his ship, no longer a shoe with one mast, had three tall masts, each thick as the biggest trees. At first sight, the inner self of Johannes stirred mightily at the complex web of ropes holding the masts as securely as would deep roots for a tree. He was awestruck at the grand after-castle that rose higher than a church. But what he admired most of the ship was the head of a unicorn that looked out at the bow. It was painted bright red with eyes of deep blue and a white, curled goatee. Sprouting from its forehead came a long, straight bowsprit, white as new-fallen snow. Spiraling grooves ran gracefully around its entire length. Who could not love such a ship?[11]

Of course, the lad had some second thoughts about ocean travel. Men went seafaring only at their own peril and suffering. He had seen ships returning home with only half of the crew, sometimes starving at that. Some ships did not return at all. He remembered all the wives of long-absent sailors in his neighborhood who tried to feed and clothe their children on nearly nothing while never giving up hope. And, didn't his first voyage to the New World with Shipmaster Block nearly end in disaster?[12]

The Unicorn was an old ship; it had never crossed an ocean; it reeked with the smell of tar, stale food, and fish; and, if gossip were true, it leaked badly. The crew was not friendly, and he had barely exchanged a word with any of them during their weeks of fitting out the ship. The last boarded, strange cargo added a new pang of doubt.

As Johannes wrestled with these misgivings, he spotted the hatch of the quarterdeck spring open. The shipmaster's head popped out for an instant. The bosun turned around sharply toward it and as quickly turned back. The hatch closed. Without a moment's hesitation, the bosun raised his head and cupped his hands around his mouth. Out came the words that the crew yearned to hear: "Readddd-yyyy the ship." The command flowed across the deck in a deep and resonating sound. There was a pause for a long, deep breath and then, "Make ready to cast away." These words set into motion the complex process of an ocean-going journey.

The bosun, a short man and as thick as a tree trunk, snapped the first mate into action. "Heave anchor." His sharp, raspy voice somehow told of years of calling orders on a ship.

"Work the capstan," barked the first mate. A hive of men shifted swiftly into position. "Heave aweigh," the first mate prodded. Men leaned against the thick bars that jutted out from the trunk of the capstan. There were two men on a bar and four bars in all. They pushed forward, straining mightily. As they walked, turning the bars round and round, the anchor chain started to wind around the barrel of the capstan.

The eight straining men sang as they plodded in that tight circle. A song for weighing anchor gave rhythm to their slow march.[13] One crisp, clear tenor voice among them rang out:

"A cottage by the Zuider Zee
A polder filled with wheat a'waving
The smell of loaves a'baking
And a churn full of butter."
Then, the other capstan turners joined in:
"We haul the anchor up
Away, away
A sailor's life is far from home
Away, away."

From the heights, Johannes watched the anchor cable straighten in the water as the winding capstan took up the slack. As the men toiled, the high-pitch chant returned:

"A windmill squeaks its merry song
A meadow filled with cows a-milking
A wife with cheese a-turning

Ten guilders in my pocket."
Again, all the voices:
"We haul the anchor up
A-way, a-way
A sailor's life is far from home
A-way, a-way."

The cable groaned noisily as it slid through the hawser-hole at the bow. The anchor was losing its grip in the mud below. Johannes felt the ship drift slowly abaft just as he heard the sharp calls of the bosun, "Hoist staysail."

"Hoist staysail," echoed the first mate. Men at the bow quickly freed a line and a small sail rose above the bowsprit. It soon puffed up in light wind.

"Brace staysail to starboard." Nimble hands quickly tied the line that kept the sail taut.

The ship turned slowly with the bow of the ship headed slowly off wind toward larboard.

"Raise anchor," called the bosun. The first mate repeated, "Raise anchor." Heavy-breathing men at the capstan stiffened with the load. With their turning the cable wrapped farther around the trunk as the dead weight at the far end began to rise.

From the bosun came another command, "Let fall the main course."

"Main course let fall," came the reply of the first mate.

In midship a dozen men sprang into action, letting loose the buntlines and martinets that wrapped around the partly unfurled main sail. The giant belly of the mainsail came down with a thunderous *swoosh* and soon, caught by a gust of wind, billowed out.

The unfurling of the sails of the mainmast reminded Johannes of a preacher in an immense white robe slowly unfolding his arms to welcome his flock to the altar. The young man on the mast was amused to have a view from the pulpit.

Bosun: "Brace main course to starboard."

First mate: "Bracing main course." He turned to his crew, "Haul! Haul away!" Men on deck tugged at the stays. A shanty known to all who go to sea brought the full force of many hands onto the sail:

"Those golden *curls,*
And sparkling *eyes,*
Two rosy *lips,*
I'm coming *home.*"

The sail came in tighter. As it did, the men pulled harder and grunted all the louder.

"In stormy *skies*
On rolling *sea,*
'Neath flapping *sails,*
It's a farm for *me.*"

The giant sail was pulled taut. It lay into the wind without so much as a wrinkle. The entire forecastle was cast in its shadow.

And so—for sail after sail (seven in all, great and small) on three masts—came the practiced ritual of raising or unfurling of canvas. Flying jibs, fore top gallant, main top gallant and last of all the mizzen spanker sails: all came to action. Each, once braced, tightened up under the gentle pressure of wind. The process unfolded with the unwavering surety that petals on a sunflower open in the break of day.

The deck and rigging, which only moments before were as still as a tomb, quickened with overlapping calls and echoes that rang from bow to stern. Men scampered up the ratlines and crept out on the yards. Others hauled in lines, hand over hand, with all their strength. They lifted and they groaned. They pushed and pulled. They sang. Each one reacted to shouted commands with a swiftness that rivaled the thunder that follows lightning.

Johannes could see his ship moving ahead, at first slowly, then ever faster with the setting of each sail. Then he felt the change of pressure in his whipstaff.

Just at the moment when the last of the sails—the spanker—was braced, the eye of the anchor burst out of the water with a tremendous gush. Another turn of the capstan brought into view the flukes, dripping of mud.

"Up and down" shouted the second mate from the forecastle deck. The anchor now hung against the hull from bowsprit to water. The bosun returned, "Bitt the cable. Mind the cat-fall."

The first mate bellowed, "Haul taut the cat-fall." A team of hands struggled to lash the anchor onto its place at the bow. "Not all day, idlers" taunted the first mate. "Put some horses into it." With another hard turn the anchor came to rest snug alongside the cathead.

Slowly, slowly, the ship under much canvas turned until it was broadside to the wind. *The Unicorn* threaded her way between the moored ships. Its bow pointed eastward toward open water of the Zuider Zee. The harbor soon lay directly astern.[14]

From his view above it all, Johannes saw the harbor slipping into the distance. Hoorn was fast becoming little more than a jagged line against a gray landscape. The familiar stench of a seaport town was slowly replaced by the exotic aroma of sea air. Even the flies were left behind.

Johannes could now hear the bow gurgle as it charged through the ripples. He saw the wake spreading out from the stern. What sat like a house a long breath before was now a raging beast with all its sails bent to the wind. Wood, hemp, and canvas worked as one in a perfect blend. Every seaman on a ship, just as every sail and every rope, had its duty. From aft, the low and steady voice of the pilot-navigator wafted across the open space, "Steadyyyy as she gooooesss." *The Unicorn* charged on. And Johannes felt part of it all. "Oh, if only my sister could see me now, sailing on my big shoe!"

The great ship squeezed her way through the narrow sand-edged gap that separated the tip of North Holland and the Island of Texel. People scattered along the dunes stopped their work to watch a square-rigger under full sail head out to sea. They stood in silence for just a moment before returning to their gardens. Peering downward, the lookout saw one small figure running along the shore. It was a boy waving his arms excitedly.

Johannes heard a high-pitch call "Goede reis!" (Have a good trip.) He returned the wave, making great circles overhead with his hat. It was not so long ago that he, too, was a boy, calling to sailors on passing ships, and dreaming of going to lands far away. His hat-waving stopped quickly as he felt his precious instrument nearly slip out of his hand. "Careful now," he reminded himself. "Drop my close-up glass and my life is over!"

As the smell of salt air and the gentle motions of the ship stroked his soul, Johannes had blurry visions of a new and exciting continent. His exotic images came with a sinking feeling. The thought of leaving his mother, father and sister, his friends, his puppy, and the hearty food and coziness of home was awful. Such is the common dilemma of departure for those who challenge the ocean on ships. It brought a sense of depression mixed with exhilaration that is spoken of among sailors as the "bitters and honey of seafaring."

Johannes began to sense the slow roll of the ship. It had been three years since the rhythm of a sea throbbed beneath his feet. Whether the strong pulsing felt deep within was his own heart beating or waves breaking against the bow, he could not tell, and he did not care. It was all the same. On his first journey, Johannes took on as an ordinary seaman. Then, he was just a cabin boy, not a full-fledged member of the crew. And on this day, he became sixteen years old. It was Sunday, the 14th day of August in the year 1616.[15]

And so, the crossing of the Atlantic Ocean began. A unicorn with dark blue eyes, a long, white, spiral-wound tusk, and newly sprouted wings led the way. The sun moved across the sky and fell into a broad pink blush below the horizon. Toward dusk, the bosun saw to it that the flowerpots were watered and placed below where they would be safe from the chill of the night's air.

The coming of darkness brought out a million stars under a sliver of moon. Breaking the unworldly stillness was the faint flapping of canvas and the soft swishing murmur at the bow. Seamen, mostly strangers to one another stood wistful and silent along the waist deck rail, each taking in the salty tang of sea air and each with his private thoughts of whatever fate may be in store for him.

CHAPTER 2

Promises

THE TRANCELIKE SPELL of wind and ship and waves ended abruptly with the bosun's cry: "All hands to weather deck. Weather deck. Now."

Within a breath's time, an assortment of rag-tag men stood crowded in the darkness on deck. Mostly, they were hardened seamen, unshaven and coarse, in tattered clothes of many faded colors. Johannes, relieved of his watch at nightfall, stood among them. Crowded together, the smell of seldom-washed bodies blended with a newly tarred ship and with the salted air to produce what men on ships know as "the fragrance of the high seas."

Hurried together, the crew stood in crowded blackness save for a single lantern. Time passed. No words were traded but for a whispered, impatient curse or two for what seemed a never-ending wait. At last, the waiting came to an end.

The hatch of the quarterdeck swung open. Out stepped a lean figure, back-lit by a small oil lamp in the helmsman's castle. Beneath a broad-brimmed hat, one could hardly make out the face. The eyes, however, seemed to be roving, and the jaw jutted forward behind the well-trimmed beard. Here was the complete picture of the ocean-going shipmaster. Yet, there was something about his appearance that spoke of another figure. There was a tremor of his head. He paced nervously back and forth across the high deck of the stern castle. At last, he stopped. Looking down toward the dark-shrouded crew, he spoke, "My name is Vroom... uuuh... Shipmaster Jacob Hendrick Vroom, remember that now." He paused for a long moment, then added, "I am from Amsterdam. My authority is the East India Company."

The voice seemed at once too high-pitched and too fragile for such an important person. Johannes well remembered the voice of Adriaen Block, skipper on his first trip to the New World three years before. He had come to cherish the first words that Master Block spoke to his crew on the night of departure. Block's booming voice spoke of dangers ahead and of the need for all the men to work together. The words that Johannes had memorized were, "As for you who are new to the sea, it will not be easy. Remember, your fate is in your own hands. I expect you, every man of you, to do your best."

Ship-master Block had scanned the faces of the crew, most all of them seasoned by hard years on ships. His head had stopped at Johannes, and his eyes had looked directly into the cabin boy's eyes. "To be a good sailor, you must learn to believe in yourself." These were encouraging words for a frightened boy on his first voyage and away from home for the first time.

Master Vroom's message to his crew was different. He started again in a shaky voice, "Every man is here for one pur-purpose... aaah... to get us to New Netherland and back. Pilot-navigator Escobar will show the way."... There was a long pause. "Mister Ruis van Vliet is bo-bosun. Jaap Steen is first mate. Second mate is "Ignatius va..." No one could make out the rest of the name. "You are mea-meant to do as they say."

His words began to quiver even more. "Mister... uuummm... Laurens Tuinstra from Univer- University at Leyden will see that the tu-tulip plants receive all the care they need. He... also... will be the ship's surgeon. But I want not one of you trouble him with your sniveling."

The words startled Johannes. Men standing before the mast glanced sideways at each other. Are they hearing right? No one dared speak but they fidgeted even more.

"*The Unicorn* has weathered many years carrying lum-lum-lumber from the North Sea and knows many a storm. She is a sturdy fluyt, every bit built in Hoorn. I will, will,... aaah, I will bring her back to Holland filled to the gunnels with pelts. I promise you that."

The shipmaster paused, paced some more, then spoke. The voice now dropped a tone and the words became more deliberate. "I expect every man of you to obey your officers with no de-delay and with no question. I will tolerate no fighting, no laziness, no drunkenness and no blas-blasphemous talk. Be certain that punishment for any violation will be swift and deserving. I promise you that, too."

He hesitated, drew himself up even taller and with both arms held forward, their pointer fingers extended, added with growing intensity in his voice, "Disobedience on my ship is a capital offense." He paused between each word, increasing the volume as he went on, "Make... no... mistake. These... are... my... rules."

The crew froze into a stack of poles. To the man, each one had joined ship to make a few guilders that would carry him for a time through a life of poverty back home. Most had little in mind but to do their duty as best they could with the least possible effort and to return home to their wives and many children in the shortest possible time without getting flogged or maimed in the process. Now they listened to the man who would control their lives until they returned to Holland. The voice was weak, but the message was strong.[16]

Master Vroom paused again, cleared his voice with a muffled cough, as if to catch his thoughts and continue his speech. His head shook a bit more and his hands were not steady. Again, he walked back and forth across the deck. He stopped suddenly. There followed a long moment of awkward stillness. Every ear strained for the next words from the stern castle. Then, barely heard was, "God ble- bless this voyage." Vroom whipped around and retreated through the hatchway on the quarterdeck. It shut behind him.

In the near blackness, heavy silence hung on the weather deck much the way a dense fog lies on an early morning meadow. One by one, the hands-on-deck melted away to return to their duties or to their berths.

It was not the stirring speech that Johannes expected from his new master on a great ship. He slowly worked his way below in the dark to find a place to sleep among the coils of rope.

CHAPTER 3

Westward Bound

At daybreak, the helmsman's bell brought the ship to life with eight jarring clangs. Johannes quickly gripped his long glass and slung a rope tied to a pail around his waist. In the pail he carried the new day's ration of hard biscuit and water. Once in his place on the foremast top, he squinted to take in the first light. Over the stern, the sun barely peaked above the horizon. Across the bow lay an unbroken expanse of water. The cloudless sky was a dazzling blue, bluer than any blue seen on the plates made in Delft. It was a sky seldom seen over sun-hungry Amsterdam.

After a wretched night in the stifling air below deck, the young sailor greeted his high station with welcome relief. The strong smells from animals, the cursing and snoring men, and the creaking of a rolling ship and plain dank filled the night with annoyances. Johannes had not been able to find an empty place atop a coil of rope, and so he slept, or tried to sleep, on hard planks beneath the tiller; it was the only space he could find among the sprawling bodies. The mammoth tiller, swinging back and forth only a fingerbreadth above his head, did not help his night's rest. Now, atop the foremast at the first blush of daylight, he yawned and tried to stretch the dampness out of his bones.

As the sun gained height, the lookout pondered the complex ship below him, with its amazing network of lines, tackles, and canvas. These things were the flesh and bones that defined his present world. His ship was larger than Captain Block's *Tijger*. It was not much longer, perhaps, but very much wider, more like a wooden shoe than a fish. The design was meant to hold as much cargo as possible and still prove worthy of stormy weather. Soon, pelts meant for coats and hats for the well-to-do all over Europe would fill its hold.

Johannes knew that his father was hopeful of a handy profit from a shipload of furs from New Netherland. That he would return home with them, Johannes had no doubt. After all, the big ship was sturdily built. Its size alone would bring it through the most terrible storm. The shipmaster, after all, knew everything there was to know about ocean voyages. At this moment, the trade wind blew favorably from astern. When returning to Hoorn, his master would find the winds for speedy sailing.[17]

Below Johannes, the bosun barked orders until he was satisfied that all the sails were sheeted round as hard to wind as they would go. Then, he ordered, "Let fly the spritsail." The great, square canvas dropped sharply from the yard and began to fill quickly. It was a difficult sail to handle, stretching as it did below the triangle of the bowsprit sail. Once filled, though, it gave a powerful thrust on a following wind. But success did not last long. Very soon afterward an erratic billow caught the sail before it could be properly braced, and the starboard clue snagged on the forestay! As it did, the unruly sail wrapped around and beat against the shrouds without mercy.

"You, up in the crow's nest," shouted the bosun between cupped hands, looking directly up at Johannes. "Out on the bowsprit with you. Let go the snag and be quick about it."

Johannes, for an instant, was stunned. He had no idea about what to do but obey he must. What's more, he was also eager to prove himself as an ordinary seaman. He quickly placed his long glass safely on the lookout platform and climbed down the ratlines. He worked his way through the forecastle shrouds and around a forest of lines and gear at the beakhead. In another instant, he started to shimmy up the bowsprit, now feeling the shudder of the tangled spritsail as it whipped wildly in the wind.

Climbing the bowsprit was not easy. The spiral groove that was carved inside it tended to twist the climber around. Yet, Johannes was pleased to show his agility to a score of onlookers, as if he were one of those high-rope performers who came now and then to the market square in Amsterdam. He fought the spiraling groove to stay on top of the bowsprit and soon found himself at the tip where the snagged sail shook most violently. At the same time, the ship pitched heavily in the slow rollers. Its prow dipped deep into the water, then rose high above it with each coming wave.

Johannes reminded himself of a basic rule of seamanship: always place one hand on something secure. Keeping this in mind, he straddled the bowsprit, gripped the forestay tightly and with the other hand reached out at the nearest part of the wayward sail. With each tug, the sail loosened a bit until the twisted leech line came free. It snapped past Johannes's head with a swoosh, and the end dangled in the sea. Now, leaning out from the bowsprit, his arm outstretched, he waited until the whipping line swung into his hand. The strong tug of the line nearly yanked him off his perch, but determination and a sturdy grip gradually brought it in.

At first, the spritsail tightened a bit as he brought in the leech line. Little by little, the wind filled portions of the sail and began to unwind it from the forestay. Suddenly, with a deafening thud, the whole sail puffed out. Then came the creak of halyards and the shouts that directed the bracing of the sail. As these events unfolded, the young man on the boom could feel the ship surge ahead. Once again, the reassuring call, "Steady as she goes" flowed across the deck. Now, Johannes, more than ever, felt truly a part of the ocean-going crew. He had done something right, something that was important, something that was good for the ship. Never before had he felt such joy in success: not in school, not in his father's trading office, and never at home.

It was in this state that the overjoyed seaman sprawled out along the bowsprit and watched the bow cut through the waves in the same way that a plow breaks the soil after a good pair of oxen. He became aware of the murmur of ripples against the ship that, along with the fluttering of the sails, makes the music and poetry of a tall ship under sail. Old time sailors said that every ship had its own sound; they spoke fondly of "the spirit of the ship." The spirit of *The Unicorn* cast a magic spell on the boy.

It was in this moment of jubilation that Johannes decided to make the most of it. He shimmied out farther on the bowsprit to the very end. With much effort and even more daring, he soon poked his head out from beneath the bowsprit sail so that it was in front of the tip of the horn.

Now, he, Ordinary Seaman Johannes van der Zee of Amsterdam, was at the forward most part of the ship. Behind him rose the dark-shadowed hull topped by a stack of white sails. Far behind that, somewhere beyond sight, was Holland. And ahead, there was nothing but water between him and the New World, not even his ship. He was at that moment in front of the world!

But in seconds things changed. Growing frightened in his awkward perch, Johannes nearly lost his footing as fierce blasts of wind hit him hard and water drenched his clothing. A rogue wave suddenly came out of nowhere![18] It rolled the ship far to starboard. Johannes countered by leaning toward port. Then, the ship rolled sharply to leeward. The unexpected movement caused him to swivel around the wet, spiral grooves on the unicorn's horn. There, he dangled beneath the bowsprit with arms and legs wrapped around for dear life.

The boy used all his strength to right himself time after time, but the smooth, wet bowsprit with the spiral groove did not let him. It was then that he thought about what a fall into the water would mean. Like most sailors, he could not swim. Even if he could, he would only watch the ship as it slowly disappeared into the horizon. No, he did not want to think about that.

How long Johannes hung there just above the splash of the bow, he could not say. He only knew that he was losing his grip on the bowsprit. Soon, his aching arms, rapidly draining of strength, would have to let go. It was then that he felt a strong tug on one ankle.

"Come on lad," came a deep, husky voice. "Up with you or else you'll not get to see the New World." Johannes looked back to see a giant of a man with a broad grin. The tugging slowly brought him along the bowsprit. Soon, Johannes lay on the forecastle deck, catching his breath and waiting for his racing heart to slow a bit.

The young sailor glanced at the man who had saved his life. He was powerfully built, balding but with a ragged, brown beard that hung across the upper half of his chest. The leather-like, speckled skin of his face spoke of many years at sea. A scar stretched across his cheek. His nose was partially missing. A gold ring dangled from one ear. Around his neck was a stout cord on which hung a row of sharp curved teeth. Johannes tried to think of the proper words to give thanks, but before he could, the man was gone.

There was no time to regain his strength. His spirit sank as he saw a new man posted at the lookout and peering through "his" long glass. He had barely recovered from the shock of being replaced when the first mate pressed him into deck service. After all, he was an ordinary seaman, just one of the crew.[19]

Johannes found himself on his knees flanked by other sailors. Each scrubbed away at the hard planks with big, flat-bottom stones. Others sloshed bucketsful of seawater onto the work. The scrubbers tried to keep ahead of the sloshers, but the buckets only seemed to come faster. As the men made their way across the planking, others came along with mops to sweep away the loosened tar and grime. One last splash of seawater left the deck clean and smooth.

The scrub-down began in the forecastle and then moved to the waist deck. The aft deck was the last to be scrubbed down. There, scrubbers were told to clean the quarterdeck quietly; the master did not wish to be awakened by their commotion.

Talking was not allowed during the process. The men had little chance of learning about each other or to complain about shipboard conditions. It was the tradition of sea-going ships, meant to produce more work and at the same time reduce the possibility of the crew plotting against their officers.

On the next morning, the knee-wrecking labor of scrubbing the deck planks would begin all over again. It would go on day after day in the same way. No chilling wind was too cold nor any blazing sun too hot to forego the chore. Only a heavy storm, when all hands were needed to control the sails, was this, the most hated of all the seamen's duties, called off. Everyone suspected, however, that the real reason was to keep the men too busy to cause trouble.

The long morning of scrubbing stirred up a powerful emptiness in the belly. At long last, eight bells rang out. Word passed quickly along, "Bowls to the galley." Those sore of knees and aching of back responded promptly.

The cook, an elf of a man named Niels, stooped in the cramped and low quarters in the forecastle. He had a deep bronzed skin and a one-tooth smile. In front of him, steaming over the coals, sat a huge black kettle. Without a word, Niels took each bowl in turn and filled it, carefully measured, with a ladleful of dark, thick, green porridge.

To Johannes, it had the familiar and agreeable smell of beans, peas, and salted pork.[20] It was the everyday meal served by the *Tijger*'s cook three years before. Certainly, a hot meal aboard ship is always a luxury. When the seas become rough, the fire goes out. Rough water always means that the next meal will consist of rancid, dry food.

Johannes looked for a quiet place to enjoy his hard-earned meal. He squeezed himself into the shadow of the shallop that lay upside down on the weather deck.[21] Once there, he found himself not alone. A young boy with curly, red hair and delicate features sat wedged between the shallop and a barrel of water. His face was ghastly pale.

"Are you...," began Johannes. Before he could say more, the boy retched again and again, then lay face down across some coiled-up lines. It was not unusual for a new sailor to become seasick, but seasickness on a calm day is not a good sign for things to come.

"Tulip!" The call came again, this time more forcefully, "Tulip!"

The boy with the red hair pulled himself up, wobbled on his feet, and still pale as a new sail, started toward the orlop hatch. The last words heard by Johannes were, "Those terrible men!"

Work began again: scraping rust off iron chains, tarring lines, and mending sails. The men kept on until twilight. Then, it was another bowl of green porridge; this time each man received a chunk of hard-dried bread with his filled bowl.

After scraping his bowl clean, Johannes sought out the man who had rescued him from a watery grave. From his size alone it was easy to recognize him in the deepening darkness. There he sat alongside the capstan smoking a long-stemmed pipe that had an enormous bowl. The smoke seemed to rise in great billows.

Johannes spoke directly, "You saved my life."

"Ah, hah. So, you want to be the first one of us to reach New Netherland. You were a fish in a net out there. I just lent a hand." There was a strong hint of Denmark in his words. "Call me Ingmar. Copenhagen is my home. First time on a ship?"

Delighted with the attention of a real sailor, Johannes gave a lively reply, "No. I crossed over one time three years ago." With this, he could not hide a sense of pride. "That time I was just a cabin boy."

"Hear me out, lad. Life aboard ship is dangerous enough, even on good days. You will see for yourself. Take no risks you do not have to. This voyage is an easy one, but anything can go wrong. Look," he said, pointing to his crooked nose and a jagged scar on his cheek: "From a scuffle about nothing."

Something the big Dane said, struck Johannes with curiosity. "Why do you say *The Unicorn* will be easy?"

"The days are warm. The wind is steady. There is plenty of food, even food that is cooked. We will reach New Netherland before the beer and meal have rotted. Do you know of Willem Barents?"[22]

"Yes. Everyone knows shipmaster Barents. His voyages to the Arctic made him famous."

Since Ingmar knew he had a good listener, he went on. "On one of his voyages to Novaya Zemlya, I found out what Arctic sailing is like. Do you know about Arctic sailing?"

"Well, no. I think it must be very wonderful."

"It is cold. And it is dangerous. We chased seals on ice floes for food and fur. One time, a snow bear chased us. Two of my friends were killed before our lances brought him down." The old sailor stroked his necklace. "See, here are his claws."

Johannes listened to the tale of danger with rapture.

"Every day, the rigging gathered ice. We climbed the ratlines to clear the shrouds and sails by beating on them with bare hands to break the ice. Sometimes in a freezing rain, the beating went on through the whole night. A top-heavy ship will go over even in the calmest weather. We were icicles ourselves, living in wet clothes and eating nothing but seal blubber for weeks at a time. The cold was the worst! Just look what frost bite can do!" He held up his left hand and then used it to point to his mangled nose.

Johannes stared at what was left of the sailor's nostrils and at the stubs of three fingers. The fingertips were missing.

"The worst thing was watching our sister ship being crushed between ice floes like a pigeon egg. We listened helplessly through the night to the groans of the ship in her final agony and to the wailing of the luckless crew. Above us, green and red lights swirled in the night sky while around us, frozen bodies piled up on the deck. Our ship could not sail. It was frozen in ice. Spending a winter in a crude shelter on an island of ice, I do not wish to do again. And all this so that a rich lady could wear a fur collar.[23]

"*The Unicorn* will enjoy an easy journey—easy, of course, if it does not meet up with a pirate ship."

The boy's eyes opened wide. "Did you ever...did you ever fight pirates?"

Ingmar looked grim. "See this?" He revealed a long scar on his right leg. "Some ten years back in the Caribbean, a pirate almost killed me. After he slashed me with his scimitar, he slipped on the bloody deck, giving me a chance to bash his skull. We Danes won that battle but, lad, we also lost quite a few comrades. But I think there is less chance of a pirate attack on this journey since we are sailing toward the west."

"Tell me," said Johannes. "*The Unicorn* is a good ship, is it not?"

"Ah, yes. It is double planked. A layer of felt between keeps out wood-eating worms. But she is an old lady, and she leaks. Besides, the bottom is round and made for shallow water. In a heavy sea, she will roll like a drunken man. The 'dragon's breath' may do us in."

"The dragon's breath? What is the dragon's breath?"

"Oh, that? When the wind blows so hard, the ship heels over to the gunnels. Spars snap apart as if they were twigs."

"But, I saw myself," Johannes interrupted, "that *The Unicorn* had new fittings."

"What you saw, lad, was a new figurehead, all carved and painted fancy. That is all. Remember, *The Unicorn* is an old hauling ship with a new face, nothing more."

The story about the ship did not ease Johannes's worry. "Surely, the investors would not send us to New Amsterdam on a ship that is not seaworthy." His words sought reassurance.

"Investing, lad, is a game. A ship is a high risk. No, investors do not care to put money into seaworthiness when they could lose it all, anyway. But, they do want to leave their mark on a successful voyage. The fine-looking *Unicorn* will serve well to interest future traders. With luck, the profits, too, will be handsome."

The comments were honest and wise. They were not the comments, though, that Johannes wanted to hear. As he thought about them later, he saw the red-haired boy pass by, still colorless in the face, carrying a bucket. From the smell, Johannes knew that it held the waste of the animals that were penned beneath the orlop deck. The boy carefully lowered the bucket over the side with a rope and raised it empty. From his own experience, Johannes knew that it would taking many more bucketloads before the chore of feeding and cleaning up after the animals was done for the day. By the end of his watch, Johannes had found a coil of rope worthy of a bed. It was tucked up in the peak of the forecastle, far enough away from the tiller swinging overhead.

Two bells rang at dawn. Johannes roused himself for his morning watch. The second mate sent him back to the lookout on the top mainmast. "Keep a sharp eye," was the second mate's only command. Again, Johannes climbed to the lookout spot with the usual items: the long glass, some hard bread, his jug of water, and a pail. Bruised knees and sorely scraped hands from the work of the day before welcomed the return of his old duty.

And so, he stayed on the narrow platform for the rest of the day, constantly looking out over the water. Whatever he was to watch out for was never clear to him. He tried to keep his eyes on the horizon, but that always remained the same: a long straight line that separated the blue-green of the ocean from the blue-blue of the sky. There was nothing more to see. There was not a cloud. The magic of his telescope no longer brought joy with only the horizon to see. He had no place to sit or walk. He was slowly beginning to realize why the newest member of the crew was given the "privilege" of serving as lookout.

Johannes followed the work of the men as they scoured the deck from head to stern, mended sails, and carved new blocks. He was beginning to feel envy for them. "What is worse," he asked no one in particular, "hard work or sheer, endless boredom?"

The second mate did not call Johannes down even as darkness fell. Had he forgotten about his lonely and hungry lookout high on the top mainmast? But evening at the station had its reward. From his lookout spot, Johannes followed the sun's gradual fall toward the earth and its slow dip behind the horizon, leaving a broad glow. He watched as the colors slowly changed from purple to black, then, as the first star appeared, then as the new moon took position. The order of things was all so familiar yet very mysterious. Soon, other stars came into view. To pass the time, Johannes began to count them as they appeared. At one hundred and twenty, he had to stop counting. He could not remember which ones he had already counted.

Eight bells announced that his watch had ended. It was midnight, and time for a morsel of food, some water, and a good sleep. Tomorrow, he feared, would bring another day exactly like this day. And all the days after that would be the same. Boredom was to be his lot; he had to learn to accept it. Boredom aside, he was determined to be the best lookout that *The Unicorn* ever had.

At the galley, Niels came to life as Johannes entered, looking for food. With his unchanging, nearly toothless smile, the cook doled out a ladle of porridge into the held-out bowl. With it came a tankard of water dipped into a barrel that sat behind the galley. After a full day aloft, the lookout had earned a rock-hard biscuit.

Guided by the light given off by burning charcoal, Johannes found a place to enjoy his long anticipated feast. He was surprised to find the cabin boy already there. The boy sat leaning against some hanging rope and, seen in the dim light, he was clutching a ragged sheet of paper.

Johannes, after a long sip of water, spoke first. "Are you feeling better?"

"A little. You can see, I am a bad seaman."

"You get used to it. Everyone at first feels the sea in his stomach."

"It is more than just being sick," returned the cabin boy. "I hate the men. They make me feed the pigs and some sheep and the chickens. I must clean up the mess. The crew makes me attend to their trifles, all the while making fun of me. They tease me about my red hair and big ears. I have a weak chin, they say. Some even believe that a redhead on board a ship is unlucky. They think I will bring a disaster on them. At least, these are the men who keep their distance from me."

Johannes tried to be helpful, as he dipped his biscuit into the water. "The duties of a cabin boy are not pleasant. But you will learn about the sea. Some day you will remember the journey in a better way."

"I know hard work and long days of it, too," came the reply, "but my nature is not one for the awful smells and the endless tormenting of life on a ship. The only blessing for a cabin boy is that I do not have to climb the masts."

"So, you cannot stand to be high, like I am all day long."

"Yes, but there is a reason. I once fell out of a tree, not a very high one. I was only bruised. Still, that fall haunts me. I often dream of falling, falling forever through space. These are dreams that wake me up in the middle of the night. They terrify me! I wake up sweating and shaking. It may sound silly to you, but I can do nothing to make these dreams go away."

"We are in the middle of the ocean. You will have to change your nature for now. There is no other way." Johannes sensed that the cabin boy did not hear what was meant to be helpful words. He added, "My name is Van der Zee, Johannes van der Zee. I come from Amsterdam."

"I am Reginald. My family name is Tilley. From Leyden. My family was in Amsterdam before. You are the first one to say anything friendly to me."

"Why did you choose to be on a long-journey ship?"

"I heard talk by sailors. They came to Leyden with pockets stuffed with guilders, spending them as quickly as they could. They told about the exciting life of ship faring and about getting rich. They told me that the cabin boy had the best life of all on a ship."

"Did they tell you that gold and silver were found along the footpaths in New Netherland?"

"Yes, they said it was easy to become rich."

"You speak Dutch in an English way."

"I am English. From Yorkshire. My father took us to Holland eight years ago. I was seven years old and my sister Elizabeth was only four."

"Why did you leave England?"

"Religion. My parents believe in God very much. In England, the king allows worship only through priests and bishops. The people in my church want to worship God directly. They went to Holland to have their own church. Each person, we believe should speak to God in his own simple way. The Bible teaches us to be pure in spirit, to read it word for word, to live by every word. We do not like the King's way of church decorations, statues, and robes. For that, they call us Separatists. Have you ever heard of us?"[24]

"Yes, my parents have mentioned them. Why did you not stay in Leyden?"

"Life was hard for me there. When I was nine years old, I started to work in a mill. We made flour. From dawn to dark, every day but Sunday, I heard that windmill clatter away. I collected the flour in big bags after it was ground to a dust. The noise of the mill made my ears ring all night. Even when I was not yet fifteen, the miller made me carry heavy bags of wheat chaff up to the chute on the top platform. That is how we fed the grinding stone. I even came down with miller's cough from the dust. Sometimes I coughed the whole day. My ears would ring all night from the noise. But climbing was the worst part. My back was sore and climbing up to the platform on a rickety ladder made me dizzy.[25]

"Now on this ship my dreams of falling come more often. Sometimes I wake up screaming as I tumble over and over." A wave of retching broke up his talking, but he continued a moment later. "And for that, I am paid a few stuivers a day. My parents take most of that. I spend what I can to buy pencils."

By now, Johannes had eaten nearly all the porridge and had begun to scrape up the rest with his softened biscuit. He tried to think of something comforting to say, but nothing came to mind.

Reginald rested his chin on his upturned hands. "Oh, this sick feeling never goes away. I would rather die."

Johannes tried to divert his attention. "What are you doing with your paper?"

The cabin boy held up a ragged piece of paper. "Just drawing. It is something I like to do. But there is so little..."

"Tulip!" came a harsh shout from the lower deck.

"That's what they call me for my red hair. It is just more teasing."

"Tulip! Where are you?" Laughter erupted from below ship.

"I must go. What will those awful people have me do now?"

With these words, the younger boy sprang up and disappeared into the pitch-dark orlop deck. In his haste, he left behind his sketch. It was tucked into a crevice between shallop and deck. Johannes held it nearer to the lighted charcoal for a closer look. He was astonished to see a view of the ship, drawn from the forecastle. It also showed the soup kettle in the foreground. Beyond that stood the main mast centered on the weather deck. There was the upside down shallop, too. Beyond that, the quarterdeck castle rose above the helm. Roughly sketched in was the pilot at his instruments. In outline was the face of the helmsman, both hands on the tiller. The lines of the ship were strong and the rigging delicate. Johannes carefully laid the rolled-up drawing above a hull knee where it would be safe from flying cinders and splash.

CHAPTER 4

A Seaman's Life

Day after day, a steady wind pushed the ship westward at good speed. Soon days and distance on the high seas merged until the men on the ships lost all sense of time. Their worlds had shrunk into the tiny space of a ship. Now, their fates depended upon the numbers and charts of their navigator.

The routine of ship care and mending went on and on without let up. Scraped raw knees and sore arms washed, scrubbed, washed, swabbed, and washed again the decks from bow to stern. Fingers stuck to one another after wrapping ropes with strings of tar to protect them against wear.[26] Eel skins covered braids of hair to keep them free of tar. Men with needles and thread attended the slightest tear in every sail. Others dangling from hoisted rope seats painted masts and yards, and God have mercy on whoever dribbled a drop of paint onto the deck.

One man on each bilge pump worked the handle to keep up with the constant trickling of water that leaked between the planks. When the main work was done, the bosun put the crew to work polishing brass on capstans, bells, buckets, and harness and cask straps until they shined enough to be fitting for a visit by the Prince of Orange.[27] Then, too, were chains and cables that had to be scraped of rust. These were the mindless tasks that were meant to keep men at sea too busy to think about hatching up any thoughts of mutiny.

Lookout duty meant relief from the labored work. But night watch was worse than hard labor. For Johannes, what had been a thrill soon became tedious. Before it was over, night watch was deadly. No moon was there to give a sliver of light. Staring into black space from the top of a mast for a whole night became a torture. The interval between the helmsman's bell seemed longer and longer. There was nothing to do but listen to the sounds of the ship break through the swells and hear the creaking and groaning of the hull. At least, on day watch he could follow the men in their work far below. Evening watch held the slowly merging spectacle of sunset turning into twilight and beyond. Now in utter blackness, save for the helmsman's small lantern, there was nothing to see, nothing to do, and nothing to report. "For what do I stand here through the night?" he asked. Some nights, by the time eight bells rang, Johannes felt he was going mad.

The helmsman marked the time. His duty was to turn a sandglass over exactly when all the sand had fallen from the top bulb to the bottom.[28] The falling meant the passing of one half an hour. With each turn of the sandglass, he rang a bell, adding an extra ring, up to eight rings. "Eight bells mean four hours," Johannes told himself, "then the count starts all over. I must stand here statue-like waiting until dawn for another set of eight bells. How I suffer from this wretched living death!"

Dawn broke and that brought the look-out something new, something strange. Just as the sun peeked above the horizon aft of the ship, Johannes spotted tiny white puffs in the far distance off the larboard beam. The puffs then vanished as suddenly as they appeared. At first, Johannes questioned his eyes. Perhaps he had gone mad, after all, in the long night. Then he saw them again and again. A look with his close-up glass told him that the puffs were not his imagination gone crazy. Johannes knew his duty, and he performed it with the full authority fitting for his place high on the mast. With his deepest voice, he called out between hands, "Tornados off larboard! Tornados off larboard!"

The bosun was up on the deck in an instant. He alerted the master who stepped onto the poop deck and raised his long silver tube to one eye. He scanned the horizon back and forth. There were no more puffs. Johannes felt his whole insides seize up. But in one last look by the bosun, the water did break in the distance. With this, Johannes heard them both laugh. "Whales!" said one. "They are only whales." Said the other, "They welcome the new day with their spray."[29] And so, Johannes, relieved and ashamed at the same time, stepped down from his long torment in the mast to face the ridicule of the entire crew. Mercifully, no one said a word about his phantom tornados although he thought he heard a snicker or two. And there was a good side to think about, "I make someone laugh where life is always so grim."

Somehow between all the chores, Johannes knew that if he were ever to be promoted from ordinary to able-bodied seaman, he would have to learn all about the sails and rigging and how to tie all the knots. Fortunately, on his first trip, he had learned a little about ropes: coiling a halyard, making an eye splice or a sheet bend, tying a square knot to reef a sail, and a clove hitch to tie to a post. Now, crouched down near the forecastle, he struggled to master the bowline. But with all his twisting and tugging, the knot always came loose.

A large hand reach down over his shoulder and grasped the learning rope. It was Ingmar. He said, laughing, "Heh, lad, let me show you my way."

Turning to face the same direction as Johannes, he held the line in his left hand. He seemed unconcerned about the missing fingertips. “Imagine, the standing line is a tree. Bend a loop on it to make a rabbit hole. The loop must lie over the tree, not under as you did. Now imagine the end of the rope is the rabbit.” It was a strange way to think about a knot. Ingmar held the end with his other hand. “The rabbit comes up out of the hole, see that? He runs behind the tree. Yes? You see that? The rabbit then goes back down into the hole.” Ingmar pulled the standing line tight.

“It is not a pretty knot, but it is good for tying to a ring. It will never let go no matter how hard you pull. Also, it will not jam. Here’s how easy it is to undo.” With a quick push of the rabbit end, Ingmar loosened the knot and it fell apart. “Learn this knot well, lad. It is the sailor’s best friend.”[30]

Even with the forced business of the bosun, there were some quiet moments after dusk to talk. Johannes and Reginald spent many evenings over their bowls of hot pea porridge. It was the same pot that had simmered since the beginning of the journey. Niels kept it full by adding salted pork, dried vegetables and water from time to time.

The English boy had slowly become accustomed to the rolling and pitching of the ship. He had gotten his “sea legs” as sailors called it. After more than a week at sea, he was able, once again, to eat without throwing up. He appeared gaunt but better in spirit and steadier in walking.

“Where did you learn to draw so well?” Johannes asked, his voice showing his amazement.

Reginald explained. “An old miller lives in my alley. Sometimes, late at night he gave me lessons along with his son. The son, who is only ten years, is very good at drawing and with paint. But his father gave me hope of learning, too. He is poor but he gave me these scraps of lead, some charcoal points, and some paper. I did not have the stuivers to buy paint."

"So, you will draw handsome ships if not command them."

"No. Never! The miller's son may become a great painter. My father would not let me waste time on what he spoke of as 'such nonsense.' He told me that artists are the poorest of the poor. Their lives mean nothing in the eyes of God. Someday, when I am older …."

"Tulip!" came a shout from below. Further talk had to wait.

Over time, Johannes learned from Reginald that foreigners in Holland had a difficult time. From the words of his new friend, "The Dutch welcome people from other countries. It is good for business. But —foreigners cannot join a guild to learn a real craft such as glassblowing or woodcarving.[31] The English and the French could never be more than common laborers in Holland. My parents bemoaned my spending a life in nothing but heavy, thoughtless work. And they did not like me to speak Dutch for fear that I will forget our mother tongue. They were afraid that someday I would marry a Dutch girl. Most of all, I think, they worried that I would lose my Puritan ways told in the Bible."

Johannes was eager to hear more, "What was your life like in England?"

"My family lived in Yorkshire. I grew up with many friends. We climbed rocks and ran through the tall grass. All day we could spend in the fields herding the cows or picking berries. Sometimes, we rafted on the river. We worked hard milking the cows and cleaning the barns and house. Yes, we were poor, but we raised our own food. I remember as children that we were content. The only regret of people in the village was that the king would not let us live by the scriptures, only by the pomp of the English church. The vicar saw to that."

"Were you sorry to go to Holland?"

"Yes. The Dutch are good people, and they like to have fun. They work hard and expect their children to do so as well. But they let them laugh and play games, even on Sundays. I wanted to make friends with Dutch boys and girls my own age, but my parents would not let me. They say that their silly behavior is ungodly."

Johannes asked, "Why did you choose to come on this ship?"

"People in our church often talk of going to the New World, either Virginia where it is English or Guiana. They have heard that these places are always sunny and warm and that the mountains and rivers are beautiful. They say that there is much food: fruit and nuts just for picking off trees, streams teaming with fish, and forests filled with game. People believe that the land is good for planting. Mostly, they want to pray to God in a place not yet poisoned by human sin. Hard work and prayer in such a place will reward them in heaven. In this way think the Puritans."

"Then," returned Johannes, "it is love of God that makes them think of the New World."

"Yes. But not only that. Last year my sister started to work in the textile mill, too. She is only eleven years old. It was like that in England. People called children 'idlers' if they did not have some work by the time they were six years old. About my sister, her name is Catherine. My parents saw her getting paler and thinner every day. Her face is dull, and she does not like to talk to anyone. They worry about her all the time. They want to go to the New World before her strength and spirit are broken altogether."

"Then, why don't they go? Ships are always looking for settlers willing to make a new life in Virginia."

"True, and the people in the church talk about it all the time. Some say it costs too much money or that the journey is too dangerous. A few people think that the foreign climate will cause sickness. Others believe it is the only hope of living a pure life according to the Bible. You have been to the New World. What is it like?"

"Life is not easy there," Johannes spoke with confidence. "But it could be a fresh start," he offered.

"Hmmmm," allowed Reginald. "If I find that the New World is as good as people say, I will go home and tell my parents. I will earn enough guilders to pay for their journey. Maybe they will forgive me for running away. Then we can all go and live there. My mother will like the silk and spices." Reginald paused, then added in a low voice, "But I am afraid of the *Wilden.*"

Johannes laughed. "Oh, I lived with the *Wilden* for a whole winter when our ship burned in the harbor. Our crew could never have lived through the terrible winter without their help. They showed us how to make bark houses. They gave us enough food to keep us from starving. They even helped our carpenters build a new ship, a small ship. We called it the *Onrust.*[32] In English, that means 'Restless.' In the spring, the ship was fit enough to take us into a great inland water. We discovered islands. We found that the land where we spent the winter was an island, a long island at that. Master Block told us that..."

But the mind of Reginald was on another worry, "Do the *Wilden* eat people?" he asked.

Johannes chuckled. "No. What have you heard? The *Wilden* are simple people but they can be kind. They are also useful for trade. How else could we get enough furs to please the craze of fashion in every country in Europe? The Dutch do not like the messy art of trapping and skinning animals; they are traders. The *Wilden* are trappers and skinners. My father says that there is much money to be made by trading in fur that the *Wilden* bring in. And they expect but a few trinkets for their trouble."

There remained a look of doubt on the face of the English boy.

Johannes explained further, "Besides, Fort Nassau way up the North River is where we will go. The men talk about a huge fort there with thick stone walls. It has cannons and many guns. Even the blast of gunpowder is enough to frighten the *Wilden* if they ever threaten. You will be safe enough.

"Once"—Johannes began to smile—"our ship passed close by some little boats in a wide part of the river. There was a boy in the last boat. He saw me waving crazily and answered with a timid hand. On a sudden whim, I shot my matchlock in the air. It was my way of greeting them. With the blast, the boy nearly jumped out of his boat. The other paddlers seemed to freeze solid. To show that I meant no harm, I tossed him a gift, my hat. It was a blue hat that my mother had made for me. Spinning, the hat skimmed across the water and plopped into the water close to his boat. The boy picked it up. What happened then, I know not for our ship pulled away. It was all over in an instant, but I will remember that moment for the rest of my life. Later, of course, the bosun scolded me for wasting gunpowder. My mother, of course, scolded me for losing my hat."

Reginald had more questions. "Is it true that the *Wilden* run around naked except for feathers and that they have no proper tools? There are no wagons or windmills. No cows and no horses. They don't even have a clock. Some of the sailors said that the *Wilden* eat strange animals from the sea and forest."

"You ask about too many things at once. The *Wilden* have no cloth; they wear clothes of leather, different from what you will see in Amsterdam. The rest is true. Still, they have clever ways of making tools from wood and stone. They are good at hunting with arrows and at making snare traps. They cannot read or write. They even think that common seashells are more valuable than gold and silver. As I said, they are a simple people."

Reginald seemed satisfied with the explanation. He asked, "What did you miss most when you were so far from home?"

"It seems silly now, but all I ever thought about through the whole winter was cheese. Living with the *Wilden* we had enough to eat, but a thick slice of Gouda for breakfast would have made me very happy."

Reginald turned his questions to more pressing issues. "Why does the water taste so terrible? I get sick with every sip, even after I scrape the green, smelly scum off the top. I cannot even eat my biscuit after softening in the water. Just this morning, I found a maggot in it."

"We have been at sea for more than three weeks," Johannes explained. "Drinking water spoils about this time. It will only get worse. No one knows why it turns bad. Some say it is from the wood in the kegs. Others say that the sea air causes plain water to rot. I have heard talk of tiny animals in water that turns it sour. Who knows?"

Then Reginald spoke in hushed tones, "Have you seen what the surgeon does with our water? Twice a day he pours some on his flowerpots. In the day, they get the best water. At night, the crew is crowded in the orlop deck while the plants take most of the space. The men hate those pots. Still, no one dares complain."

Johannes knew that they should not be talking about this and he replied with an equally soft voice, almost a whisper, "Do the men say why we bring the pots?"

"Oh, yes. The men say that in each pot there is a tulip bulb. You can already see the shoots. The surgeon thinks they will grow well in New Netherland. You know that tulips with beautiful streaks of colors fetch a high price. Merchants think there is a fortune to be made with tulips. They say that the surgeon cares more about those plants than he does about anyone on ship. So, the tulips have good water while we thirst."[33]

"Cheer up, Reginald. If you cannot drink the water, you can always have beer. Beer does not spoil as quickly as water does."

Reginald scoffed at this idea, but the need for something to drink was powerful. The first mate allowed each man two pints of beer a day. Johannes drew his ration for the cabin boy.

"Try this," said Johannes, returning and pressing a mug toward him.

Reginald sipped, then gulped it down as if he had just come upon an oasis in the desert. He paused and with suds on his lips said, "I think my father would rather I die of thirst than drink beer."

"No worry. Every seaman must drink beer to live through a long journey. It stays fresh longer than water. Your father will..."

At that instant, there was a cry from above. Heard then was jiggling of the rigging. A dark form came plunging down.

TTTTHUDDDDDDD.

Two sets of eyes flashed over to a sailor sprawled out on his back across the main deck just in front of them. The fallen sailor did not move except for slow, gasping breaths. A trickle of blood came from one ear. One leg flared out unnaturally from the knee. Tar spilled out of a pot lying on its side nearby. Crewmen quickly tried to revive the fallen man with slaps to the face and sharp calls, "Antoine! Antoine!" Someone splashed a pail of seawater on his head. It made no difference. His half-opened eyes remained unblinking.

At once, the bosun summoned the surgeon. He was a long time coming, from three bells to four bells. He looked over the limp figure, pulled open the eyelids fully, lifted each arm and leg one by one and, in turn, let them flop lifelessly back to the deck as if those of a rag doll.

"Careless, but the idler will be fit for duty by tomorrow," declared the surgeon with a tone of assurance. "Take him below. Find a blanket for him. Give him an extra beer when he wakes." Done, the men quickly returned to their chores. First among chores was scrubbing up the spilled tar.

Johannes pointed to a short board that dangled from the upper main course yard. "See, that is a seaman's chair," he explained to his friend. "A sailor uses it to pull himself up into the spars." Johannes saw that the short board, the seat, was attached to only one line. "So that is why he fell. His knot on the other side pulled free. If only he had tied a bowline! That would never have come loose." He turned to look at Reginald and saw an ashen face. "You need not worry. You heard what the surgeon said. He will recover by tomorrow."

The cabin boy stood weaving from side to side as if the ship were in heavy swells, yet the sea was calm. He shuffled hand over hand along the rail until he came to the stairs. As he struggled to climb down into the hold, his legs gave out at the knees. Johannes rushed over to steady him. He guided his friend to the plank that Reginald called his bed. Johannes's last words of the night were, "Next time, you must drink beer more slowly."

The first news of morning was that the fallen sailor had died. He came from the coast of Flanders, but he had gone to Holland looking for a better life. Few knew anything about him except that he was a fisherman, not yet thirty years old, who had sailed on a long journey only once before. He had come on this one with the promise of better providing for his wife and children. No one knew how many children there were waiting for him in Amsterdam. They said he was a religious man, a Huguenot from the Belgian territory perhaps, but he kept his belief to himself.

Burial at sea was a simple affair. Friends wrapped the body in a tattered brown sailcloth which was weighted at the foot end with a ballast stone. Except for the helmsman, the entire crew gathered around the deceased. Also missing were the shipmaster and the surgeon.

Johannes's thoughts raced ahead as he stared at the canvas-covered body lying still before him. He had never talked to this sailor, and he had seldom seen him talking with any of the others. But Johannes had always marveled at how quick and nimble he was on the ratlines, how he was always in sight pulling on a line or hefting a barrel, and how he never complained. A silent sailor, he was bent in ways that made him different from all the others. Spare moments he had spent crouched up in a corner of the forecastle with his nose in a book.

Johannes was struck by how the soft sailcloth clung to the face. The nose was sharp as in life, and the chin, as square. In between, he half expected to see the sailcloth draw in, then puff out with a deep breath. The unnatural crook of one leg broke up the long flowing line of cloth that covered the body. Here, he thought, was a man meant to climb, to run, to laugh, and to rear children. He had a mind picture of Antoine's children eagerly waiting at the shore as *The Unicorn* returned to harbor in Hoorn. But there was no movement of the cloth.

The last words for Antoine were those said by the pilot-navigator. He held a silver cross high up about his head. A droning voice pleaded, "We who commit the body of this man to the sea beseech God to grant his soul everlasting paradise."

With these words, four sailors lifted the canvas coffin and hurled it over the rail. Johannes and Reginald, standing together silently and solemnly, watched the splash. The body plunged feet-first and quickly vanished into a watery grave. In an instant, all traces of a man were gone.

The next part of the ceremony was holding an auction. The sea bag of Antoine was brought up to the deck and its contents spread out: one nautical tool, a fid, that Johannes had learned, was a tool used to separate strands of rope. Then there were two pairs of socks, a woolen hat, and a wooden cross. Bidding for each possession went on fiercely. The last item, a small book, went without a bid. Perhaps, out of respect to the deceased and perhaps out of curiosity, Johannes shouted above the crowd, "One guilder." He was the only bidder. A quick look through its pages told that there were no pictures. It was not printed in Dutch but rather, Johannes guessed, in French.

The steward kept close track of every transaction. At the end of the trip, he could deduct the cost of each item from the highest-bidder's salary. For Johannes, when he returned to Hoorn, his payment for months of toil would be lessened by one guilder.

Afterwards, the men returned to their chores on deck or on the high poles. They were exceptionally quiet. Perhaps each was heavy in mind with his own fate, mindful of the narrow path between life and death that every sailor dreads. It was the way of life that men on ships have known since the beginning of time.

CHAPTER 5

Dead Man's Breath

IT WAS THE thirty-fourth day since leaving the port. The drudgery of everyday that is common to seafaring had become well established. Mindless work, rancid food, sickness and boredom had taken its toll on the sailors. Tempers were short and grumbling long, however muted.

Music is said to sooth the savage beast, and the sailor who played the concertina did his best. During the first two or three weeks of the journey, dances were held from time to time, and at twilight many of the men used whatever energy was left in them to kick up their heels and to sing in gruff voices with sense of melody, harmony, and rhythm long gone. At this point of the journey, everyone was tired of the musician's songs, and few felt the urge to dance or sing.

It was in this state of lifelessness that tensions among the crew grew to the breaking point. A fight broke out between two seamen quarrelling about their rations of food. One struck the other with a belaying pin across the forehead, and his scalp split open. The ship's surgeon was called from his books and flowerpots to treat the bloodied head. Treatment was a splash of seawater over the gash and an old piece of sailcloth wrapped round and round.

The master was true to his word. Both men soon found themselves confined to the lower hold in the bow, their days to be spent in the darkness and humidity, lying on top of the anchor chain to which they themselves were chained.

Another incident was about disrespectful language to the bosun. It came from a seaman named Julius Hansen, a German from *Ostfriesland,* who was forced to nourish the tulips day after day with the best-kept drinking water. Old Tuinstra, the tulip-surgeon, watched every move so that not a sip of that precious liquid was taken, nor a drop spilled. The seaman complained about this outrage to the bosun who asked him to say no more about it, but to do what he was told.

People standing on the after deck where the conversation took place heard the seaman say, "We are more important than tulips," pleaded Julius. "A word from you could stop this madness now."

The bosun shot back, "I told you to be quiet. Do your duty. That is all asked of you."

Mumbling so it could barely be heard, the seaman retorted, "The tulips will be beautiful, but we will all die from thirst." But the bosun did hear.

Not a turn of the sandglass later, the entire crew was called to stand on the waist deck and to witness discipline at sea. The protesting offender was dragged by a half dozen of his crewmates and lashed to the main mast. There, Julius was condemned to receive twenty strokes of a braided rope across his bare back. The crew watched passively as each lash brought a piercing scream and a splatter of blood and flesh. By the time the flogging had ended, men standing alongside were speckled in red.[34]

Johannes had seen sailors suffer before, but none so needlessly. His disgust with the harsh punishment was matched by the look of glee in the second mate's face as he rendered every stroke with full force. However strict former Shipmaster Block had been with his crew, he never--Johannes remembered--allowed his officers to abuse the men like this. The young sailor turned away from the horror and saw Reginald, ashen white and rocking on his heels. Before Johannes could catch him, the boy knees buckled, and he fell in a heap to the deck.

Twenty blows it was, not one fewer. Toward the end, the poor wretch's screams grew weaker and weaker. Afterward, he hung limp in his bonds as if life itself had flittered away. The body recoiled with a spasm when a bucket of seawater was thrown against the freshly opened skin. "Now, get him out of here," the bosun commanded. Shipmates were allowed to cut him away and carry him off to the stifling hold below. "There," the bosun went on, "the cheeky sailor will think over his words to an officer, and he had better appear for duty in the morning or suffer a less kindly fate."

The lesson for the crew did not need words: anyone who wishes to challenge the officers will bear the full brunt of shipboard punishment. The torment of one will serve as an example for the whole. Unsuspecting, the whole ship was about to endure another form of torment, this one forced on them by nature. It would spare neither crew nor officers.

Even as the ceremony for the back-talking sailor unfolded, the wind gradually lessened, and a mist slowly rolled in toward the ship. Soon, the craft was bathed in a fog so thick that one could scarcely see from one beam of the ship across to the other side. The sails hung limply, and all sounds of the ship's progress in the water ceased.

"Lodeman, what say you?" shouted the first mate. The lodeman from the bow threw his chip log into the water and then ran abaft to haul in its line, timing the run as best he could. Many times the task was repeated. "Well?" demanded the first mate.

The lodeman had an answer. "Speed, under one knot."[35]

Through it all, the bosun directed Johannes back up into the foremast. There, Johannes stood in his barrel throne unable to see the bow of the ship through the fog. Staring for hours at a time seemed more pointless than all the deck scraping and brass polishing. Occasionally, the fog parted enough to see a patch of a flat, gray sea ahead; it lasted but a moment.

On the third of those endless days, watch was broken by a sharp inhuman squeal that came from the fog-shrouded afterdeck. Johannes's inside froze with the sound. The squeal gradually weakened to a gurgling grunt, then stopped altogether. Death-like silence followed. Johannes shuttered to imagine the cause.

After day four under the heavy veil, the fog lifted and with it, the spirits of the men as well. But the wind did not return. The sails drooped. Nothing like this had ever happened to Johannes on his voyage three years before. It was new even to Ingmar. "The old sailors call it 'Dead Man's Breath.' I like it not. The Dead Man's Breath is a weather breeder."[36] Johannes was left to ponder the meaning of Ingmar's words.

The ship sat in the flat sea like a rock in a meadow. The depression and listlessness of the men deepened with each hour. The bosun tried to overcome the mood by pressing on them more useless and wearisome work. The decks were scrubbed twice a day, the rust chipped from chains and the shrouds and seams between planks re-tarred.

The added chores, like The Deadman's Breath, went on day after day for six more days. It was during the beginning of this period that Johannes, relieved of his mast duties for the moment, summoned the courage to speak to the pilot-navigator about a long secret dream. He approached the pilot at a time when he found him alone, scanning the horizon. Johannes had often practiced a speech during his long watches atop the mast. Now, this was his chance, and he braced himself.

"Pilot-Navigator Escobar. My name is Johannes van der Zee." The tall man in the long, black robe did not turn. Johannes steadied and went on, "I am an ordinary seaman, but I wish to become a shipmaster."

"Oh, so you do, do you?"

"Yes, more than anything else in the world."

"That much?"

"It is true. Will you teach me how to use your instruments? I am a hard worker. I am good with numbers." Johannes waiting anxiously for a reply, his heart chugging like vanes of a windmill during a gale. "Oh, sir, I will be most happy if you would," Johannes added with his most refined touch.

"'Tis a long way from an ordinary seaman to a shipmaster," returned the master-pilot as he stood peering along his cross-staff.[37] He turned slowly toward Johannes and stared at him for a moment that seemed like a whole day to the young sailor. He said in his deep voice in Dutch with heavy Portuguese accent, "Have you put your life in the hands of Jesus, son?"

Johannes stammered with the unexpected question. "Yes, yes, I think so." His mind had been on ships and the sea and not on the Heavenly Spirit. "My mother and father go to church all the time," he responded. "Sometimes I go with them." It was a truthful answer, but Johannes suspected that it was not what the master-pilot wanted to hear. He added with confidence one more point, "I am good with the long-glass."

"The long-glass! That is a vile instrument." It was not what Johannes had expected to hear. Pilot-Navigator Escobar explained,

"No man can change the Universe. There is news of a man in Italy who claims that he saw through his long-glass moons moving around the planet Jupiter. He says that the earth moves around the sun in the same way. Rubbish! The earth is the center of the Universe. God made it so. It is blasphemy, son, pure blasphemy."

With these words, Escobar handed the cross-staff to Johannes who had by now given up hope of learning navigation. It was the measuring device that Johannes had seen Escobar use many times. Johannes held the delicate instrument carefully in both hands as if it were a newly hatched crane, just fallen from its nest. "Sight along the staff," the ship's officer began. "Hold the rod so that it lines up with the horizon." Johannes did as he was told. "There. Now move the vane back and forth until the upper edge lines up on the sun."

The fiery thrill of trying the instrument was quickly doused. The sighting forced Johannes to look directly into the sun. Its brightness struck him like with painful shock, and he withdrew his head by impulse. His vision blurred for an instant. Slowly, his eyes returned to normal, first as a series of spots. Then, more and more ordinary things came into focus.

"Try again," implored the pilot-navigator.

Johannes kept trying but the brilliant sunlight spoiled his eyesight. Struggling, he finally fixed an angle between the sun and horizon. The pilot noted a number on the cross-staff, then referred to his quadrant. "You said you were good with numbers. Here is an instrument to find latitude. You may thank seagoing people for plotting it for hundreds of years. The quadrant has served seamen well." He then unrolled a chart, jotting down a point. "We are here, along this line. That is latitude."

Johannes, still seeing sparks from the assault on his eyes, saw the pilot's hand point out a place on the map. "How close are we to the New World?" he asked, pretending as if nothing ever happened.

"See this line?" The pilot pointed to a horizontal line on his chart. "Here. We are somewhere between these points." His hand traced a segment that spanned almost half of the ocean. "I cannot tell the longitude exactly without knowing the true speed of the ship. Without a clock, we only have the guesses from the chip log. I can tell where we will come to land, but I cannot tell when we will get there. I have faith that someday God will give sailors a clock that will work even on a rolling ship. By comparing our time with that of a land point, we can know the longitude."[38]

Johannes stood awed by what was known of the sea. Still, what astounded him even more was how much trouble it was to find out. He rubbed his eyes to clear them of the sunspots. It helped to close them for a spell.

Escobar finally spoke, "Do you still care to learn navigation?"

"Yes. I think so." This time, however, the answer did not sound sure.

"Remember, God through his only begotten son leads us across the ocean. Our instruments we use, but it is we who are the instruments of the Almighty."

Johannes was left wondering what these words meant. Did he say the wrong things? Should he never have spoken out? He had too much time to think about the encounter, and in his mind, it took an ugly turn. For being so bold to speak to the pilot-navigator, he imagined that he would be thrashed against the mainmast and thrown into the lower hold to rot away. He could almost feel the lashes against his back.

At soup time, Johannes expressed his concerns to Ingmar. "No harm would come from it. Iberians believe that God directs everything. I saw you with the cross-staff. Many a navigator has lost an eye with it. Something else," he added. "Be careful, the crew does not take kindly to favorites among the officers."

Johannes did not find much comfort in these words. Reginald, joining him with his bowl, interrupted his musing over them. They had not talked for days. "Are you getting used to the way of seafaring?" inquired Johannes.

"A little. The men are not tormenting me as much. Now, everyone calls me 'Tulip' but I don't mind anymore."

"Good."

"My days are better now," Reginald confessed. "I care not for that awful pig anymore. It disappeared during the night." Johannes knew the cause of the awful squeal heard early that morning. "There are only six chickens now," Reginald went on. "We started with thirty. I don't know where they go, but I don't care."

Johannes, once a cabin boy, knew where they went. The choice meat was for the master and the officers. The rest went into the pot. He thought it best not to tell Reginald, whose beliefs as a Separatist honored the myth of fairness for all.

In a whisper, Reginald pointed out the obvious, "But the food is getting worse. There are now so many maggots in my biscuits that it is hard to see the biscuits."

"Are you drinking the beer?" Johannes asked.

"Yes. It is not bad. I drink slowly, as you told me. The water tastes too vile." He asked Johannes, "Do you like this life?"

"No," returned Johannes after a thoughtful pause. "Still, there is something about being a sailor that gets in your skin. You can curse it every minute on board ship, but when you get back to the common chores of land life, all you can think about is returning to sea. It happened to me. It may happen to you."

"No, I think not," came the quick answer. "But why did you come on this journey?"

Johannes tried to explain something that he did not fully understand himself. "I come from Amsterdam.[39] It is a big city, and my family has a comfortable life. My father is a merchant. He finds good profit in furs from America. Workers in Amsterdam cut them and sew them into long coats and hats. People of great wealth find them quite stylish. My father sells them in France and as far away as Russia. The royal families in St. Petersburg and Moscow are his best customers. He even buys back furs when the coarse outer hair on them is worn out. What is left is the plush inner hair. Used furs are pressed into felt to make hats.[40] All this business back and forth requires good bookkeeping."

"But you do not tell me why you chose this horrible life to get away from bookkeeping."

"Can you read?" asked Johannes.

A little startled by the question, Reginald answered, "Of course. Parents from England make their children work hard to learn to read. Even my little sister can read the Bible. Why do you ask?"

"My father tried to make a merchant out of me. My uncle already makes much money at furs by tending to feltmaking. They want me to join them. I have a good memory and am quick with numbers, but I cannot read well. My teachers thought I could read, but I brought to memory all the pages by having my friends read them to me. It was easy to pretend that I was reading them myself. My teacher or my father never realized it."

"Isn't knowing numbers good for business?" asked Reginald.

"Yes, and here is the truth. I am too restless for bookkeeping. My father's shop faced the Zuider Zee. When I worked in his shop, I spent most of the day watching the boats. Day after day, all I could think of was becoming a master. Imagine me, master of an ocean-going ship. My father suspected my mind was not on his ledgers; I made too many mistakes for someone who was clever with numbers. Only after much pleading did he allow me to go on my first voyage. This time, he spoke to Master Vroom who let me join the crew. Father thinks I will get seafaring out of my head with one more trip. Anyway, I would rather fight the whims of nature than argue with quarreling traders over furs."

"What is your family name?" inquired Reginald.

"Van der Zee."

"That means 'from the sea.' If you are from the sea, why is your father against a sailor's life?"

"My grandfather was a ship master. Between voyages, he often told my sister and me stories of fishing and hunting for seals and walruses in the ice of the North Sea, about ship-tossing storms, and about the hard lives of men who sailed with him. Once he showed us a long ivory tusk that had a spiral groove. The last time I saw my grandfather was at the dock in Amsterdam. We watched his ship disappear into the Zuider Zee. That was five or six years ago. We never saw or heard from him again."

"And because of that your father turned against life on ships," returned the English boy.

"He did, but I can tell you that he made a small fortune when he sold that spiraled tusk to a rich bishop. And now he makes a good living selling things from the sea, but he is always safe. No freezing hands high on the yardarm. No maggot-infested bread. Our canal house in Amsterdam is roomy and comfortable. I have my own bed."

"Then, why do you leave it?"

"Because life there is a bore." Johannes reflected for a moment, then added, "My father owns part of this ship."

"Really? Which part?" asked Reginald.

"I don't know. It is not a real part. It is something called an 'investment.' I only know that he is interested in the ship coming home safely with a full hold of furs. His profit will be ten times greater than the guilders he invested. This ship is much wider that the one I traveled on three years ago; the design is meant to stuff more pelts in the hold. Ingmar says that the ship is yet to be tested in a storm. You say that you hate high places. My great fear is drowning. I awake some nights from a fitful dream, being underwater and about to take that last irresistible breath. I know not why. Perhaps I had an incident at lakeside when I was a small child. Who knows?"

Reginald skirted the unhappy subject of drowning and asked if their ship could get lost in the ocean.

"No, I think not," returned Johannes. "Pilot-Navigator Escobar is very good with his instruments and charts."

Changing the subject once again, Reginald asked Johannes, "Do you have a drawing of yourself?"

"No, of course not. Only rich people have those."

"I am drawing your likeness," the boy said with an air of shyness. "It is almost done. I hope you do not mind."

"Honestly!" Johannes was flattered. "How did you...?"

Eight bells sounded, and it was time for Johannes to take watch on the main topmast once again. Just as he took his first step on the ratline, the bosun called, "Master Vroom wants to see you now. Be quick about it." The voice had a tone that raised suspicion of trouble ahead.

Johannes's heart jumped. His mind said, "It is about punishment for talking to Pilot-Navigator Escobar." His legs stiffened. Breathing stopped for a moment. He forced himself onto the afterdeck, trying not to call attention to himself. He paused for an instant before the hatch that led to the master's quarters. Filled with equal amounts of curiosity and fear, he rapped on the hatch cover. It was the hardest single act he had ever done.

"Yes?" came from inside.

Johannes froze.

"Yes!" Now, the voice was louder, and it sounded annoyed, "Come in!"

Johannes entered, holding his hat in one hand, and bowing properly.

The shipmaster sat at a wide table, his back toward Johannes, his head looking down. Johannes stood there awkwardly. The master drew points on a chart and connected them with a wooden ruler.

Johannes stood anxiously for a long time waiting for a word from the master who appeared lost in his charts. The young seaman was aghast on seeing the huge space of the master's quarters: the full width of the stern. The ceiling was high enough to stand in. Narrow beams of light streamed through small glass windows placed across the transom. There were velvet-covered chairs, a cupboard with china and goblets, and shining swords. Against one wall sat a bathtub. A matted sofa in bright purple was placed just below the windows. On it sprawled a little white, curly-haired dog, its head turning from side to side with curiosity. The shipmaster, totally absorbed in his charts, gave Johannes ample time to look over the scene.

Finally, Master Vroom spoke without turning to look, "Are you the Van der Zee lad?"

"Yes, Master." Johannes' s voice faltered a little.

"I know your father. A fur trader. Rich man."

This bit of information gave Johannes a sense of connection with his past. He waited for more, but there only followed another long period of silent charting. Johannes spotted a large, open book alongside the charts. He also saw a large pewter mug on the table. Next to it sat a white plate picked clean except for the bones of pork chops. In a bowl at Master Vroom's feet were pieces of meat that the dog could not finish.

When Johannes had thought that Master Vroom had forgotten him completely, even after a few quiet but well performed coughs, he heard, "So you want to become a shipmaster?"

"Oh, yes. That would give me great joy," the answer shot back.

Then came another long wait. The master scribbled away on his book. Johannes heard one bell, then two bells. By then, the master leaned back and stared up at the ceiling. It was in this mood that Johannes wondered if he were asleep or in a kind of trance. The shaking of his hands and head was barely noticeable. After an eternity, three bells sounded. The clang startled the master back to life. Without turning, he said, "You can go now."

"It has been a great honor, Master Vroom," was the well-mannered reply.

Johannes bowed politely, passed through the hatch, and up the steps onto the deck. He had the rest of the night curled up in the bow to think about the encounter with the man who held his life in his hands. By morning, he still had not made any sense out of his meeting, and he cursed himself forever having mentioned his dream of becoming a shipmaster.

The ship made no headway for nine days as The Deadman's Breath continued to exert its misery. The sun beat down. The humid holds were stifling. Water was hopelessly stale, and the beer was getting so. The men were ever more irritable and ready to abuse anyone of lesser rank. This showed mostly in the first mate who threatened the men at the slightest infraction.

As if the dreadful calm was not enough punishment, the curse of sea-farers came aboard ship. One of the sailors had become listless and weak. The bosun found many purple marks spread over his legs and abdomen. The sailor had stopped eating biscuits because chewing made his mouth bleed. It was two days before the bosun could persuade the surgeon to see him. His verdict, "Scurvy. It happens first to the laziest ones." The pitiful sailor looked for words that would heal his wounds. Instead, he heard, "There is nothing to do about it. For now, you must continue your duties."[41]

Johannes had heard about scurvy before, always in foreboding tones, and always on long voyages. He had not encountered the sickness, however, on Block's ship. He went to Ingmar to learn more about this strange illness.

"Ah, lad, we call it 'the bite of the devil.' First, the devil takes little nibbles out of the skin here and there. In a few days, there are great slivers of putrid flesh, and the poor soul is left a walking skeleton. The gums blacken and bleed, teeth loosen, the breath is foul, and the joints everywhere are painful and swollen.

"I had scurvy once," Ingmar continued. "It was during our terrible winter on Novaya Zemlya. Look here," he said as he pulled up his pant leg to show a ragged scar. "I got that when we boarded a Spanish ship in the battle. That was before you were born, my lad. Years later with Master Barents, we hunted on the northern ice. We ate only seal meat for more than three months. The old wound, already healed into a strong scar, opened and festered. On that journey, half of the crew died from the 'bite of the devil.' People say it comes from the salt air. I say it is from something wanting in food. Back home in Copenhagen, the wound healed as if touched by an angel."

"Surely, the surgeon can give this sailor something that will help."

"No, nothing. Once it starts on a ship, it spreads fast. But Satan will stop his nibbling when we reach land. It will be too late for this man. I expect he will not last more than a day or two. More will soon follow."

It was on this, the ninth morning with no forward progress, that the cry of "mermaid" was heard. Some of the men pointing excitedly at huge sea creatures that followed the ship. They had seen them up close and described their long, black hair, white skin, long tapered body and wide speckled tail. These, they said, were women who try to tempt sailors into the sea. Now and then, one of the creatures sprang completely out of the water.

Johannes caught sight of them in his telescope. Never before had he seen anything like these creatures, but he knew one thing, they were not women. At that very moment, the bosun called Johannes to the main deck. Surprised, the young sailor's feet were heavy with dread as they carried him toward the helm. It must be about using the telescope.

"The pilot-navigator wants you to take the helm." Johannes was struck dumbfounded. "Quick, now. The helmsman will show you what to do."

"Me! A helmsman?" The thought astonished Johannes.

Johannes knew that the man at the tiller was not much older than himself. Still a boy, the coarseness of his scaling face, the long, bushy beard and gold ring in his ear told of his being a well-seasoned seaman. "My name is De Vries, Jan de Vries. Stand here. Both hands on the whipstaff. Keep your eyes on the main course sail."

De Vries explained, "Feel the motion of the ship as she rolls and pitches. Keep her headed so that the main course sail is always full. If the starboard leech begins to luff, push the tiller toward larboard. The tiller goes toward starboard if the larboard leech begins to luff. The second mate stands on the stern castle. He will give you headings. You get them from the compass. 'N' means north and so on. He will give you a heading for the compass. Follow his instruction."

"Whatever you do," continued the helmsman, "do not forget to turn the sandglass." On the binnacle stood a vertical glass tube in which sand spilled from the top end to the bottom. "As soon as the sand runs out, turn it and let it run the other way. Then, ring the bell. It takes a half hour for all the sand to run out. Here is the rope for the bell. One ring is added each time until eight bells. After eight bells, you start all over again. Understand?"

Johannes shrugged.

"Never forget to keep your eyes on the sand glass and never forget how many rings are coming. The men will not pay much attention to a mistake in steering, but they will have no mercy if they think that a bell is one minute late."

"I can do that," Johannes responded with increasing confidence.

"A-fore you is the compass." For Johannes, this was the most famous invention in the whole world, and he now had the privilege of seeing one for the first time. It was really a bowl of water with a needle floating in it. Letters were inscribed all around the bowl: N, E, S, W, alone and in combinations. The whole was enclosed in a glass dome, and it stood on a pedestal just in front of the tiller.[42]

"See how the needle points to SSW. Keep it that way until the second mate gives another direction." A quick look on the quarter deck spotted no second mate.

With this briefing, the helmsman De Vries left to catch up on his sleep. Johannes suddenly found himself in control of the ship, not sure which way to push the handle, what to look for, whom to ask for help, or why he was there.

Johannes' s view from the helm was little more than the base of the main mast. The course sail hung from the yard as limply as an old shirt. Moving the whipstaff from one side to another seemed not to make a difference in the direction of the ship.

What he had learned so far about the art of navigation was that the ship finds its way half way across the earth with a blinding rod and slot, a needle that floats on water, a glass that pours sand from one side to another, a view that is like being inside a deep cave and a lifeless handle to steer. As he reflected on the words of the pilot-navigator, he came to realize that the Almighty must have had a strong hand in the process of navigation.

Here he was, Johannes van der Zee, an ordinary seaman, sixteen years old, at the helm of a great ship somewhere in an infinite ocean. No matter that the ship had not a whiff of breeze and that it responded not a speck to his touch, it was he who held the whipstaff. Had not great voyagers—Columbus, Magellan, Cabot, and Barents—done the same on their explorations around the world? Dead Man's Breath or no Dead Man's Breath, this was the most exciting time he had ever known.

CHAPTER 6

Dragon's Breath

Through the long, steaming hot night, Johannes stood at the helm, both hands clasped tightly to the whipstaff. The officers slept in their quarters; the crew sprawled across the deck seeking any breath of fresh air. Johannes knew that he— and he alone—was the only person awake on the ship.

In time, the new helmsman heard himself say, "This ship did not roll or pitch. I hear no sound of buffeting sails. The hull does not creak. Even my magic needle lies like a twig on a rock. There are no commands from above. There is not a whisper of wind. Here I am steering a great ship that behaves like a dead horse."

The absence of any life quelled his expectations of adventure. A long, sweltering night turned into a kind of nightmare, as if he were shut up in a tomb. To top it all, his eyes were getting heavier and heavier. Even though he knew that sleeping at the helm was a capital offense, he caught himself in a doze and had to shake his head with great force.

After another turn of the glass, he said aloud, "These falling grains of sand are alive. Yet even their falling seems to be slowing up." When the last grain of sand had passed through, he gave the rope that hung from the bell a good yank. Each clang resounded across the rigging and continued, he imagined, across the water to the New World.

A small measure of relief came with the first blush of dawn. With it came a slight puff from nowhere. Although it was still too dark to see the rigging, Johannes heard the billowing of the maincourse sail. It caused the yard to snap with a crack. It was a fleeting moment that broke up the monotony of the lonely duty. With the breeze came a refreshing coolness.

Puffs gradually became more frequent, and it was not long before the maincourse sail was filled by a steadier wind. Now the tiller gave more resistance. At times, it swung away from his guiding hand. The needle on the compass drifted toward SWW. Johannes felt the ship coming back to life. Now, this was exciting! All he had to remember was to push toward starboard for one direction of luff and larboard for another direction of luff. But which was which; he was not sure. He looked above him on the quarterdeck for help, but no one was there.

With the slowly brightening day, Johannes watched a low-lying bank of dark clouds drift toward the ship. It was not long before stronger gusts made the yard of the maincourse sail shudder. Johannes began to hear other sails come to life. Suddenly, there was a starboard luff in the main sail, and he pushed the whipstaff toward the larboard. The edges of the course sail quivered. Before he could act in proper response, the wind caught the sail from behind, knocking the yard toward the other side with a resounding bang. "Where is the master? Where were the other officers? Why is everyone sleeping?" he said aloud.

The struggle with the whipstaff increased, and the ship began to roll sharply. For an ordinary seaman dreaming of becoming a shipmaster, it was a nightmare within a nightmare.

At last, Johannes heard the call, "All hands." It was the cutting voice of the bosun on the edge of panic. The command echoed in the orlop deck. Soon came footsteps of scampering seamen. The wind strengthened. Flesh-pelting rain added to the turmoil. In the growing light, Johannes saw the sea welling up into snowy crests that broke into a soapy foam. The ship rose to them as they crashed against the hull before rolling away to leeward.

De Vries, ashen faced, entered the helm and grabbed the whipstaff from Johannes. The master then appeared on the quarterdeck and motioned for Johannes to go out onto the weather deck. There he found frenzied action from bow to stern. Men hurried up ratlines to furl the madly buffeting sails. Others closed hatches. The cook doused the galley fire. The steward's men secured the kegs stowed on deck with double lashes.

By now, swirling rain fell in blinding sheets. The wind had gained enough force and the waves enough height to place a fully canvassed ship in danger. The first sails to be brought in were the course sails. The fury of the wind was matched by the fury at which the men went about their work. The spritsails were the next. The mizzen sail was only partly furled against the boom so that it could serve as a weathervane, keeping the bow pointed windward.[43]

The bosun then sent men up the main and fore masts to bring in the topsails. As they were spread across the yards, the master appeared on the quarterdeck. Through the rain, all could see that he wore the full regalia of his office: broad-brimmed, peaked hat, decorated sash, and long boots. "No, Mister van Vliet," he yelled loudly. "Not the topsails." The stammer in Master Vroom's voice had gone, as he called between his cupped hands. "Stay the topsails. Too many days lost already. We will sail through the storm with topsails and mizzen."

The bosun called the men down from the ratlines. Every face among them had a questioning expression as if to say, "Does the master want to kill us all?"

The ship staggered through the breaking seas. The weather deck was awash. Men clutched whatever they could to stay aboard.

The bosun called up the two men confined in steerage. They were brought to the deck and forced to work the bilge pumps. The twisting action of rough water on the ship was letting water pour in between the boards. Fast pumping was necessary to keep afloat. But these wretched men, after nearly two weeks in chains in darkness and nearly starving, had little energy to apply to the task. Still, all other hands were needed for the rigging.

In all the action, Johannes stood immobile, not knowing what to do. He followed a line of black clouds that was rapidly approaching from starboard forequarter. Beneath the clouds, the waves crested, and the wind blew foamy spray off the crests. He heard someone murmur as he past, "The Dragon's Breath comes for a visit."

Reginald, crouching behind the shallop, called to Johannes. "What goes here?"

"We are getting a bit of a storm, that's all," Johannes replied, trying to sound a well-seasoned sailor. The loud roar of wind passing across the ship and a whine in the shrouds, however, did not give much assurance. The ship began a rocking action that set one's balance awry. "So, this is a ship made for shallow water," thought Johannes. "Ingmar was right about too much roll in heavy seas."

The water churned ever more, bring crashing waves as tall as the hull and tipping the ship to her gunnels. At times, it nosed up on a swell only to plunge into the trough, putting the stern high up and the bow cutting into the water as if it were a plough.

In the deepest troughs, the men on deck could not see over the crests of swells on either side, as if the seas were smothering the ship. But the ship did rise and, now and then and for the briefest moment, lifted high out of its natural element and sat atop a mountain-sized crest. Water drained off the ship in cascades as she rose, only to bury the deck once again as she slid down into a watery canyon between mountainous swells.

Wave after wave slapped against the bow, cascaded down the forecastle and spilled out at the waist deck with an eruption of spray and foam. Now, two men struggled with the whipstaff, each lashed to his own station. Seamen on deck held onto the standing rigging for dear life as great rushes of water pour past them.

Through it all, Johannes noticed golden sunbeams that pierced the highest waves just as they broke against the ship. He had never been at sea in serious storm before, but he knew deep inside himself that *The Unicorn* was sturdy and seaworthy, and that Pilot-Navigator Escobar was a splendid navigator. There was no need to worry, even as the ship labored heavily. A glance at Reginald, however, found him shaking pitifully as he clutched the rail.

Through the torrents of rain, Johannes saw that one of the men at the bilge pump, the one with the head wound, had collapsed. The second mate screamed for him to arise, but he did not move.

Suddenly, there was a cannon-like boom heard coming from above. Even in the middle of a gale, all eyes flashed skyward. There, the top main spar had broken in two. Shreds of the topsail snapped with vengeance. Heard more than seen, parts of the broken spar dangled crazily between mast and shrouds, threatening to inflict further damage.

The bosun, standing on the weather deck, quickly grasped the situation. He drew out a long dagger from his belt and handed it to the closest of two figures standing nearby with arms hooked around the standing rig. The figure was Johannes who took the knife. The bosun snatched a knife from the second mate and gave it to the second figure. This was Reginald. He hesitated to reach out, but the knife was forced on him.

Yelling, the bosun commanded, "Quick, up the rigging. Cut away the spar before we lose the mast." He then disappeared into the swirling rain.

One look at his face told Johannes that his friend was paralyzed with terror. "Come, Reginald. You must do it. I will help. You cannot stay here. The punishment will be worse than a little climb."

Johannes held the handle of the knife in his teeth as he had seen other sailors do, grasped the ratlines and started up, step by step. "Just do what I do," said Johannes. Reginald faltered. "You must come," Johannes persisted.

"Up with you," came the no-nonsense voice of the second mate.

The white-faced boy started slowly up the ratlines of the main mast. He was but a step behind Johannes. Even the ratlines shook with each clang of the spars.

Johannes coaxed his friend along, reaching down from time to time. "Keep both hands on the lines. Change your grip after each step. Always have one hand on the stay. Believe in your hands; they will not fail you. Do not look down!"

The climb was too slow for the officers, and more muffled shouting urged the climbers on. Up and up, deliberately, they went. Johannes shouted through the howling wind, "You are doing fine, Reginald. Keep coming."

As Johannes spoke these words, the ship dove into another trough just as the crest of the on-coming wave broke. A wall of water struck the ship from the starboard bow and sliced across the ship. Both boys braced themselves as the sea struck their legs and then exploded onto the deck. "Quickly, Reginald, quickly, up," shouted Johannes.

Together the two climbed higher, Johannes staying just ahead of the other boy. At last they reached the topsail spar. The roll and pitch of the ship was amplified high in the mast and both felt the reeling of the ship as if they were riding a wild stallion gone mad.

When, at last, the two had gained a foothold near the flailing topsail spar, a strip of canvas whipped so hard, stinging, against the face of Johannes that he nearly lost his hold on the ratline. With practice, one hand tight around the line, the other slashing away at the canvas, Johannes slowly cut away the shreds which then blew off into the sea. Dodging the swinging spar parts, Johannes slashed one of its lines, then struggled with another. With that, the spar soared out into the storm. "Cut the lines over there," he shouted to Reginald. But there followed no action. Reginald stood frozen against the rigging, both arms wrapped around the ratlines, not mindful of the section of spar that swayed just above his head. There was no knife. It was merciful, thought Johannes, that the rain was too thick for the officers to see their cabin boy crippled with fear. He dared not even think about the terrible punishment awaiting the loss of a knife.

It was at this moment that the ship caught a wave broadside, a giant wave among all the other giant waves. It gave the ship one enormous, shuttering roll. The tip of the mast tipped so far over that it seemed to touch the sea itself. Then it whipped back with such a force that the next wave collapsed onto the ship. Its splash reached as high as the two struggling for a hold on the topmast.

As the wall of water cleared, Johannes looked for Reginald. But the cabin boy was no longer there. There had been no shout. He had just vanished. Johannes tried not to believe his eyes. "I have heard of men falling unharmed into a billowed sail." It was a futile hope, but it was his only one. Yet, Johannes knew the truth. Reginald had run away from home for a better life, and now he had no life at all.

Johannes watched in further horror as the remaining broken topmain spar continued to smash against the main mast with every roll of the ship. "And soon we will have no ship," the certainty of total disaster now unavoidable. He forced himself to reach across, leaning way out, and cut away the lines. This time, the spar fell straight down, causing a crash somewhere on deck. The cut lines came back to thrash him. Johannes quickly retreated down the ladder of rope.

His task done and back on the reeling deck, Johannes came upon an astounding sight. Many of the seamen, atheists to the core, were on their knees, heads bowed into hands, praying.

The storm lasted throughout the day. Gradually, through a long night, it blew itself out. The wonder was how the ship rode such heavy seas at all. Of course, the planks leaked profusely with the twisting strain on the hull. Exhausted men kept the bilge pumps working constantly to relieve the hold of seawater. Johannes welcomed the chance to tire himself on pump duty. It was the only way he knew to get his mind off the greatest loss he had ever known.

CHAPTER 7

Ship's Log

The following entries are extracted from the log kept by Shipmaster Jacob Hendrick Vroom. They are official notes, written in Old Dutch hand, along with pencil sketches. This ship's log was discovered on June 30, 1881 among the records of the Dutch West Indies Company in Hoorn. Reproduced here are English translations of the some of the original pages in Dutch.[14]

20 September 1616: 32 days out. The want of a breath of wind continues, now in its sixth day. Speed less than one knot. Sweltering heat. No sign of relief. Many porpoises sighted.

21 September: A savage storm tosses the ship.

22 September:
Morning: Wind NE at 310 degrees, 12 knots, gusty; Swells 10–12 feet high, and 20 feet apart. Heading 196 degrees. Speed 8 knots.

Fairly calm seas after great commotion began early morning 21 Sept with heavy northeasterly wind. Forced to run southerly course under bare poles, losing much headway. Swells crashed over forecastle. In troughs, swells as high as top of main spar. Bosun was slow in taking in topmain sail breaking spar, causing much panic among crew and peril to the ship. Sails cut away and broken spar released. So ferocious was the sea that old sailors trembled, and god-fearing men—and those who suddenly became god-fearing—knelt in prayer. Only divine providence allowed me to save the ship from total destruction.

Report of damage: Two barrels of water on waist deck crushed and contents lost. Attempts at catching rainwater in basins not successful because of severe rolling. One anchor torn loose and beaten against hull until catted with great effort. Hatchway on aft castle stoved. Wash flooded hold. Water in bilge is more than 30 centimeters deep. Bags of meal soaked. Pumps worked constantly with some effect. Shallop stoved in, may be ruined beyond repair.

Pots with tulip bulbs broken and soil scattered, most lost. Mister Tuinstra is in a terrible mood, crying and moaning from quarterdeck. He will talk to no one. Life's savings went into bulbs, and he expected to make a king's fortune if they grew well in New Netherland. I fear he has gone mad.

One able seaman suffers arm injury with protruding bones from fall. Surgeon urges carpenter to amputate arm to prevent gangrene. Sailor refuses.

One ordinary seaman struck on forehead by whipping topsail halyard, one eye is crushed. Examined by surgeon. Cabin boy lost overboard.

Midday: Heading W at 180 degrees. Wind SSW at 10-15 knots. Swells: 6-8 feet. Speed 6 knots. Seas now roiling but able to use main course and top mainsail of foremast. Ship rides more stable with spanker unfurled. Bilge water down to 9 inches.

Fresh provisions are gone. Salt junk and biscuits left, but in small amounts. Water gone. Bosun reports that helmsman was asleep on duty when storm arose. Punishment to be decided.

Sunset: Gannett sighted heading 'SWW,' causes great excitement. Passes directly over ship just above mast. Master-pilot observes water dripping from mouth, a sign of land nearby. Expect to sight landfall within one or two days. Lookout on main mast given telescope.

Evening: Sea calm with steady blow at 8 knots, speed 4 knots. Heading 190 degrees. All sails unfurled and carrying. Auction of cabin boy's possessions. No valuable items. Sketches of ship and crew found, placed in ship's chronicle. Twilight sets in as if the sea had never heard of a storm.

CHAPTER 8

Devil's Bite

The storm had passed. The days following brought a gusty breeze from the southwest. With it, the bellies of the sails filled, flattened, then filled as if the ship itself were breathing. The pilot-navigator now had a steady ship and clear skies to make his sightings. With the sun at mid-day and the North Star at night, he could locate the ship's position again. Sail makers and carpenters busily repaired the storm-torn canvas and broken spars. Below deck, men again tied the barrels and crates that had come loose.

But all was not well on the ship. As it slowly glided along that measureless ocean, men on board, one after another, moved more slowly. They talked less. They tended to lie around at any chance. Many bled from their teeth. Dark spots appeared here and there on arms and legs. Some had swollen knees and elbows so painful that they could hardly move. The Bite of the Devil was rapidly working its way through the crew. Each day, the laborious duties of ship handling were left to fewer and fewer.

Pulling his pant-leg to mid-thigh, Ingmar directed Johannes's attention to the old leg wound. "See, it bleeds again. This always happens on a long voyage."

"Does it hurt?" was the boy's predictable response.

"No, but I know that I will be bitten in the same way if we are at sea much longer. Have you noticed that the devil does not often bite Dutch sailors? No one understands why. On this point, luck is with you."

Johannes came to wonder, too, why he might be spared. He had heard so many reasons for the Devil's Bite: the sea air, the terrible food, lack of proper sleep. Some even believed that it was caused by laziness. Others said what spoiled the sailors was the same thing that spoiled the water, although no one knew why. And why not affect the Dutch? The men from England, Denmark, and Ireland all did the same tasks, breathed the same air, drank the same water and beer and ate most of the same foods as the Dutch. All worked hard, the bosun and first and second mates saw to that. It was a mystery.[45]

Back on the top foremast, the lookout passed each day as all the previous days. He swept his big eye aimlessly from one end of the horizon to another without ever a change in the view of water. He shuffled round and round in his tiny round perch; he counted the stitches in the sail that fluttered just above him; he watched with envy the men below with their freedom of real work. For Johannes, the experience could be summed up in one word: monotony.

Monotony, that is, until the seventieth day at sea when a tiny dark patch popped into his lens. It fell directly in the ship's way. "Another false tornado," thought Johannes, "another mermaid." This time, he chose to remain silent. But the patch was steady, not like the on and off spout of a whale. As the ship closed in, he kept his big eye on his finding with fanatical intensity. Soon, Johannes could see that the waves were breaking over it. Still, he held back. It was not long until he could make out through his telescope what looked like the branch of a tree. "Yes, a tree branch it is. I am sure," he told himself with an air of confidence. It was time, now, to act, to perform the duty that was expected of a worthy seaman high in a lookout.

Calling out between hands bent around his mouth and with a voice that sprang from deep within his chest, Johannes announced for all to hear, "BOOM TAK, BOOM TAK." This time, the voice rang with assurance. His sighting was no mistake. The bosun rushed up onto the forecastle. By then, the ship was close enough for him to spot the tree branch patch with the naked eye.

Johannes waited spellbound until the object passed abeam. He saw that fresh leaves clung to the branch. "Keep a sharp eye for land," yelled the bosun. Later in the day, the ship encountered more branches and then some floating seaweed. By evening, there appeared the most exciting of all the early hints of land ahead: shore birds. A dozen or so squawking gulls circled round and round *The Unicorn.*

Sweeping now continuously along the endless horizon with his glass, the lookout found a hazy whitish line that stretched out along the horizon and faded into the sky. It was just before sunset, and he had to squint against the glare. Slowly, Johannes became more and more certain of its reality. Ahead was a white, sand-lined shore, now with a red sun falling partly behind the dunes. He focused repeatedly at the thrilling sight.

At this moment, Johannes felt that his whole life had led to this point. He was duty-bound and privileged to announce to the world—which consisted at the time of twenty men on a ship—that they had at last crossed the ocean. Once again, Johannes called out in his best full-throated voice pressed between hands: "*LAND IN ZICHT!*" Again, "*LAND IN ZICHT!*" A moment later *Land in Zicht!* spread across the weather deck and down into the orlop. No, it was not a whale sounding. Johannes took pride in his sighting. After all, it was he who first saw the end of what for so long had seemed like never-ending water.

It was not a long time before the naked eye could make out the white-rimmed coastal line. Master Pilot-Navigator Escobar looked over his charts with exacting care. He sent out two welcomed words: "Cape Cod."[46] A joyous shout arose from the deck. A few men sank to their knees in prayer. Those able-bodied enough to see land for themselves ran toward the bow for a better look. Those unfortunates stricken by the Devil's Bite found the strength to pull up for the viewing. They knew that fresh food would soon end their suffering if they could live that long.

The pilot-navigator's calculations had been close. Now the ship must turn south, clear the shoals and only then continue a westerly passage. Soon came the command:

"Hard to larboard."

"Hard to larboard," came the helmsman's voice, and the ship veered to south.

"Maintain 180 degrees compass."

"Compass reads 90," answered the helmsman a few moments later.

"Maintain course until clear of the shoals."

"Maintaining course."

Sails were trimmed and braced. As night fell, the pilot Escobar announced, "All is well," to anyone within earshot.

What Johannes saw of land as the ship slipped broadside was a brilliant line of white sand dunes that stretched across the flattened land. Still standing in his bucket at the top of the foremast, he had the best view of the New World. Even with the gathering darkness of a vanishing sun, there was enough light to outline land. What he heard when the ship had sailed well past the landmass was, "Helm hard to starboard."

"Starboard helm" came the answer.

"Hold at 270 degrees."

Soon came the reply, "Reading 270 degrees and holding." Of course, the turn meant sails were to be trimmed and braced once again.

Not long afterwards, Master Vroom, now dressed in the finery of his office, stood on the quarterdeck. Two lanterns placed on the capstan showed him standing tall, complete with ruffle, cape, and broad-brimmed hat on which stood straight up a long, feathered plume. He spoke not but rather strode back and forth with a haughty grin of pride, having led his ship across an ocean.

And so, the ship bore directly west along the distant shoreline to starboard. The excitement of arriving in the New World was now just as great to Johannes as it was three years before when his ship had followed the same course. His eyes were heavy after more than a day without sleep, yet the thrill of arriving held his spirit up. On this journey, Johannes was a seasoned hand. After all, he had been there before. He knew what to expect. At least, he thought he knew what to expect.

By moonlight *The Unicorn* slipped quietly and steadily along coastal land on the starboard. It was at the first light of dawn that the ship came to land straight ahead. The wonderful sight brought more cheers.[47]

"Bear on 360 degrees" came new instructions from the Master-Pilot.

Echoes and fresh setting of sail followed. Now on a northern tack, the ship passed between stretches of land not half a league wide.[48] It led into an immense harbor with some islands.[49] There ahead was the island of the Manhattoes people.[50] It was the place where, Johannes easily recalled, he had spent a winter.

This time, however, the trees were no longer green. Their leaves were brilliant hues of red and yellow! "Fire," cried the men who had never witnessed the colors of New World autumn. Smoke from small domed houses curled up into the sky.

No canoes came out to greet the ship. Only a few people were standing silently along the shoreline. All seemed strange after the lively welcome that Johannes remembered when many canoes and people waving from the shore greeted the ship of Master Block.

Johannes hoped to stop at the island where the Manhattoes had helped them during that first journey: by providing food, dwelling space and firewood these *Wilden* had made it possible for Shipmaster Block and his crew to survive a harsh winter. Johannes remembered clearly that this was also the place where these same native people helped the crew build the small ship, *Onrust.* The *Wilden* there were friends. He could thank them once again. Instead, to his great disappointment, *The Unicorn* bypassed the island and headed upriver in the morning sunlight.

What about food for the men suffering from scurvy? Fresh food, everyone knew, would take the spell out of the Devil's Bite. Instead, the Master chose to reach his destination upriver without delay.

At the northern tip of the island, the land rose steeply in a wooded ridge.[51] Just beyond it, Johannes remembered a small river that led into the North River. It was the river that separated the trading island from the mainland. Finding this river told Shipmaster Block that the expanse of land was an island. The river appears on a map drawn on the following year.[52]

On the other side of the North River was a long stretch of immense cliffs that rose sharply at the river's edge. The morning sun cast them in an eerie reddish-brown glow. Zigzagging up and down were cracks that gave the cliffs an appearance of a wall of wooden posts that circled around a fort. The stony wall dwarfed the ship that had seemed so huge in harbor of Hoorn.[53]

CHAPTER 9

The North River

There was a good southwesterly breeze on that first morning in New Netherland. The river was wide. A long reach made sailing easy.[54] As *The Unicorn* made way on an up-flowing current, Johannes recognized more of the sights as they came into view. Who could forget that place just upriver on the starboard? This was the spot where water cascading over great boulders sprayed high before spilling into the North River.[55]

Steady on the same reach, the ship came to a place in the river, beyond the cliff of rocks, that was even wider. It was as broad as a sea, though not as broad as the Zuider Zee.[56] Here the land gradually rose from each shore. The reds and yellow of autumnal foliage covered the landscape in colorful splendor.

It was here on his first voyage that Johannes first saw native people up close. Block's ship, the *Tijger*, came upon some canoes in mid-river. "Yes, this is where I frightened a boy in the last canoe," thought Johannes, reliving the story he had told Reginald. "I wonder if the *Wilde* still has my hat, and if he even knew what it was for."

Rocks that sparkled brightly came from hills on the starboard where the river narrowed a bit.[57] With a fresh setting of sails, the ship came to land just beyond a place that jutted out into the river.[58] Here, many canoes came to greet the ship. The mood was friendly. Master Vroom ordered that the ship be hove to. Trading across the rail was soon brisk. For hoes and axes and glass beads, the crew took in corn, meat, and other victuals.

Surely the fresh food would undo the devil's terrible wounds. Two men suffering from scurvy had already died during the voyage upriver. Within a day or two of having fresh food, others suffering from scurvy, among them Ingmar, could scamper up into the rigging and haul heavy lines as if never stricken.

By evening, *The Unicorn* approached a place in the river where it narrows and takes gentle turns, first to larboard, then starboard. Mountains stood on both sides.[59] By then the current had changed direction. "Such a strange river," the lookout reminded himself. Fast running currents pressed against the ship, impeding its progress. As darkness fell, pilot-navigator Escobar signaled to come about for a night mooring.

Closer toward shore on the western side, away from the strongest current, the ship played out its anchor. Sails were furled. For the first time in more than two months at sea, the men could enjoy a long night's sleep. But first, the bodies of two men done in by scurvy were brought up from the hold. Wrapped in tattered sailcloth and weighted down with ballast stones, they were thrown into the river. The ceremony was brief. A noisy auction soon followed.

By early morning on the following day, the anchor had been raised. The journey upriver was underway. The day was gray with a light, chilling rain, but progress was speedy in a flood tide and a following wind. Mountains rose behind both shores. How impressed a boy from Holland had been to see highlands for the first time, and he was thrilled to see them once again. Was he to believe the stories of sailors that goblins lived in these mountains? That goblins did not like ships? That they caused baffling winds to bewilder the crew? That they make the skies thunder?

Superstitious or not, the sailors suddenly found themselves in a facing wind and were hard-pressed to set sails to it. No sooner were sails trimmed and braced, a heavier blast came directly over the larboard beam. Commands came rapidly for sailors in rigging and on deck as the ship worked through the passageway between mountains. Looking down from the top foremast, Johannes saw that the men and officers who had been bad-tempered for weeks now worked together like parts of a village clock!

A forested mountain rose directly up from the river on the starboard side. Across the way were other mountains set farther back. A stream snaked between the massive green. "I think," said Johannes aloud where no one could hear, "that this must be the most beautiful place in the whole world." As an afterthought, he said, "And I have the best view of it all."

Up ahead where the river narrowed even more, Johannes could see a sharp curve of the river to the larboard, then a sharp turn to the starboard. He knew that here the current was the strongest and most changeable, and the winds were even more so. It is the reason why sailors called this part of the river "World's End." It meant the hurried adjusting of sails to keep in mid-river. Through it all, every man, weakened or not, was called upon to give his utmost effort. Even Shipmaster Vroom stood out on the quarterdeck.

Leaving the double curve behind and entering a wider, calmer river, the ship approached a sight that had before captured the imagination of Johannes. Near the top of a sharp-rising mountain on the starboard shore, there was a rocky overhang. Just below and in the middle of the overhand, lay a long, bare rock.

Below that there was a broad prominence where tall trees grew. The whole made a face, its eyes in deep shadows that followed Johannes, as it had done before, all along that stretch of the river.

Continuing upriver beyond the mountains, the ship was now in a wider, gentler, straighter river. Depths, however, were uncertain. Even in such a big river, there was always the impending disaster of going aground. Here the safety of the ship depended upon the leadsman, the hard-working man who must throw the lead weight over the ship's bow until it dangles from a long line or until it strikes bottom. He then must haul it up and count the knots on the line. Done every minute or so, he calls out the measurements of depth. The numbers, Escobar puts in his book. All who have had duty as a leadsman know the aching of the arms and the sore hands that are sure to follow.[60]

Progress of the ship was steady. Flatlands with many island marshes and dense with birds came into view. Sometimes, despite the untiring effort of the leadsman, there came the unsettling sound of the hull scrapping against mud. Even so, in mid-river at low tide, the ship became stuck on a sand bar. Shipmaster Vroom appeared at once on the quarterdeck and scolded the leadsman for his bungling. The bosun ordered the shallop put into the water. The effort took all hands to lift the shallop and gently slide it into the water. With six straining men on oars and a rising tide, *The Unicorn* floated free once again. From then on, the ship towed the shallop from the stern.

On one long reach, a familiar smell wafted across the ship in an easterly wind. It came from clover that caused every man on board to think of the fields of home. From that time on, the reach has been known as Claverack.[61]

CHAPTER 10

Fort Nassau

The Unicorn came to a cleared land on the western shore, its destination at last: Castle Island. Here on the island was Fort Nassau. It was not the great fortress of masonry that Johannes had expected. What he saw, instead, was a small wooden cabin that looked more like a fisherman's hut. Around it was a palisade, yet incomplete, of upright poles. "This is Fort Nassau?" he asked himself. "This is the place where I told Reginald he would be safe within its walls!"[62]

On shore, there came loud cheering and a great waving of arms by men dressed in rags and appearing famished. These were the homesick men who spent the winter collecting beaver pelts.

When it reached the island, the ship turned abruptly with the sails trimmed along the wind. Thus hoved to, the larboardside anchor was released and the ship spun around to face into the wind.

With anchor set and sails furled, men crowded into the shallop bound for shore. There, their feet touched ground for the first time since Hoorn. The first steps ashore where clumps of grass met the sandy beach brought a sensation of firmness that had been forgotten on their always rolling, pitching world at sea.

There were hugs of joy among the scrawny men ashore and the newly-arrived. “What news,” they said, “What news?” But the crew soon discovered that they were there not for amusement or information.

Shipmaster Vroom ordered the pelts accumulated through the winter be brought to the ship. The order brought a flurry of activity. The work of off-loading goods and on-loading pelts could not wait. One of those chosen by the mate for the exchange was Johannes. He feared the shallop as he knew not how to swim.

Soon the sailors had packed the shallop with items for trading with the *Wilden*. There were kettles, knives, beads, hoes, and axes. There were also rolls of duffel, a thick and coarse woolen cloth with nap on both sides. These had been woven in Leyden, perhaps Johannes imagined, by the sister of Reginald.

Johannes found the cabin so filled with pelts that there was hardly any room for the men who had been left there many months ago. They were piled almost to the top of two small windows, keeping the room in near darkness. The only open space was in front of a stone fireplace. With every passing day, the accumulated pelts meant that much less living space so that, by now, there was hardly room inside to turn around.

On return to the ship, the sailors piled the shallop so high with beaver pelts that the oarsmen could barely see above them. Once lifted on board ship, the pelts were packed tightly in the hold.

On one exchange, the shallop had been so over-loaded with pelts that it became top heavy. As it came alongside *The Unicorn*, a sudden gust caused the shallop to tip over. Within an instant, the river was strewn with furs that floated rapidly downriver and with struggling sailors, including Johannes, hanging onto the shallop for dear life.

The mate, seeing the pelts float away, quickly assembled those who could swim. There were only four swimmers among all the sailors. These he sent into the water to retrieve the pelts. Others walked and waded along the shore to pick up the pelts that had blown to land. Under the stern eyes of Master Vroom and the bellowing bosun, the effort continued until every single pelt had been picked up. Each was placed on the deck to dry. Meanwhile, Johannes, in sheer terror, hung on to the side of the upturned shallop until it was hauled ashore.

The capsized shallop had put another day into the voyage upriver, a delay that put the master in a foul mood. Eventually, all the furs were packed tightly into the hold, beginning at the bow and moving toward the stern. Load after load were packed below deck until there was scarcely any room from the crew to sleep. The terrible smells of rancid animal skins added to the awful air below.

Master Vroom came ashore on the last trip. He called together six crewmen, including Johannes, and one of the men who had spent more than four months in the cabin. "You men will stay here at Fort Nassau," the shipmaster announced. "You will do your best to trade pelts for trinkets at a good price. When a ship returns in the spring, you will return to Holland. See that you have enough fur to fill the ship hold. The shallop will bring your seabags from the ship along with some barrels of dried meat and lard. You will have some muskets with sufficient powder. There is plenty of game in the forest. The river is teeming with fish. Starve, you will not if you keep your wits about you."

The announcement brought a gasp of disapproval from the men. All gasped, that is, all but Johannes who thought the assignment might prove exciting.

"What is your name?" Master Vroom inquired of the fur trader.

"Joost van Hoofddorp" came the answer in a hesitant voice.

"Good. You are Dutch. You have experience. You will be in command."

The seaman's face turned white, and he collapsed to his knees. He pleaded, crying, "But Master Vroom, I must return to my home. I have a wife, four children, and a crippled mother. They will starve without me. Spare them, I beg of you, Sir."

"I see no reason to change my order. Your family will get along as all the peasants somehow do. You in the orange jacket," said the shipmaster, turning toward another man. "you will be next in command should anything happen to Mister van Hoofddorp. The color of your jacket tells me you are from Holland." With these words, Master Vroom turned toward the shallop, placed himself in the tight area made for him at the bow, and waited to be rowed to the ship, never looking back.

CHAPTER 11

Fur Traders

***The Unicorn* weighed** anchor at high tide and with a favorable westerly wind. The sailors assigned to stay at Castle Island watched *The Unicorn* as it passed out of sight downriver, the tip of the mast and long yellow banner the last to disappear. The seamen-become-woodsmen now had to fend for themselves through the long winter. The men, feeling abandoned, were ill prepared to endure what was ahead. Only their leader had experience in the wilderness, and he had collapsed into a sobbing heap.

Johannes went to the fortress that was, really, just a crudely built cabin. The hinges on the door had rusted badly. He looked inside. It was dark, lit only by a small glassless window with light streaming in from the edges of a hemp curtain. The house was empty aside from some pewter mugs and plates, some blankets, a barrel, and some odds and ends stashed in one corner.

It was at nightfall before Joost found his voice and could speak to the men. They gathered at the doorway for whatever comfort they could get from their new, dubious leader. "I will do my best," said Joost. "It will not be easy." Each man knew that somehow the group had to stay together to survive the many months of isolation ahead. Each gave his name: Cornelius De Gant, Rut Schermerhoorn,

Lars Svenssen, Dietrich Jäger, Sean Doyle, and, of course, Johannes van der Zee.

Joost explained, "Food is our greatest concern. We can hunt and catch some fish. I tell you now, winter is terrible. We depend on trading with the *Wilden*, but they are not easy to deal with." He went on to say that the *Wilden* belonged to a tribe called Mahicans. They spoke the language of the Algonquin. Although they were friendly, and they did not steal, everyone had to be careful not to offend them. Also, there were strict orders from the East India Company that there would be no trading for beer, rum, firearms, or gunpowder.

The men busied themselves cutting firewood, reinforcing the palisades, placing shingles on the badly damaged roof. Quarreling began almost at once as their new leader proved weak for the role.

That first night in the cabin was a relief for Johannes. Room enough, straw for a mattress, and a woolen blanket. What he liked not was the sound of snoring men.

The early morning fog slowly lifted, leaving a thick film of moisture on the grass and a death-like silence in the air. Johannes went to the edge of the clearing to attend to nature's necessity. As he turned back toward the cabin, he saw something that sent a chill running up and down his spine.

CHAPTER 12

Mahicans

Standing just inside the clearing were some *Wilden.* They stood firm as if trees, some with their arms folded in front. Tar-black hair hung below their shoulders. Each man was covered from head to foot with animal skins and a furry shawl draped over the shoulders. Their faces were decorated with ink, black or red.[63]

Instinct told Johannes to run, but it took a moment for his legs to respond. When they did, he raced toward the cabin, shouting excitedly, "The Mahicans. They are here. There must be ten, no twelve, no maybe fifteen of them."

Joost and the sailors-turned-traders rose quickly and prepared to meet their visitors. Together, they stood just beyond the cabin and beckoned the Mahicans to approach.

Rut shouldered his musket. "No," cried out Joost. "Put it down. Firearms make *Wilden* nervous. We have nothing to fear." Rut put his musket down but carried it slung over one arm. The traders slowly approached the *Wilden,* each of the newcomers suspicious of some kind of trick. Johannes, now more composed, counted them. There were twelve. Their faces were stern, but no spears or bows could be seen.

One of the Mahicans, an aged man with long white hair bedecked with feathers, stepped forward and raised one arm. Joost, in turn, raised his. The gestures, he knew, were the formal beginning of friendly talks for trade. First came words for trading. Both spoke slowly. Joost, had learned some of the Algonquin language. The *Wilden* had learned a few words in Dutch. The exchange came down to counting on fingers, a nod for agreement, a headshake for disagreement. Five fingers extended five times.

Joost sent four of the men back to the cabin to fetch two kettles, four hoes, an axe, and four pieces of duffel. For these, he told them, the Mahicans would bring twenty beaver skins.

The Mahicans gingerly touched the items and then passed them around to each other, all the while feeling muted admiration for a sharp edge, a smooth surface, or a soft texture.

It was during this time of examining tools and cloth that one of the Mahicans quietly slipped away and wandered toward the trading post. Rut kept an eye on him as he looked into the cabin and then entered it. Rut followed. All was quiet for a moment, then, ...

BOOOoooooom

Everyone gasped as they turned to see a furry figure fly out of the door, take another step and collapse face down into the dirt path. From the unnatural, unmoving position in which one arm was thrust beneath the body, they knew that the man was already dead. Blood trickled from his gaping mouth. Still in the hand of the flung-out arm was a pewter plate than was imbedded sideways into the ground by the impact of the fall.

Rut stood there next to the face-down man, grinning, with a trail of smoke coming from his matchlock. The Mahicans braced themselves for a moment, then like of flock of crows startled by hunters, disappeared into the forest. The traders, with equal haste withdrew into the cabin, stepping over the body sprawled out just before the door. A thick wooden bar was quickly propped across the door from inside.

A deep sickness suddenly came on Johannes. It was like seasickness only worse. The awful echo of the firearm's blast in his ears would not stop. He felt his heart pounding in a wild flutter as if it were about to leap out of his chest. He breathed rapidly and deeply, but still could not get enough air. The life-force seemed to drain out of body and, just as his vision began to fade into a vague grayness, he reeled and fell to the dirt-packed floor with a thud.

Even in this state of shock, Johannes could hear the words of Joost. "Why did you do that?"

Rut answered, "I had to."

"You had to?"

"Of course. I saw him though the shutter. He was about to steal something. You can see for yourself, still in his hand."

"So, for that you killed him. For a pewter plate? Suppose he just was only curious about our things? The *Wilden* are very curious people."

Rut now remained silent and Joost continued. There was an understated rage detected in his voice. "Rut, you are new here. You do not know *Wilden*. You may think that you have protected us with your gunpowder. I think you may cause the death of all of us. The Mahicans will not forget."

A chill went through the air. The men squatted or paced nervously. It took no further words for everyone to realize that their situation at Fort Nassau, their first morning, was not good. A long silence, aside from the shuffling of restless men, followed. It was long enough for Johannes to catch his breath and clear his head. He wanted to think that he was awakening from a terrible nightmare but a quick look at his cabin mates told a different story.

"What should we do now?" asked Dietrich.

Cornelius offered his opinion, "We have good firearms, even a few flintlocks. We also have a good supply of gunpowder. We can defend ourselves."

Joost, trying to control his anger, quashed this notion instantly. "No, remember that these people are all around us. We need to go outside, to hunt, and to raise a garden. They will attack us day after day until we are all dead." There followed a general shrug of hopelessness. "And remember that death is better than capture by the *Wilden*." This thought provoked a shudder even among men accustomed to harsh living at the edge of dying.

Another plan came from the Irish sailor, Sean. "We could escape at night through the forest and find our way downriver to Nutten Island where it is safe."

It was not a useful idea. Joost explained, "You know nothing of living in the forest. The Mahicans will follow us all the way and watch us starve to death one by one."

"Suppose we use the timber from the cabin to make a raft," added Lars. "I used to make rafts in Oslo with my friends. We could easily float away on the out-going tide."

"That way," snapped Joost, "we will find arrows whizzing toward us all along the river." He paused before adding, "And what happens if by some miracle you reach Nutten Island? You will be tried as a traitor for abandoning your post. Need I remind you what happens to traitors?"

After a long silence save for heavy breathing, Joost shared his most chilling thought. "I believe that the *Wilden* will come to us tonight. They will have torches, and soon our cabin will become a torch. You may wish to stay inside."

Thus, it was in this state of desperate indecision that Joost came up with a plan, at least for the moment. "We will have a lookout at each window. Our only hope is that the noise of our firearms, should they appear, will frighten them away. If they do not come during the night, I will go to them tomorrow. Perhaps we can settle the matter, though I know not how."

Evening soon cast the trading post in darkness. Lookouts were urged to keep alert every moment through their watch. One window faced the river on the east, the other toward the forest on the west. The traders were blind on two sides. They settled in anxiously for a long night inside their tiny, four-sided world.

It was during the night that Johannes was poked awake to stand watch at the westerly facing window. He stared out into the black space, a night without moon or stars. He looked for torches. He listened for the crackle of footsteps. But all remained dark and silent around the fragile fortress.

Johannes had much time to think about why he was there. He was meant to become a shipmaster, not a trader. But it seemed not to matter now. His fate, along with that of the others, seemed already determined. He thought of his family and the safety and comfort of his canal home in Amsterdam. He thought of Reginald.

In time, the outline of the forest emerged from the darkness. The new day brought more details of the world around them into view: the garden, a stack of firewood, boulders, a half-built shallop. Johannes was relieved that they had not all perished by arrow or by fire.

Lars was the first to leave the cabin to attend to necessities. "Only one at a time," Joost had cautioned. "If the *Wilden* are out there waiting for us, they will get only one." It was not a comforting thought.

Lars lifted the bar that secured their door and squeezed out. Just as the bar was again dropped, there was a shriek from Lars followed by frantic pounding. He was quickly let inside, and the door again barred.

Gasping for breath, his brow sweating, his face snow-white, Lars managed to say, "Gone!"

"What is gone?" came a bevy of questions.

"The *Wilde's* body. It's gone."

The men looked at one another in total disbelief, all with the same thought. "So, the *Wilden* came during the night and took it away right under our noses."

With this thought, the door was again flung open for a second look. Just outside were red stains on the ground and near it a pewter plate, standing on edge in the ground. And next to that was a stack of beaver pelts. They counted twenty.

CHAPTER 13

The Bargain

The discoveries of the morning left no doubt that the mysterious people who lived around them were also clever. As the morning passed into afternoon, there was no more talk about how they could get out of their situation alive. But in the end, everyone thought of himself as a dead man. How they would die was not yet decided. That was just a matter of waiting.

Rut, haunted by his thoughtless action, whimpered as if a child. As a lad, he had sailed under the flag of Sir Francis Drake, the most famous of the Queen's shipmasters. He had fought the Spanish, even boarded their ships with firearms ablaze and sword flashing. He had not given much thought to the poor souls at the other end of these weapons. Now that his rashness was responsible for their present sorry state of affairs, killing had taken on a very different meaning.

Of course, the men knew that they could not hide behind the thin plank walls of their cabin for the whole winter. Furthermore, they knew that they could not collect more pelts unless they could restore the friendly relationship with the *Wilden*. They had to make amends to the Mahicans.

It was after nightfall that Joost announced what was their only hope. "Someone must go to the Mahicans. We can take gifts and show our good will. The chance of failure, though, is great."

"I will go, too," volunteered Cornelius.

"And I," Johannes shot out eagerly. "We will go with you."

"No, I must go alone," said Joost. "Only I know some words of their tongue. In the past, the Mahicans trusted me, and one person will not be so threatening. Though there is little chance of success, it is our only hope. With luck, perhaps, I may strike some bargain. At first light, I will go into their village, not far from here. I will return before sundown."

"And what if you do not return?" asked Lars.

"Then wait another day. If you do not see me by nightfall, you can believe that I have come to grievous harm. You will all be on your own."

It was at daybreak when Joost started off on his dire mission. Inside his sack were a few morsels of food and a blanket and a string of beads of many colors for a gift. His last words were, "If I fail to return, you must decide among yourselves a plan of escape. None of you knows how to get through these terrible winters. I think each one of you should start out for New Amsterdam alone and not at the same time. Stay close to the river, but within the cover of the forest. In this way, the *Wilden* will have to split up their numbers to track you. Be aware, that they are good at tracking. Like me, leave your muskets behind. With luck, you may find some berries and eggs along the way."

With these words, Joost departed. The men watched him cross the clearing and disappear into the forest beyond. He did not look back. With Joost gone, the talk centered around what would happen should they fall into the hands of the *Wilden.* All had heard rumors from seamen returning from the New World, but many of the stories about prisoners were too ghastly to believe. Each story added to the fright.

The night did come but their leader did not. It was with great anxiety that they waited a second day without his appearance. By evening, the men had to choose their fate. They must decide who would go first and in what order the others should follow. They knew that they must keep along the general direction of the river but, to avoid detection, stay as far away from it as they could.

Some suggested during the long night of decision-making, that they draw straws to determine their order of escape. Others thought that those most physically fit or those who were oldest should go first. In the end, they decided that Rut should go first since he had a wife and six children in Delft. He would leave at the first light of day. The others would follow as directed. Of course, by logic, Johannes was the last to leave since he had no wife and no children to support. He was also the youngest. Johannes would be the last to see that the fire was kept up so that any watching *Wilden* would think that they were all huddled inside. All knew that anyone reaching New Amsterdam still had to gain the sympathy of the traders there.

Dawn came. Rut slipped away into the wilderness. Not long after, Dietrich was ready to leave. But just before he stepped from the cabin, Cornelius, at the necessities pit, spotted Joost in the distance. He was returning along with three *Wilden*, each burdened by a load of pelts strapped to their backs. It was a sight that none could have imagined.

The Mahicans unloaded their burdens by the side of the cabin. Joost calmly counted them under the watchful eyes of both hunters and traders. There were thirty pelts, not more, not fewer. The Mahicans were pleased to see that the traders were pleased. What the traders were not prepared for is what happened next.

While the Mahicans waited expectantly, Joost walked into the cabin and came out with one of the matchlocks. His crew looked on with astonishment. They were about to be even more astonished as Joost handed both the firearm and a pouch of gunpowder to one of the *Wilden*. It was but another instant before the Mahicans disappeared back into the forest.

"Have you gone mad?" bellowed the crowd around Joost. They demanded an explanation. It came quickly.

Joost had his men sit near the heap of pelts. He said, "The Mahicans are good bargainers. You know that our chance of success was slim. They had not yet decided among themselves how they would avenge the death of one of their bravest. You can believe, however, that vengeance was coming. It took much persuading to convince them that the killing was a mistake by an innocent man who did not understand the actions of their tribesman."

The men glanced at each other fitfully.

Joost went on, "I promised that we will not threaten them. But promises were not enough to satisfy them. I could not spare our lives without including a gun in this first trade. At first, they demanded two firearms but finally agreed to only one. I saw no other choice. Do you?"

A look of uncertain approval passed from face to face.

"We still have four matchlocks and three flintlocks with a good supply of powder," Cornelius offered. "Rut did not take a firearm."

"Rut!" someone yelled. In the excitement of the moment, they had all forgotten about Rut.

Dietrich said, "He is far away by now. We would never catch up with him."

Joost, taken back by the new challenge, replied, "You are right. Only the Mahicans can find him now. I fear that they will not be kind to him. We had best not tell them."

Cornelius replied, "We could give them something useful for their trouble. It may save his life."

"I think they will ask for another musket," returned Lars. "I fear it will be aimed at us."

"Perhaps," said Joost. "That is our risk. I will do what I can. But later I must tell you of a promise that the Mahicans made." It was a promise that the men needed to hear at that moment.

Joost then explained, "There have been five shiploads of fur taken from this trading post over the last five years. Now, the beaver dams disappear from the territory of the Mahicans. The gathering of pelts is becoming ever more difficult. The Mahicans will bring in as many as they can. They will be requesting more tools and trinkets to trade for their hard-to-get furs. It is up to us to fill the returning ship. I, for one, do not want to face the shipmaster next spring who finds us with a cabin almost empty of pelts."

"What can we do?" queried someone.

"What we can do is convince the Mahicans that beaver pelts can be brought in from another tribe."

"Will the Mahicans agree to that?"

"I am not sure. But I did learn that a large tribe lives along a river not far from here. It spills into the North River. Their hunters will have a fresh supply of peltry. We could start trading with them. A problem is that the Mahicans have been long-time enemies with this other tribe, called the Mohawks. The Mahicans will promise them safe passage to our trading post. In return, they have insisted that we provide them with two firearms. After much arguing, they would accept nothing less. Hoes, kettles, and blankets would not do. Since we cannot gather beaver pelts ourselves, it a necessary bargain."

"Have you already agreed?" asked Cornelius.

"Yes, the chief will send a messenger into Mohawk territory. My promise was to provide them with the firearms and powder at the arrival of the first Mohawks with furs to trade."

The thought of arming the *Wilden* with European weapons sent a shiver through the men. Joost had more to say on the transaction. "Our safety will not be at risk if we behave as honorable traders. Do you all hear that?"

"Yes," came the soft reply.

And so, it was with mixed feelings that the men went to sleep that night. They would live another day. The price exacted, though, may yet prove their downfall. But that worry was for another day. For the moment, each man could enjoy the luxury of sleeping on a soft bed of beaver fur.

CHAPTER 14

Mohawks

The newcomers along the North River were soon caught up in the many tasks of frontier life. Busy and free of the worry of massacre, the days of autumn passed agreeably. Food at first was abundant. Squash from last spring's planting had ripened on the vine. Potatoes only waited for their digging. Wild apples were not far away. After spoiled meat and their maggot-infested diet on the ship, the change was welcome.

One of the most interesting foods was one that the Mahicans had taught the traders to grow. It grew on a tall stalk, almost as high as a man and was wrapped in a heavy covering with delicate tassels at the upper end. Inside were tiny yellow seeds lined up in neat rows. Those with good front teeth enjoyed it most.

The Mahicans came every day. They showed the traders how to build a small smoke house. They showed them how to cook meat slowly so that it would last all winter. The Mahicans also offered to show them how to make spring traps to catch rabbits, raccoons, and squirrels.

Each day or two, *Wilden* arrived with more pelts. The number brought in, however, was shrinking, sometimes only ten at a time. While the stack of furs stowed in the cabin grew, Joost did not believe that they would have a shipload by spring. Thus, he reminded the Mahicans of their promises. They now agreed to seek out the help of their enemies, the Mohawks, but first they wanted to have the firearms. After much head shaking and hand talking, Joost gave them one, the other to come on the first arrival of the Mohawks. And so. the pact was settled.

More than two weeks passed before the Mohawks arrived. When they did, there were six, arriving by canoes. Each canoe was stacked with furs to the gunnels. On shore, the Mohawks walked toward the trading post. With their appearance, the Mahicans vanished except for their elderly chief and three others.

The Mohawks differed from the Mahicans only in one way: decorations of the body. Some had one half of the scalp bare of hair or wore just a strip of hair running over the center of the head. All but the single boy had large tattoos in black or red on their faces: stripes, arrows, a hand, or a leaf. One had a black tattoo that went from the center of the forehead where the roach ended, around the nose to the chin.[64]

Icy stares were exchanged between Mahicans and Mohawks. Still, no weapons were brandished and there were no acts of hostility. Whatever bargain was made between the tribes was of no concern to the men of the trading post. The pelts had started to arrive, and the traders were happy. There were one hundred and eighty in all in this first trade. Among the beaver were much prized furs of mountain lions and otters.

Joost was quick to welcome the Mohawks. They spoke a different language from that of the Mahicans and so negotiations depended entirely on hand talk. The Mohawks were soon looking over metal tools and cloth. Each piece was eyed and fondled with intense interest by one man, then passed on to another. They tested the strength of the hoe handle, the sharpness of the axes and knives, and the softness of the duffel.

One of the Mohawks stood out. He was the tallest of them, had a delicate face and slender and nimble body. He was also clearly the youngest, about the same age as Johannes. A pointed feather poked down from his headband. But what caught the attention of Johannes was that the boy's eyes never seemed to leave his. Indeed, the constant stare was unnerving, a stare that was noticed by the other traders as well.

The negotiations went smoothly. The Mohawks seemed satisfied with their assortment of pots, sharp tools, and duffel. It was not long before these were stowed in their canoes. Just as they about to paddle away, the young Mohawk approached Johannes, pulled the feather from his headband and handed it to Johannes. Johannes was mystified, an astonishing gesture that brought surprised laughter from both sides of the traders. Not to be outdone in gift giving, however, he gave in to his impulsive nature, ran inside the cabin and a moment later returned with a rolled-up paper. It was his portrait that Reginald had sketched. This, he handed to the Mohawk to the amusement of all the onlookers.

As the band of canoes pushed off upriver, the Mohawk boy turned, held up the rolled paper high and waved. It was a strange image that haunted Johannes for many days to come.

CHAPTER 15

Cabin Fever

WINTER CAME QUICKLY to Fort Nassau. Cold winds blew in from the north and swirled around the little house. Now and then a snow flurry appeared. There was yet much hard work to do to prepare the house, cut firewood, and store food to survive the winter.

Johannes had looked forward to seeing the heaped-up snow, spending carefree days in a warm house, and sharing stories with men who had traveled the world on ships. There would be endless time to enjoy the leisurely life rather than look at endless columns of figures in his father's shop or at the edge of an unchanging horizon. But being with five quick-tempered cabin-mates all crowded into a tiny space was not as much fun as he had imagined. And with each batch of pelts stowed, the space for living became even smaller. In addition, it soon became clear, that the smaller the space, the more irritable the men became.

With a critical eye, Johannes examined one of the pelts and fondled it with great pride. He thought of his clever father who would be one of the buyers. There in Holland, *mijnheer* van der Zee would arrange to have them made into fine coats and would earn a great deal of money. He would earn even more guilders and stuivers when felt hats were made. His father's great wealth was based largely on the ever-mounting stacks of brown pelts.

Joost, to his credit, kept tight control over the food. Mostly, the men took lard from a rancid barrel and layered it on hard tack. Vegetables and meat were eaten more sparingly to last through the winter. A stew simmered constantly, one thing added, then another: a potato, a turnip, and after a successful hunt, a skinned squirrel or pigeon. Snow replaced the boiled-off water. In time, though, the taste of the stew made some stomachs turn over. A fish was a welcome addition to mealtime but catching one was more a matter of luck than skill.

The fire, kept low on an open hearth, needed a constant supply of wood. A sudden shift in the wind brought a cloud of smoke back down the chimney. If coughing was music, the cabin housed an orchestra.

With the toilet at the edge of the clearing, every trip for the necessity was an adventure in the bitter cold. As the depth of snow increased through the winter, the necessity became ever more troublesome.

The winter proved long and disagreeable as everyone tried to cope with each passing day. In the first few weeks of winter, they were talkative. They told stories of strange sightings, cruel and clever shipmasters, shipwrecks, whales, and sea creatures that looked like women. It was often difficult to tell where truth left, and when fantasy took over. They spoke of home life and the plight of a careworn family, of their children, and their hopes for a happier life.

Sean sang, playing along with his concertina. Strange tunes from his country they were, but at least, at first, they provided a distraction. Cornelius sang songs of his homeland, Wallonia.

Eventually, the same songs constantly repeated became annoying. It was Lars who seemed to have an endless supply of Viking legends, one more far-fetched than another. The life story of each man, including Joost, was told with endless, rambling repetition, some turning to the sea to escape a serious trouble at home, others forced onto the ship in a drunken confusion. Dietrich had expected a quick profit for his trouble. Lars knew no life other than seafaring. Johannes added his own story, but the facial expressions and comments of his listeners told him that they could not understand the frustrations of the son of a city merchant.

Left over by the previous traders were two books. They were children's books, one about a poor girl who became a princess, another the stories of a boy no bigger than a thumb. Only Johannes knew how to read. Reading for him, however, was limited. Still his cabin mates insisted that he make the best of it. As he struggled with each word, he regretted the time he spent daydreaming in school when he could have learned properly. He found it easier to make up stories around the drawings in the books.

Johannes brought out Antoine's book from his sea bag. He knew not a word of French and there were no drawings in it. Dietrich spoke a little French, but he could read in no language.

Their constant complaining and quarreling threatened their survival. To break up the boredom and tension of the cramped cabin, on sunny days Johannes bundled up in duffel and made long treks along the river or into the forest. Such great trees were a marvel to a boy from Holland. Deeper into the winter, with the snow drifted high against the house, the men withdrew more into themselves, talking less, easily brought to quarrel.

What Johannes hated most was the boredom; every day there was nothing to do but wait. He thought about home. He pondered wasting his life on adventures that seemed exciting at first but soon turned tedious, to say nothing of the danger and hardships.

There was one diversion from the cruel monotony of long winter months. It happened on December 6, before the deepening snow bound them to indoors. It was about high noon when a thumping on the door startled everyone. It was opened—and there stood *Sinterklaas.* His long robe was a length of duffel and his bishop's miter was a beaver pelt. In one hand, he carried a flintlock and in the other, a fat goose. Cornelius had not forgotten that it was The Feast of Saint Nicholas.[65]

In no time, the goose was plucked, stuffed with potatoes and spices, and baked over the open fire. It was Johannes's job to turn the spit over and over so that it would burn. The thought of a Christmas goose in this far-away world was enough to cheer even the most depressed of the traders.

As the men enjoyed the drumsticks and all the meat they could find on the roast, their holiday mood improved. Someone suggested gifts. "Why not open Rut's sea bag," Dietrich ventured. "Everyone will receive a gift. Rut won't need them anymore."

Joost resisted at first but with continued insistence finally gave in. To Johannes, it was a dreadful idea, but he had to go along with the spirit of the rest. To make the search more interesting, all agreed that each man would reach in and take out one item until all were gone. It was a game of luck and one that picked up the mood of the cabin-bound men.

First, out came a woolen scarf. Next was a shoe-sized ship that Rut had been whittling from scrap wood at restful times during the journey. Then came a shirt and next a tightly rolled flag of The United Provinces of New Netherland. The game continued until the sea bag was empty of Rut's worldly possessions: a pair of woolen socks, a necklace made of seashells, some tiny wooden ships and a deck of cards.

Johannes was last to reach into the sea bag; he felt something at the bottom that was hard and half-rounded. Even before he pulled it out, he knew what it was: the magnifying lens that Rut had purchased in Amsterdam. He used it to carve small details on his model ship. Johannes had no idea what he would do with a lens.

The long days wore on. Games with Rut's cards often grew unruly. Petty squabbles were part of everyday life. The monotony of unchanging cycles of day after day became absolute. They saw the same unshaven faces and unwashed bodies, looked at the same walls, heard the same voices. The books were read, the life-stories told, the games of cards played. No one could stand to hear the concertina player's songs one more time. Each man sunk into a state of depression, withdrawn within himself, so that he uttered barely a word the whole day. He knew that the next day would be exactly like the previous day, except that the snow piled against the cabin would be a little higher. This boredom would go on and on until spring or until everyone went completely mad.[66]

Johannes toyed with his gift, the close-up lens. He found his shirt was close-woven while the duffel had a loose weave. Did that account for their differences in softness? He examined the grains of oak planks and found the fibers twisted tightly. Those of the pine, on the other hand, were loose. Was this the difference between a hard wood and a soft wood? A dead ant found in one corner was smooth all over; a moth was covered with a hairy skin. Now, no object in that cabin was beyond the scrutiny of a close-up lens. The differences in seeing things too small for the plain eye became a fascination for the young sailor. He had already mastered the far-looking lens from the foremast. Now, he held a new close-looking world in his hands.[67]

Before winter's end, the supply of food was nearly gone. The traders were forced to take drastic measures. They agreed with the Mahicans to exchange corn and meat for some of their own: spare boots, shirts, and gold earrings. To persuade a man to give up his prized possession required of Joost the tact of the Dutch diplomat to France. Even more, the Mahicans wanted a flintlock, not a matchlock as a bargaining chip.[68]

CHAPTER 16

A Bridge

Slowly, the days drew longer and the chill from the north winds slackened a bit. The river churned from breaking ice. By midday when the sun was bright, the ground had thawed. It was on one of those balmy days of early spring that Johannes set out to chop another supply of firewood. The snow lay in heaps around the stockade but in the open sun and the wind-exposed garden, bare earth showed through in muddy puddles.

The young woodchopper liked the feeling of reaching high into the air with a sharp axe and bringing it down sharply and forcefully onto an upturned log. Again and again he struck, and the sound resounded across the field with a faint echo. When his blow struck the log just right, it split with a crack. As he got more practice, his log splits became neater and the wood piled up more easily.

Johannes worked on that bright morning with a touch of sweat over his brow. He did not think of the boredom of his cabin or of the comfort of his home in Amsterdam. The thought of Gouda cheese barely came up in his head. The feel of metal striking wood and the smells of early spring were enough to fill all sensations.

Yet, during this work, he became strangely aware of someone in his presence, the kind of unexplainable awareness that sometimes happens to a person alone.

Suddenly, Johannes heard a low growl coming from behind him. His head whipped around. Standing there not more than a long jump away was an enormous wolf. Johannes had never seen a wolf up close; its piercing stare, pulled back ears and toothy snarl turned his insides to ice. Instinctively, Johannes lifted his axe high overhead with both arms and was ready to bring it down, but his raised arms were frozen in fear.

Even before he could release his arms in defense against the wild beast, another figure caught the corner of his eye. His body spun toward it. There at the edge of the field not twenty steps away stood a tall *Wilde.* He stood tall, his arms folded in front, his face broadened into a grin. He had a long bow slung across a shoulder. If this strange encounter were not enough, there sitting on his head was a broad-brimmed blue hat. Even for a traveler who had been thrice across an ocean, the sight was astonishing.

The *Wilde* was a Mohawk. Red stripes on his cheeks and style of leggings told Johannes that. And suddenly, Johannes realized something else: it was the young man who had come to the trading house just before winter set in, the one whose haunting eyes followed him everywhere, the one who gave him the feather from his headband.

The Mohawk slowly lifted his left hand up while the grip of Johannes tightened on the still-raised axe. The hand reached up and lifted the hat from his head. The arm drew back and with a snap threw the hat toward Johannes. The hat skimmed along the ground like a low-flying owl, plopping down among the wood chips at Johannes's feet. Puzzled, Johannes slowly relaxed his grip on the axe, lowered his arms and bent to pick the hat up. It somehow looked familiar. More astonishing, inside the brim were the initials JvdZ.

His mind raced to explain this extraordinary affair. In a flash, it all became clear. The hat was his! His mother had sewn in his initials for good luck. It was the hat that he had tossed at passing canoes three years before.

With these thoughts jumbling in his head at one time, Johannes broke into a chuckle. Soon, both the young men found themselves sharing a cautious laugh. The Mohawk took a few bold steps toward the Dutchman and raised his right arm so that it made a sharp angle at the elbow. Johannes took steps toward the Mohawk and hooked his arm around. All the time, the wolf stood silently, turning its head from side to side as if trying to comprehend the amazing events and commenting with a bark now and then.

Here stood two young men, one from a world of ruffled collars, the other from a world of animal skins, locked-arm-in-arm and, for the moment, forming a bridge over a muddy puddle as if the ocean itself between their worlds had shrunk.

All at once, Johannes felt the loose-flowing frame of the *Wilde* suddenly tense. The *Wilde* pulled back. His face stiffened. In an instant the laughing, stomping, and barking came to an end. In the silence that followed, Johannes heard a click. Then another click. He whirled around and found himself staring into the muzzles of two long muskets. There, not ten steps away stood Dietrich and Sean, their matchlocks held deadly horizontal, pointing straight at them.

"Stand aside, Van der Zee," bellowed Dietrich.

"Be quick about it, if you do not want to feel hot lead," Sean snarled.

Johannes felt a chill run from his feet straight up to his neck. The strength of the moment before drained away much in the way that snow melts in a flame. His chest tightened. He tried to speak but the voice was caught somewhere deep inside my throat.

Dietrich persisted, "Step away, Van der Zee, I say again."

Johannes struggled to find some words but could only say "No! No!" The hunters moved a few steps closer. He shouted "Wait!" and held up his palms on outstretched arms.

His words only seemed to make the faces of the men more flushed. Their grips on the weapons tightened. A string of squirrels and pigeons dangling from their necks spoke of their success with firearms.

"You are in the way, boy," yelled Dietrich.

"Stop!" Johannes pleaded. "You must listen to me. The *Wilde* means no harm."

The hunters did not listen, but instead, they began to circle around the pair to gain a clearer aim on the *Wilde*. Johannes groped with ways to make his trading partners yield. Yet, he had seen enough of the struggle between Good and Evil on ships to feel the hopelessness in their situation. But if there were any surprises of that day, he was hardly prepared for what was about to happen.

The *Wilde* broke away from Johannes and with slow, deliberate steps walked straight toward the hunters. He stopped but an arm's length from the ends of their long barrels. He pulled himself up to his full height and stretched his arms out to the sides. The wolf stood unmoving at his side. Then the *Wilde* turned toward Johannes, his back to the hunters. Johannes held his breath in horror and waited for a deafening blast that was about to come. But, the amazed woodsmen held their fire.

In the faces of his trading partners, he saw only hostility. In the face of the *Wilde*, Johannes saw something else. It was not the expression of fear or of hatred. Instead, his delicate, bronzed features had a calm, peaceful expression. The eyes seemed fixed past the guns and past the gunmen, as if he were staring into a space and time far beyond the reach of mortals. It was the same gaze that Johannes had seen so many times in that of Pilot-Navigator, Francisco Escobar, as he looked at the fog-bound sea, determined and fearless in the search of direction by divine guidance.

The young sailor's thoughts stumbled over each other as he tried to find a way to break the impasse. Finally, he blurted out, "Shipmaster Adriaen Block knows this *Wilde.* We saw him once paddling on the river." The men with their heavy flintlocks looked puzzled, but they did not move. "See, my cap," he went on, putting the blue cap on his head and pointing to it over and over. "He is only returning it to me."

"You talk crazy, Van der Zee. The smoky cabin has taken away your reason."

With this remark, Johannes felt bolder. "I tell you again, this is my friend. Put down your flintlocks," he demanded.

Dietrich spoke sharply, "Van der Zee, we are here to trade, not to make friends."

All the time, the *Wilde* stood stiff, arms out, like a tree with two branches. Further emboldened by his courage, Johannes said, "Making enemies will not get us any more furs, either." And to his surprise, the point of Jacob's gun slowly lowered. Sean's soon followed.

Slowly, the arms of the *Wilde* came down. He turned, and slowly made his way to the edge of the forest, never looking back. The grizzled wolf followed silently. The three speechless traders watched until the young *Wilde* reached the dense underbrush and disappeared into the trees.

"We thought the *Wilde* and the wolf were trying to kill you," claimed Dietrich.

"You should be grateful," uttered Sean. "We tried to save your life."

There was no use arguing with such men, thought Johannes. They had seen life only through harsh and cruel realities. They met this uncertain new land unwillingly with mistrust, expecting danger at any moment. They chose to find safety in gunpowder.

The men did not tarry long but soon returned to the warmth of the cabin. Johannes was left alone with his thoughts and with his blue cap. It had traveled far, and it was fine as ever. For Johannes, it became more than just a beautiful cap; it was a bridge between two worlds.

CHAPTER 17

Words

THE INCIDENT WITH the Mohawk had caused unspoken but unrelenting tension between Johannes and his so-called rescuers. Joost was unable to sort out whose story was right and whose was wrong. Johannes came to believe that the other men sided with Dietrich and Sean. Until now, he had stayed clear of the petty quarrels and jealousies that kept the men agitated. Now, he could not rid himself of rage. Even so, he kept it to himself. He spent every waking day outside of the cabin by himself, taking long walks into the forest and along the river. Wood-splitting and digging the garden were springtime chores that got him away from the others. Only after dark did he return to the cabin and then he kept to himself.

At dawn, three or four days after the incident with the blue cap, a rap on the door awakened everyone. They were astonished to see just outside the same *Wilde*. This time, he had a full-sized antlered deer slung across his shoulders. He lowered the deer and squatted beside it, a broad smile across his face. He pointed to the mortal wound where his arrow struck.

The men were suddenly in a joyous mood. They would have venison for dinner at last, not squirrel and rabbit! Although they had discharged plenty of gunpowder from their precious flintlocks and had suffered frostbitten toes, the men had never been able to shoot a deer. The animal was just too skittish for the hunter's aim. Making things worse, in addition, was its increased trading value: the Mahicans were now demanding too high a price for a deer. Now, success with the lowly bow and arrow lay before their eyes.

The *Wilde* took his leave moments later. He just stood up, turned and soon melted into the distant trees.

It was the following day that Johannes tried to clear his head in the solitude of the forest. Somehow, the cawing of crows, the rustling of the pines and the smell of their needles provided a comfort that he needed. It was in this state of deep thought that he was startled by a figure standing next to him. It was again the *Wilde* boy again smiling and again with his wolf.

He beckoned Johannes to follow. The young seaman-turned-trader was led to a lean-to made of pine boughs and bark. Nearby was a small circle of stones centered with glowing ashes. The boys sat together, laughing, trying to understand each other with hand gestures, hopelessly at first.

The *Wilde* then drew a bird on the bare fireside ground with a stick. Its features were carefully detailed with a giant feather at its hind end. He pointed to the tail, then to himself. Johannes delighted to learn that his name was "Feather." Pointing again and again with hand signs, the *Wilde* got the idea across that his name was "Tail Feather."

Johannes could not draw a picture of his own name, so he voiced it: Yo-HAN-nes, pointing to himself. What came back was Ho-HAN-nes. With a little practice, Tail Feather got it almost right. The *Y* sound starting the Dutch boy's name, though, was difficult for Tail Feather to say. There came more laughter with each try.

And so, day after day, Johannes went into the forest under the pretense of hunting and collecting specimens. Each day, the boys practiced words. Johannes found that he had a very attentive student who seemed eager to learn his language and, more, his ways. Johannes picked up Mohawk words much more slowly, but learned to follow animal tracks, shoot an arrow, and build a fire with a stone that made sparks.

Of course, all his companions noticed the absence of Johannes for much of the day, every day. The fact that he came back each day with a rabbit or raccoon from trapping did not allay suspicions that something else was going on besides hunting, something they feared: becoming too friendly with the *Wilden*. At night around the hearth, Johannes spoke of his ventures exploring along the river. These stories were not enough to quench idle gossip.

Still, Johannes continued his daily meetings with the Mohawk. It was not many weeks before they could speak with some understanding, mixing up two languages and topping off conversations with hand signs. What Johannes eventually learned was that his newfound friend was curious about the ways of the traders who had come to his land. He wanted to learn where they came from. What did the traders do with so many furs? The two boys told each other of family, village, and things they liked. They laughed about the comical moments that happened while they tried to exchange information. Throughout these daily encounters, Tail Feather kept a low fire so that no smoke arose to reveal his whereabouts to the Mahicans or the traders.

One day, Tail Feather announced, “Tomorrow, I go to my village in mountains.” Before Johannes could jump to volunteer to accompany him, Tail Feather said, “You go with me.”

The idea was thrilling. A new adventure. What stories to tell back in Amsterdam! "Yes! Yes, I will go," Johannes replied. He questioned, "How long will it take?"

"Ten days to my village. Six days to return. You stay in my village as long as you like."

Johannes was puzzled. "Why ten days going and six days back?"

"The river" was the answer. "Walk part way going, canoe all the way back."

It was a simple explanation. But Johannes anticipated a problem. Would Joost give him permission? There is work to be done at the trading post. The men needed the game that he brings home every day. Of course, it would be easy to just disappear for so many days. That would mean desertion. The punishment for desertion is... Johannes did not even want to think about that. Suddenly, an idea popped into this head. "Tail Feather! Go with me to the trading post. I will ask my chief about going to your village."

The two reached the cabin by nightfall. The men were leery of the *Wilde* yet they showed no hostility. The wolf at his side caused the biggest anxiety. Joost beckoned Tail Feather inside. KyKoo curled up in sleep just outside the door.

Many questions were asked of Tail Feather by the light of the hearth and for quite some time Johannes patiently helped to provide answers. After what seemed to be a long, long time, he dared to approach Joost with his own special message: "Tail Feather wants me to go to his village. It will be a journey of many days."

Joost did not answer immediately. Instead, he poured some hot water into his cup and took some long sips. Finally, he spoke, "We have already lost one man. I do not care to lose another. The ice in the river is breaking up. In a few weeks, a ship will arrive."

Johannes added, "In the Mohawk village I will see that his people send more pelts."

Joost found this argument persuasive as he looked around at the half empty store of furs. "So be it, but you must return within twenty days, not a day later."

The *Wilde* departed with KyKoo. There was a great sense of relief with the departure, as the men did not dare venture out for their necessities while the wolf was still lying just outside their door. By early morning, Johannes had put his things together and started off toward Tail Feather's lean-to. Just as he left, with well wishes from all, Joost handed Johannes one of the flintlocks and a pouch of powder. Johannes did not choose to carry a weapon; he had fired one only once before. Still, Joost insisted. "Always keep some powder in the breech," he cautioned. "You never know what dangers come without warning."

The boys met at the lean-to. Tail Feather was displeased that Johannes carried the musket but grudgingly allowed him to take it. The journey began with a quick walk to the river.

CHAPTER 18

The Falls

Tail Feather, with KyKoo following close behind, led Johannes to the river. There, the trek hugged the riverbank to an iced-over marsh. As they came to a clump of branches and reeds that bordered on a stream, Tail Feather began to pull the brush aside. There, to his astonishment, Johannes saw a long, slender boat made of bark. It was a canoe with paddles and a basket sitting on the bottom.

First, Tail Feather entered the canoe at the stern. With the grace of a dancer, he first held onto each side of the canoe, then flung the far leg over and stepped in the center of the hull. He then pulled the near leg in. Next, he helped KyKoo step in where the wolf found a comfortable spot in the canoe's waist, its middle. Tail Feather beckoned Johannes to step into the bow.

"Will it hold us?" Johannes asked.

"You will soon see."

Johannes, somehow overcoming his fright, followed the same actions but not like a dancer. The little craft tipped sharply on receiving his weight, but it soon steadied. The boys were ready to begin their adventure.

Johannes quickly picked up the knack of paddling a canoe as Tail Feather set the course from behind. The canoe was kept close to shore where the downriver current against them was not strong. The canoe that rocked so easily when sitting, to his surprise, was stable when it moved along at a good speed. At times, a headwind impeded their progress while it churned up waves. Yet, the canoe proved seaworthy.

By high sun, the canoe had progressed to where a large river joined their river. They were now in earshot of a distant, deep roar that seemed to make the whole earth tremble. Johannes turned, pointing toward the roar with a questioning expression. Tail Feather did not answer but instead swerved the canoe into the adjoining river. They paddled past two small islands, and then carried their canoe over small rapids. With the canoe in the water again and headed upstream, the paddlers were soon looking at spray that crossed the entire river. Above it there hung a rainbow. At a closer distance, Johannes could make out a gigantic ledge over which poured more water than he ever could have imagined. This exhilarating sight amidst the thunderous roar and the chilling mist was a moment to celebrate, to remember forever.[69]

Johannes came up with an idea! Once again, he would surely impress Tail Feather. With this thought, he took up his flintlock and standing placed it against his shoulder pointing toward the sky. In almost the same instant, he let flint strike powder.

The blast set forth a strong recoil. With it, the canoe tipped sharply, took in water and in a flash, was upside down.

Johannes found himself floundering in frigid water. Thrashing about, gulping water with each frantic breath, he tried in vain to sound out a call for a helping hand as he floated downstream. Sputtering for air, energy quickly fading, his vision graying, he had a glimpse of Tail Feather on shore just moments before the water took him under. The *Wilde* was laughing too hard to even stand. Johannes thought of one last thing before that final gulp that would send him into a watery grave: it was about the treachery played upon him by this savage.

But Johannes did not drown. His first conscious feeling was of violent shivering. He was unable to speak. Slowly, he regained his sense to realize that he was now on the shore. He was lying naked on a mound of dried grass. A layer of grass had been piled on top. One quick look around took in the canoe. Next to it were the basket and the paddles. There, too, was his duffel sea bag. His flintlock was nowhere in sight.

His tormentor was now completely crazy. He squatted nearby as he scratched some stones together. A few sparks ignited a small pile of twigs. He added larger and larger pieces of wood until a fire was ablaze. Was he, Johannes thought, about to be roasted? Johannes next saw Tail Feather hanging his clothes on branches placed around the fire. It was not long before the life-giving warmth began to take effect. The shivering slowed.

Johannes reflected on what happened, but the details only came bit by bit. He knew that he had done something stupid. He knew, too, that this *Wilde* had rescued him from certain death. But why had Tail Feather let him nearly drown? Why did he think it all so funny? Why did he go through the trouble of rescuing him? Perhaps to enjoy another near-death trial?

Yes, the Dutch sailor was alive. For that, Johannes was thankful. Yet, he was troubled. He felt strangely alone in a strange place. What was on the mind of his friend? His flintlock lay at the bottom of the river. Now he had no way to protect himself.

His thoughts then skipped to Joost and the pain he was sure to endure for returning to the trading post without his firearm. Perhaps drowning would be the more pleasant fate. It was perhaps this thought more than any other that persuaded Johannes to continue his journey and to put as much distance between himself and the traders as possible.

It was the following day before the boys set off together in their canoe. No words had been spoken. Having seen the place of the great falls, the now silent travelers returned to the North River, heading upriver. A wall of misunderstanding had come between the two. Neither one knew how to talk of the strange events of the day before. The tension between the two seemed to mount with every paddle stroke.

Finally, after they pulled ashore to sleep that night, Johannes said, "I was foolish." Foolish was not a word they learned in either language but the idea of stupid or silly was conveyed with gestures. He then posed a question, "Why did you save me?"

"Ho-han-nes, you are my friend. Why do you seem not..." he struggled to find the word, "... eh, happy?"

"As I was going underwater, I saw you onshore laughing."

"Oh," Tail Feather started to explain. The answer, in fact, was quite simple. It was one that Johannes had not thought of after reliving the terrible experience a thousand times in his mind. "You splash the way a funny person, a clown, would. In my head, you were making fun."

"But I was drowning. I know not how to swim!"

The Mohawk was puzzled. "You cross great water in a ship and know not how to swim. That is sad."

Johannes found no fault in this reasoning. He told himself, "I am just an ordinary seaman. Not many of us know how to swim. If we fall off the ship, it will not turn around to rescue us. It is better to die quickly than try to swim across an ocean. Seamen live by staying out of the water, not falling into it." All this he could not explain in simple language.

What was missing in the exchange of words and hands was

gratitude for his rescue. To put right this oversight, Johannes said with great sincerity in his voice, "I am happy. I give thanks to you for saving my life, for bringing in the canoe and paddles, even my sea bag. I know that you, too, could have died in that cold water." Tail Feather looked a bit puzzled. Not knowing if his companion understood his words, Johannes extended his hand slowly in Tail Feather's direction and smiled. Tail Feather smiled back.

It was on the third day of paddling that the downward current had become too powerful for paddles. They had to abandon the canoe and depend on their feet to take them the rest of the way. At Tail Feather's instructions, the boys pulled the canoe to the edge of a marsh where higher ground gave rise to a hardwood forest. They came to a place where two giant-sized, gray, oval-shaped boulders stood side by side. Between them rushed a babbling stream that spilled into the marsh.

Tail Feather motioned for Johannes to hold the canoe near the falling stream. He then ran to collect rocks found beneath the trees. With each return, he placed the rocks in the canoe, and the paddles at the bottom. "Now," thought Johannes, "who has gone crazy?" Trip after trip brought enough rocks to weigh the canoe down until it sank and was hidden in the stream. The basket and the sea bag now became packs for carrying. Ahead were many days of hard walking but with promise of wonderful sights along the way.

CHAPTER 19

The Trek

On foot, they stayed close to the riverbank while at the same time remaining hidden at the edge of the forest. Tail Feather led the way at a fast pace, KyKoo lolling just behind. Johannes did his best to keep up and, at first, he did quite well for someone accustomed to a ship or confined to a cabin. Still, his companion never became impatient.

The three crossed grassy marshes and meadows with high reeds, climbed ridges, squeezed through thick pine forests and over and under fallen trees, and at times emerged on high ledges with a long view. All the way, they exchanged words of their languages, teaching each other the names of trees, animals, and weather conditions. They learned the names of feelings (thirst, hunger, pain) and actions (walk, run, jump, swim).

Johannes soon realized that his companion of the forest learned the words in Dutch much more quickly than he could learn them in Mohawk. Those words were long. Some words were made from many small words. In ordinary talking, the Mohawk spoke as if singing. In every way, the language of the *Wilden*, Johannes slowly realized, was as fully developed and as complete as his own.

Around a small fire after nightfall, the two talked about their families. Tail Feather seemed to understand that Johannes had one sister who was younger than he was, that his mother and father were very severe, that his father was a trader in furs. Johannes got from Tail Feather that he had two nearly grown-up sisters who were twins. He also had a sister who was still little. Her name was "Sky Flower." Three winters ago, his father traveled this same river but never returned. For him, his mother sheds tears every day.

"How old are you? How many years do you have?" Johannes asked, carefully explaining his questions in winters passed. The question was difficult to convey but the answer was even more baffling for him. It seemed that Tail Feather did not know.

Frequent stops were made to gather food, but it was of a kind that was hidden to a seaman's eye. There were nuts and berries. Now and then, a nest with eggs was found. These were eaten raw, a delicacy to Tail Feather. For Johannes eating raw eggs was at first disgusting. But there is an old saying, "Hunger is the best sauce."

Nights were spent on a thick layer of pine boughs lying on top of a layer of moss. Johannes rolled up in his blanket, using his sea bag as a pillow. Tail Feather slept beneath a bearskin, always with KyKoo at his side.

Tail Feather had a custom of plunging into the water every morning, even for a moment. He did so on first awakening, no matter how cold. Johannes, on the other hand, held back. He never found frequent bathing necessary. It was not the way of his people. Bodies in Holland and on ships had strong odors. That was expected. *Wilden* did not.

After days of hard trekking, Johannes was only too aware of a problem. The leather of his shoes became stiff from frequent soaking and drying. To make matters worse, the soles had worn so thin that the balls of his feet were exposed. Tail Feather saw him falling behind and limping. He pulled out a pair of plain moccasins from his basket and handed them over. Johannes found them a good fit. What was strange was that he could feel the ground beneath each footstep. Tail Feather showed how it was possible to walk silently through the forest with moccasins since a snap of a twig or crunch of a leaf could be avoided from the feel. Johannes also realized knowing how to and doing were two different things. Walking in silence took much practice.

At one point as they crossed a creek, Tail Feather pointed to a massive pile of sticks. "Sit here and watch," he instructed. Before long, a furry animal swam up the creek pushing sticks in its mouth. These, the animal placed alongside the pile of wood. All around were stumps of trees as if the forest had been just cleared. But the cuts were not those of an axe or saw. "Now you see where your pelts came from."[70]

"So, these are beavers?" Johannes cried out in disbelief. He had somehow put out of mind that each pelt stowed at Fort Nassau and each pelt that his father bought and sold was once an animal. It was an animal that worked hard to cut wood with its teeth, to build strong houses for its family and somehow survive the winter. Its thick, plush fur was meant for something besides a fancy coat and wide-brimmed hat.

"How are the beavers caught?" was a question for Tail Feather. Here is how Johannes understood the answer. A hunter swims to the stick house and breaks through its the thick wall. There, he snatches all the beavers inside. They bite and struggle. In winter, it is cold. Then there is the work of stripping the fur and scraping the inside clean. Getting beaver pelts is not easy.

Here at the creek was a lesson for Johannes: why beaver pelts were becoming scarcer. He realized that it must take a long time for a beaver to make a house in mid-stream and raise its young there. Yet, Dutch merchants were hungry for more and more pelts. There were only so many beavers. As more ships came with metal knives and blankets to exchange for pelts, the beavers would disappear altogether. Johannes now had some troubling thoughts about the purpose of Fort Nassau.

Most of the walking kept them in deep forest where detection was least likely. Now and again they would come to the river's edge. What drew them to it was the sound of rushing water. They now had come to a place where cascades gushed over rock ledges and sped in dizzying whirlpools and foam. Some huge rocks lying in mid-river were partially exposed in the spray. What caught Johannes's attention was the fact that these rocks were different from any that he had seen before. They were flat on top. To him, they looked like dinner tables that were large enough to seat a hundred people at each one. But the water that swirled around top and poured over the side would surely spoil a royal feast.[71]

Tail Feather yelled over the water's roar, "Follow me!" With these words, he set his basket down, stepped onto a flat rock at the shore and from there leaped onto a series of other rocks until he reached the table rock in mid-river. KyKoo, instead, partly jumped and partly swam. Then both walked directly into the wall of water that poured over one edge and disappeared. Johannes could not believe his eyes. Was this magic?

Of course, Johannes followed across the slippery, flat rocks, though not as agilely as his trail leader. It took some courage to plunge through the falling water but when he did, he saw Tail Feather and KyKoo standing in a huge cave. A moment later his friend's big grin strangely disappeared. Looking around, Johannes realized that they were in a massive room larger than any he had ever known in Holland (except for his church). Above them was the continuous growl of the river. Another surprise: Tail Feather let out a blood-curdling yell, *Aaahoo.* It echoed throughout the chamber with the kind of hollow sound heard in a conch shell. And he soon found a reason for the disappearing grin. Johannes had forgotten to leave his sea bag behind. Now it was soaked along with the blanket inside.

They emerged from the underwater, under-rock cave, passing again under the falling water. In his excitement and with a water-heavy blanket, Johannes took an unsteady step on the slanted flat rock. Within seconds his legs melted underneath him. To cushion his fall, he struck his right arm sharply against the rock. As he slid into the cold, raging water around him, he felt a powerful grip on the wrist of his other arm. Tail Feather held on and carefully pulled him onto solid footing. Together, they made their way back to shore.

By now, he felt a strong throbbing in the arm. It was not long before pain was added to the throbbing. Johannes looked closer at his injury and saw that his arm near the wrist was curved like a spoon. To add to his chill and sopping misery he now had a broken arm.

Tail Feather quickly pulled a piece of bark off a fallen elm tree and with Johannes's long knife shaped it into two strips. With lengths of leather thong, he wrapped the bark strips snugly around the misshapen arm. Inside, a thin pad of moss provided a soft cushion for the skin against the bark. While Johannes lay there in agony, Tail Feather went into the forest, returning with some leaves that he ground between two round stones. These he gave to Johannes with water in a cup made from bark. "The leaves will lessen the pain. It is my fault," confessed Tail Feather. "There was no need to stray off our path, even for a look at a strange sight."

"No, no," answered Johannes. "Being in the cave, hearing your voice boom over the roar of the water above is a memory that will last me the rest of my life. A broken arm will be forgotten in a few weeks." Tail Feather nodded.

It was another day before Johannes felt recovered enough to continue the walk. But first, Tail Feather unrolled one of his deerskins from his basket and cut a palm-wide strip. This, he tied into a loop, placing it around the neck of Johannes and gently sliding the forearm in. "Now," he reassured, "your arm will not bounce with every step. We will go more slowly from here on."

There were no more side trips, but there were some wonderful places to see up ahead. At one point, a river poured into the North River from the left side. The joining river was as wide as the main one. Just beyond, the river narrowed sharply into a roaring gorge. Above were great overhanging ledges. Tail Feather kept creeping along the rocky edges until standing directly beneath the most protruding overhang. Johannes followed along stepping from stone to stone. "Here," said Tail Feather, "Mahicans with fearful masks have their dances by fire."[72]

"There," pointing upriver, he said, "the river rushes over boulders in a spraying roar. One night on foot and without moon, we carried our canoes down here under the noses of the fire dancers." One look at the cascade ahead made Johannes shudder as he listened to the amazing feat.

"Watch for holes in these smooth rocks," cautioned Tail Feather as they moved along. Johannes was dumbfounded to see round depressions in the shelf of rock; they were knee deep and smooth inside. "One of our men stepped in one that dark night. His hurt leg brought us much trouble."

From here on, the river flowed gently along high sandy banks. It snaked through marshes. In places, where the river widened a bit, trees came up to the narrow shoreline. Everywhere, soaring birds, flitting birds, wading birds, and swimming birds squawked and sang and peeped and quacked. Giant frogs jumped out of the way. Muskrats skittered into shoreline holes. Never had Johannes seen a place so filled with life. Night in the marshes brought new sounds. Johannes knew not which animals made them.

With two more days of the journey, Johannes came upon a sight as stunning as any he had ever seen. It was along a shallow part of the river where water raced across a rock-lined bottom. On the right side, the shore rose slowly under shrubs and small trees. On the left side, a high wall of jagged rock rose straight up. The wall was blue. Was he becoming delirious? Splashing down from the top was a small waterfall. They stopped to rest and to take it all in.[73]

Ten days of walking brought them to a high ridge. There in the far distance were a few trails of smoke that spiraled up against a cloudless sky. Up closer, they could make out a cluster of bark houses that sat scattered within a thick wall of standing poles. Johannes was astonished at the length of these bark houses. The thrill of visiting a Mohawk village sent him into a mood of exhilaration, the same kind of feeling he had when he first spotted land from atop the foremast of *The Unicorn.*

Johannes welcomed the end of his journey. They had eaten nothing but a few berries, nuts, and some roots over the past several days, walking steadily with barely a rest until full darkness made it too dangerous. The anticipation of entering a Mohawk village—no Netherlander or, as far as he knew, any other European had done so before—was enough to make him forget about the hardship of travel and his aching arm and weary legs.[74]

CHAPTER 20

The Look-Through-Stone

THE FAST SINKING sun had barely touched the distant mountaintops when the trekkers came to the high and thick fence that enclosed the village. Tail Feather found the secret entry point with no difficulty. Well hidden by intertwining saplings and branches, the opening led into a winding narrow passageway. Johannes dutifully followed his guide, pushing aside smaller branches, twigs, and assorted old foliage.

Inside, a cluster of a dozen or so longhouses greeted them. The houses reminded Johannes of the loaves of bread that sit in every bakery shop window in Amsterdam. A tall post stood in the center of the sprawl. On top of the post sat the skull of an antlered animal.

It was but an instant later that a small child spotted the new arrivals. She let out a high-pitched yell, "*Gy-yahhh.*" Within another instant, young and old crowded excitedly around the two boys. There was much joy on seeing Tail Feather smiling and sound in body. But their joy was overshadowed by their timid curiosity on seeing a tall boy with a white face topped with long, flowing yellow hair. Others quickly gathered.

One of the women strode toward Tail Feather with a look that told Johannes that she was his mother. Despite her broad smile, Johannes thought it was a sad face, and the lines around her eyes told of long endured grief. Beside her were two grown-up girls who looked exactly the same. Johannes had guessed right. These were Tail Feather's sisters. Johannes remembered that Tail Feather had mentioned them when the boys were telling each other about their families with words and much hand talk. Each of the sisters held onto one hand of a toddler. "Hmmm," he thought, "so, here is Sky Flower."

Johannes glanced around anxiously at the throng pressing around him. Yet, in the excitement, no one spoke. In truth, there was an eerie silence. Johannes saw that most of the men wore only a leather breechcloth. Their chests were bare despite the chill in the air. Bold designs in black or red designs marked many faces. Large shells hung from the necks. Women wore full-length soft leather; the sleeves and hems ended in long strips. The smallest children wore nothing at all.

The people of the village kept a respectable distance from Johannes. Yet, no one in the village missed any of the strange details in the newcomer. It was not only his lack of skin color, his yellow hair, the hair on his chin, or his blue eyes. They were even more astonished by his long, woolen shirt and pantaloons.

Suddenly, the crowd split into two to make a pathway. Chief Red Sun stepped out of the longest of the longhouses. He wore a headdress of antlers. His shoulder-to-foot cloak shimmered in an array of colors in the fading light of day.[75]

The stately figure edged forward in long, slow steps. Chief Red Sun came to stand squarely but a footstep in front of Tail Feather. He folded his arms high in front, his feet placed tightly together. Chief Red Sun spoke slowly, "We are happy that our brave young man has returned safely from his journey." With his eyes directly focused on Tail Feather, he continued, "We hope that you have learned much about the ways of trading people who come to the River-That-Flows-Two Ways." Chief Red Sun waited for a reply. Of course, Johannes understood barely a word.

Tail Feather answered after an uneasy hesitation. "Yes, I have learned about some things of their ways." Another pause followed, then, "See, I have brought one of the traders to our village. He has come to meet our people and to learn about our ways." Straining to say it right, Tail Feather added, "His name is Ho-Han-nes." Johannes, through it all, remained mystified but amused by the exchange of words.

Then, moving aside to stand before Johannes, Chief Red Sun carefully looked the young man over from head to toe. Stepping back a step and glancing toward Tail Feather, Chief Red Sun announced, "Tell your friend that he is welcome in our village. I see that he has been hurt." It was simple language, and Tail Feather could put these words into Dutch. Chief Red Sun went on, "Tell Ho-Han-nes that our people greet him in friendship. We trust that he will find a peace here within our village." Again, the translation came in words and gestures. Chief Red Sun spoke once again, "Tell your friend that we are happy to share all that we have. Our shaman will tend to his arm."

Taking a few more steps backward, Chief Red Sun stated, "Now, our young brave and the stranger must rest from a long journey. We will see that there is enough honey, meat, and cornmeal to bring back your strength. Tomorrow, we will all gather at the meeting circle. Ho-Han-nes can tell us about his own village far away." With these words, the chief unlocked his arms, turned around and slowly strode toward his longhouse at the far end of the village. The pathway between people did not close again until he had entered the longhouse.

During the welcoming, Johannes kept scanning the amazing sight before him. The houses were narrow. Some were as long as *The Unicorn.* White smoke rose lazily from several openings along the arched roofs. Outdoor fires between longhouses glowed beneath wooden frames. Nearby, a pot hung from a stake. Fish lay on racks scattered all over. Animal skins, big and small were stretched out on other racks and on the ground.

Tail Feather led Johannes to his own longhouse for a closer look. Overlapping rough bark covered it all. Over the slabs of bark, saplings bent tightly. At one end of the longhouse, hanging strips of animal hides made an entryway. Just above the entryway were the carved heads of forest animals.

Inside, narrow shafts of sunlight streamed in from holes in the curved roof and from an open entryway at the far end. Still, the longhouse was chokingly dark. There were six small fires along the entire length, each within a ring of stones.

At first glance, everything seemed cluttered as Johannes's eyes adjusted to the dim light. Along the walls on both sides, there were two levels of platforms. Cornstalks hung from every corner and between rows of platform beds. Furs were stuffed here and there. Bows and spears poked out from high on the walls. The dirt floor was partly covered by woven mats. Johannes saw no polished wood, no decorated wooden doors, no tables, and no chairs as would be found in any proper house in Holland.

First impression aside, Johannes came to realize that every item, just as he would find that every person, had its place within the clutter of the longhouse. As he tried to sleep that night on one of the upper platforms—and on a well-satisfied stomach—he marveled at his chance of being in a world apart from anything he could ever imagine. Even the crowded, smoky space within the longhouse was of no greater discomfort than the hold of a rolling, pitching ship or in a cabin full of irritable, land-bound sailors. And, the mattress of woven reeds was better than a coil of salty hemp rope, if a bit noisier. "Surely," he mused, "I have a story to tell back in Amsterdam!" He worried, though, "Will anyone believe me?"

In the early morning of the next day, people of the village gathered around the meeting circle. They hunkered down facing the sun and stretched out to receive its warmth. Passed from hand to hand was the drawing of Johannes so that each person could compare it with the visitor. *Aaahhh* with a nod of the head meant the likeness was true, and many were heard.

Johannes found himself standing beside the meeting post, uneasy as the center of attention. He tried to count the number of people who encircled him but he quickly lost count. Perhaps there were sixty or seventy. Perhaps even more. There he stood shifting from foot to foot, not knowing what to do with his hands. Tail Feather stood at his side. Behind them, a fire leapt and sputtered.

Again, Chief Red Sun, dressed in his full regalia of deer antlers and turkey cloak, appeared. His way of speaking, as always, reflected the dignity of his position as leader of his people. "Today we greet a man from across the great water. Our people are honored with his visit to our little village. Today Ho-Han-nes will tell us about the world from which he comes. We must listen with care." Having spoken, Chief Red Sun melted into the crowd, leaving all eyes focused on the uneasy youth with long-flowing yellow hair.

Of course, Johannes knew not of what Chief Red Sun spoke. But from the eager faces all around, it was clear that everyone wanted to hear his story. For the first time in his life, he felt important. There was only one problem. He did not know what to say.

As Tail Feather motioned for his friend to start, Johannes stood looking at the sea of expectant faces. This moment is when he froze, but not from the cold. It was the chill of having to say something before all those people. There followed a long, awkward silence. Johannes rocked back and forth from one foot to the other. He felt his breath tighten. He wrung his hands together fretfully and moved them from hips to shoulders to forehead. All the while, the crowd waited eagerly for words about a world they could not even imagine, but words that did not come easily to their honored visitor.

Tail Feather knew well the burden of being tongue-tied. At last, he broke the silence. "Let them ask questions," he whispered. "You can answer them to me. I will speak in my tongue."

"Good. I will try." Johannes braced himself. He felt his heart beating in his throat. His throat felt somewhere deep down in his chest. Ready or not, the questions came: many and often.

"How far away is your village?" was the first.

"Far, far away."

Tail Feather suggested, "Try to tell them how far."

"Our ship crossing the Great Water took fifty-four days to go from my village to your land." Johannes saw his friend trying to describe a ship with hands and the number of passing moons.

These facts brought a gasp from listeners.

"How big is your village across the Great Water?" came the next question.

"It is a village as big as one hundred of your villages." Johannes answered. Tail Feather spoke these words in Mohawk. There were more gasps.

"What is the name of your village?"

Replied Johannes, "My village is called Amsterdam. It is in the province of Holland. Holland belongs to the United Provinces of The Netherlands."[76]

Tail Feather struggled to say the right words. Only blank faces stared back.

"What is your house like?" asked a man with a black palm tattooed on one cheek.

"My house has three floors, one above the other, connected by stairs. Some houses in my village rise higher than your tallest tree." He tried his best to explain tall houses. The version by Tail Feather puzzled everyone.

"Who is in your family?" one of the younger people asked.

"My father is a merchant. He sells things, like furs and pearls, in exchange for silver." Of course, there was no word in Mohawk for "merchant" but Tail Feather used the idea of trading to convey the meaning.

Johannes paused for the translation, then went on. "My mother cooks all our food, washes clothes, scrubs floors, and, at night, reads to my sister and me."

Tail Feather struggled with the words. More baffled looks came from his audience.

Johannes, finding public speaking getting easier with practice, continued, "My sister is eleven years old. She goes to school to learn to read and to study numbers."

Tail Feather cautioned Johannes, "I cannot say these things in my language."

There was another question, "Do you live in the forest or in the mountains?"

"No, the land where I live has no forest. The land is flat everywhere. There are no mountains."

"No forest! No mountains! How can that be?" The idea struck everyone as quite odd.

"Do you live near a river?" came a question from an elder.

"No. I live near a great lake. It is so wide that I cannot see the other side."

The people who lived alongside a mountain lake were astonished.

"Our land lies lower that the water around it," Johannes went on.

Tail Feather, puzzled, said, "Tell me one more time. I did not understand."

Johannes tried a better explanation. "There is water all around my village. It is higher than the ground where our houses are built."

The Mohawk version took some time to complete; it stirred up some doubtful looks. The air of mystery about this place across the ocean deepened further.

"Is it magic?" one asked.

"No, it is not magic."

"Is your land always flooded?"

"No," came the confident answer. "Our people build dikes. These are huge mounds built around the village. The dikes keep water out."

There came a flood of questions. All seemed to ask, "Where does the water go?"

"We have windmills. The windmills work all the time to pump the water out of the land." Johannes explained his meaning with whirling arms and mouthing the swishing sound of pumps. Tail Feather, of course, did his best to explain in his language exactly as he heard it in Dutch. Yet, Johannes could sense that the listeners, though intent on listening, were mystified. He thought to describe further.

"Windmills are huge buildings of six or eight sides. They have vanes, like huge paddles, and the vanes carry sails. The sails go round and round in the wind. They turn gears that go to pumps. The pumps bring water from the land, over the dikes to the canals."

Tail Feather did not even try to put all this in Mohawk. He motioned to Johannes with both palms held forward and head shaking that these things cannot be imagined. He must think about something else to say about his home across the Great Water.

"What animals do you hunt?" was asked more than once.

"We do not hunt. We grow our animals for food." It was one more answer that astonished the crowd.

"We have cows. A cow so high and so round at the middle" he said with hands working along with words. "Cows have horns." Going through the motions, Johannes added, "Milk we get from the cow is good to drink," gesturing as if milking the cow. The listeners listened with amusement.

"Other animals called horses pull wagons. Wagons have wheels."

Turning to Tail Feather, Johannes said, "Tell them that in my country, there are great mills that weave cloth from wool. The wool comes from hairy animals called sheep." He saw no reaction from any of the listeners as his words spilled into Mohawk, but he remained undaunted. "We have fine jewels made from silver and gold and diamonds, not from seashells." He paused for translation. "Our woodworkers build the finest ships in the ocean. It was one of these ships that brought me and twenty men across the great water to your shore."

The people strained for Tail Feather's version. Tail Feather strained to tell them. The expressions, as before, were vacant.

After a time, Johannes realized that the more he described his world in Holland, the greater was the confusion and the greater the disbelief. Even gestures, by now, were becoming hopeless.

"What do children in your village like to do?" a child asked.

"In winter," Johannes said holding his shivering fists against his chest to mean winter, "I skate." With this answer, he showed the movements of skating for all to see. The problem is that his feet were stuck on the ground. Never had he felt sillier.

Johannes, the able-bodied seaman and fearless lookout on a tall mast, nevertheless was not easily deterred. "Painters of Holland are known all over the world for their beautiful pictures of countryside and people, even paintings of children."[77] He knew from stares all around that no one understood.

He would try once more, "In Holland, we have great inventors. They make a glass to bring far things closer and another glass that makes small things big." Tail Feather, struggling with the translation, could not dispel the look of blankness among the audience.

By now, Johannes tried to think of some merciful way out of his terrible predicament. Suddenly, an idea popped into his head. Of course! His magnifying lens: the one drawn from the sea bag of Rut. He rushed to the longhouse to fetch the lens, leaving the bewildered people wondering aloud about their strange visitor. "Have we offended him?" they whispered.

Johannes, breathless, returned only a moment later. Now, he held up his lens for all to see. Hardly larger than a man's fist, it sparkled in the sunlight. Even more striking, it was as clear as water. "This glass comes from my village. I will show how it works." With this promise, a renewed expression of curiosity spread across many faces.

Johannes placed the lens close over one of his eyes and turned from side to side so everyone could see. The crowd stared unblinkingly at the eye that now was much bigger than the other. When the lens was taken away, the eye came back to the same size as before.

Johannes asked who would like to be the first to try his powerful look-through stone. A young boy in front stood up. Without spoken words, Johannes had him hold the lens a distance from a caterpillar that had climbed onto the meeting post. The boy was astonished and even a bit frightened to see that the caterpillar had suddenly grown much larger. Once the lens was taken away, the caterpillar returned to ordinary size. The boy then examined his fingernail and then a grain of sand. With each sighting came a gleeful surprise.

Eager hands quickly passed the lens from person to person. There was delight and fascination as each one stared at a bead, a tip of a porcupine quill, or a pine needle.

Everyone knew that the white stranger came from a world where there were many wonderful things. These were so different from the world of forests and mountains that no one could understand what the stranger, trying his best to explain, told them. Yet, the simple glass from Holland told of a power—unlike anything they had known —within the grasp of Johannes.

When the visitor finally retrieved the lens from the hands of the awe-stricken observers, he held it close to a dried oak leaf. A tiny bright spot suddenly appeared on the leaf. It moved over the leaf as if it were a dancing ant. People circled tightly around for a closer look. If the tiny bright spot were not amazing enough, the leaf suddenly burst into flame. The little blaze stunned the crowd into silence. But not for long. Soon, there were spirited words exchanged throughout the crowd. Some shook their heads in total disbelief. Others wondered what other magic the stranger possessed.

Chief Red Sun had seen it all. At last, he came to the meeting post, held his arms upward at full height. His solemn voice rang out, "We have heard of things of great wonder in the motherland of our honored visitor. We have much to learn. We have seen the power of his look-through-stone that makes things bigger. We have seen how it makes fire. I hope that such things of which he speaks will one day make a better life for our people. We give thanks to Ho-Han-nes." Everyone murmured in agreement. "Remember, too," he reminded the listeners, "we are rich in the simple gifts of the Great Spirit." Turning to Tail Feather, the Chief announced, "Your friend from the far side of this universe is welcome to all that we can offer."

Once these words were put into some semblance of Dutch by Tail Feather, the whole assembly quickly vanished. Tail Feather announced to Johannes: "Mother has made ready some venison."

"No, not now. I will come later. I have need to be here by myself for a time." With these words, Johannes soon found himself alone. He sat on a fireside log staring for a long time into the still red, popping embers. The thought came repeatedly, "I have failed. Telling about my world in Holland was dreadful. No one understands. How can they believe? And it is all so simple." Still with these lingering thoughts, Johannes was drawn toward the scent of roasted venison.

CHAPTER 21

Strawberries

The people of the village soon accepted Johannes as one of them. Their care made it easy for him to adjust to life in the Mohawk village. He wandered freely from cookfire to cookfire, sampling the food, chatting mostly with hands with the fire tender. He meandered into the forest for long, lazy walks with Tail Feather and KyKoo. He sat beside the elders as they talked about village plans. The medicine healer came to him every day to look at his broken arm, sometimes making a new birch bark cast. At the nighttime storytellings, Johannes understood more from the movements of the storyteller than from the words.

Slowly, some Mohawk words became familiar to the boy from Holland but he found them difficult to say; one word, he learned, could express several ideas. Yet Johannes delighted in the musical sound of spoken Mohawk.

It was among the children that Johannes stirred up the most excitement. They followed his every move, day after day, always asking questions. How did he find Tail Feather? Why did he want to visit their village? Who are the white men who come in giant canoes with wings? What do they do with so many furs? When will he return to his village with its high houses and whirling arms?

Why...? What...? How...? The children were always patient to hear answers, no matter how their guest struggled to find the words in their Mohawk tongue.

Of course, every boy wanted to get his hands on the look-through stone that causes a leaf to burst into flame. Every girl wanted to hold the stone that made little things look bigger. Each one passed it back to Johannes who then passed on to another set of eager hands.

Johannes noticed things about the people, too, as they moved between longhouses and to the lake and to the fields. Most all appeared in perfect health; no one was too stout and no one too thin. Their skin was smooth and the color of bronze. No one had pockmarks. This sight alone was strange for nearly everyone in Holland had at least a few; some had many. Even he had them. A badly curved back on one white-haired man, a slow, painful shuffle by an older woman, and the limp arm of a child were signs that the *Wilden* were not entirely free of bodily suffering.

Johannes saw that every person had some task. One task calling for many hands was keeping the fires lit, both inside the longhouses and outside. Men mended fishnets and chipped stones for a sharp edge. Women scraped fresh hides, pounded corn and tended to the cooking. He saw how they heated water by putting white-hot stones into pots made of clay.

There was one pot that sat directly over the fire. Johannes felt some pride on learning that it was an iron kettle that a ship had brought from Holland to Fort Nassau the previous fall. For it, he learned, the Mohawks traded twenty beaver pelts.

The mother of Tail Feather, whose name was Morning Blossom, tended to the needs of Johannes. She offered meat, berries, and cornmeal bread covered with maple syrup. She wove a thick mattress for his platform bed. During the night, she washed his shirt and pants and hung them near the inside fire to dry. Yet, Morning Blossom seldom spoke to him. When she did, she spoke slowly and in a quiet voice as if carrying a great sadness.

As the days went on in the Mohawk village, Tail Feather reminded Johannes, "The time comes soon for you to return to your fort."

"To be truthful, I wish not to go back but it is necessary. I will follow the river and try to remember your ways of finding food."

"No, you will not go alone. I will go with you. But first we must build a canoe."

Until now, Johannes planned to return to Fort Nassau alone, simply finding his way downriver. Why should his friend go all that way only to retrace his steps? But Johannes knew that he had to leave the river's edge near unfriendly people and that he might not find his way. He was unsure if he had the skills needed to survive in the forest or—because he was afraid of water—to paddle alone. With these thoughts, he gratefully agreed to help with the canoe. Besides, he was interested to see how these woodland people would build something as complex as a boat.

Canoe building began in the forest. Tail Feather carried an axe. Its iron head, attached to a gently curved piece of ash, was another prize from his first journey to the trading post.

Certain kinds of wood were needed. A long limb from a maple tree, curved at the end, would make the keel; branches of birch could be bent for the frame; and bark from the birch would be the canoe's skin. To hold them altogether, they teased out cord from the roots of a spruce tree.

On a flat stretch of land near the lake, Tail Feather outlined the canoe-to-be with stakes pounded into the ground. He stretched the support frame around the stakes. After passing the birch branches through steam from a continually heated pot, he could bend the ribs and gunnels between the stakes without breaking them. The shape of the canoe quickly came into being.

In the bending and shaping, Tail Feather explained, "Making a canoe is something my grandfather taught me. I learned much from him." Johannes nodded; he understood. "It is easy to drown in a fast-flowing river," the canoe-maker went on. "Before we take the canoe downriver, you must learn how to swim."

The thought chilled Johannes. Going into the water was something that he had dreaded since childhood. "No, there are some things I will not do," he told himself. Tail Feather sensed his resistance, but he was firm. Besides, Johannes knew that Tail Feather was right about this matter, and so he agreed.

Lessons for swimming did not go easily. The lake water was ice cold. Yet a host of children accompanied him to the lakeshore, and each plunged in without an instant's hesitation. Within moments, the water was churning with a host of yelling, laughing children, beckoning the traveler who crossed an ocean to join them in their little stream. Even the little sister of Tail Feather, Sky Flower, a mere toddler, was among the high-spirited swimmers.

Halfheartedly, Johannes put the toes of one foot in the water but pulled back. The chill and his life-long dislike of being in water above his ankles weighed heavily in his mind. At the same time he became aware of Tail Feather's sisters who stood quietly beside him. Each extended a hand and gently led him deeper into the water. Although his fright increased with each step, Johannes did his best to keep his panic inside.

With two eager helpers at his side and twenty or more children cheering him on, there was no possibility of turning around. "I am brave," he told himself. "Didn't I climb to the top of the foremast almost every day for fifty-four days? Hadn't I untangled the spritsail from *The Unicorn's* horn? Who cut away the thrashing sails and tied down the broken spar in a fierce storm?" His unspoken words were self-convincing enough. "No, I am not a coward! Acting like one now would be worse than dying." Now determined, he resolved, "I will do it. I will learn to swim."

The three stopped in waist-deep water. "*Si-kat-ken-se,*" one of the twins called, then took a deep breath and bent forward so that her head was beneath the water. She held it there for a long moment, then turned to the side, blew air out and as quickly drew in another gulp of air. This she did repeatedly, turning from one side to the other with each breath. Her sister followed. They made dunking look easy. They motioned for Johannes to try.

Johannes now had to face his life-long nightmare. There was no way to back out without bringing everlasting disgrace upon himself. His first dunk resulted in a gulp of water and a quick surfacing followed by a sputtering cough. He knew that he should try again and, after recovering from his first dip, he did. This attempt was more successful although he could only stay under water for one breath. After several attempts and much encouragement from the sisters and the applauding children, he had mastered the art of lifting his head from side to side to exhale, then inhale before plunging in again. He found himself laughing for the first time in a long, long time. But then shivering and blue lips and fingernail beds told everyone it was time to return to shore and to dry off. "*En-yor-henne,*" the girls said in unison. Gesturing the arm motions of swimming, they repeated, "*En-yor-henne.*" Johannes understood, "Tomorrow, another lesson in swimming."

Several days of dunking tested Johannes before he found the courage to lift his legs while his face was in the water. For a moment, he felt as if he were flying, or as in dreams, falling from a great height. For a moment he was panic-stricken. As always, steady arms were there to support him and to ease his fear.

Each day the twins had a new lesson for Johannes: floating, legs only kicking, arms only flung overhead then down, and using both arms and legs at once. Johannes took them all in. While he still did not like the idea of being in water, he was beginning to enjoy his lessons. Tail Feather's sisters were cheerful, laughing all the time and, above all, patient. Their hands were gentle but strong.

There was a second profit from his everyday plunge. Johannes felt cleaner than ever before. The accumulated grime and tar from his long voyage slowly disappeared. In Holland, bathing was not common. Sometimes the time between baths went for many months. Dutch people believed that washing removes some vital energy from the body, or some such notion, as Johannes recalled. On an ocean voyage, a bath meant little more than a splash with a pail of seawater; few of the seamen bothered.

The lessons also created a growing bond between Johannes and the look-the-same sisters. He noticed one of them laughed more easily, was a bit hastier, was first to try something new. As the twins held Johannes in the water to practice leg or arm strokes, she was the one who was the second to let go. Her voice, too, was slightly different, perhaps a bit softer and at times almost whispered. She spoke a little more slowly than her sister, but her smile came sooner. And when it came, there was no dimple on one cheek as her sister's smile brought. And with these little differences, Johannes learned that this was Awakens Corn, not Laughing Rain.

The twins were eager to learn some words of Johannes's language. He, in turn, was as eager to teach them. They started with words for things of most interest to them: items of clothing, colors, features of the face and hair. Johannes pointed out each thing, saying its name carefully twice. They repeated the Dutch word, often many times to get the pronunciation just right. He was amazed at how quickly they learned, even faster than Tail Feather.

Meanwhile, the steady work of Tail Feather with the now-and-then help of Johannes gave their canoe shape. The ribs were fitted and tied to gunnels. Crosspieces bonded the sides. Tail Feather's long strands of cedar strips held together the patches of birch bark that covered the hull. Pitch, a sticky, black sap from pine trees, was gathered to seal cracks between bark pieces.

In the days of bending and stretching and fitting and sewing and sealing, the two canoe-makers often had an onlooker. It was Awakens Corn who came to see their progress. She did not speak but instead stood quietly by, then, after a time, disappeared just as silently. Tail Feather hardly ever noticed his sister's coming and going. Johannes, on the other hand, was fully aware of Awakens Corn's interest. He was always careful to look busy and fully absorbed in the business of canoe making. Of course, it was during those brief visits that his clumsiness showed most: his stone hammer always seemed to split a pounded stake, his bent birch strip sprang out of place, or he knocked over the pot of pine pitch.

Heavy rains slowed the canoe maker's progress, although Tail Feather worked during spells when the pouring let up. Time inside the longhouse was filled with inside chores: making backpack baskets, weaving mats, pounding corn into meal, making journey cakes and the endless tasks always needed to care for a village. Everyone, especially the children, looked forward to the telling stories at nighttime that somehow always seemed more drawn out and more fantastic when rain beat against the longhouse.

Three days of sopping rain brought something else. Softly-Running-Stream, an old woman known for her watchful eye on woodland plants, reported that the rain had brought out a plentiful crop of strawberries. From the news, an idea sprang into the heads of the twins at the same time. They talked it over and agreed on a plan. They would ask Johannes if he would like to go strawberry-picking in the morning. "Strawberries," they said, "add fine flavor to journey cakes." Johannes was quick to accept their invitation. Tail Feather hesitated a moment before saying, "Yes, go. The canoe is finished, except for pitching the seams. I can do that."

Johannes fell asleep that night with joyful thoughts of strawberries. To top it all, the twins had a surprise. Laughing Rain handed him a gift: a soft and smooth leather shirt made from doe hide. Johannes tried it on at once. The shirt had long sleeves. It came down almost to his knees. Awakens Corn presented him with a pair of moccasins. These, fitting perfectly, were of tough buckskin. Red and blue stitching trimmed the edges. For these, the well-traveled Dutch sailor was more than willing to shed his tattered, smelly blouse and his old moccasins.

Morning came. The sky was heavy and dull gray at the horizon, but the rain had stopped. At dawn Johannes put on his new shirt and moccasins. He was eager to gather strawberries. His face fell when Tail Feather announced unexpectedly, "Sky Flower did not eat her morning porridge; her forehead felt too warm to touch. Laughing Rain promised to stay with her. She will make a good herbal brew and braid her hair."

"We will all stay here," offered Awakens Corn. "There is always another hide to scrape or a newly molded pot to cure. We can pick strawberries another day." Understanding but a few of these words, Johannes prepared himself for a terrible disappointment.

"No. You two must go," replied Laughing Rain. "Awakens Corn, you always know where the strawberries grow best. And I think Ho-Han-nes would be sad if we went back on our invitation. Besides, strawberries may not be as plentiful later."

Then Laughing Rain took her sister aside and beyond earshot of Johannes, whispered, "You must return by high sun." Their mother standing by had heard it all and, with a nod, approved. Laughing Rain confided that gossip about her and the yellow haired one was already in the air. "Whatever you do, do not overstay," she pleaded. Awakens Corn murmured agreeably.

The strawberry search began with a walk along the lake. Just before they turned into the forest, a throaty call came from the lake. There, a loon rising from the lake brought their gazes to where tiny ripples sparkled across the water, broken by the half-flying, running start of flight. Their eyes followed the loon until it vanished in the distant sky.

The trek into the forest followed a meandering mountain stream. Along the way, birds and running animals scooted out of the underbrush and soon vanished. Awakens Corn and Johannes, laughing, tried to outdo each other in imitating the chatter of the squirrel, the caw of a crow, and the bleat of a bullfrog.

Suddenly, Awakens Corn thrust out one arm across the chest of Johannes to hold him back. There up ahead, not twenty or thirty paces beyond, was a full-grown black bear. "*Shhhrrr,*" she commanded in her softest voice. The bear stood on its hind legs, its forward legs scratching frantically at the bark of a tree. Johannes had never seen a bear before except one chained and growling at a town fair. The sight brought up frightful boyhood memories from stories of fabled, giant monsters with gnashing teeth and long, tearing claws. "Run!" Johannes said in a strained, terrified voice. Instead, Awakens Corn held him back, pulling him closer so that the two together would appear double in size. Johannes felt his heart racing as never before. Awakens Corn appeared as calm as if she were watching a child play.

It was not but a moment later that the bear lifted its head. Its nostrils flared. The bear came down on all fours, took steps toward the pair, and stopped. What was it thinking as it stared at the figure with two heads? The massive head of the bear rocked slowly from one side to another. The bear yawned. The pure white teeth gleamed long and sharp. Then, as if bored, the bear turned and quietly and slowly loped away. To Johannes, it seemed to take a complete emptying of the sandglass before the bear disappeared into the forest. "*Whewww,*" he murmured. Awakens Corn smiled, pinched his sleeve, and once again led the way toward the strawberry field.

Awakens Corn and Johannes continued alongside the stream, sometimes crossing it for better footing over rocks. Along the way, they picked up shiny and colorful pebbles—green, blue, reddish—that lay along the streambed. In time, they came to a pond. Teeming in the clear water of the pond were fish, more fish than Johannes had ever seen in one place. Beyond that, the stream opened into a clearing with stands of tall grass.[78]

Just as they emerged from the canopy of the trees, streaks of sunlight splayed out around billowing clouds. There at the edge of the forest, the two spotted the object of their quest: a meadow of strawberries. There were more strawberries than stars in the sky. Of course, Johannes nibbled on one. The bitterness caught him by surprise. Awakens Corn chuckled on seeing his mouth pucker up. She tried to tell him with hand talk that the berries would taste much better after boiling and with a topping of maple syrup. From his expression, Awakens Corn knew that Johannes was not entirely certain that he agreed. In this instance, however, it did not matter.

Another surprise: Johannes came upon a clump of mushrooms that were a brilliant red. He stooped to pick one. Awakens Corn tapped the back of his grasping hand sharply with the tips of her fingers. "*Yah! Yah! Yah ki' on-ek-wenhas!*" She pretended to eat one. Hand pressed against abdomen, she gestured as to throw up. Then with her eyes shut tight, she let her head droop down on one shoulder, pretending to fall dead. Johannes quickly learned that red mushrooms were not good to eat.

Picking strawberries is a slow, bent-over task that causes the back to tire quickly. Yet, the pickers kept at it until their baskets could hold no more. By then, it was time to forget about back aches and eat some corn biscuits that Laughing Rain had tucked in one of the baskets. They agreed to walk back to the pond to rest and enjoy their biscuits.

The sun had reached a high point by the time they returned to the pond. There, the cold water sipped from cupped palms was refreshing. They sat on a flattened boulder covered with large, green-gray patches of lichen. It lay part on land and part in the pond. The swishing of the fish and the hopping of water bugs could easily be seen. The boulder had a pleasant warmth to touch. It was a good place to be.

The two strawberry pickers sat with their baskets between them. Their eyes met for an instant. "You believe the bird has spirit?" Awakens Corn asked, combining Mohawk and hand speak.

"Believe" was one of those difficult words to translate, but he had learned the sign from Tail Feather: the pointer finger of the closed hand against the chest, then to the head. "Spirit" was conveyed with outstretched fingers of one arm wiggling and slowly rising above the head.

The question startled Johannes. He stared quizzically into space, not knowing what to say. After some hesitation, he answered, "*Hen' en.* I believe bird have spirit."

Awakens Corn added, pointing, "This rock has spirit? You believe?"

This time, he did not answer.

"Believe tree have spirit?" she went on, laughing softly. "Believe lake have spirit?"

"*Yah*, meaning 'No' in my language," confessed Johannes. "There can be no spirit in a rock or in a tree."

There followed a long silence while the sun moved from behind a cloud. The entire landscape from grass, across the water, to the far-away mountaintops was bathed in brilliant color.

"Believe in Hee-sus, Son of One-Great-Spirit?" came the next question.

Hearing it, the eyelids of Johannes popped fully open, his head spun around to face her. "You know about Jesus?" his voice raised in astonishment.

Awakens Corn, delighted with the reaction of surprise, explained, "Two or three winters ago, a man of great height and with hair bright red on face came to our village. He spoke about One-Great-Spirit. One-Great-Spirit had son named Hesus. His thinking was strange. What is your thinking?" she said with both palms held upward toward him, as to invite his honest opinion.

Johannes had not given much thought to such beliefs about the Son of God. Even those long hours in church every Sunday of his boyhood were times to daydream. Reginald had told him how the worship of Jesus was the center of his own family's world. Johannes feared that his own father worshipped the guilder, spending his waking hours praying that his treasure would multiply. Still, the idea that every animal, every plant, every rock had a spirit was strange, too. He answered after a long pause, "My thoughts are jumbled about spirits." With eyes turned up, Johannes made a circling motion at the side of his head with his pointer finger. It was a sign that needed no further explanation.

With this answer, Awakens Corn laughed aloud, quite satisfied. She placed two fingers on her sleeve, then pointed them at her eyes, then to the sky, then to the eyes of Johannes. Her face brightened even more, but Johannes was perplexed. She performed the action once again, this time more slowly, followed by two clinched hands with arms crossed in front. Johannes knew then, "She likes my blue eyes." His face flushed in the full light of the sun.

The brilliant sunshine, after so many days of damp wetness, was too tempting to ignore. Johannes chose to move from the boulder to a patch of thick grass where he stretched out in the warming sun. Awakens Corn knelt beside him. He closed his eyes for a moment, and in a state of being half awake and half asleep, felt the moment too blissful to be real.

Awakens Corn did not speak. Instead, with a trace of smile, she reached to pull out a blade of marsh grass. Ever so slowly, she ran its feathery tip across the forehead of Johannes, over one eyebrow, then down one cheek, beneath the hairy chin and up the other cheek. For Johannes, a ship crossing an ocean brought no greater adventure. The grassy fluff, in fact, was making a journey around the world on his face. The full sun filtered through his closed eyelids, and what he saw—of all things—was the hated sandglass. Now, instead of wishing that the sand would fall quickly, he wished that each grain would dally for a long while before deciding to drop into the lower chamber. The tuft had crossed his other eyebrow and returned to the forehead. The journey across an ocean took no longer than a long-held breath.

The spell was suddenly broken by a sneeze. With it, amusement washed across the face of Awakens Corn. Johannes had never been close to a grown-up girl before; he did not know that such a person could be so gentle.

Lengthening shadows gave notice of the passing day. It was far beyond a proper time to retrace their steps toward the village. Awakens Corn and Johannes glanced back at the grassy shore, picked up their baskets and started out into the forest. They spoke hardly a word. Perhaps hands held a bit longer than was needed to help step over slippery rocks and fallen trees. Perhaps one hand placed on the shoulder of the leader in the narrowest paths was not always necessary. Both had the same thought, "This day has been the best day of my whole life." Neither knew how, nor dared, to put the thought into words.

Twilight had already crept upon Awakens Corn and Johannes when they arrived at the passageway through the village's palisaded wall. Awakens Corn stopped short. She pointed to a single, bright star that sat just above a line of trees. She pointed to herself, then to the star, then to Johannes, then back to herself. She then clasped her hands tightly together. What did she mean? Johannes took these signs to say, "The star will always be the spirit that goes with us."[79]

As Awakens Corn and Johannes walked along the pathway between longhouses in the dimming light, people kept busy at their tasks. No one glanced up to greet them. Frolicking children did not run after Johannes, teeming with questions, as they had done before. No one seemed to care about their baskets filled with strawberries. Awakens Corn pulled aside the entry hide of her longhouse and a hand reached out to take her baskets. No one spoke.

Johannes sensed that something had changed. Tail Feather stood silently at the entrance. His expression seemed fixed. At length, he announced in a firm voice, "In the morning, we will start downriver."

CHAPTER 22

White Water

A SHARP TUG on the toe stirred Johannes from sleep. The whispered voice of Tail Feather directed, "Follow me." Only the faint glow of ashes could be seen in the darkness. A bit puzzled, he sat on the side of his platform bed and rubbed the sand out of his eyes. He stood for a moment until his legs were steady. Then he started out.

A pinkish blush in the sky over a line of trees told of breaking dawn. Tail Feather and KyKoo led the way through the narrow passageway in the wall of trees. Leaves crinkled underfoot and chilling, dew-wet branches of the underbrush swept across arms and legs as they made their way to the lake.

The purpose of the early morning trek puzzled Johannes. They headed toward the place where the lake spills into the river. There, he saw their new canoe, tethered to a leaning tree, bobbing gently in the rippling water. "So," Johannes reassured himself, "He wants me to see our handiwork." Indeed, he had much admiration for the making of a canoe that floated so evenly on fast-flowing ripples.

Johannes also noted that the canoe was fully laden for a long trip. The hand of Tail Feather motioned for him to get into the bow. There was just enough space on each end for paddlers. In the mid-section, a smaller space was left for a well-tucked-in wolf.

Suddenly, as he kneeled admiring in the perfect canoe, the meaning of the mysterious dawn walk came to Johannes. The thought caused his insides to sink to the bottom of the stream. He knew now that Tail Feather meant to take him away from the village without ceremony, to return to the cabin of bad-tempered traders. There would be no great speech by Chief Red Sun. No crowds would wave them off. There would be no dances. Kind words of departing were not to be. Where was Awakens Corn?

In another instant, Tail Feather released the canoe into the current made powerful by heavy rains of many days. The canoe plunged ahead at a furious speed into the mist of a morning fog. Splashes against mid-stream boulders rose high into the air. In the dappled light of the rising sun, all that the paddlers saw of the shoreline was flashing green. Now and then, the canoe skipped jarringly over a hidden boulder. A quick swerve around or a sudden all-heads-down was needed to pass under a tree that had toppled into the water.

"You have become good at paddling," Tail Feather shouted above the raging water. The downcast face of Johannes changed into a broad beam. Of course! Hadn't he worked the whipstaff of his great ship, *The Unicorn*, during a great storm? Here, it was only a canoe. Paddling a canoe, he admitted, was more fun. And, now bouncing along the rapids, there was no sandglass to vex his soul. But now, he began to realize that he was in a mighty contest between his paddle and the half-submerged rocks and fallen trees.

Tail Feather meant to go far that first day. The swift-running river and a sun-filled sky after so many days of rain favored the paddlers. They did not stop until near dusk when hunger, weary arms and sore knees brought the canoe into a small, well-hidden inlet. There, they laid woven mats on a thick bed of moss and rolled out their bearskins on top of these. Journey cakes with strawberries were then soaked until soft. All that remained to complete the day was a full night's sleep.

Yet, Johannes could hold back a burning question no longer, "Why did we leave the village, why in such a hurry, why so secret?"

Tail Feather did not reply. Rather, he wandered off into the thicket, returning with an armful of pine boughs. These he carefully layered between the deer hides and the moss. Still, the question of Johannes weighed heavily on them both. As they settled for the night, he posed it once again, "Why?"

"I think you know," came the reply.

"No, I can think of no reason."

There was a long and painful pause before more was said. "The reason is you and my sister."

"Awakens Corn and me? Do your people have bad feelings about us?"

Tail Feather's voice betrayed the well-disguised anguish in his answer. "Know that everyone likes you. All want to know more about the world of Ho-Han-nes. They think you care about our people, will not deceive them, as the other traders have. But some, mostly the elders, will not accept mixing your world with our world. It is about our ancestors and about ancestors to come. You and Awakens Corn threaten to change that."

Johannes gulped at this idea. "But,..." his words trailed off as the words of Tail Feather sunk in. "But,....," he started again, "someday..." Even this thought he could not finish as images of swimming, strawberry picking, a journey across the ocean on a tuft of grass whirled in his head. There was, he knew, no more to say. And so, the travelers, with KyKoo snug between them, tried to sleep. Johannes could not take his eyes of the evening star that slowly moved across the horizon.

The sky at daybreak was clear, save for some low-lying clouds downriver. Leaning-over trees and submerged boulders were few. The canoe went far that day. Drizzle, nevertheless, began during that night and put an end to restful sleep. By the morning light of the third day, the drizzle had turned to a sprinkle. Not long after the canoe was underway, sprinkles became a downpour. At times, rain fell too heavily to see dangers ahead. Water taken aboard made the canoe float lower. Paddle commands gave a sluggish response. The wind decided not to let rain outdo it. Powerful and swirling gusts threatened to topple the canoe.

The time had come to find a high spot of ground, empty the canoe and turn it over for a shelter. Inside the turned-over canoe, there was room for Tail Feather and Johannes lying toe to toe. There, above the marshland and beneath the canoe, the two travelers hunkered down, wet but out of the chilling rain. They both were glad, finally, to lie down on thick-padded beds that were well above the soggy ground. They had woven mats underneath them and bearskins on top. KyKoo, her thick fur shedding the raindrops, appeared content enough as she crouched in the thick grass just outside.

Wind and rain kept up for all that day and through the next day and through the day after that. There was little else to do but talk. Tail Feather had become quite good at speaking Dutch. Johannes's understanding of Iroquois lagged far behind. Each spoke slowly, combining languages. Always, flying hands filled in spaces between shared words. Talk beneath the upside down canoe was almost continuous through the day and far into the night.

Tail Feather had harbored some troubling questions. Now he found the moment to ask, "How does your big village lie below the water around it?"

Johannes tried but was not able to explain dikes in words. He chose, instead, to show how building walls of earth keep out water. For this, he put a hickory nut in a small puddle within arm's length of the canoe. "My house," he pointed out, "is the nut." Of course, Tail Feather remained baffled. Then, Johannes stretched one hand out to pick up a short, stout stick. With it, he pushed mud into mounds around the puddle. The nut sat even deeper in the water. Next, he used the stick to splash water out of the puddle. Soon, the nut sat on mud almost free of water. Johannes smiled. Tail Feather nodded at the explanation without words. Of course, rain soon filled up the puddle again. There were no tiny windmills there on the marshland to pump out the water.

Tail Feather's curiosity kept coming back to life in Amsterdam. "Talk to me about the houses with wings," he said.

"The windmill? A mill is a place to make things. The power comes from the wind." Johannes held a leaf and blew against it. "See how the wind drives it." Spinning the leaf around, he showed how its stem could turn a stick. In a windmill, the leaf is one of the vanes and the stick is a pole.

"How does the turning stick raise water?"

"It works on a pump."

"A pump? How does a pump work?"

Johannes tried to describe the action of a pump. In truth, he had never thought much about pumps before. He simply answered, "I know not." After a thoughtful pause, Tail Feather still wanted to know more about his friend's world. "Tell me how your people make houses higher than trees."

"Tall houses are made from laying many bricks on top of one another."

"Bricks?"

"Yes. Bricks are long blocks made from clay."

"But clay is too soft to make a house. We must use strong saplings and bark."

"True, but the clay is heated to make it hard, the way your women make a pot."

"I do not understand," Tail Feather persisted. "Pots made from heating clay break easily. They cannot take fire the way your iron pots do."

"Bricks in Holland are hard and last forever, even in fire. They are made in a hot fire."

"Fires are hot."

"Yes, they are hot," came the reply, "But for a good brick, the molded clay must be cured in a fire that is hotter than most fires. For this, brick-makers use a kiln."

"Kiln?"

"Yes, stones or bricks are built up around a fire pit to hold in the heat. Bellows makes the fire even hotter."

"Bellows? Your people have too many things. What are bellows?"

"Bellows are bags made from animal skins. Squeezing bellows forces a blast of air over the fire. It pumps air."

"Again, pumps. Wonderful things, these pumps. You must know how they work?"

Again, Johannes could not explain. "I never gave them much attention before. They just do what they are made for."

Tail Feather held off asking more questions when he realized that learning about this strange place, Holland, was more than he could grasp at one time. Johannes used the opening to ask his own questions.

"How do you make houses that are warm on the coldest day and do not leak in the rainiest night?"

It was Tail Feather, now, who had to answer. He thought of the great effort made to weave tight mats of grass to place underneath the sheets of elm bark, not only on the roof but on the sides as well and how the mats overlap. It was too much to explain and so he said, "They just do what they are made for."

"Then, how are animal hides so soft and long-lasting for clothes and shoes?" came the next question.

This time, Tail Feather knew he could explain without words. One hand sign came quickly after another, but they were easy for Johannes to follow. "Deer. Arrow. Shoot. Take hide. Scrape. (Here, he indicated heavy labor.) Dry in sun. Boil in water with brain of deer. Smoke. Pound with round stone. Dry in sun. Cut with sharp edge of stone. Sew with long tendon of deer hind leg." Then, he added in voice, "Laughing Rain is good at making soft leather. Awakens Corn hates this work. Instead, she likes to work with clay, to make pots and bowls that are good to look at." Johannes nodded with an understanding smile.

The conversations went on in this manner as the two companions hunkered beneath the canoe. There were many questions with almost as many answers. In this way, they learned something about the life of the other. Johannes told about school where children learned to read and to use numbers. He told of books, candles, musical instruments, oil painting, skates that go fast on ice, cows and tall houses, all common to every child in The Netherlands.

Tail Feather, in turn, told how he hunted in winter on snowshoes and how his people used flint for sharp edges and to make sparks. He described the "Three Sisters" and explained why squash, corn, and beans are planted together in little hills. He told how people get sweet sap from a tree and how it is boiled into a tasty treat. Tail Feather showed how he and his friends make an icy trough for the game of snow snake and see who could throw the "snake" the farthest along it.

Of course, there were many questions about the giant "Snow Goose Canoe." Johannes did his best to tell about an ocean-going ship made from hundreds of giant trees; what sails did and how ropes turned the sails to gather wind. He told about how it was to be in an ocean where there was no land to see. There was a pilot on the ship who could find the way on a long journey with nothing but water from horizon to horizon. Listening with a sliver of skepticism, Tail Feather found the strangest story was the one about a moving needle: it always pointed in the same way.

On the second night beneath the canoe, the patter of rain suddenly was no longer heard. Then a full moon broke away from a cloud. It bathed the shoreline in light, casting its waving reflection across the river. This was the time when Tail Feather asked his knowledgeable friend about something that had long haunted him. "You know about Grandmother Moon?"

"I know a little," was the reply.

"Why," Tail Feather pressed on, "moon come on one side of sky and go away on other side? How moon go from round to thin? Why moon hate sun, most always in sky at different times? I think about since small boy."

Johannes knew that he was in for a long night. He began, "First you must know about the Earth. There are high places called mountains and running water called..."

Tail Feather stopped him there. "What is Earth?

Restarting, Johannes went on, "Earth is all the land and water that we live on. They say it is round like a pot but with no neck. It is so wide that our ship took fifty-four days to cross from my land to yours on the ocean. There is another side of Earth where ships take even longer to cross the ocean."

The idea of a round Earth brought a long period of silence and disbelief. In time, Tail Feather gathered his wits enough to say, "You speak of something too strange to even think about. My people say that—when the world was only sky and water—earth began on back of giant turtle. I believe Sky Woman fell from the sky. The water animals brought her soil and from her body grew the Three Sisters, corn and squash and beans. From her, all people began. Which of us speaks true?"

"Yes, Awakens Corn told me about that beautiful story. I say only what people of my world have learned from the stars. I do not understand much of it."

"But you speak of a ball. If we live on top, how do we go around the sides?"

"No, there is no top. There are no sides. There is no bottom. Something holds us close to the ground everywhere." He sensed that a better answer was expected, but he had none. "I can jump off the ground, but I always come back down."

"What of birds? They stay in the air."

"I know not what keeps birds in the air. Gulls barely flap their wings."

"What of moon? Is Grandmother Moon also a round pot?"

Here, Johannes knew a bit. "Yes. Moon is round like Earth. It is far, far away. It circles around the Earth one time every day."

"What makes it grow, then get smaller...become a ball and each night slowly change into a line?

"The moon is always the same size. The sun shines on only part of it, as a cookfire lights up only one side of a pot. This, my father taught me: the sun goes around the Earth and the moon goes around the Earth. The shape and size of the moon do not change. We see only the part where the Earth does not hide it and where the sun can light it."

Johannes offered another explanation. "Some wise men who study the sky tell us something different. They say that the sun is the center of a great spinning world and the Earth circles the sun. Such an idea, my father told me, is against God. The whole universe..."

"I listen to you," interrupted Tail Feather, "but what my people say how the world is, I believe more. Our story is stronger. My father said it makes us one with our ancestors from the beginning of time."

Johannes was curious that in the village he had not seen Tail Father's father. An answer came after a long and thoughtful wait.

"My father paddled with me to Water-With-No-End three years ago. We went there to trade flint stone and copper for shell beads. There were eight of us in four canoes. He was in the same canoe as I was when we came upon your great ship."

"But I remember seeing only three canoes," returned Johannes.

"True. One of the canoes carrying an injured paddler had already gone to Water-With-No-End."

"What did your father think about our ship?"

"Like the others, he thought it was a spirit from another world. Our people do not make that long journey now. It has become too dangerous. But during the many days of paddling and nights spent along the shore, my father taught me much about the river. Many sights there were of places and things told about in the children's telling stories. He paddled with me to see a skyflower, in the same place where our canoe tipped over. You must remember that colorful picture in the sky!"

"Oh, yes. How could I forget?"

Tail Feather continued with his story. "I showed you the cascade where the stone has deep holes. Talks-Like-Thunder stepped into one of these in the dark and hurt his ankle. After our return paddle he tried to continue with us on foot but his ankle had not healed enough. My father stayed behind to help. We never saw either of them again. Every day that passed after the rest of us returned to the village was a torment."

"Is that why your mother always looks so sad?"

"Yes, our elders teach us to go on with life without mourning the past, and so we try. Out of respect, I am not even supposed to say my father's name until the name is passed on. Perhaps one of my children will carry the name. But my mother still believes my father will return one day."

"What do you think?"

"What do I think about what?"

"Do you think your father will come back?"

"No. The time since has been too long. I do not want to think about what may have happened to him and Talks-Like-Thunder if the Mahicans found them."

There was a long wait in silence before Tail Feather went on. "The long paddle with my father will always be the best memory of my life. He believed in me, though I felt useless at the time. Father told me much about his life, how he came into the village and got his name, about my birth, about the time that my twin sisters were born, about how my grandfather was injured and about the other men on their journey." With the telling, Johannes learned much of the life of a Mohawk boy.

The morning of the fourth day under the canoe brought bright sunshine. The young men stretched their cramped arms and legs. Looking around, they found the marshland flooded. The only place left above water was the knob of land where their unturned boat rested. From the underbrush, they quickly retrieved some of the baskets that had floated off. The canoe was soon readied for travel.

"We have lost some days," Tail Feather said. "The river is swollen from so much rain. We will go fast now."

"Good. I have now been away from the trading post far too many days. I return without his precious flintlock. Joost will have some frightful punishment waiting for me."

Although battered downriver by submerged rocks, the strong canoe held fast. Often along the way, the paddlers had to unpack it and carry it around waterfalls and rapids. The journey continued.

CHAPTER 23

The Chase

In the ever-widening river and beyond the last of the great falls, there were few rocks to upset the canoe. While not so fast or as exciting, traveling was carefree.

Johannes now felt himself as part of the canoe, skimming through what not many days before meant paddling around a tangle of branches, shallow boulders, and foaming eddies. Yet, even in a calmer river, his buckskin clothes never seemed to dry. His food was nothing but tasteless journey cakes softened by soaking in water. They had no berries. Even so, Johannes felt in high spirits as they neared Fort Nassau. He was certain that they would arrive at the trading post within a few days.

The boy from Holland had, nevertheless, growing regret on realizing that his days in Mohawk land had come an end. Soon he would spend long days in a smelly, smoke-filled cabin with coarse and boring men who cared little for each other. Gone would be his traveling companion who had proven faithful and kind.

It was in such a mood of mixed feelings that the canoe sped along the riverbank to lessen the wind coming directly up-river. Along one steep bank where the river narrowed, it turned sharply. Just around the bend, some men huddled around a cookfire. A stag deer hung head-down from a nearby limb. The men, as surprised as were the paddlers, jumped to their feet. From them came a volley of shouts and agitated gestures. They were not friendly. KyKoo growled back.

"Paddle" cried Tail Feather. "Paddle hard. As fast as you can." The canoe approached and then shot past the startled hunters within a stone's throw. The men reached for their bows. But the canoe sped away and was out of range of arrows before any of the hunters could take aim.

Still, the paddlers could hear shouting as the hunters chased them on foot. It was an unnerving moment, and Johannes glanced back to see how close their pursuers were. Just ahead, a fallen tree, bleached white in the sun and its branches laden with sticks and leaves, blocked that side of the shoreline.

A quick flip of Johannes' paddle would have cleared the tree easily, but his head was turned at that moment. Tail Feather's strongest stroke could not turn the canoe in time. The bow struck the tip of an underwater branch. The canoe veered violently. It crashed sideways into the tree. Tail Feather grabbed one of the tall branches to keep the canoe upright, but the force of the current capsized the top-heavy craft within an instant.

The paddlers-turned-swimmers tried to free the canoe from the tree, but it was tightly tangled within its branches. As they struggled, an arrow struck mid-canoe with resounding *thwaaak*.

"Swim!" shouted Tail Feather. Johannes began to swim toward shore. "No!" screamed Tail Feather, "Swim out into the river," even while Johannes was having all he could do to keep his head above water. In mid-river, Tail Feather, Johannes, and Kykoo found the current stronger and a better way to put some distance between themselves and the hunters. But the water was too cold to continue for long. The swimmers felt their arms and legs tighten up.

"Now, swim to shore," shouted Tail Feather where the shore made a sharp bend. "Run, we must." The swimmers pulled themselves onto a rocky bank, shivering and panting.

"Follow me!" Tail Feather with Johannes and Kykoo close behind began a shaky sprint. "We will head out of the marsh into the forest. If we can walk through the night, we may lose them."

And so, the escape began. The three ran across the thick marsh grass, skipping over streams toward the edge of the pines. A quick look behind revealed a trail of bent over grass. Once inside the woodland, they raced around fallen trees, across deep ravines, and up onto cliffs.

Tail Feather said not a word. He kept off patches of snow and mud as best he could to lessen footprints. In short time his fast pace became too much for his friend. Johannes was out of breath and his legs were sore. Tail Feather paused to let him rest. But rests were brief. Dusk came and then the darkness. There was just enough light from the moon to show the general terrain, and so they scampered, climbed, and crashed through the night. Branches slashed the face, briars tore skin and clothing alike, legs bumped against rocks, and feet tripped over exposed roots and fallen limbs.

Breathless, Johannes found the moment to ask, "Why do they chase us?"

Tail Feather, leading the way, did not answer until they came to a thicket too dense to pass in the dark. "We are near the river now. I can hear it. We can rest here until there is a little light." He hunkered down with KyKoo at his side and tried to answer the long-hanging question. "Tribes can be natural enemies. Bad feelings may have happened long ago, and they never go away." There was a long pause. Johannes thought his friend had gone to sleep, something that was impossible for him to do. But Tail Feather spoke more. "Hunters find stalking humans more fun than deer. A Mohawk and a white face would be big trophies to boast about."

Johannes had long dreamed of commanding a great ship across the ocean and returning with fabulous riches. Instead, he found himself racing through the woods at night like a hunted animal, soaked through, cold, empty of strength, scratches everywhere and feet in torn moccasins too sore for walking. It was now that Johannes realized how fast life can change from splendid to miserable. His only hope of seeing another day was to keep up with his friend, the same *Wilde* whom he had frightened a few years before just for fun.

As daylight came, Tail Feather climbed high into the tallest pine tree to find his bearings. Looking up at the figure scanning the horizon with one hand shielding his eyes from the rising sun, Johannes could not find a trace of tiredness or fear in his companion.

Back on ground, Tail Feather, described their situation. "We have walked far from the river. We need to be close by it to find our way. Running can bring us there by high sun. We must stay at the edge of forest. They would see us along the marsh."

"Did you see any hunters?"

"No, only their smoke far away. For certain, they intend to pursue us. They stayed the night by a fire along the riverbank."

"They will never catch us now," said the always-hopeful Johannes.

"Remember," cautioned Tail Feather, "The hunters have food. They are rested. They have extra moccasins with thick soles. They have many arrows and they are warm. The broken twigs and ruffled leaves from our footsteps show them the way. Take care how you step and move through the bushes to leave no print or broken branches."

"What will happen if they catch us?" Johannes could not imagine anything so bad.

"For now, it is best you do not know," came the puzzling answer.

"I still think they will give up when they see how fast we are."

"No. Hunters know the ways of the wolf pack. Wolves follow an elk until it becomes so tired it cannot lift its horns or kick with sharp hooves. Then, the pack closes in for the kill. Sometimes, a chase takes many days. Wolves never give up the chase. Hunters, too, will not give up. We will give them a good chase."

The hunters and their prey continued for another day. The hunters rested at night while the prey continued to plod through the forest. From a treetop view the next morning, the weary prey found that the hunters were closing in.

The new day was a repetition of the day before. Johannes was reaching the point of painful exhaustion when he had to think about placing one foot in front of the other. His companion encouraged him from time to time to keep on, but by now words no longer helped. It was in this manner that he struggled through another night.

By first light of the following day, Johannes rested while his friend shimmied up another tall tree for a look. This time, he remained in the tree for a long time, searching this way and that. At last, Tail Feather came down with news of their situation. It was not good.

"We are near the river now. The forest gives way to marshlands just downriver. The hunter's smoke is not far behind us. I saw two of them. They have gone ahead along the riverbank to look for us to come out of the forest." The news had passed beyond the limit of Johannes's youthful optimism.

Another day of hard walking was ahead, to be interrupted only for an occasional drink from a stream. To add to his misery, Johannes became aware of a terrible itching on his arms and face. Scratching only worsened the itch.

As night approached, they stayed near the edge of the forest where they could hear the water rushing along the overflowing river. A quarter moon gave just enough light for his guide to find a path between bushes and boulders. To his surprise and just as he was about to fall face first into the earth, he heard Tail Feather say, "We will rest here for the night."

Thankful for the chance, the sailor-turned-woodsman lay down on a thick clump of moss and tried to forget their troubles. But the itching had worsened, and his legs were scratchy as well. In the darkness, he felt tiny bumps everywhere on his skin, and the more he scratched, the more he itched. During the long and restless night, Johannes was gripped with the maddening rawness over his whole body.[80]

By the first light, a hand shook Johannes with the words, "We go now." He tried to open his eyes, but they seemed stuck. His whole face seemed swollen tight. His lips were puffy, and he could barely talk.

One look told Tail Feather that their troubles were deepening. "Tell me, what is wrong with me?" Johannes demanded.

The answer: "You have the three-leaf itch. Stay here. Do not scratch." Johannes heard his footsteps rapidly disappear into the distance.

Johannes cried out "Why do you leave me?" There was no answer. He shouted, "Don't let me alone. I cannot see." Again, no answer. Johannes knew he had been abandoned. Even KyKoo had vanished. As if being sore all over, exhausted, hungry, and itching terribly were not enough, now he could not see. It seemed that just as every possible misfortune had befallen him all at one time, his friend had left him to join the hunters. Perhaps, he thought, Tail Feather intended to betray him all along.

By now, the itching was everywhere. Sometimes it was worse around the neck, then the ankle. At other times, the itching was more agonizing over the arms or on the back. Then it was the thighs or under the chin. Scratching with his long fingernails only heightened the suffering. Still, Johannes could not keep from scratching.

The time had come when Johannes was resigned to reality. He was dying. He had come to a time when he was ready to welcome death. It was the only escape from his misery. Preachers, he remembered, often spoke of the eternal peace found in heaven. Even in this cursed wilderness, there must be a heaven where there is no itching.

Johannes sat there for endless time feeling as wretched as anyone could possibly feel. A bird, perched somewhere in the upper branches, seemed to taunt him further with its cheery song.

He began to think aloud and in a calm voice said, "So this is what death is like. I may be dead already!" He tried to reflect on what evil deeds he had done to deserve such punishment. "Once, I frightened my sister with a dead snake. I dozed off at church almost every Sunday. My teacher often scolded me for talking in class. Did he know that I was memorizing my friends' readings to me, not learning to read myself? Who knows how many careless mistakes I made in father's bookkeeping? Yet, was I so bad that I deserve such a terrible afterlife? I have never stolen anything, I have never hurt anyone, and I have never lied about anything, well, anything important."

A slowly approaching rustling of leaves interrupted these thoughts. The sound was for certain one of the hunters. It came ever closer, then for a moment, there was complete silence. Johannes dropped his head and waited for the blow that would put an end to his suffering. But none came. He used both thumbs to push one swollen eyelid up just a crack. It was not a hunter! It was a strange animal, somewhat bigger than a cat and black as coal. From its pointed snout, a wide stripe of white ran along the back to a long, bushy tail. "Now," he thought," even animals play tricks on me."[81]

Johannes acted in a way that anyone so startled and so desperate would do. Flinging a fistful of moss toward the creature, he shouted, "Go away. You can see I have enough trouble." Just when the boy thought that no human being could endure any more, his condition was soon to worsen.

The animal reacted in a way that any wild creature would react to an offense. It brought into action its strongest defense. In this instance, as Johannes was soon to observe, it faced away and lifted its tail. Out flew a glistening spray. Afterwards, the animal quickly scurried into the underbrush.

A moment later, Johannes smelled something so awful, so dreadful, it seemed to cut through his nostrils. His insides were so unsettled from it that he began to choke, to throw up. Never in his whole life had he ever known such a strong smell. He felt as if a thousand rotten eggs mixed with putrefied meat and fish had been dumped upon his head. The odor so foul soon overpowered his itching, tiredness, and hunger.

It was in this bleak situation that the sailor from Holland curled up in the leaves and wept. "Oh, how I long to be back in the trading cabin with my dear friends. What joy it would be to stand in a barrel atop a foremast and search the empty horizon day after day! How sweet would be the smell of the orlop deck. No weather deck could be too long to scrub with a smooth stone; I would happily do that so that the most finicky bosun could admire my work. How wonderful it would be to sit in our little home in Amsterdam, talking all day with my mother and father and to take my sister on walks along the seashore. Why, I would joyfully go to church and listen to every word spoken. No sermon could be too long. The preacher could speak of how many angels could dance on the head of a pin for hours. I would give father's rows of numbers the highest attention the whole day. No, I do not need to be master of a great ship. Not even an able-bodied seaman. Those were foolish dreams. If I were just an ordinary person who milks cows and tends to windmills, that would be such a wonderful life."

In this frame of mind, Johannes heard light footsteps approaching. This time they were surely those of a hunter. Through his closed-shut eyelids, he made out a dark figure pass in front. Again, he wished for a merciful end. Instead, he heard the voice of Tail Feather say, "Here, Ho-Han-nes, it is a plant that will help you. It grows not in deep forest, only along streams."[82]

With these words, Johannes felt a hand press a leaf against his face. The hand rubbed firmly but most carefully around the eyes. Then, it was the turn of an arm and a leg. A pressed leaf passed over his chest and back. As Tail Feather smeared the oil of the plant onto the skin of Johannes, he casually said, "You had a visitor."

"Yes. It was a huge black cat with a..."

Interrupted Tail Feather, "I know."

By high sun, tiny slits appeared between the lids of Johannes. He could see again with a narrow view. It was enough to avoid walking into trees or stepping into deep holes. With the improvement, the chase started again. Johannes had rested and, even with some trouble seeing, he could keep up. At times, in the distance, they heard the echoing calls of men.

Tail Feather reported, "I saw the river. It is running hard. I know where we are." The news brought a glimmer of hope.

By sundown, the runners had come to the edge of the forest. Beyond was the marshland, but only the tallest tufts of grass were seen here and there. Clearly, it was flooded. Beyond the marsh, a swift current marked the broad river where uprooted trees floated past.

Tail Feather chose to follow the river by keeping to places where the forest and marsh met, always with KyKoo loping along just behind. Johannes tried his best to keep up. At times, they squeezed through thick underbrush and at times splashed in the knee-deep water of the drowned marshland.

Breathless and bone-weary, Johannes was ready to give up. He stopped running just as they came to a high rise of huge boulders. Tail Feather shouted to Johannes and signaled to KyKoo, "Wait here." He scampered up the cliff, scaling one boulder at a time.

Johannes, bent over hands on knees, gasped for air. He watched Tail Feather gain the cliff top and shield his view from the sun's glare with one hand. From the distance, Johannes saw him point quickly with outstretched arm toward a place on the marsh before returning.

Tail Feather partly jumped and partly slid down the slabs of rock until he was back on level ground, saying, "Follow me." Johannes did his best. They sloshed out into the marsh. Kykoo half swam, half leaped along. Shouts from their pursuers told of the distance between them narrowing.

"Why are we going out into the open?" called out Johannes. "The forest was our only chance to hide." There was no answer. But farther on, they came to two great boulders rising above the flood. It was there that Tail Feather took a deep breath and plunged into the water. Tail Feather had gone completely mad!

Johannes saw that Tail Feather was engaged with something strange underwater, as if he were planting corn or adjusting his moccasin. A moment later he came up for another breath followed by another plunge. The action was repeated many times. As he did so, the voices of the hunters were heard even closer.

"Of all times for my friend to go crazy again" an anxious Johannes wondered, but paused, remembering the way Tail Feather had found his canoe after leaving Fort Nassau. As the voices of the enemy became louder, the tip of a canoe broke the surface. Tail Feather pulled out rock after rock. Soon, the canoe was floating at the gunnels.

"Quick, now," he shouted. "Turn it over with me." With each of the boys on an end, the canoe was lifted to its side, emptying water, then upside down. Along with the water, some more rocks fell out and, with them, two paddles. Tail Feather held one side of the canoe while Johannes climbed into the bow from the other side. He then lifted Kykoo into the center and slid to the stern.

As the boys looked back, they saw three men sloshing toward them. A fourth held back to draw his bowstring. Shouted Tail Feather. "Paddle for your life." Further persuasion was not needed.

The canoe charged across the flooded marsh but soon bumped onto a barely submerged mound of grass. The canoe, hung up, began to turn sideways. Tail Feather used his paddle to push off. Just as the canoe slid free, KyKoo let out a snarling growl. Tail Feather felt his paddle caught. Looking back, he saw one of the men with a two-handed grip on its blade. Tail Feather gave a sharp twist to loosen it. *Craaaack!*

Kneeling, Tail Feather found himself holding the handle of his paddle. The hunter, waist deep in water, held the blade. For an instant that must have seemed like a day, the two were eye to eye. In another instant, the hunter lunged to grab the stern. At that same instant, a stroke from Johannes's paddle drove the canoe just beyond his grasp. Swift paddling soon brought the canoe well beyond reach. Even a one-paddle canoe is faster than a runner in deep water.

The danger, though, was not over. An arrow whistled between KyKoo and Tail Feather. It struck on the inside of the canoe near the keel. Water poured around the feathered end. Tail Feather stuck one big toe snuggly against the shaft. The toe-plug brought the leak to a trickle.

The enraged voices of the hunters faded. Soon, the canoe had crossed the marsh and was beyond their reach and arrows. The canoe moved into the fast flow of mid-river.

It is hopeful to think that during their narrow escape on the flooded marshland, the terrible itching of Johannes was entirely forgotten. Now safe and skimming along easily in the wide river, he felt his skin come alive with renewed torment.

CHAPTER 24

The Flood

Easy paddle strokes and a following wind sped the canoe along in the fast-moving current. Paddling at the bow, Johannes tried in vain to keep the canoe from turning from side to side. "Give me your paddle," the other boy directed. Paddling from the stern, he could bear a truer course in the direction of the wind.

About sundown, Johannes thought that a few sights along the way were familiar. He recognized the outlet of the river where he had seen the rainbow. It was the same place where his own folly nearly caused him to drown. What was different now was the high water that flooded the shoreline and pounded against the riverbanks. The river at this place was normally but a gurgle. Now it was a hissing roar.[83]

The ferocity of the flood was evident in the many uprooted trees that floated along. A family of raccoons crowded on a trunk. On another floating tree, a bear cub perched on a branch. A wide-eyed stag, carried in the rushing water, was seen struggling to reach the shore.

Now and then a great swell came from behind. It lifted the stern of the canoe with a rude shake, then pitched the bow up before passing on down-river. Tail Feather angled the canoe into each swell to keep from being swamped.

Johannes knew that this was not an ordinary tide but the result of days and days of heavy rain on top of a strong spring sun that melted the mountain snow. Water from rain and snow that had melted together now poured into the river in the same way he had seen it gush through a broken dike back in Holland.

Just as the sun touched the horizon, the canoe reached a point at which the trading post would come into view any moment. Johannes became increasingly uneasy about the high water. After all, the little fort on Castle Island had been built on a low-lying plateau where loading furs onto a ship would be easy. As the canoe at last came within sighting range of the trading post, he saw something that would haunt him for the rest of his life. There in the distance, swirling water surrounded the cabin. On top, the men—there were six of them altogether—straddled the peak of the roof. One (it was still too far away to tell which one) held his hands in the posture of prayer. Another rocked his body with great agitation. The others sat motionless along the peak.

"Six people?" Johannes questioned himself. "There were only five people when I left."

Someone on the roof spotted the canoe. He pointed. In an instant, all arms were flapping madly. There in his orange shirt was Rut. As the canoe neared, Johannes and Tail Feather began to hear desperate shouts. "Help us! Help us!"

"What can we do?" the Dutch boy, turning toward his clever friend, asked with desperation. There was no answer. It was just at this moment that a great roar came from behind. Johannes whipped his head around and saw a massive swell bearing down on the canoe. Tail Feather kept the stern pointed at an angle into its foaming front. Johannes put both hands firmly on the gunnel. The wave carried the canoe up as if it were a twig in a mountain stream then, as suddenly, dropped into a deep furrow before moving on downriver.

It was not long before the giant swell reached the cabin. The paddlers looked on helplessly as the men took hold of each other for protection against the fast-coming surge. Johannes had one last image of the trading post and of the seamen who accompanied him to the new world: all was rising to the top of the wall of water, then tumbling into foam. In a blink, cabin and men were gone. Johannes knew that not one of them could swim.

The canoe veered around bobbing branches and trees toward the site. Tail Feather and Johannes found nothing but churning water. There was neither a trace of the building nor of the men who lived in it.

Dispirited, the young men turned their canoe toward land and brought it to the edge of the forest that bordered their now-flooded garden. Tail Feather stepped onto dry land and pulled the canoe, stern first, up onto a mossy patch. Johannes stayed slumped over in the canoe. He could not stop himself from weeping.

Poor Joost had been forced to stay at Fort Nassau another half year despite his pitiful plea to the shipmaster. He might have returned to the family he left many months before. Yet, he had done his best throughout the long winter to keep the hot-tempered men from each other's throats. Sean will never play his concertina again. Half-decent, young Cornelius will never sing again in his beloved Wallonia. Even the irritable Dietrich and Lars had their good sides. Both men had hoped that by *Sinterklaas* and Christmas they would have enough coins to take home to their families in Hamburg and Oslo and finally be able to end their wretched poverty. And Rut—he must have returned from a failed attempt to escape.

The calm voice of his Mohawk companion sounded over his muffled sobs. "Listen to me, friend. My grandfather told me, 'when you lose an important person in your life, that person can live on through you.' I know you are strong. You must return to your people. You must tell your story. They must learn how their men lived and how they died. You will be a stronger person for the telling. They will be stronger for the hearing."

Johannes found his composure and looked Tail Feather directly in the eyes. He remained silent but his mind spoke, "These words come from a person who has spent his life in the forest and knows nothing of civilization, someone who has no alphabet or calendar, someone who does not even know his age, someone who believes that every animal and tree has a spirit. Yet, no one in Holland or on an ocean-going ship has ever said anything to me with more wisdom."

Johannes spoke from his heart, "I will do as you say. Thank you."

"Thank you? What means thank you?"

Johannes tried to explain. "It means: I know that you have said good words to me and that you have helped me. I am happy about that."

Tail Feather was a bit puzzled by this explanation. "We have no word for 'thank you' in Mohawk tongue. To do good things in our clan is expected of everyone."

"I must remember that," his friend answered, equally puzzled.

The body requires food, warmth, and sleep. Of these, the two chose sleep. They lay on the spongy-wet forest floor atop some brush and dozed off. Kykoo, too. Whatever tomorrow would bring, well..., at least for the moment, they were safe.

CHAPTER 25

Destiny

Early morning light streamed through the trees. Dawn brought an end to a terrible night of shivering and scratching for Johannes. A whine from KyKoo caused him to open his eyes. Standing at his feet were four men, motionless as tree trunks with arms folded in front. "The hunters?" thought Johannes. "They have caught us at last."

Tail Feather leapt to his feet. He stepped toward the men. In a like gesture of boldness, he held his arms folded before him. KyKoo growled at his side with her toothy snarl. The standoff at the edge of the forest played out as the sun peaked over a ridge across the river.

Slowly, as he stood, his head clearing from sleep, Johannes recognized all the men. They were the ones who came to the trading post when he first arrived. It was in autumn last. They were Mahicans. "Are these the men who chased us?" he asked himself.

The tallest of the men, one with two eagle feathers in his headband, raised a hand. Not speaking, he beckoned Tail Feather and Johannes to go with them. The two, hardly at ease about what fate might be lying ahead, had no choice.

It was not a long walk through a winding valley between gentle hills before they came to a village. No palisade guarded the village. Altogether, about twenty houses lay scattered here and there on flat, raised ground. Most houses were circular and peaked like a cone; some were dome-shaped. A few, though, were of the longhouse style; these were not so long as the longhouses in a Mohawk village. The largest of them may have had room for two or three families only, not ten or twelve families, as in Tahawus.

Centered within the sprawl of houses was a huge fire. Stout posts encircled the fire. On top of each post sat the skull of a large animal.

The people of the village instantly circled around the strangers with great curiosity. What added to the eeriness for Johannes was the stillness of the village. No one spoke. Even the three or four wolves there watched from a distance without so much as a growl. KyKoo stood calmly by Tail Feather.

Seafaring men in the New World often spoke about what the *Wilden* do with captives. These prisoners, they said, were fed well, painted and decorated. There were dances and speeches to honor them. The rituals were said to be stretched out for days. During these days of ceremonies, the tribe was not kind to the captive for they were tormented in the most gruesome ways. In the end, the captives welcomed death. These stories Johannes always took to be too horrible to be true. As the fire blazed and the people surrounding him stared in silence, Johannes grew more certain he would become an unwilling participant in the ceremony.

Johannes and Tail Feather were led to the largest longhouse. A double layer of bearskins was laid out for them to sit on. Inside, the space was dark but warm. Shivering soon passed. The warmth, agreeable as it was, worsened the itch of Johannes. He could not help scratching. All the time he tried his best to disguise it from the multitude of Mahicans who had crowded into the longhouse.

The welcoming began with a gourd full of warm, spicy broth. Freshly boiled pieces of venison came next. Then followed cakes of cornmeal soaked in maple syrup. Tail Feather ate heartily. He appeared to have no qualms about whatever their fate may be. It was not long before Johannes was feeling a bit easier about his prospects of living another day.

By using his hands to communicate, the tall man with two eagle feathers inquired of Tail Feather, "Who are you?"

Replied Tail Feather, "I am Mohawk."

"Why do you come to Mahican land?"

"I bring my friend. He comes to be with his people at the trading post. But we saw a great wave swallow them all."

Another man, one with a sharp voice, joined in, "The pact between Mahicans and Mohawks for safe passage to trade is no more. Trading stopped when something terrible happened."

Two-Eagle-Feathers explained. "A great canoe with wings came to our land. It left a new set of men. They killed one of ours. It was at the time of the first snowfall. We traded little after that."

A shuddering chill rippled through the limbs of Johannes when Tail Feather explained the words. He was further dumbfounded when Two-Eagle-Feathers turned to him and asked, "Who are you?"

Tail Feather responded in sign, "My friend is one of the trading people."

"No, no," came an agitated response. "We watch the hairy faces closely. He is not one of them."

"Yes. He is one of the traders. He traveled with me to see my village, a village near the mountain called Cloud-Splitter."

Doubting eyes among the crowd found one another. "No, we do not believe you," said Two-Eagle-Feathers.

The Mahicans looked stonily at Johannes. His prospect for observing the morbid rites of the *Wilden* loomed heavily once again in his mind. Tail Feather did his best to assure the Mahicans that Johannes was exactly who he said he was. Then, Tail Feather glanced at Johannes. Of course! His friend's face was still swollen, bumpy and scratched beyond recognition. With that realization, Tail Feather broke into a hearty laugh. The Mahicans again looked at each other for meaning in this strange outburst. The hands of Tail Feather flew to tell this story of the itching disease. As he did, a trace of smile came on the face of his listeners. Soon, all joined in with laughter.

Johannes, not understanding, was hardly amused. "Tail Feather laughs with them. So, he has planned my fate all along," he thought. He felt his heart drop to his feet on discovering this treachery. He thought, "Now my friend will help the Mahicans in some monstrous ritual with me at the center of it all." Johannes then made a quick promise to himself. "I will be brave. I will show these *Wilden* that people from Holland can be honorable to the end."

All did not go as Johannes had imagined in those awful flashes of thought. Tail Feather explained why the Mahicans did not recognize him. They remember you now." Johannes, one can easily imagine, breathed more easily with the account.

There was more hand-talk. Tail Feather explained: "Two-Eagle-Feathers told me that the chief of this clan is Talks-With-Wise-Voice. He has sent for the chief's shaman. He says that the shaman knows what helps fire in the skin."

Then began a string of speeches. Some were solemn; others were agitated with much waving of arms. Worried, Johannes whispered to Tail Feather, "What are they saying?"

"I can understand only a word now and then. It is something about a festival tomorrow."

"Are these the hunters who tried to catch us?"

"No, of that I am sure."

It seemed that every Mahican crammed in the small longhouse had something to say. After the last them had spoken, the hide flaps over the entryway were pulled aside. In stepped a man with loose, pure white hair that fell well below his shoulders. His was a deeply wrinkled face. He walked stiffly as the crowd pushed back to make a passageway.

The elder spotted Johannes crouched in the far end. He went directly toward him stopping but half a step away. There he stood erect as a meeting post, feet together, hands held together at his waist. There was a moment of suspense before he guided Johannes to his feet. He studied the face with great care. He looked behind his ears, under the chin, at the tongue, behind the neck. One at a time, he examined each arm and each leg. He lifted Johannes's shirt to look at his torso, front and back. With each part, hc mumbled softly to himself before passing on to the next part. This, thought Johannes, is the way a butcher looks over a farmer's pig before the sale. His manner fixed in the mind of Johannes that he was being sized up for the roasting skewer.

Having completed his head-to-toe inspection, the shaman nodded respectfully to Johannes. He turned to Chief Talks-With-Wise-Voice and spoke in a quiet way before bowing and exiting the longhouse.

Hand-talk around some smoldering embers went on until late into the night. The Mahicans told Tail Feather about how they watched the hairy faces throughout the winter as the traders tried to hunt, trap, and gather berries and nest eggs. It was clear to them that the white-faces were woefully lacking in natural skills. The Mahicans knew that winter in the cabin meant near starvation. They wondered, too, why no one came to them to ask for help.

As the account of winter around Fort Nassau came bit by bit from the mouths and hands of one, the others nodded or murmured in agreement.

Tail Feather learned that the Mahicans thought that the traders of fur were a bit dim-witted. There was much nodding with this telling. True it was that the traders made fine axes and kettles, that they traveled great waters in giant canoes without paddles, and that they carried fiery sticks. Yet, they wore strange clothes. They knew nothing of body decorations. They also smelled. With hand-talk Tail Feather told about the arrival of these strangers four winters before. The Mahicans knew it was foolish of them to build their house on low land at the river's edge.

Johannes asked Tail Feather to inquire if they knew anything about Rut. Had they found him? Was he the sixth man on the roof? Here is what they signed:

"Some of us followed your man from the day he left the trading house. We were curious about his purpose. He never knew that we followed him. He did not know the secrets of the forest. Instead, he wandered along the river for four days before collapsing for want of food, sleep, and shelter. Our men carried him to our village. We gave him nourishment and rest. During that time, this man uttered not one word. After many days, we returned him to his own people. They rejoiced on seeing him. Then, turning their backs on us, all went into the trading house, barring the door from inside.

"I pity Rut," thought Johannes. "He would have been better off if they had just let him die peacefully in the forest. He would have been saved from drowning." After thinking more about it, though, Johannes admitted that the acts of the Mahicans were kind. They were not what a stranger and enemy could expect in Holland.

While the night talkers went on, a woman—not old, not young— entered the longhouse. She was tall and slender, decorated only with a small necklace of shell beads. All features of her face were delicate. Her hair fell loosely around her shoulders.

The woman first went to Chief Talks-With-Wise-Voice and bowed, a slight nod of the head that signaled both respect and self-pride. She then bowed in the same way to Tail Feather who, somewhat surprised, stood to receive her. The woman then turned to Johannes who remained sitting and uneasy. But, her eyes, reflecting from the glow of the low-lit fire, were soft and comforting.

Standing a half step away from Johannes, she placed a wooden bowl at his side. In it was a paste as white as newly fallen snow. Pointing first to herself, she extended both hands, palms down and fingers, separated and jiggling. Next, she lifted both her arms with fingers spread straight up, and then let them fall slowly toward her waist. Even Johannes knew the message the meaning: Her name is Gentle-Rain-Falling.

Without hesitation, Gentle-Rain-Falling took a gob of paste with her fingertips. She started on Johannes's forehead, then around the eyes taking care not to put any on the lids. The nose and cheeks were next. Her broad fingertip touch was gentle and slow moving. The paste went onto every puffed-up spot of angry welts. She even rubbed the paste between the fingers where the itching was most maddening. Soon Johannes resembled a scrawny snowman. All the time, he listened to the deep-toned chanting of many voices. By now, Johannes was even more certain that the paint was the decoration before the sacrificial ritual as sailors had warned.

Gentle-Rain-Falling guided Johannes to stand. She continued pasting on his back, chest, abdomen, and legs. Once the body was covered and the paste used up, she bowed to Johannes, and again to Tail Feather and lastly to Talks-With-Wise-Voice. After that she quickly departed.

There was another side to the body painting that Johannes had not expected. His itching eased a bit. It was not long before he hardly needed to scratch. Another thought came to him, "Could it be that I am wrong about a sacrifice? Is it possible that the Mahicans are...?" It was during this thought that his exhaustion and freedom from terrible itching took over. He fell asleep.

One by one, the men left the longhouse. Tail Feather was alone with his friend. He, too, needed sleep, and it was not long in coming. KyKoo, as she always did, slept in the open but close to the entryway.

The mind plays tricks during times of great anxiety. Johannes dreamed that night. But he did not dream about some imagined hideous rites of wilderness people. Instead, he dreamed of one summer when he was a boy and visited his cousins, Thomas and Janine, who lived on a farm in Aalsmeer.[84] His dream took him into the fields. There they picnicked by a stream with bread and freshly made cheese, topped with raspberries picked along the way. They waded into a cool pool where they watched and wondered as tiny, silvery fish nibbled at their toes. The dream ended suddenly just as the picnic ended that day long ago when a black snake slithered out from beneath the log.

Johannes opened his eyes in time to see the first glimmer of daylight through the smoke hole. The light began to trace the outline of ears of corn and baskets that hung along the walls. Renewed worry about his fate came upon awakening. He stepped outside the longhouse to find the village still asleep. All was still among the longhouses. Only stares of wide-awake wolves greeted him. Within the meeting posts, the blazing fire of the previous night was but a faint glow.

"Now is my best chance to escape," Johannes concluded. "First find the canoe. Next slide it into the flooded marsh. Paddle out into mid-river. Do this before anyone knows I am gone." He hesitated, thinking better of the idea. "No," he told himself. "I will not get far. The Mahicans will sooner or later catch up with me. They will treat me even more vengefully. Worse, they will think me a coward." Another plan came to mind, "Yes, I could paddle across the river, let loose the canoe and walk to Water-With-No-End. They will think me drowned." He thought again about that plan, "No. I am still too weak. I will never reach the trading village."

It was in this uncertain mind that Johannes wandered to the edge of the village. There he found a path and followed it as it twisted and turned upward to a hilltop. From there, he could see the swollen river speckled with floating branches. Across the way, there was a pink blush that stretched across the entire highlands beyond the river. "This may be the last sunrise I will ever see," he thought aloud. "I also believe it is the most beautiful sight I have ever seen." As if there were not beauty enough, Johannes followed a soaring eagle with white head until it landed at the top of the tallest pine tree in the distance.

The sight did something to Johannes's state of mind. "The Mahicans have been good to me. Am I only imagining that they intend to harm me, to have fun at my misery?" He watched with fascination as the pink skyline slowly faded, and the sun floated over the horizon. "Now," he knew, "it is too late to break away. The whole village will be awake." He pondered further, then came to accept whatever fate the Mahicans had in mind for him. He had to return along the path and see for himself. "If the clan has bad intentions about me, I am doomed. If I am mistaken, I will be ashamed of my feelings." With these thoughts, Johannes returned to the village, telling himself that every coin has two sides. He will soon find out which side turns up when the coin is tossed.

Johannes found the villagers up and about. The central fire was ablaze once again. Many clay pots hung near small cookfires among the dwellings. People had already started their daily chores: scraping hides, pounding meal, and mending fishnets.

Tail Feather appeared. "We looked for you. Finally, one of the children spotted you on top of a hill. She was frightened for a moment," he said with a chuckle. "She thought you were a ghost; your face is painted all white."

Johannes did not speak his thought, "So they think that I scare the *Wilden*! What a curious affair!"

"Did you have a good view?"

"Yes, a wonderful view. I could see the river and how it curves into the distant hills. No place in Holland has such a grand view."

"You must eat now. Soon you need all of your strength."

The comment gave further worry to Johannes. But he went with Tail Feather to the cookfire of Gentle-Rain-Falling. There, with turtle shells, they dipped into the stew. Beans and squash were mixed with fish and the meat from small animals, perhaps a squirrel or pigeon. In addition, Gentle-Rain-Falling offered them smoked venison and corn bread stuffed with berries. A flattened log served as a bench on which the two savored the meal. KyKoo ate, too. She always waited for the meat to cool, then bit through it noisily, bones and all. And as always, the children, silent but watchful, pressed quietly around them.

His hunger satisfied, Johannes stretched out on the bench and closed his eyes to enjoy the warmth of the early morning sun. It was not long before shadows passed before his closed eyes. They were not those of the ever-curious children. Instead, they were the shadows of men. These were the same men who, on the day before, had led the exhausted paddlers from the waterfront to the longhouse. Johannes could see on some of the serious faces the trace of a grin. Tail Feather announced with little feeling, "The men want you to follow them." If he had been on edge of panic before, his jitters were further stirred.

"So, my time has come," thought Johannes. "All along, my distrust has been right." He told himself, "I will not be a coward." At the same time, he did not feel brave, rather more like a rabbit than a great black bear. Whatever was to come, Johannes did as he was told; he followed in the footsteps of the men. Tail Feather, with KyKoo of course, walked just behind him. The slow walk in single file took them toward the blazing fire within the meeting posts. The worst moment for Johannes had come. He struggled to breath in against a constricted chest. Inside his chest, he felt a dozen shipbuilding carpenters pounding away. The file did not stop at the fire but passed beyond toward the river. The walk at last led to the place where the forest and the marsh meet. Just where they had left it, sat the canoe.

The Mahicans looked the canoe over with great care, turned it sideways, then over and finally right side up. They signed to Tail Feather. Tail Feather raised his right hand to heart level with thumb and pointing finger extended, meaning that he understood. With the exchange, muddy feet made their way back to the village.

Johannes was afraid to ask what that exchange was about. He need not have asked, for Tail Feather, along the way, told him, "In a few days, when you are rested and stronger, we will continue our journey to Water-With-No-End."

The head of Johannes was rattled with this news.

Tail Feather added, "The Mahicans say the canoe is worthy of a long journey. Look, they have patched the hole made by the arrow. There is another paddle. The rolled bundles of deerskin hold a good supply of journey cakes. What do you think of that?"

Johannes could not reply for lack of words. It is easy to imagine that his breathing was fuller and that the carpenters inside his chest had gone home after a long day's work.

CHAPTER 26

Reflections

Days in the land of the Mahicans passed quickly for both young men. They had rested and were well-fed. While work was not expected of them, they did help with the clearing of land for spring planting. Shrubs and roots needed pulling. Many rocks, big and small, had to be removed. Hoes of stone and bone loosened the earth. Mostly, however, the two companions spent the days, which were warm and almost cloudless, walking lazily along the riverbank or into the forest.

On one long walk into the forest, Johannes heard a story that was not easy to believe. Tail Feather had not talked much about himself but on this day, he told about a custom in his clan. He spoke first by showing signs of growing into manhood, at the time when he undertook a "Dream Quest." That ritual required boys to be sent alone into the forest in the winter for seven days. "I took a vow not to eat anything during this time. I was allowed to drink from a stream to quench my thirst. My clothing was light and my moccasins without linings. I carried no bow and arrow and no spear."

"How did you keep from freezing?"

"By hard walking or running in daylight. I chased deer, climbed ledges and trees, and crossed streams on fallen trees. To walk over deep snow, I made wide foot loops from birch branches. At night, I slept undercover. My grandfather taught me how to build a shelter of saplings and evergreen boughs topped with snow."

"Why does your clan make you suffer so?" seemed a proper question for Johannes to ask.

"It was my duty," came the expected answer. "I had to wait for the clan spirit to come in a dream. The spirit may be in the form of a bird, a raccoon, a bear, a fish, or a tree. One never knows which one. The character of the spirit helps a boy leave his boyhood and find direction as a man."

"Of course," the next question begged asked, "Did your clan spirit appear?"

"Yes, more than once."

"What spirit was it?"

"That, our custom allows me to tell only the sachem. He advises on such matters."

"Could you find things to eat beneath the snow?"

"Remember my promise not to eat?"

"What if you became lost?"

"We learn as children to remember the hills and the rocks and streams along the way. How moss grows on one side of a tree helps us find the way, too. On a long journey, we learn to tell direction from the sun and from the stars."

Johannes was fully aware of the hardiness of his friend who never complained and who never seemed to tire. Still, he strained to believe that anyone could live through such a terrible time. "And you were only a boy then?" he questioned.

"Yes. Every boy must go through a Dream Quest. If a boy should weaken, a dream spirit will not come to him. He will bear the burden of separation from the forest spirit world for a lifetime. He will then be like a woman."[85]

"But women work hard. They are noble in spirit and comforting in mind," protested Johannes.

"You are right, my friend," Tail Feather answered. "I just tell you what it is like in my world."

Johannes lapsed into thoughtful silence. When at last he spoke, he said, "The *Wilden* take life too seriously. Your people are clever at weaving and making pottery. The canoes and bows and arrows are wonderful things. Your longhouses are warm during the coldest nights. Clearing fields and planting gardens is not easy with tools of stone. Even fishing is tormenting, standing with nets in ice-cold streams. Then, you must also suffer to follow your traditions. I do not think that you just have fun."

"No, no. We play games," Tail Feather interrupted. "Footraces, wrestling, snow snake— they are all part of growing up. Now, we have a new game played with a netted stick and leather ball."

"But even your games are hard played as if life itself depended on them," returned Johannes. "In your village, I never saw one person laugh aloud. No one makes up funny stories or plays tricks on one another. Life is not easy in Holland, but we had fun, sometimes just being silly."

Tail Feather did not respond to the challenge. Johannes took his lack of response to be the end of the exchange.

Suddenly, Tail Feather asked, "Are you ready?"

"Ready?"

"Yes. To paddle to Water-With-No-End? You call it the Island of Hills."

"Ready!" By now, Johannes was flushed with vigor. His rash was nearly gone. One more layer of paste that night might be the last. He longed to speak to a Hollander again and hear his feet shuffle on the deck of a homeward bound ship.

"Then we will leave this village at first light of day. Do you agree?"

"Yes, only not together. I will go alone. You have already done much for me. No one could ask of you more." Johannes spoke boldly, wanting to prove that he had entered manhood, too. Yet, there was an awkward hesitation in his voice.

"You may need help. I will go with you."

"But I can find Island of Hills. I will travel only at night to keep from being seen. There are no more rapids or waterfalls. I will not get lost. The journey will be easy." Again, these words did not come out as strong as they were meant to.

Tail Feather explained, "I have another reason to go to the Island of Hills. When I was there some winters ago, the Spirit of a Snake gave me a terrible sickness. People of the Shorakkopochs cared for me in a deep cave. One of them tended me day and night. I told her of KyKoo. Now, I will bring KyKoo to her. I think she will like that."

"Then, we will go together to the Island of Hills," Johannes responded with a sense of relief in his voice. "You can come, too, on the winged canoe. We will cross the ocean. You will see that I speak true about my big village in Amsterdam."

"No," was the quick and resolute answer. "My world is in the forest and waters of our land. Trapped on your great canoe for a long journey would take away my right thinking," Tail Feather said, making circles on the side of his head with his pointing finger.

"But you must come. You will see many wonderful things in my land," insisted Johannes.

"What you speak is true. No, I could not feel good on a land that is below the water. I wonder about your story of houses with great arms that turn in the wind and pump water. You tell of making fire even more hot. Things you speak of in your world have no place in mine. For now, a visit to yours with my mind's eye is enough. When I leave my village, I can hear the wind calling me back. That is my good feeling." There, the discussion about Tail Feather visiting Holland ended.

The last afternoon at the village of the Mahicans was unusually balmy. The two agreed to take one last walk into the forest. Not much was said as they, with KyKoo, chose to follow a well-worn path. In time, they came to a monstrously big oak that had fallen across the path. The upturned roots, laden with earth and stones, made a wall as high as two men. Behind the root wall, there was still a patch of snow, never touched by the sun, yellowing with the stain of leaves.

Tail Feather stopped abruptly to examine some animal prints that lay across the snow patch. "We will have a lesson about tracking animals," Tail Feather announced. "What are these?" he asked of Johannes.

"They are made from hooves. Each hoof is pointed and split in two."

"Good. And what animal made them?"

"Hmmm. They are small, so it must be a deer, not a moose or elk."

"You are right. Look closely. See that the prints are narrow. They were made by a doe, a doe about two winters of age. She was tired and running slowly. You can tell because the tracks are farther apart than walking tracks and too close for a full running tracks.

"Yes, I see that..., I think." Even so, Johannes was not so sure he had grasped all these signs in the snow.

Tail Feather went on. "Wolves probably chased her. She was lucky to get away because her leg was hurt." Tail Feather pretended to limp. He went on: "See the bow-arm hoof. It turns out. Not good. The doe cannot lift her leg in the right way." Then pointing to a long groove in the snow, he continued, "See how the hoof drags in the snow.

"She came by here well after sun-up on this morning. See the snow around the edges of each footprint. The edge on the sun side is soft from melting snow. Other side is sharp, still frozen. By this night both edges will be smooth from melting ground warmth."

"You know much about the forest," Johannes commented.

"Now we must look closer," Tail Feather continued, crouching down over the footprints. "Her legs in back sink very deep in the snow. The front legs, not so deep. That means a baby will come soon, maybe in next round moon." Tail Feather carefully tested several of the hoof prints for firmness by lightly pressing with his extended long finger. "I think she will have a twin birth. She is doubly lucky not to be wolf food by now."

Johannes was amazed by these insights from tiny signs.

Tail Feather then walked beyond the snow patch to where, in the open sunlight, the wet leaves had been ruffled. "This is where she stopped to rest. "Ah ha!" Pointing to her droppings, he went on: "their shape and smell mean there was much water in her body. I think she was caught in swift current and nearly drowned."

Johannes could only shake his head in admiration of such wisdom.

His woodlands teacher had not finished, "The shade of green on the droppings tells me she ate fresh marsh grass, not salty, like the grass along this river. The fresh kind grows only along the River-Between-Mountains, near the place where deer like to graze—where we saw the rainbow. Haaa! So, the doe lost her footing in the wet ground, probably from the lame leg, and was swept into the river."

Johannes was speechless.

The explanation continued. "I think... fast waters carried her to the trading house. She waded up to dry land and rested there. Wolves found her. What do you think?"

The listener was too astonished to answer.

"There is something else. One eye is hurt, the eye on the arrow-arm side."

This last bit of information stunned Johannes. "How can you tell that?" he stammered.

"It is simple. Follow me." Tail Feather walked a bit farther along the tracks. "A few strands of hair on some of these bushes tell the story. A deer with sight in both eyes would not have brushed its sides against these."

Both eyes of Johannes were white all around from astonishment.

"You can remember all that?" Tail Feather asked.

"I think so." The voice of Johannes wavered a bit.

"Then you will learn about tracking by going over all these signs by yourself. I show you animal tracks. You tell me their meaning."

"What a good idea!"

Once the lesson was agreed upon, Tail Feather led them some distance until they came upon another set of animal tracks that crossed a brook. These were small footprints with toes. "See what you can make out of these," he instructed. This said, he and KyKoo wandered away, leaving Johannes for his first wilderness test.

"Of course, I can remember something about animal tracks," Johannes told himself. "Didn't I pretend to read in school by memorizing what my classmates read aloud? I learned the name of every sail and every line on a great ship. Animal tracks will be easy."

Johannes immediately occupied himself in the studious application of his newfound lore. To this end, he went onto all fours, using every sense that he could engage, looking for shades of color and texture and to find those tell-tale signs pointed out by his Mohawk friend. It was not long, though, before he had to admit, "I can find none of them." They are just the footprints of some animal. Misty hopes of living in the way of the *Wilden,* at least for the moment, were not to be. With this admission, he turned to find Tail Feather and KyKoo and admit his failure as a woodsman.

They were not far away, standing alongside the fallen tree trunk. Standing is not quite accurate, for Tail Feather was bent over, hands on knees, stamping his feet and laughing hysterically. Tears streamed down his cheeks. His teeth sparkled in a crescent moon grin. He spotted Johannes and ran toward him with open arms. Tail Feather flung them around Johannes in a tight hug as if to keep from collapsing from laughter.

At first, Johannes was bewildered by these strange antics. It took but a moment to realize that he had been drawn into an impossible feat of deduction. And so, realizing that he had been duped, he joined in on the laughing. He knew that there was no need to give an account of the lesson found in the animal footprints. Johannes's lesson for the day was just this: *Wilden* do have fun. They can be mischievous, like the coyote. Tail Feather told Johannes that his tracking trick had been guided by the spirit of a coyote.

During this delirious hilarity, KyKoo disappeared. For her to leave Tail Feather's side was extraordinary. In time, the two collected themselves and began to search. The search ended where wolves left muddy prints and patches of pressed down small plants where they rested. There, they found KyKoo sniffing around in wide circles. At times, she stared stiff-legged at tracks that led into the thicket, letting out a mournful whine.

"KyKoo has acted this way before," Tail Feather worried aloud. "The first time, she went into the forest. She did not come back for many days. Scratches and cuts were all over. Big patches of hair had been torn away. One ear was missing. For now, we must take her to the village and keep her from going into the forest."

With much coaxing and some pulling and pushing and a little carrying, Tail Feather and Johannes steered KyKoo in the direction of their longhouse. Her wide-eyed squirming prevented them from taking her inside, no matter how they tried. Instead, Tail Feather gathered enough venison from generous Mahicans to overfeed KyKoo. "When she hears the wolves at night, KyKoo may be too stuffed to answer their call," he explained. "That is all we can do to keep her with us."

Tail Feather told how KyKoo had gone into the forest another time. It was the time when he had paddled to Water-With-No-End. She was not seen from one full moon to the next. Later, KyKoo acted strangely, letting no one near her. Finally, she presented the village with two pups.

Surprised Johannes asked, "What happened to the puppies?"

"At first, KyKoo protected them with a growl should anyone come close. As the days passed, my sisters won her trust little by little. They gave the pups much attention. When the pups were half grown, they often wandered into the forest, returning by sundown to eat. Then, one day they never returned. Laughing Rain and Awakens Corn cried for days."

"What about KyKoo?"

"I was told that KyKoo was not saddened. Animals know when it is time to let their young ones go free."

As evening approached, the two friends waited to catch sight of the first star in the sky. It was just then that Gentle-Rain-Falling came to the longhouse. This time, she came with her children, a girl about Sky Flower's age and a boy in a cradleboard. She also brought a shirt and pair of moccasins for each guest. They were plain, without a bit of decoration, but they were well stitched.

Johannes had almost forgotten about his three-leaf itch. The skin was still angry in places that had been scratched raw. These places called for another layer of paste. Gentle-Rain-Falling, if anything, was even more painstaking with her skin painting than on nights before.

On previous times when she came to the end of her work, she nodded slightly with a quick knee-dip and left. This time, she signed something to Tail Feather. Tail Feather in turn relayed her message to Johannes, "Gentle-Rain-Falling wants to tell you about her husband."

"Yes, I would like to hear about him," rejoined Johannes.

There were more exchanges of hand talk. When Tail Feather had it all in mind, he said, "Gentle-Rain-Falling tells us that her husband knew the men who first came here two winters ago. He found much good in their ways. He watched them build their cabin. He helped them make a chimney from stones. He liked their tools of hard metal. They were friends. He went into their cabin many times."

Johannes was moved by this story. "Why hadn't Joost told us about her husband?" he told himself.

Gentle-Rain-Falling had more to tell. Again, Tail Feather unraveled the signs. "She has a question about the man they found in the forest."

"Rut! Of course, tell her to ask whatever she would like."

Tail Feather relayed her question, "Why did he kill my husband with his thunder stick?"

With the question, Johannes suddenly felt as giddy as at the time the awful event happened. A powerful chill overcame him.

He could not get enough air even though he was breathing fast and deep. He rocked unsteadily as if he were to faint.

Since that incident, Johannes had tried to keep it out of his mind. He was sickened by Rut's act. Like the rest of the traders, however, he thought only of how the affair caused trouble for them. He did not think about the man himself, as a husband and father. He could not explain why. At the time, the traders and the *Wilden* were in a different world, though they stood together on a small part of it. One man's impulsive distrust turned deadly just because of another man's simple curiosity. The full impact of the terrible moment now came down on Johannes as he looked at Gentle-Rain-Falling and her small children.

His best answer to the unanswerable was, "I cannot give a reason." He stammered, "It just happened." Johannes was ashamed to have such a weak explanation for something so terrible. After Tail Feather's signing explanation, Gentle-Rain-Falling dipped and nodded a bit deeper than before. She and her children then quietly disappeared into the night.

Johannes paced back and forth from one end of the longhouse to the other. He tried to make sense out of why people do not trust each other, and why they fight. He could find no excuse for his countrymen's action. They came to the New World to trade tools and trinkets for furs. What they accomplished instead was to make enemies.

Tail Feather tried to calm down his agitated friend. "You are not to blame. All the Mahicans know that." The comment helped but did not relieve Johannes of the entire burden of guilt. He needed to search further into the bad feelings between people. His thoughts slowly turned inward, and then, in a sickening and overwhelming sense of anguish, as if he were again being pulled underwater, Johannes remembered that he, too, was guilty of the same thing. He had misinterpreted the actions of his loyal Mohawk friend three times before: when he thought he was being left to drown, when he thought he was abandoned just when his itching was at its worst, and when, on this day, he imagined he was being marched to his death. Oh, how easy it was to let fear turn to distrust!

His tormented thoughts wandered next to the distrust between nations in Europe, causing senseless and destructive wars to all concerned. All for some pieces of land or to avenge a petty offense! Sometimes at the whim of a bored king who wanted adventure! Was it the same in the New World?

"Why do the Mahicans and the Mohawks fight?" Johannes asked.

"Conflict between our people goes back a long time," said Tail Feather. "There was a clash, a battle, no one knows. Quarrels can happen over things of no importance. From then on, revenge followed attack, and that led to more attacks and more revenge. Sometimes a raid is only so that a warrior can touch the scalp lock of an enemy; that act proves him brave."

"But the Mohawks brought furs into Mahican land. There was no fighting."

"It is true. Here is why: the Mahicans quickly ruined nearby beaver lodges when the Hairy Faces came to trade pelts for kettles and axes. There were many beavers along the River-Between-Mountains. That is the Land of the Mohawks. The Mahicans agreed with the traders to give safe passage to Mohawks bearing furs. For so many pelts brought to the trading place, so many tools would be given to the Mahicans. So, was that clever?"

"Yes, clever. Is that why you came to our trading post?"

"Yes. Our people heard that beaver pelts were valuable to traders. The skins are small. They make good mittens, but little else. We still do not know why they are so important for people who come from across the ocean."

Remembering that he had tried to explain this to Reginald, Johannes sighed and started once more. "Pelts from beavers are stitched together to make coats. The fur is warm and soft. People who wear them feel stylish and want to be admired. They exchange beaver pelts at high values. My father works in this exchange trade. When the coats are worn down, hat-makers use steam and heavy smooth irons to press the fur into thick and dense layers. It is called 'felt.' You have seen felt hats with wide brims that some of the men at the trading post wore." Johannes hoped that his listener had understood at least half of this explanation!

"Hmmm," was Tail Feather's only comment.

"Trading stopped, but the Mahicans were kind to us, you a Mohawk, me a white face. Why?"

"We were no threat. It is their way to help two half-starved rabbits."

Later into the night, Johannes said, "I have a question for you."

His reply, "You sleep, now, Ho-Han-nes." Tail Feather had already crawled beneath his bearskin. He added, "We start another long journey tomorrow. We may not sleep in a warm house again for many days." There followed a long, long silence. At last, he said, "Well, what is your question?"

"What do you think of me now?" asked Johannes.

"Of you? What is your meaning?"

"We have traveled far together. Have I been a terrible bother?"

Tail Feather chuckled quietly with the question. He thought for a while before answering. "No, you have been good. I have learned much about the world from you. You are my friend."

"Do you speak the truth?"

"Of course. Sometimes, it is true, you act like a child. But you learn quickly. In time, you may become a good Mohawk," he said in with a half-mocking tone.

Johannes was amused with the thought. "You must know that I was happy to visit your village and to journey with you," he replied, forgetting for the moment some of the details. He thought of adding his lingering suspicion that Tail Feather planned with the Mahicans to roast him in a tribal sacrifice. "No, no, that thought will wait for another day."

"There is still something that I do not understand," Johannes admitted on this last night together.

"You must tell me," replied his friend.

"Well, why did the hunters pursue us for four days? Did we offend them? Are we enemies?"

"No, I think not," said Tail Feather. "Hunting is a way of life for woodland people. From hunting comes our meat and our furs for clothing. To be a good hunter takes much practice. You know that animals are swift and clever. There is also much excitement during a hunt."

Johannes interrupted, "Then why did they chase us? And nearly catch us?"

"Because we were now the prey and they, the predators. I think that the hunters enjoyed the chase as much as you hated it."

"Would they kill us?"

"Perhaps not. More likely, they would take us to their village. Remember, too, that they would like to have our canoe."

The voice of Johannes rose with this terrible thought. "And then what would they do with us?"

"We would be required to do hard work until we proved worthy enough to become a member of their clan, and then marry us to their women."

"Do not fret, my friend," said Tail Feather. "We did escape. I should tell you that I found some pleasure from the excitement of escape." With this, the head of Johannes spun in disbelief.

Sleep, so needed for the day to come, did not come easily to Johannes. Instead he tossed awake through the night. His days with the *Wilden* came back over and over. What did he think of them? Here his thoughts were jumbled. "They are a simple people. They are one with the forest and river. In such a primitive life, they do not use an alphabet and so there is no writing. They live in crude huts of bark. Their clothes are leather and fur. They have no cloth, no plates or chairs. There is no school for children. They do not even have money. Time is measured not by clocks but by the sun and moon and by the passing of seasons. Tail Feather does not know how old he is."

There was another side to think about. "The *Wilden* know the secrets of the wilderness. They survive in these terrible winters. They believe in spiritual beings in the sky, streams, trees, and rocks. Their faith is fully as strong as that of Catholics and Reformists in their belief in one God and the holiness of his only Son on Earth, Jesus. Their sense of loyalty to one another is beyond doubt. Looking back, I know that Tail Feather saved my life many times. Each time, he put his own life in danger."

Johannes's thoughts turned to home. "With luck, we will soon meet a ship in New Amsterdam. I could be home by *Sinterklaasavond*. The celebration will surely include a chocolate *J*. Mother and Father will want to hear all about my journey even if it takes a whole year to tell. My sister, Catherine, would surely like to hear about Reginald and his drawings. Will she be surprised that I learned how to swim?"

Of course, he would go to Leyden to see the grieving Father and Mother of Reginald. "I will tell them how brave their son was to climb with him to the top of a mast in a raging sea. They should know that he did his duty until the final moment. I will tell them that their son was a true friend. They will be happy that he spent his last days doing what he loved best: his charcoal on paper that brought the ship and the sailors who sailed on it to life. They can remember him as a fine artist. If only I had one of his drawings to show them."

Visions of his own future now tumbled wildly around in his imagination. "Will my father welcome me back to his business? I will promise to be careful to write every number in its rightful place. Someday I, too, will be a gentleman, wearing velvet shirts, pantaloons with silver buckles at the knees, a cape, and great felt hat with broad brim. People will see me strut along river Amstel and know that I am satisfied with life. On cold nights, I will sit by a roaring fireside and read the most important books in Holland." No, he promised himself, he would no longer spend endless days looking out from the top foremast into blank space. He need never drink foul water again. Nor taste stale beer. No more eating maggot-ridden bread. No, never again. He would never be chased by hunters nor suffer from the three-leaf itch. Gone are the days when...

The eyes of Johannes closed in slumber, and this last thought was never finished. Although he fell asleep with the promise of a comfortable life ahead, he awoke to the terrifying images of a dreadful dream.

He dreamed that a giant book of accounting opened above his head. From between its pages, a flock of numbers tumbled out. The numbers all had different colors. Their shapes were horribly twisted. All the purple Number Twos had pointed wings and swirled in tight circles around his head, stinging him everywhere. The Eights were green, and had many legs, like a caterpillar; they crawled across his face, prickling him with every footstep. Red

Number Sevens had talons and sharp teeth that pecked at his nose. Yellow Nines, shaped like ears, covered each ear and echoed the thunderous sounds of waves splashing over a deck and the high-pitched whistling of shrouds in winds without pity. The Number Threes were black. They curled tightly around each big toe with the middle part dug into the skin. Trying to pull them off only made them more painful. Worse, a thick blue Zero hung around his neck and slowly grew tighter. Johannes awoke with a start, cold sweat on his forehead, taking deep noisy breaths, his heart racing. Sleep after the attack of numbers was impossible.

He tried to forget about the nightmare, but it lingered in his mind. "Were the horrid numbers telling me that a life in a counting house was not meant for me?" The longhouse was still dark. Embers no longer glowed. He peered through the entryway hides and saw a faint trace of light stretching across the far tree line. Despite the chill in the air, he walked to the edge of the village to watch dawn unfolding.

Johannes was not alone. Trailing just behind was KyKoo. As he found a log for a seat, the wolf crouched down alongside. It was the first time that she had come to him. He reached out and put one arm around her shoulders. There, side-by-side, the two silently viewed the slow beginning of the day. By now, a long bank of overlapping pink clouds filled in the space between distant mountaintops.

As the sky slowly lightened, some rounded clouds replaced the long, flattened clouds that rimmed the ragged horizon. One of these new clouds, more oval than the rest, rose above them. With but a little imagination, Johannes saw it take on the shape of a face. Eyes were darkened puffs near the top. A long upward curl along the bottom made a smiling mouth. He saw in that cloud the face of Awakens Corn.

Suddenly, Johannes felt he was being twisted topsy-turvy. Now came a new plan. He would go back to Tahawus. He would become a *Wilde*! Even Tail Feather said he would become a good Mohawk. "He can teach me everything about their way of life. I will learn to speak their tongue as fine as they do. I will learn to make a bow and arrow and to make a fine canoe. I will learn everything there is to know about hunting, building a snow house, and finding my way through the wilderness. I will become a good Mohawk."

Second thoughts then began to edge out the vision of living forever in the "New World." "No, I cannot do that," Johannes told himself. "The clan will not welcome me. Not now, anyway. I must continue on downriver and return to the Old World."

"Help me decide, KyKoo." With these words, the wolf looked up wistfully with her golden eyes. "You always know the right thing to do."

Then a new thought came to him. It was really an old thought but one reborn. There is a Third World, one that connects the other two—the world of ships. In that world, he vowed, he would carry out his life's work.

"There will be another Fort Nassau and more furs to trade for kettles and axes. Dutch ships will return, perhaps English and Danish and French as well. The people of Europe will learn to respect and even admire the great character of people they now call "savages." We have much to learn from the people who live in bark houses with mats on bare ground but are truer in their thinking than the most pompous merchant or preacher in Holland. Their ideas of spirits are no less nor more complex than the scriptures of the Reformed Church that guide all proper Christians. The *Wilden* children run freely and often naked. They enjoy their childhood, and they do not make trouble."

The wolf crouched patiently even as these powerful reflections possessed Johannes. "KyKoo, do you know how cruel a Dutchman can be against another Dutchman and how the rope lashes the back of a common sailor for speaking against a senseless injustice?"

As a bank of clouds nestled along the ridge of mountains turned bright pink, the thoughts of Johannes swirled ever faster. "It is a false religion when sailors believe in God only when their ship is tormented by a great storm. My own father deceives buyers, and even me, with fables of unicorns. A spiral tusk from an Arctic whale fetches a handsome price when it is said to come from a unicorn. I can never forget how our heartless shipmaster abandoned unwilling men at Fort Nassau. Our children—even young ones—must labor at mind-numbing work all day and then spend one day in seven at an endless sermon. Do you hear that, KyKoo?"

Something else came to mind. He had never heard a *Wilde* complain. Not one word of complaint ever came from Tail Feather. But ever since he could remember, Johannes had heard people in Holland grumble. If it was not about the rain or the cold, it was about a painful knee or about not having enough money. Surely, the *Wilden* had needs and at times suffered much. These miseries they kept to themselves.

These far apart ideas whirled about in his head. He knew it was time to give serious thought into preparing for grown-up life. And so, a decision was made there on the log facing the rising sun. "I will study the art of sailing. I must learn to be good at the compass and cross staff. I will become perfect at making charts. Of course, these skills mean learning much about mathematics and even reading and writing. But I can do it."

Johannes knew only too well that life on a ship is neither easy nor safe. But after many voyages, he told himself, "I will become first mate, then bosun and someday, shipmaster. I promise to be a stern master but not a cruel one. I will not send a frightened cabin boy aloft in a storm to his death. I will not make any sailor suffer needlessly. I will keep my log true to facts."

This he promised KyKoo, "One day, I will have my own ship. Its name will stand out boldly in gold at the bow: Evening Star. I will sail up the North River. Awakens Corn will pick strawberries with me again. She will come aboard my fine ship. Do you think that Tail Feather would let you come, too?" With this new thought, he pulled the wolf a little closer. Together, they watched the leading edge of a red sun peer just over the mountaintops.

PART II

Notes About the Story

List of Notes in Book 3, *Johannes van der Zee*

Chapter	Note	Title of Note
1	1	Landlubber's Dictionary
	2	Hoorn
	3	Dutch East India Company
	4	Telescope
	5	Weathercock
	6	Wilden
	7	New Netherland
	8	Golden Age of Maritime Holland
	9	Ship's Officers
	10	Fluyt
	11	Unicorn
	12	Shipmaster Adriaen Block
	13	Sea Shanties
	14	The Zuider Zee
	15	World Events of 1616
2	16	Life for the Common Person
3	17	Trade Winds
	18	The Rogue Wave
	19	The Crew
	20	Shipboard Cuisine
	21	Shallop
	22	Barents Sea
	23	The Northern Lights
	24	Religious Tensions
	25	Windmills
4	26	Tar
	27	Maurice of Nassau, Prince of Orange
	28	The Sandglass
	29	Monsters of the Sea

Chapter	Note	Title of Note
	30	Knots
	31	The Dutch: Guild Members and Others
	32	*Onrust*
	33	Tulips
5	34	Discipline at Sea
	35	Chiprock Reach
	36	Dead Man's Breath
	37	Cross-staff
	38	Position of the Earth
	39	Amsterdam
	40	Fur Trade
	41	Scurvy
	42	Compass
6	43	Storm at Sea
7	44	Ship's Log
8	45	Dutch Luck
	46	Cape Cod
	47	Lower New York Bay
	48	The Narrows
	49	Upper New York Bay
	50	New Amsterdam
	51	Washington Heights
	52	Harlem River
	53	Palisades
9	54	Chiprock Reach, Again
	55	Saw Mill River
	56	Tappan Zee
	57	Sing Sing
	58	Croton Point
	59	Hudson Highlands
	60	Leadsman
	61	Claverack
10	62	Fort Nassau
12	63	Mahicans (Mohicans)
14	64	Mohawks
15	65	*Sint Nicolaas/Sinterklaas*
	66	Cabin Fever
	67	Magnifying Glass
	68	Firearms

The Notes

CHAPTER 1: OUTWARD BOUND

1-1 The Landlubber's Dictionary of the Square Rigger

Translation: Explanation of terms used on tall ships for "lovers of land." This mini-dictionary covers terms found throughout the story. An underlined term is a "<u>loan word</u>," adapted directly into English from the Dutch seafaring tradition.

abaft: toward the stern of the ship.
aft: the hind part (or stern) of the ship.
athwartship: across the width of a ship.
ballast: heavy weights, usually stones or lead pieces, placed along the keel to stabilize an unloaded, top-heavy ship.
belay: to secure a line onto belaying pins along the pin rails and fife rails (U-shaped at foot of mast).
bend: to make fast (or tie securely), an item such as a sail or anchor cable. The term bend is also used for a knot that holds one rope to another.
bilge: the lowermost part of the inner hull.
block: a piece of wood with sheaves (wheels) through which the lines (ropes) are rove (threaded). A block changes the direction of force applied by the line rove through it.
boom: a long timber that holds the foot of a sail.
bow: the foremost part of the hull or deck (rhymes with "cow").
bowsprit: a long spar projecting forward of the bow.
brace: part of running rigging by which the sail's yard is pivoted and held to point of the wind.

buoy: a floating object, used as a nautical marker, mooring, or personal floatation device.

buntlines: lines that take a tuck in a sail.

capstan: a barrel-shaped mechanism on deck around which are wound heavy lines or cables. Heavy spokes (or bars) radiate from the top (or drumhead) on which force is exerted to turn the capstan.

carvel: also, caravel. A hull constructed by laying planks edge to edge rather than overlapping. The design reduced the weight of a ship but required reinforcement by inner supporting structures.

castle: closed 'rooms' built on the deck. Aftercastle and forecastle (often shortened to "focs'l") are examples.

caboose: formerly, the galley of a ship.

cat-head: timbers projecting from the bow of a ship where the raised anchor is secured.

close-hauled: in sailing, to head as close as possible into the wind.

course sail: the lower sail of a mast.

dead-eye: a round block of wood with three holes through which is run a series of lines for stronger purchase (force or leverage) on shrouds. "Dead-eye" comes from the block's resemblance to a sheep's skull with two eye sockets and nasal opening.

deck: any of the planked floors of a ship, from the Dutch word *dek*. The weather deck lies between the forward forecastle and the aft quarterdeck.

fid: a small cone-shaped tool used to separate tight strands of rope, as in splicing or untying knots.

fluyt: a bulky ship designed and built in Holland that combines the efficiency and ease of handling as a small ship but has the carrying capacity of a large ship.

fore: refers to anything at the forward end of the ship. The word "before" is interchangeable.

forecastle: the built-up deck toward the bow, often designed for the galley and quarters for part of the crew.

foremast: On a ship with more than one mast, the foremast is the one closest to the bow

gasket: a small line that secures a furled sail to its yard.

gunwhale: (pronounced "gunnel"). The edge of the upper deck or hull. "Gunwhale awash" means that the boat or ship is heeled or tipped so far over that the one edge meets the water line.

halyard: a line used to raise a spar, sail or flag (or haul the yard).

hand: a working person on a ship (or one unit of work).

hatch: a small door that leads to the hold or quarters of a ship. A hatchway is a series of steps between decks.

hawser: a heavy rope, cable, or chain on a ship that is attached to the anchor or to the dock; hawsehole: the opening at the bow where the hawser is passed.

head: the toilet of a ship. In olden ships, it was placed at the forward part of the ship (the head) where the breeze coming from aft carries odors away from the ship.

helm: the apparatus by which a ship is steered. It includes whipstaff (or wheel), tiller, and rudder. The helmsman is one who operates the helm.

hove to: sails set parallel to the direction of the wind in order to spill the wind and keep the ship at a standstill.

keel: the central structural beam of a vessel that extends from bow to stern and around which the rest of the hull is built.

larboard: toward the left side of the ship when facing forward. On modern ships, the term "port" has replaced this name, to avoid being confused with "starboard," a similar sounding word. Origin: Dutch words for loading (*lade*) and side (*boord*).

lateen: a triangular-shaped sail flown from the mizzen mast. The yard that holds the sail pivots against the mast. This sail is of ancient Arabic origin.

latitude: a point on earth defined by its north-south location. It is defined by a number in degrees: zero degrees at the equator and ninety degrees at the pole.

leeward: away from the wind.

line: when a rope is assigned to a task on board ship it is no longer called a rope; it becomes a "line." An exception: aboard ship, a rope that is attached to a pail is still called a "rope."

longitude: a position on earth defined by an east-west location. Zero degree denotes a position on the same meridian as Greenwich, England. Degrees increase going both east and west. In the mid-Pacific Ocean over Taveuni, one of the Fiji Islands, the meridian is 180 degrees going mid-way.

luff: the forward edge of a fore and aft sail. Also, the fluttering motion of a sail as it points into the wind.

marline: a light-weight line made by twisting strands of rope (from *marlijn*, or tie-line).

mizzen: the aftermost mast.

oakum: fibers used to stuff into seams between planks to make water-tight seals.

quarter deck: the upper part of the ship behind the main mast.

reach: wind coming toward the side of the ship. It is a "broad reach" when the wind comes directly from the side.

ratline: roped steps tied on the shrouds that form a ladder up the mast.

rigging: refers to all fixed lines (ropes, on land) of two basic types.

standing lines: the securely seized shrouds and stays that hold up the masts and spars.

running lines: the lines used to haul spars and sails, and which move through blocks.

rudder: a vertical surface, of wood in olden ships; steers the vessel from the stern.

schooner: a two-masted ship. From the Dutch word for shoe, *schoen.*

scow: a flat bottom, working vessel used for hauling cargo in shallow water.

shallop: a small boat, usually rowed, carried on a larger boat and used to approach shore or explore shallow areas.

sheet: a line used to set a sail.

shroud: a set of lines that support the mast.

skipper: the master of a ship.

sloop: a small vessel with a single mast and fore and aft rigged sails.

spanker: a sail attached to the aft-most mast on a square-rigged ship. It lines up in a fore-and-aft orientation along the length of the ship. It adds surface for gaining wind power and helps to stabilize the steering of the ship.

spar: timbers that make up the fixed support of the sails and rigging, including the mast, yard, boom and sprit.

spritsail: a square sail bent to a yard and suspended below the bowsprit.

starboard: the right side of the ship looking forward. It is the side of the steering gear on old ships; from the Dutch words for steer (*stuur*) and side (*boord*).

stay: lines that secure a mast to the forward or after section of the ship. Forestay and aftstay are more specific terms.

stern: the rearmost part of the ship. Sternway: movement of the ship to stern.

taffrail: the often-decorated rail around the stern of a ship.

tacking: moving across the wind, helped by the spanker and rudder to kick the stern downwind.

tackle: a mechanism to increase power and control of a line by running it through a block.

tiller: a beam mechanism that connects the actual steering post or wheel to the rudder.

top mast: the mast above the lower mast and fixed at its base with a trestle tree.

topmast castle: the platform (often enclosed) on the upper mast where a look-out is stationed; called, simply, the "top."

tumblehome: the curved inward topsides of the hull.

waist-deck: the portion of the deck at midship.

weigh: to lift a heavy weight, usually referring to an anchor.

windward: toward the wind.

whipstaff: the vertical post by which the helmsman steers the ship.

yard: a long spar attacked to the mast at its center point where square sails are spread.

yacht: a single-masted, small ship often used for pleasure and rigged with fore-and-aft sails; a radical innovation of the time.

1-2 Hoorn

Although Amsterdam was the major commercial center of 17th century Holland (and now in modern times, of the Netherlands), its location on an inland sea proved to be less than desirable: its harbor was too shallow for large, heavily loaded ships headed for the open water. This disadvantage led to the growth of a new port at the trading center of Hoorn about thirty miles to the northwest. The water depth at this location was more advantageous for ocean-going ships. Hoorn soon welcomed ships from all over Holland. Today the city wall around it is mostly gone, but one of its old towers has been restored; it is now a restaurant called *Restaurant de Hoofdtoren Hoorn.*

What's in a name? In 1616, a pair of Dutch ships from Hoorn rounded for the first time the point at the southernmost island at the tip of South America. The island was named for one of the ships, the schooner Hoorn. This ship, alas, was destroyed there by fire. Now, Cape Horn is better known worldwide than its namesake. It is a place where howling winds and thunderous waves have caused many a tall ship to flounder on its way to and from the Pacific Ocean. For sailors, "Rounding the Horn" is what climbing Mt. Everest is to mountaineers.

1-3 Dutch East India Company

In 1602, the Government of the Dutch Republic granted a group of merchants temporary permission to trade in foreign lands with autonomy in its business dealings. Called the Dutch East India Company, it enjoyed a monopoly for 21 years. From its headquarters in Hoorn it carried out extensive trading in South America and Oceania, including Indonesia and Japan.

The Company's investors also sent a few ships to North America to find a short way to the Far East while keeping a good distance between them and the Spanish fleet. They did not find that elusive Northwest Passage nor did they did find much of high value there. The ship *Half Moon* (*Halve Maen*), skippered by Henry Hudson in 1609, was one such exploration. Hudson's historic sail up an unchartered river resulted in nothing for him but bitter disappointment. He never knew that the river would eventually bear his name or that the river would become one of the most important in the world. But one lowly trophy brought back from the New World piqued the interest of his company: beaver pelts.

A second shipping company, the Dutch West India Company, received a charter in 1621 to trade in the New World. The government granted it the right to ply the West Indies and the New Netherland territories for promoting trade and, incidentally, for seeding the lands with settlers.

1-4 Telescope

No one knows who invented the telescope, but the first one appeared in 1608. The honor of invention is most probably a Dutch maker of eyeglasses (spectacles), Hans Lippershey. It is said that he got the idea from two children who were playing with lenses in his shop. They found that by looking through two lenses at just the right distance apart, a weathercock in a distant steeple appeared much closer and much bigger. One can barely imagine their astonished delight. The commercial aspects were not lost on the optician. He lined up the two lenses and fixed them at the proper distance, then enclosing them in a metal tube. For viewing, closer to the eye was a lens with an inward curve (a concave lens). At the far end, the lens had an outward curve (a convex lens). This, then, was the original telescope.

The first telescopes brought distance closer by a factor of three to four times. Galileo, a practical mathematician in Padua, Italy, soon improved the optics by refining the lenses. In 1610, he constructed an instrument with a magnifying capacity of thirteen times. This, he called the *perspicillum* but later adapted the name *telescopio* (meaning to "look far off"). Even this new-found power, however, barely matches that of telescopes found in today's toy stores. With it, nevertheless, Galileo could observe ships from shore while they were still far out at sea.

Moving to Florence, Galileo studied the "high prominences, deep valleys, and chasms" on the moon. He determined that the Milky Way was made up of countless stars. Most importantly, he discovered "stars" that moved around Jupiter, concluding that these were moons that revolved around the planet. All this was done with an instrument through which he could look at the heavens with thirteen times greater detail than any mortal had even done before him.

Actually, his notion about the moons circling around a planet got Galileo in hot water. Could the Sun be the center of the Universe with the Earth a planet moving about it rather than the other way around? The idea did not sit well with the Church in Rome. In 1633 it hauled Galileo before the Inquisition and forced him to renounce his findings.

1-5 Weathercock

The direction of wind is revealed by a weathervane. For reliability, it is mounted on a high place to avoid interference from ground structures. In most communities, the highest points are the steeples of churches. This was certainly true in the Middle Ages when weathervanes, in the shape of animal figures, were commonplace. Most common of all animal figures was the rooster (or cockerel). The time-honored connection between this creature and the Church goes back to a prophesy of Jesus, heralded by the crowing of a cockerel. The museum in Hoorn exhibits a gold-plated weathercock that was blown down from a steeple in a storm years ago.

Weathervanes turn on a vertical rod. The weight on each side is the same, but the surface area is different: small and pointed on one side and large and broad on the other. With this arrangement, the head of the rooster faces into the wind and the tail away.

1-6 *Wilden*

"*Wilden*" (plural of *Wilde*) is the Dutch name for savages. The word was used to refer to someone uneducated or unsophisticated. The term did not have today's implications of a blood-thirsty barbarian. The Dutch letter ***w*** sounds something like the English ***v*** but is pronounced softer: as in *vilden.*

1-7 New Netherland

In the early days of transoceanic exploration, countries claimed as their own any new territory that their employee-explorers came upon. Of course, the mapmakers of the nations were extremely liberal with their drawings of these discoveries. In the New World of North America, the Dutch claimed all the land between the English colonies in Virginia and Cape Cod. This territory they called *New Netherland* (in Dutch, *Nieuw Nederland*). Note that the plural form for the mother country (e.g., The Netherlands) was not used for its American extension. Dutch settlers in 1628 named present-day Manhattan Island and its environs *New Amsterdam.* Lacking sufficient numbers of settlers to develop this vast area, the Dutch were soon overwhelmed by the rapidly expanding English population. In 1664 England had full control of the colony.

1-8 The Golden Age of Maritime Holland

Other than fertile soil, The Netherlands (or *Nederland* meaning "low country") had little to brag about in natural resources. Essential timber, minerals and building material were scarce. Even the farmlands were always in danger of flooding unless protected by dikes and continuous pumping.

With a flair for organization, record keeping, and civic discipline, however, the Dutch turned to seafaring to bring in the raw materials to support its country. They proved themselves worthy long-distance traders, using the cash flow to invest in further ventures. Grain from Poland, copper and iron from Sweden, and timber from Norway kept the nation well supplied. Ships from Brazil brought sugar and rum; from Virginia came tobacco. As a bargaining chip, the Dutch brought slaves from Africa.

Ships laden with silks and fine porcelains anchored in Hoorn or Amsterdam after a voyage of a year or two to the Far East. They also brought spices: pepper, ginger, nutmeg, cinnamon, and the most valuable of them all them, cloves.

The merchants shipped the bulk of imported goods to other countries to trade for lumber and industrial items, including cannon and gunpowder. In the process, the Dutch became the most important middlemen in Europe during the seventeenth century.

What gave the country its hard currency to develop a powerful navy and a high living standard was the discovery of a way to preserve fish (in particular, herring) in ships on long voyages. Performed on board, the process consisted of gutting (removing the viscera) and curing the fish in heavily salted water. When later dried, the salted fish kept indefinitely. Altogether, the fish and the exotic items were things that the Dutch could easily trade in the Scandinavian countries and in Germany and Russia. These faraway marketplaces proved highly profitable.

Religion played a heavy role in European trade and beyond. During the 16th and 17th centuries, a fierce religious struggle raged on the continent. The Dutch, seeking reformation of Christian principles, could hold off the long tentacles of Catholic Spain simply because of its success in commerce. All told, the people of the Dutch Republic enjoyed seventy years of high prosperity with relative freedom from war, a monumental achievement at the time.

Sea trading has always been a risky business. As tight-fisted as they may have been in financial concerns, the Dutch were caught up, ironically, in speculation. Some made a fortune overnight investing in the "wind and sea" of foreign trade. On a single journey, the lucky stay-at-home speculator could retreat to a comfortable estate in the country to count his guilders. Needless-to-say, the dangers of storm, mutiny, and rivals on the high seas could make an instant pauper out of the wealthiest investor of them all. Yet, it was the seamen aboard their ships who undertook the actual risks for long-distance trade and who suffered the unimaginable hardships of the life at sea. Not surprisingly, they received pitifully small monetary rewards for their trouble.

1-9 Ship's Officers

The following is a brief description of the duties of the managerial staff on a tall ship in the 17th century.

Master: The commanding officer of a sailing ship at sea was the unquestioned ruler of a small kingdom. He had unrestricted power. He was the chief administrator and decision maker. He set the tone of the ship by his sense of discipline and purpose. He enjoyed the most spacious of quarters and saw to it that certain comforts (bed, good food, wine) were available to ease the inconveniences of a long voyage.

The shipmaster often left the details of sailing to his officers. Despite the special comforts, his position of Top Command was a lonely one. It was generally believed that familiarity with the officers and crew would sap away discipline. Since maintaining strict discipline was, after all, the mainstay for preventing an onboard disaster—namely mutiny—the master tended to stay to himself.

How the shipmaster sets the tone and fate of a ship is well represented in history: Captains Block and Cook through their logs, and in literature: Ahab (*Moby Dick*), Bligh (*Mutiny on the Bounty*), and Queeg (*The Caine Mutiny*).

The Dutch, by the way, did not use the term 'captain' for a commercial ship's executive officer at the time of this story. Instead, that title was used to designate a leader of a military unit, which may have been aboard a warship.

Pilot or Pilot-Navigator: It was the pilot of a ship who set the course and made navigational adjustments. To do so in the days of tall ships meant being able to plot a course with crude instruments and to refer to mathematical tables. In the early 1600s these were uncommon skills.

Early Dutch shippers often employed foreign master-pilots for ocean journeys. Henry Hudson of England was such an example. Hudson had already had the experience of two explorations under English sponsorship into the Arctic. The Dutch more commonly engaged navigators from Spain and Portugal, those who had experience in the South American and Pacific trade.

Bosun: He was the chief officer, responsible for carrying out the orders of the master rapidly and effectively. He oversaw the crew and expected immediate obedience to his every command. The bosun oversaw loading of the ship and safekeeping of cargo. He was the sailing master who saw to it that the sails were raised, trimmed, and furled as needed along the way. Additional duties may have included keeping the ship's log, navigation, or looking after the ship's stores. (Incidentally, the word bosun comes from 'boatswain.' In the language of the ancient Nordics, 'swain" meant a boy or servant. Later in Middle English, it came to be the attendant of a knight.)

First mate: The bosun depended upon the first mate to maintain the crew's performance efficiently. He commanded with authority and meted out discipline as he saw fit.

Second mate: The next position in the chain of command was the second mate. He held an awkward position between officers and crew. He gave orders passed down from the bosun or first mate. Most often, he was disliked (to be polite) by both officers and crew. He also had to perform the daily chores of the crewmembers, such as scraping, tarring, and climbing the rigging.

Scientist-surgeon: Ships sailing to exotic places sometimes carried an observer trained in one of the natural sciences. He was usually excused from other duties required of the officers and crew. Charles Darwin, sailing on the *Beagle* in the 1830s was such a passenger.

In addition, the naturalist in the Age of Sail often found himself the ship's doctor. Most likely, he had little formal medical training. All too often, he had none. Indeed, medical practice in the seventeenth century was hardly a science, and all told, a doctor, practicing by the standards of the day, probably did more harm than good. Stopping bleeding and setting fractures were the outstanding exceptions.

Clerk: The person accountable for all cargo, keeping exact tally of every item going and coming, was the clerk. The clerk was also known as the merchant, purser, factor, or supercargo. He probably had no duties aboard ship other than looking out for trade goods with an eagle eye. He saw to it that expendable supplies of food and beer, meted out by the steward, did not dwindle too fast. He reported directly back to the financial backers at the end of the voyage. One can imagine that the clerk was none too popular with the crew.

1-10 Fluyt

Cost-minded shipbuilders of 16th-17th century Dutch provinces developed a cargo carrier that was cheaper to construct than those of other European seagoing countries. It was meant to be simpler to operate, required a smaller crew and yet carried an impressive load.

The shipwrights came up with the fluyt, a bulky 3-masted ship, designed to combine the efficiency of a small ship with the carrying capability of a much larger one. The first fluyt was built in the village of Hoorn in 1595. The name may come from *Vlie-boot* (fly-boat), perhaps after the *Vlie,* a shipping channel leading from the Wadden Sea into the North Sea.

The bow and the stern of the fluyt's hull as well as its bottom were rounded. It is said that the bow was shaped like the head of the cod, and the stern, like that of the mackerel's tail. Hydrodynamics at the time was based more on opinion than on science. Not much is known about the designs and methods of shipbuilding because there were no blueprints. Ship designs were usually made and preserved by families who worked without written plans. Since there were no patent laws, competitors could steal anything put on paper.

In any case, the design of the fluyt gave a shallow draft, allowing the ship to enter the not-so-deep harbors of the Netherlands. The tub-like shape also increased the space for payload, compared with the *V*-shaped English and French hulls of the time. The dip at the waist deck of the weather deck (between the fore and aft castles) and the curving inward of the upper hull (called the "tumblehome") added to the overall likeness of the fluyt to a wooden shoe.

The Dutch were clever master designers in the shipyard. They created laborsaving devices such as cranes to lift heavy beams and, of course, windmills to saw timbers into planks. They also devised the money-saving design of the tumblehome. To get to the Baltic Sea, Dutch ships had to pass through the *Sont* (or Sound), a narrow passageway through Denmark. The Danes exacted a tax on every passing ship and charged according to the width of the vessel amidship. The curved-in tumblehome of the fluyt reduced the deck space, thus saving tax money without losing space for cargo.

A small forest went into building a single sea-going ship. About one hundred fully grown trees of different types were required for a three-master of average size. Trees, however, were not plentiful in Holland so that the Dutch had to import timber from Sweden, Norway and other northern countries.

Shipwrights chose sturdy oak to make the keel and major supporting timbers. They cut the "knees" (*L*-shaped trusses between the beams and the timbers) at the joining of a major limb to the trunk. On the other hand, they chose pine for the upper planking and decks because it was light and easy to work. They used wooden pegs (which did not rust as nails do) below the water line. They caulked seams with strands of oakum, filled with melted pitch, and overlaid them with thick tar.

Masts came from giant trees as straight as could be and of the strongest wood. Shipwrights secured the log to the hull straight up by a complex system of shrouds (on the sides) and stays (fore and aft). To make a mast even taller, they added a second tree trunk, stepped higher up and footed on a 'trestle tree.' The two trunks were lashed securely together. On the largest ships, a mast may have been made from three trunks.

The forestay of the foremast was attached to the bowsprit, a long spar that projected from the prow. In this way, the foremast was better supported against a headwind.

A long triangular sail, the forestay sail, flew from the foremast stay, helping to steer the ship. Flown below the forestay sail in good weather and a following wind was a square spritsail. It was, however, awkward and difficult to keep billowed out, and many a sailor fell into the sea in his attempt to keep it filled with wind.

Dutch shipbuilders gradually reduced the size of the huge lower course sails that were difficult to handle and always in the way of deck workers. Eventually these sails were discarded altogether. Driving power was supplemented by other square sails attached higher up on topmasts. An elaborate system of winches and tackle enabled the crew to attend to one sail at a time, all from the deck.

The mast aft of the ship, called the 'mizzen,' carried a triangular sail mounted on a long spar that hung fore and aft. Known as a lateen rig, the sail acted to stabilize the ship in a balanced sail plan. This important sail was nevertheless difficult to maneuver in the fluyt since the forward tip of the boom extended beyond the mainmast to achieve balance. Consequently, it had to be dipped around the mast every time the ship changed course into a new tack.

At the upper fore mast and main mast, a circular platform, or "top" was built for the man on watch. It was sometimes partly enclosed to protect the lookout from the weather and from falling.

The fluyt was slow, but capacity, not speed, was the higher priority for a non-warship. It was reliable and efficient for a ship of the day. With good maintenance, it could last for twenty years. The "cockleshell" became the most important merchant ship in Dutch maritime fleet throughout the 17th century. Sadly, there is no blueprint of a fluyt built in the early seventeenth century. There are many, wonderful paintings of the fluyt but none of them show the interior details.

Ornaments on ships from The Netherlands were restrained compared with those found on Spanish, French, and English ships. Even the frugal Dutch, however, splurged on figureheads, those beautifully carved women, famous captains or ship owners, and lions or whimsical creatures that adorned the bow of ships. These images in wood were believed by sailors and investors to be the guiding spirit of the vessel. One such figurehead may have been the unicorn. And while it's there, why not use its unique horn for a bowsprit?

1-11 Unicorn

The myth of a powerful and mysterious creature with one horn that grows from the forehead weaves its way throughout history. Unicorns were said to have existed in one form or another since antiquity. Chronicles of ancient Greece mention the unicorn, as do those of India where it had a human form. In China, Persia, Russia, and Europe it was a donkey, ox, antelope or wolf. Common to all notions of the unicorn was the belief that it had magical powers, and these powers could be used to the advantage of people.

The familiar version in the western mind of this beautifully strange beast emerged during the Middle Ages. It was that of a small, horse-like figure with a beard and with the cloven (or split) hooves of a goat. Its body was milky white, while the head and horn were of many colors. Most distinctive in the unicorn in medieval paintings, engravings, carvings, and tapestries was the long, straight and gracefully tapered horn with a spiral groove running along its length.

In the European fables, the unicorn is usually a solitary beast, so shy that it had rarely been seen by humans. Its habitat was the remote part of a deep forest where it would never eat a beautiful flower. The unicorn was thought too fleet of foot for hunters to catch. It was easily charmed, however, by a young and pure maiden. One of the most appealing images handed down through the ages is that of a unicorn in a dappled glade resting its horn on the lap of a beautiful maiden.

In the King James's versions of the Old Testament unicorns are mentioned several times. In these, it was a symbol of Jesus, representing him to be noble, innocent, courageous, beneficent, and persecuted. Other sites refer instead to the Virgin Mary: compassionate, pure, and virtuous.

Europeans of medieval times believed that the horn of a unicorn possessed miraculous properties. It protected humans from poisons. The unicorn was often depicted in art putting its horn into water tainted by a snake so that other animals could safely drink it. The horn itself protected humans from poisoning, a common form of murder at the time. Cups and spoons carved from the unicorn's horn were used by royalty and the otherwise rich (those most likely to be poisoned). Many believed that the horn would "sweat" when placed next to poisoned food; in this way, it detected a mischievous deed of a contender for the throne or estate. In the medieval mind, the horn was not only a protector from and detector of deadly drugs, but also a powerful agent for deterring disease. Bites from rabid dogs or scorpions, seizures, fevers, and other morbid conditions could be successfully treated with powder filed from the unicorn's horn.

The physical concept of the unicorn has a basis of reality. In Asia, the image probably comes from the Indian rhinoceros with its single stubby horn. In Africa, it may be the eland, a large antelope with long, slightly curved and twisted horns that may appear as a single horn when observed in profile. In Europe, the model was the tusk of the narwhal of the Arctic Sea.

The narwhal is small by whale standards, although the adult may weigh more than 3,000 pounds. Its most distinguishing feature is a straight "horn" with a groove that coils around it from one end to the other. Actually, the horn of the narwhal is a hollow tusk. It is an overgrown canine tooth that arises from the upper jaw, U-turns around, and pierces the upper lip. It only appears to arise from the fore-skull. The structure is, therefore, enamel, the stuff of teeth. Thus, it is ivory and not a horn at all. Horns, in fact, are akin to the nails. That is, they are made of keratin.

The largest narwhals may have tusks as long as eight feet, nearly as long as the body. Grooves spiral around the tusk from bottom to tip. What the narwhal does with such a remarkable appendage is not certain. Some say it is used to stir up mud on the bottom of the sea in its search for food, although females, which seldom have a tusk, seem to be just as well fed. Another theory is that it is useful for fighting, though there are no confirming observations. That the narwhal uses its tusk to spear fish is simply fanciful. Sightings of a "forest of narwhal horns" waving in spaces between ice floes suggest that it is used to poke breathing holes through the ice. That the tusk is fragile, however, weakens support of all these arguments. It may be that the tusk is a sign of male dominance in mating rituals.

One can imagine some cagey Viking traders sailing to more southern and Mediterranean seaports 500 years ago, hauling a supply of narwhal tusks and coming up with a little con game. A story of its magic properties wrapped up in the myth of a horn-bearing forest creature could bring a handsome price. The story fit nicely with what medieval people wanted to believe: a mystical beast (never seen) that could protect them against poison and disease. It is enough to say that in the 16th and 17th centuries Europe, an intact horn from the "sea unicorn" brought ten to twenty times its weight in gold. Kings, popes and wealthy merchants paid fabulous sums for what they believed was the intact horn of the fabulous unicorn. One writer stated in 1609 that a good unicorn horn was worth "half a city." It is not much of a stretch to think that frugal Dutch traders, with their northern fleet and their marketing sites throughout the seaports of Europe, became caught up in the deception.

Not even discovery of the narwhal and its long and tightly twisted horn by Arctic explorers in 1577 made a smidgen's difference in the European's unshakable belief in unicorns. The deception by traders to hide the fact that the horn was only the tooth of a marine animal continued to buoy up the price up for centuries. Even today, a perfect narwhal tusk, sold illegally, can fetch a few thousand U.S. dollars

Threads have been woven into the unicorn story in priceless treasures that hang at the Cloisters, the Medieval Division of the Metropolitan Museum of Art in New York. Probably constructed in Belgium in the 1500s, the tapestries were rescued from service as winter covers for apples by a wealthy French Duke in the next century. In a series of seven large panels, the "Hunt of the Unicorn" portrays Christ symbolically: pursued by hunters, captured, tormented, sacrificed, and resurrected and finally to rest forever in a heavenly garden of a thousand flowers. Standing in the same room as the tapestries is a long, tapered ivory tusk with spiral grooves.

1-12 Shipmaster Adriaen Block

In 1613 the Dutch shipmaster Adriaen Block sailed up the North River to present-day Albany, thus duplicating the journey of Henry Hudson four years before. His purpose, then and on three previous trips, was not to find a navigable route to the riches of the Orient but rather to load up to the gunnels with furs. Here, the traders found no English or French competition in the scramble for beaver pelts.

On this fourth voyage, Block and his crew were successful in acquiring pelts, but unfortunate in having fire break out on his ship, *Tijger;* it burned to the water line while at mooring in New York Bay. Part of the *Tijger's* crew returned to Holland on a competitor's ship, while Block and a few others spent the winter on Manhattan Island. Their survival and their work to make a small yacht of thirty feet in length must have depended greatly on the help of the local natives. New lumber cuttings and some timbers from the burned ship went into the project. Sadly, we know precious little about this historical experience on Manhattan Island. What we do know is that, when spring came, the intrepid Block sailed his improvised boat, called the *Onrust* up the East River into Long Island Sound.

Block's map of the area, drawn with amazingly accurate detail, is a priceless historical treasure. Called the "Figurative Map on Vellum," it contains the first known mention of the name *Nieuw Nederlandt.* (See also Note 4-32)

1-13 Sea Shanties

While wind is the fuel of a sailing ship, the task of harnessing it requires human muscle. For complex and strenuous operations requiring many hands, harmony of action is critical. Rhythmic chants and songs, known as shanties, helped coordinate heavy push and pull work. From this tradition, we have inherited a wealth of handed-down lore about the life of a seaman.

There were many kinds of shanties sung aboard sailing ships, each adapted to the pace and heaviness of the work required. The capstan shanties were meant for the slow and steady effort to haul in a long heavy chain with a giant anchor dangling on the end. Halyard shanties were short with accentuated words for the instant of pull. There were chants and songs for pumping the bilge, turning the windlass, and the innumerable other chores of manning a tall ship. Some were more for personal reflection and an expression of the seaboard ordeal. In face of homesickness, physical hardships, and the death of mates, they served as morale boosters.

Perhaps the best known of them all is this centuries-old shanty:

Solo voice:	*In Amsterdam there lived a maid,*
	And she was mistress of her trade,
Chorus:	*I'll go no more a-roving with you, fair maid!*
	A-roving, a-roving,

	Since rovings' been my ruin,
	I'll go no more a-roving with you, fair maid!
Solo voice:	*This last six months I've been to sea,*
	And boys, this maid looked good to me.
Chorus:	*(repeat)*
Solo voice:	*Her cheeks were like the roses red,*
	and her eyes were like twin stars at night.
Chorus:	*(repeat)*

This shanty goes on into many stanzas. The next is particularly telling of the sailor's story:

Solo voice:	*Around Cape Horn through frost an' snow*
	An' up that' coast to Callao [California].

1-14 Zuider Zee (Dutch: *Zuiderzee* or *Underseen*)

In ancient times a huge, freshwater lake was created in the "Lowlands" (Netherlands). During the Middle Ages it eroded its way into the North Sea, transforming the lake into a saltwater bay, called the Zuider Zee (or the South Sea). This bay became the passageway for seagoing ships leaving the heart of the country. Fishing villages became safe harbors, with some eventually morphing into cities such as Amsterdam and Hoorn.

To get to the New World, tall ships would leave the Zuider Zee, head north, pass through a narrow slit around the hilly island of Texel into the North Sea, and turn south through the English Channel. On reaching the White Cliffs of Dover, they would make a right-hand turn and enter the Atlantic Ocean.

Periodic storms caused frequent flooding of the Zuider Zee, and sometimes caused great loss of life and immense damage to gardens and buildings. To tame the bay, the Dutch undertook one of the largest engineering projects in world history: a dam. Boulder clay dug from the lake bottom, sand, basalt rocks, and enormous mats made from willow branches formed various layers. Completed in 1932 after four years, the dam is twenty miles (thirty-two-kilometers) long. It turned the largest part of the bay back into a freshwater lake, called Lake IJsselmeer. The seaward part, remaining salt-water, is known today as the Wadden Sea *(Waddenzee).*

1-15 World Events in 1616

Shipmaster Willem Schouten and Amsterdam merchant Jacob Le Maire round the tip of South America and name it "Cape Hoorn" for one of the ships lost by fire.

John Smith, leader of the first English colony in the New World writes *A Description of New England.* In it he records much of the settlers's experiences in Jamestown, Virginia.

Astronomer Willebrord Snellius of Holland formulates the basic laws of refraction (the science of light passing through lenses).

William Harvey of England lectures on the circulation of the blood, the startling concept that bridges the ancient world of medicine with the modern.

Flemish painter Paul Rubens completes his masterpiece, *The Lion Hunter.*

Sir Walter Raleigh, freed from prison, leads an expedition to South America to find "El Dorado" (the Man of Gold) and bring home fabulous riches.

Samuel de Champlain attacks a band of Iroquois warriors (wearing wooden armor) on Lake Champlain. It provokes lasting Iroquois enmity against the French.

Pocahontas, newly married to John Rolfe, sails for England, dying there a year later from smallpox.

CHAPTER 2: PROMISES

2-16 Life for the Common Person

The happy faces shown in European paintings of the early seventeenth century hardly show the misery in which most people lived. Generally, throughout Europe, a lad took on the occupation of his father, no matter how lowly, with no hope of ever improving his lot. A girl was expected to marry within her class, have children, and tend strictly and solely to household matters. Period. For most people, life's destiny was taken up with the menial tasks of farming, fishing, or one of the crafts.

Inhabitants of Dutch Republic at the time enjoyed a standard of living that was a bit higher than those of other countries in Europe. The hard-working laborer could make a decent living, providing the essentials but without luxuries. Children had available the opportunity for a basic education. Indeed, recruiting young men in Holland to leave their "comforts" to take on the hardships and dangers of seafaring was difficult. Many ships sailed out of the ports of Amsterdam and Hoorn with mostly a foreign crew.

Because land was expensive in all the Seven United Provinces of The Dutch Republic, houses tended to be tall and narrow, thus getting the most live-in space for the plot. Taxes along the canals were based upon frontage, a system that encouraged housebuilders to extend way back. A scarcity of wood meant that furniture was pricey.

The principle food for the poor was peas and beans. These grew in backyard gardens in rich soil. Bread, too, was relatively cheap. Costly was meat, so it was not part of the regular diet.

Clothing stretched the peasant's budget, especially when colored. Most people wore brown. Woolens were fairly warm, and they resisted wetting. Once wet, however, it took a bright sunshine to dry them out. Bright sunshine in Holland was not an everyday event. Shoes were carved from willow, a soft wood. Not only were they practical for the wet ground of

Holland, they were inexpensive. A pair of wooden shoes lasted only about six weeks.

Life in Dutch Republic was probably at a higher standard than anywhere else in Europe, so that Dutch settlers in the New World were generally refugees from other countries. In 1624, a ship arrived in New Amsterdam, later Manhattan Island, with thirty families of Walloons (Protestant refugees from southern Belgium, fleeing from religious persecution). Some were left on the island while others were taken upriver to settle around the trading post, Fort Orange, in present-day Albany.

CHAPTER 3: WESTWARD BOUND

3-17 Trade Winds

Understanding the trade winds is not easy for the amateur meteorologist or navigator, even in the 21st century. But shipmasters found them 400 years ago and used them to great advantage in their speed across the ocean.

Surface air at the equator increases its temperature over the hot belt of the equator, causing it to rise. In the northern hemisphere, the air moves toward the North Pole in the upper atmosphere. Denser and cooler surface air from the northern regions flows toward the equator to fill the vacuum. The spin of the earth easterly gives the air mass a westerly direction. A mirror image of this motion occurs in the southern hemisphere.

The meticulous plotting and recording of navigators on the Atlantic Ocean from the time of Columbus provided data from which nautical maps were constructed. Of course, winds are highly variable owing to prevailing ocean currents and the lumps and wrinkles of the land masses. The shipmaster heading for the Americas did the best he could with his charts and position-finding to slip into a hefty west-to-east breeze. Contrary winds were sought on returning, usually along a more southern route.

3-18 Rogue Wave

Ocean waves are caused by wind skimming the surface of the water. They are highest when currents of wind and water move in opposite directions. Sometimes a wave occurs that is much higher than others. When such a wave is twice as high or higher, it is called a "rogue wave."

Once in a blue moon, a rogue wave is very high. Passengers on the Italian cruise liner SS Michelangelo in 1966 experienced such a devastating encounter. A totally unexpected wave stove in some of the superstructure where the ship is controlled. Throughout history, many ships that have simply vanished in the high seas may have met grief from such a monster wave.

There are differing explanations for a rogue wave. One is that it comes from a summation of waves of two intersecting currents. Another holds that the rogue wave is a result a combination of waves, one traveling faster and catching up with another. Some contend that high winds that travel in the same direction as strong currents impart additional energy into the water. Scientists have put a mathematical spin on the possibility of forming freakish waves. Whatever the cause, by the way, it is not the same as a tsunami, a gigantic wave produced by an earthquake on the ocean floor.

3-19 Crew

By crew is meant those who perform the laborious work aboard ship under direction of officers.

Enlistment of foreign crewmembers for the Dutch Fleet was common. The reason was simple: The Dutch enjoyed the highest standard of living in Europe. While life was austere by modern standards for the majority, people there had little incentive to leave the simple comforts of a small farm or shop to endure the rigors and uncertainties of sea life. A sailor's pay was generally poor, often determined by the profit made. Sometimes, pay was reduced as punishment for some trivial offense.

Even though it was prohibited by Dutch law, owners of ships recruited (or perhaps more accurately, bamboozled) seamen from Scandinavia, Germany, England, Scotland, and Ireland. Roman Catholics were generally not acceptable because of their religious beliefs. The ship's owners found it necessary to hire foreigners for positions requiring critical experience. Henry Hudson, from England, stands as a good example. Navigators and ship's officers from Spain and Portugal were most experienced in long journeys.

There were several categories of crewmembers:

Able seaman: He was the most experienced of the working crew. He was skilled at making chafing gear, tying knots, reefing, furling, setting sail and steering the ship as well as climbing masts to reeve the running rigging.

Ordinary seaman: He was generally unskilled but expected to learn knots and perform menial tasks. The most undesirable of the ship's chores generally fell upon the ordinary seaman.

Cook: The forecastle was the cook's world where he kept a galley fire going during calm seas. He added water, vegetables, and salted meat or fish to the soup as the pot emptied. He saw that each man received his share and not a drop more. The more evenly he distributed soup, biscuits, and water or beer, the less likely were quarrels among the crew to erupt.

Carpenter: Traditionally called "chips," the ship's carpenter repaired woodwork on decks, spars, shallops, and bulkheads. He sealed all hatches and kept the machinery of the steering, windlasses, and anchor lifts in good working order. He was also responsible for repairing barrels that were often damaged during high seas. Of course, the carpenter was always called upon to devise ingenious ways of fixing broken parts.

Sailmaker: Whenever sails became shredded in high winds, someone had to repair them. The sailmaker did this with a knife, tarred flax for twine, and a long, pointed, triangular needle called a fid. He raised new and strong sails when high winds were anticipated, and he chose old canvas for kinder winds. In addition, the sailmaker found many uses for old sails too worn for sailing: one was to create coffins for those not returning home.

Steward: Responsible for the pantry and stores, the steward was a critical member of the crew. He allotted the amount and kind of food allowed the crew for any given day. Most importantly, he kept account of the supply of water and beer. A generous steward would allow an extra ration one day a week (usually Saturday or Sunday). A steward's additional responsibility was to serve the shipmaster, ever aware of his demanding needs. He reported directly to the clerk.

Cabin boy: The youngest of all and one at the lowest rank was the cabin boy. His chores were menial although a kindly officer or crewman might teach a green hand to tie simple knots, braid a line or some such ordinary skill. For many a cabin boy, the harsh experience was the first step toward becoming a ship officer. For others, it provided a powerful message: never go on a ship again.

3-20 Shipboard Cuisine

Food: Food on long ocean journeys was not something to boast about. First of all, it had to be cheap because the investors saw little point in feeding sailors expensive foods. On a practical level, it had to resist spoiling. This meant generally carrying preserved food. Most notable was dried beef and pork layered with salt and saltpeter and loaded aboard in 300-pound casks. Called "salt horse" or "salt junk," the meat was as red as a flannel shirt, and hard and tough. It could have been two or three years old. To soften the meat required soaking for a day or two in seawater. It was then boiled to further soften it and to take out some of the taste of brine.

Fresh meat, a luxury at sea, was available from time to time. Ships often carried live chickens, pigs, sheep, and cows for slaughter along the way. One can assume that the officers had first choice of the better cuts of meat, while the fat and tough parts were given to the sailors. Commonly for dinner, the men got dried fish that had been salted and stored in barrels.

Flour, combined with salt and water and baked in a flat pan, made a cheap food that became the standard fare for sailors. They called it "hard tack." And hard it was! The men softened it by soaking. After a few weeks at sea, maggots generally infested the hard tack. The tapping often heard during meals was from the spoon crushing maggots before each bite.

Duff bread was more or less a delicacy. Cooks made it from flour, lard, yeast, and seawater. An extra treat may have been some added chopped pork.

Dried vegetables and fruit stored well. These were garlic, onion, grapes, prunes, figs, walnuts, and hazelnuts. Potatoes resisted spoiling. Rice and barley were durable, but they eventually germinated. Cheese, often a year or two old, was stone hard. Butter, oil, and fat turned rancid early on the voyage.

Only in smooth seas were fires for cooking safe on board a ship Then, the cook maintained a continuous brew of peas, garlic, onion, and sometimes salted pork. Animal parts were added with each slaughter of the live ones. As the porridge was consumed, more water and more food were added to top it off. From this custom comes the well-known ditty:

Peas porridge hot.
Peas porridge cold.
Peas porridge in the pot
Nine days old.

Rats, cockroaches, fleas, lice, and other vermin somehow got on board ship as if they had been born there (and perhaps were). They competed for the food supply. Some blamed these uninvited guests for causing food to spoil. When food for the crew became scarce, these critters became the food.

Beverages: Bacteria and molds grow in stagnant water. Accordingly, a keg of water will spoil after about 14 days. Of course, men aboard a tall ship considered it drinkable long after that. There were many thoughts on why water spoiled but no one at the time knew a way to preserve it. On long voyages, sailors caught rain in canvas flats to replenish their water with a fresh supply.

Beer lasted longer than water onboard ship. Beer was the mainstay on Dutch ships. When it was of poor quality and low-alcohol content, it was called "duff." Generally, one pint of beer was allotted to each crewman each day.

Beer, unwittingly, is made under strict hygienic control since it is the action of yeast, a fungus, on the carbohydrates of various grains that produces alcohol. Competing microorganisms interfere with the process. Brewing, therefore, requires rigid cleanliness to control bacteria and molds, thereby extending the freshness by a week or two beyond that of water. Wine and rum, drinks that do not readily spoil, were generally not available to members of the crew.

3-21 The Shallop

Many tall ships carried a small somewhat flat-bottomed boat for rowing. Some shallops had one or two masts to provide the option of rowing or sailing, or both. It was *not* intended as a lifeboat. A catastrophe at sea was just that: a catastrophe. The possibility of the crew, or a chosen part of the crew, rowing itself to safety was remote. Rather, the shallop was meant to explore shallows and rivers that were inaccessible to the mother ship.

In 1608, John Smith and his rowers explored the Chesapeake Bay in their shallop. Smith had the foresight to transport it to the Virginia colony in easy-to-pack pieces with "portions easy to fit together."

Hudson's *Half Moon* sailed as far as Albany in 1609. His shallop explored farther north, going about seven miles to present-day Troy. This excursion proved that the Hudson River was, indeed, a river, not a strait between two oceans. A shallop was useful whenever a ship ran aground; oarsmen would strain their muscles to haul the ship away from sandbars.

3-22 Barents Sea

Go north from the island of Texel, through the North Sea to enter the Norwegian Sea, you will eventually come to the long islands of Novaya Zemlya. Here shipmaster Willem Barents, searching for a Northeast Passage to the Orient, found great numbers of whales and seals. It was on this third Arctic voyage, in 1596, that the ship became icebound. Barents and his crew were forced to suffer through a winter.

The meticulous charting of Barents provided important information on the geography and weather of what was then called the Murman Sea. A map drawn in 1853 honored the explorer with a change of name. In more recent times, explorers in geology have found huge resources of oil in the Barents Sea. Offshore drilling for oil began there in the 1970s.

3-23 Northern Lights

Thermonuclear reactions in the sun emit electrically charged particles, mostly electrons from the fusion of hydrogen and helium. The particles shoot out at unthinkable speeds, known as solar wind. Most directed toward the Earth deflect off the outer atmosphere, but some collide with atoms and molecules, transferring their energy to them. The energized atoms and molecules of the atmosphere (mostly oxygen and nitrogen) then degrade back into a lower energy state. When this occurs, the energy lost is given off as light. The result, seen from the ground, is a fascinating glow in the sky known as the "aurora" after Aurora, the Roman goddess of dawn.

Because the magnetic force generated by the Earth's core guides the solar wind, the auroras center around the magnetic north and south poles. In the northern hemisphere, the display of light is called the "aurora borealis," a name coined in 1621 by the French physicist and astronomer, Pierre Gassendi. Boreas was the Roman god of the north wind.

Benjamin Franklin, with his usual prescience, conjectured that the "mystery of the northern lights" was an electrical phenomenon. The various colors of the aurora depend upon the predominant particles in the atmosphere and the distance from earth. Oxygen tends toward green when the aurora is closer than 150 miles and reddish when farther away. Nitrogen is blue at less than sixty miles and purple, more than sixty miles away. Whatever the geophysical explanation, the aurora borealis is one awesome sight.

3-24 Religious Tensions

England: Merry England of yore was merry for the rich but not so merry for the poor. For them, 99 % of the population, there was negligible opportunity to improve their economic plight or social position. Religion, too, offered no prospect for a status change. The poor were expected to attend church, with fines exacted for missing a Sunday.

From the time of Henry VIII, government and religion were inseparable. In 1534, then Catholic England severed its ties with the main church in Rome all because of the king's "great matter" which happened to be an issue of his marriage. The new Anglican Church of England, however, continued the Roman Catholic traditions of pomp of ceremony, the hierarchy of cardinal, bishop, and professional clergymen, and their interpretation of the Bible. According to Anglican gospel, God appointed the king who then wielded full authority by "divine right." Any criticism of the Church by members of the public was a direct affront to the king and was therefore a serious infraction.

Not surprisingly, discontent with the Anglican Church emerged. The attitude coincided with a growing protest of Catholicism that began in Germany. Some rejected the pomp, the hierarchy, and the biblical teachings imposed by the church. They chose to take a new route to worship God. They insisted—at their peril—to reform the church by adapting literal readings of the New Testament, by having parishioners elect their own ministers and elders, and by abandoning pomp for simple prayer, extemporaneous sermons, and adapting a plain style of everyday life.

Even among the reformists, however, there was disagreement. Some advocated purifying the church from within England. These became known as the Puritans. Others believed that the only way to shake off the yoke of the Anglican Church was to go to another country. These were the Separatists.

The Dutch Republic: A pact of 1579 called "The Union of Utrecht" brought together seven provinces in the so-called Low Countries. (Holland was one of these Dutch provinces.) This was the first true republican form of government since that of ancient Greece. In the pact, signers agreed that the United Provinces would thereafter tolerate religions of all faiths. In practice, it meant that the state allowed Christians, Muslims, and Jews to practice their faiths as they saw them, provided that these practices did not interfere with the state. Catholics, however, did not enjoy such freedom. Singled out, they were not allowed to worship in public. In addition, Catholics had a difficult time just finding work.

The openness of Dutch hospitality resulted in Protestants pouring in from neighboring countries. They were fleeing strict and punitive Catholic doctrine. Most notably, Huguenots came from France and Walloons from what is Belgium today. They also came from Portugal and the German states. In 1608, Separatists from England came to the Low Countries or the Netherlands. They encountered no trouble with authority, they found work, and their children could attend school.

Yet, all was not perfect for the Separatists in Amsterdam and Leyden. Coming from the farmlands of Yorkshire, they were accustomed to open spaces among meadows and trees, not the houses elbow-to-elbow along canals, the crowded and smelly streets, and the sheer boredom of factory work. The foreigners could not enter the guilds of Dutch craftsmen and had to accept the low salaries of the working poor. And perhaps, most importantly, the Separatists heard their children speaking Dutch while adopting the behavior of the Dutch classmates who were quite undisciplined by English standards. These troubling conditions underscored the gradually developing idea that they should begin a new life where there were not such impediments. The empty coasts and forests of America beckoned.

They envisioned a "shining city upon a hill." These were to become the Pilgrims of New England, although the term "pilgrim" was not used for them until a hundred years later.

3-25 Windmills

There is no symbol more Dutch than the windmill. Yet, the Dutch did not invent the windmill. The Crusaders observed such strange machines in the Middle East and brought the idea back to the "Low Countries." Since the 13th century, windmills driven by sailcloth on huge vanes rattled, clanked, and groaned all over the land, taking advantage of the wind that runs across the flatlands throughout the year.

On the Nile, the windmill was developed as a means for bringing water from the river up onto the farmlands. In the Dutch Republic it was introduced for exactly the opposite purpose: to remove water from sea-level land that had been surrounded by mounds of earth (dikes) and to pour it back into the sea. Thus, below sea-level farms (polders) were created from land previously awash. It is said that a massive system of dikes and windmills have wrested about a third of the total real estate of the country from the grip of the sea.

Over time, the inventive Dutch found many uses for their free energy. By the 1600s, their mills were grinding wheat, sawing timber, pressing oil from seeds of hemp and flax, making glue from animal parts, and mixing the natural materials that make up gunpowder, malt, mustard, and snuff. Paint, dyes, and perfume were made from red sandalwood, campeche wood, ache, graphite, chalk camarilla, arsenic, and vitriol.

Windmills crushed hempseed to squeeze out lamp oil. Paper they made white by filtering pulp through sand and crushed seashells. Glue they made from hides and bones fed into a windmill. Fitted with several vertically moving saws, the windmills cut a single log into planks in one pass. This invention of the sawmill gave the Dutch a leg up on shipbuilding.

In many ways, the operator of a windmill confronted the same challenges as the master of a sailing ship. He had to point the sails according to the direction of the wind and trim them according to its strength. He constantly needed to repair worn sails, maintain all the clanking parts, and keep the turning axles and gears in efficient working order. Of course, the shipmaster encountered many inescapable occupational hazards on every journey. At least, the windmill operator did not have to worry about a mutinous crew or drowning. The constant loud clatter and rumbling of the mill, however, led to a condition known as "miller's deafness" that spared the shipmaster.

CHAPTER 4: A SEAMAN'S LIFE

4-26 Tar

Tar is a sticky, black, oily substance that requires high temperatures to extract from coal. Without tar or something like it, there would be no wooden boats. Tar stuffed between cracks in planks prevented leaking. Worked into rope, it protected against rotting.

"Idle" moments aboard ship often found sailors assigned to applying tar to every crack in sight. Once stuck to their hands and clothing and without any solvent, sailors just had to let it wear off. It is little wonder, then, that the sailors became known as tars.

4-27 Maurice of Nassau, Prince of Orange (1567-1625)

The names Nassau and Orange honor one of the stadtholders (or chief executive officers) of the United Provinces of the Dutch Republic. This man was Maurice of Nassau, a German nobleman born in the County/Countship of Nassau (now in Hesse, Germany). In German, his name was *Moritz von Oranien.* He inherited huge estates and land in the Dutch provinces and in the region called Provence (now in southern France). The latter was the feudal principality of Orange.

In the Dutch Republic Maurice became known as *Maurits, Prins van Oranje*, a title inherited from his father, William of Orange. He became a commander in the war for Dutch independence from Spain. As "stadtholder" or community leader he was appreciated for his wise and benevolent leadership. He became so popular that even Henry Hudson referred to the river that was eventually named after him as "Prince Maurice's River." Similarly, the island of Mauritius in the Indian Ocean is named after him. The family dynasty, the House of Orange-Nassau, continues today in family lines such as those of the Grand Duke of Luxembourg and the King of the Netherlands.

4-28 Sandglass

The helmsman had a simple, age-old instrument known as the sandglass with which he kept track of time. Sand spilled from one bulb to another through a narrow connection in an enclosed system, emptying every half hour. He then rang a bell and turned the sandglass over to start again. Each half hour added one more ring to the sounding. For example, one hour was two rings. Eight rings announced the end of a four-hour duty. After eight, the count began all over again. A "glass" meant four hours.

4-29 Monsters of the Seas

Ocean-going seamen were a superstitious lot. There were endless tales of great monsters lurching about that could gobble up a whole shipload of men. Furthermore, the "middlemen" of the Middle East—those who profited from bringing spices and silks from the Orient to Europe—told of dangerous monsters lurking in the oceans. Fear, they reasoned, would keep European ships from finding their own way to the Orient.

Sea monsters drawn on old world maps stretch the imagination to the extremes. Whales breaching, creating enormous spray, and the cavorting of dolphins gave some visual substance to these myths. Most enduring of all is the mermaid. A mermaid, in sightings by sailors throughout the world, was always a beautiful woman in the top half and a fish at the bottom, never the other way around. Columbus claims to have seen three "female forms" in waters of the Caribbean, although he seemed disappointed that they were not as lovely as legend had him to expect.

4-30 Knots

Square knot. The square knot is pretty for its symmetry. It is strong but may slip under high pressure. It easily jams, making it difficult to undo. It is a useful knot for reefing and furling sails where high tension is not required.

Granny. This is a variation of the square knot with the second loop formed in an opposite direction from the first. This configuration gives an asymmetrical appearance in contrast to that of the square knot. The granny is not as secure as the square. Surgeons may prefer the granny because it is moveable and therefore able to be snugged up directly against a blood vessel.

Clove hitch. This simple knot is used to place around a post where it is possible to reach over the top. Some experience, however, is required to get the overlapping parts correct.

Bowline. Also called the fisherman's knot, it is one of the seaman's most important knots. It provides a loop that can be fixed around another loop or ring. It is easy to tie (once you get the hang of it), will not pull loose regardless of tension, and will not jam.

It is possible to become truly ecstatic about the utility, beauty, and philosophy of knots. This allure can be experienced in Clifford Ashley's classic book, *The Ashley Book of Knots.* There are 3,900 knots described with 7,000 illustrations in addition to interesting related historical and literary information.

4-31 The Dutch: Guild Members and Others

Craftsmen in the Netherlands protected their trades by forming guilds. Leathermakers (shoes, saddles), tinsmiths, makers of knives and clocks, opticians, jewelers, and potters all had their own guilds. Perhaps most exclusive of all were the guilds of artists such as painters, sculptors, engravers.

To belong to a guild, one had to work as an apprentice for at least three years. The pay was limited, the hours endless, and the work exacting, all under the close eye of a master. Getting married was prohibited.

The next step up was the journeyman who could work for any guild member for several years. After gaining the title of free master, the craftsman could establish his own workshop and take on an apprentice.

The master with his own shop, staff, and security was a formidable figure of the Dutch economy. In fact, the achievements of all the guild masters in the arts, industry, and practical science of the 17th century were truly spectacular.

The ordinary Dutchman in the Age of Exploration had no inkling of what Native Americans were like. A few were kidnapped, taken to Holland and there paraded as novelties. Verrazzano and Columbus had already engaged in this exploitation. There seemed more interest in them as a curiosity (like a "bird of paradise") rather than a "window" into another culture. There are no detailed accounts of the interaction between Europeans and these "exotic" humans. Isn't an opportunity to learn about an unworldly alien what every student of anthropology or linguistics dreams of? These subjects, alas, were hardly in their infancy at the time.

The Dutch settlers on the Hudson later came to call the Native Americans *Mahikanders,* which means "River Indians." The name morphed into the more popular *Maaquas.* The reference is far from accurate, however, since the Algonquin nations extended into vast territories away from the Hudson River, both south to Virginia and northeast to Maine.

4-32 *Onrust*

In 1613 Adriaen Block's original ship, the *Tijger,* (also referred to as *Tyger* and *Tyiger)* reached the southwestern shore of what is today called

Manhattan Island. Just as it was ready to sail back to Holland with a vast cargo of furs, it was destroyed by a fire, burning to the water line. The shipmaster and the crew managed to survive the winter, it is thought, only through the help of the local inhabitants (Lenapes and Manhattoes). During the winter of 1614 they built a small boat in the style of a Dutch sloop, using some parts from the original ship. They named it *Onrust* or "Restless."

With this improvised ship of about thirty feet in length, Block explored Long Island Sound. Along the way, he "discovered" and named Block Island, Fishers Island, and Rhode Island. He sailed the Connecticut River to a few miles beyond present-day Hartford, finding shoreline maize growing in palisaded villages. He went as far as Narragansett Bay and may have reached Cape Cod. He then turned west and emerged from the Sound where the Harlem River enters the Hudson River at Spuyten Duyvil. Thus, he was the first European to document that Manhattan Island was indeed an island. This fact is clearly shown in his map, drawn a few years later.

Partly based upon the sightings of Block in 1614, the Dutch, with the authority of "right of discovery," claimed territory between English Virginia and French Canada. The claim escalated the fur trade and led to Dutch attempts to bring in settlers.

Regarding the *Onrust*: it was abandoned when a sister ship took on Block and his crew for the journey back to the province of Holland. A team of 21st century volunteers has built a replica ship *Onrust*, keeping to the design of a Dutch yacht. Like the original, it has a single mast with one sail toward the bow (a jib) and two sails aft on a boom. The bulky design of the ship permitted carrying a large cargo while the rigging—where all sail adjustments were controlled from the deck—required but a small crew. As much as possible the modern builders used traditional methods and tools throughout the construction. Most of the work was done in a historic Dutch barn in Rotterdam Junction, New York. The replica was finished in time to join the Parade of Tall Ships in October 2009, celebrating the quadricentennial of Henry Hudson's Voyage of Discovery.

4-33 Tulips

The great university in Leyden, founded in 1575 by William of Orange, maintained a botanical garden boasting specimens brought from around the world. From the beginning, botanists studied plant structure, behavior, and propagation. In addition, they searched for any medicinal value. One such plant turned out to be of special interest but in a way that defied prediction.

In 1559, the Dutch ambassador to Augsburg in Bavaria received some bulbs from the ambassador from Istanbul, Turkey. Brought to the Leyden garden, the bulbs produced the colorful flowers that we all know as tulips. What fascinated the faculty was the great variations in patterns of colors that appeared with succeeding generations. Its fickle genetics promoted great interest within academic circles. One night, alas, burglars climbed the garden fence and made off with the best bulbs and plants. It was not long afterwards that tulip growing was widespread throughout Netherlands. One wonders if this was the first horticultural crime.

Up to this time, only the wealthy had flowers growing around their homes. Ordinary people had to use garden space for food crops. But the ease of growing tulips along with their spectacular beauty gave commoners a new joy, brightening a pathway or a table with color.

The increasing popularity of tulip-growing inflated the value over the years. Because the color and pattern of the flower could not be predicted from a bulb, there came a fad of betting on the outcome, ironically by the tight-fisted Dutch. With increasing speculation, the price of bulbs spiraled upward. Investing in bulbs began even when they were still in the ground waiting for spring to blossom. It reached a high point in 1636 when the price of tulip bulbs rose dramatically.

Blossoms of one color were common and dirt cheap. Those with splashes of color fetched a higher price. The more expensive ones had flames of yellow on a red or violet flower. Even dearer was a white flower with a purple or red flame. The most prized of all was the "Semper Augustus," a flower with stripes of red and white. It brought a king's ransom.

The speculation had come to an absurd wave of buying and selling, a period in Dutch history known as *tulip mania.* Theories of what really produced the most beautiful flowers were plentiful as were recipes for sale that "insured" the bulb would produce such magic. Money, cattle, and even entire farms were put up for collateral in anticipation of valuable new varieties. Some speculators with a winning bulb gained a fortune overnight. Others were just as quickly impoverished.

In 1636 there were some hints that the financial stability of the tulip business was becoming undone. A year later, the roof fell in. It was the world's first market crash. The province of Holland and the entire Dutch Republic slowly recovered from recession. By then, prices for tulip bulbs had reached a point that a commoner could afford. Nevertheless, the financial crash created a plethora of moral literature aimed at the greedy and the gullible. It pointed out the folly of believing in future plantings without the blessing of the Lord. Of interest, a family emblem created by R. Visscher featured a tulip with the words, "A fool and his money are soon parted."

At the time of *tulip mania* and long after, no one knew that the beautiful patterns of the blossom were caused by an infection. An agent responsible for diseases of plant viruses was not discovered until 1930 when crystals were isolated from a spoiled tobacco leaf. The crystals transmitted to normal plants induced the disease. The discovery sent shock waves into the scientific and religious worlds: how could a particle no more impressive than a crystal of sugar or salt be alive and capable of causing infection as had been proven in bacteria? The electron microscope, invented in the late 1920s, made possible a look at the agent, now called a virus. And so, the beautiful streaks on a tulip that commanded the whims of Dutch society and its money was the work of a virus. The tulip, infected or not, is still beautiful.

CHAPTER 5: DEAD MAN'S BREATH

5-34 Discipline at Sea

Tight living space in any situation causes tension. On a tall ship, the tension was obvious. The main worry of maritime officers was mutiny (the big *M* word on a ship). On long journeys, mutiny was not uncommon. After all, the men were required to perform tasks that were unpleasant in the extreme day after day. Often, they were on board against their will or were induced to sail by deception. Moreover, and not to be overlooked, the sailors greatly outnumbered the officers.

Command relied on heavy disciple and savage punishment for offenders. Jan Maat (the common name for a Dutch sailor) worked all day and in any weather at any job regardless of hardship or danger. He obeyed without grumbling. He was otherwise beaten into submission.

What offenses were serious onboard ship? Stealing food, beer, rum, or water was a biggie—also a quarrel or fight with a shipmate or another person. Seasoned sailors knew better than to spit, drop a bucket from aloft, or use disrespectful language to an officer. Over-friendliness observed in a pair of sailors was more than just frowned upon. The most serious offense, however, was any behavior suggesting that a sailor was organizing others to rebel against the officer.

The shipmaster ruled by threat of frightful punishment, typically under full view of the entire crew. Even a humane master doled out or allowed his officers to inflict dunking to near drowning, flogging, or chaining ("in irons") with only stale bread and water for days on end. Although known as a kindly shipmaster, Captain James Cook, on his great ocean voyages, occasionally meted out back-lacerating lashes on misbehaving seamen.

5-35 Chiprock Reach

A navigator estimated the speed of a ship with a simple device known as the "chip." It was a triangular piece of wood with lead weights, all attached to a thin line. When tossed into the water from a moving ship, the chip's drag made it nearly stationary, (similar to a kite aloft, pulling along the line). On the line were knots or markers at measured distances. These played out as the ship moved forward for one half a minute, measured by a sand glass. The number of knots pulled out was then counted and multiplied by 120. This number gave the speed of the ship in "knots per hour." From speed was calculated the distance traveled. The method, known as "dead reckoning" was not very accurate because of the variability of winds and current.

5-36 Dead Man's Breath

Every sailor dreads those helpless times when there is no wind. Ships on ocean journeys are becalmed for days, meaning they do not move. Sails hang limp. There is an eerie silence. Deprivation and boredom reign. When the calm goes on for days, tensions rise among crewmembers and officers worry.

There is no better description of a calm at sea than in Samuel Taylor Coleridge's famous poem, *The Rime of the Ancient Mariner* (1798).

Drop down the breeze, the sails dropped down,
'Twas sad as sad could be;
And we did speak only to break
The silence of the sea!
All in a hot and copper sky,
The bloody sun, at noon,
Right up above the mast did stand,
No bigger than the moon.
Day after day, day after day
We stuck, nor breath nor motion;
As idle as a painted ship
Upon a painted ocean.

Water, water, everywhere
And all the boards did shrink,
Water, water, everywhere
Nor any drop to drink.

A calm at sea is now called the doldrums, meaning dull. A 19th century word, it applies as well to the mental state of listlessness or, more plainly, down in the dumps.

5-37 Cross-Staff

The cross-staff is a simple instrument that performs a huge job. Invented by Arabian navigators in ancient times, it has a vane (or cross-piece) that slides along a "yardstick." The observer lines up the vertical vane so that the bottom is on the horizon and the top is on the sun or a star. The measured distance on the yardstick then provides an angle. The degrees of the angle, calculated by trigonometry, are noted on a chart. Knowing the degree derived from the sun at noon or the Polar star, the navigator can tell his position on a north-south axis with an amazing degree of accuracy.

Having to look directly into the sun was a decided disadvantage of the cross-staff. Many observations about noontime were necessary to determine the exact moment when the sun reached its highest point in the sky. The task could not have been good for the eye. It may be the reason why the pirate is so often depicted with a patch over one eye. A later variation of the cross-staff mercifully overcame this problem by using the shadow of the sun to determine its maximum angle between sun and horizon.

The cross-staff had other problems as well. It required the observer to line up top and bottom of the vane at the same time. Of course, when the sky was overcast, the cross-staff was useless.

The sexton, invented in the mid-1700s, has replaced the cross-staff. It has both a mirror and a pointer that move along an arc. Modern ones have added a telescope for more precise viewing.

5-38 Position on Earth

Latitude: The position of a ship in relationship to the north and south poles was determined with fair accuracy by shipmasters of old. For example, a ship coming from Hoorn and going to New Amsterdam could be guided remarkably close to the entrance of the bay between Long Island and Sandy Hook. The key was a point in the sky that was constant in reference to the position of the ship. This point was the North Star, a star of average brightness but one of extraordinary importance. Also called the Pole Star or Polaris, the North Star being directly over the North Pole does not move with all the other stars revolving around it. In effect, the North Star is "a nail in the heavens."

Observed from the Equator, the North Star lies on the horizon and is referred to as zero degrees. Directly under the North Star is 90 degrees. New Amsterdam, the destination in our story, is at 41 degrees latitude.

The North Star can be located on any clear night. First locate the Big Dipper, the most obvious grouping of stars. Using the two stars at the outer edge of the bowl, count five distances away. That will bring you directly to the North Star. It is the last star in the handle of the Little Dipper. While the dippers change their positions throughout the year, their bowls always seem to be pouring something from one to the other.

The North Star is 2,000 times brighter than our sun. It is only due to its great distance from earth that it appears as a rather unobtrusive star. While a good telescope can pick a close companion star, NASA's Hubble Space Telescope has identified a third star, even closer. Thus, Polaris is part of a triple star system.

An overcast sky at night, of course, rendered locating the North Star impossible. What navigators used, instead, were the sightings of the sun at high noon. These observations required a persistent eye to follow the sun until it reached its highest point in the sky, then started to descend. From the angle between sun and horizon at high point, position was determined from a chart. This method was inaccurate at best, challenging on a rolling ship and useless on a cloudy day.

Longitude: Since there was no fixed reference point equivalent to the North Star, knowing one's location in a transoceanic voyage along an east-west line depended on determining speed and distance. The variability of winds and currents made such determinations inaccurate. What was needed was a ship-borne clock. Because the earth rotates 360 degrees in a day (or 15 degrees each hour), a workable clock could keep track of distance covered. However, the only available clock, pendulum-driven, was impossible to use on a ship in constant motion.

Not being very sure about the ship's east-west position meant that it could literally bump into land during the night or in dense fog. Many ships came to grief because the navigator was unsure of his position east-and-west. For example, in 1707, a collision with one of the Isles of Scilly off Land's End, the southwestern coast of England, wrecked an entire fleet of ships with great loss of life.

What was needed was a marine chronometer; this was basically a clock that functioned accurately during the rolls, pitches and yaws of a ship. Such did not come into use until a century and a half after our story. After many years of dogged work, an English clockmaker, John Harrison, put his masterpiece on a ship making a transoceanic journey to Jamaica in 1761. By knowing the time on arrival, the navigator determined the distance between origin and destination within two geographical miles.

With a reference point of zero degrees longitude at the Royal Observatory in Greenwich, England, Hoorn in Holland is 5 degrees west. To reach New Amsterdam, proceed along a latitude of 40 degrees until arriving at the longitude 74 degrees west. You will then be smack dab in the Lower Bay of New York between the end of Sandy Hook in New Jersey and Rockaway Point in New York. Turn right, head through the Narrows in the Upper Bay of New York, and you're almost there.

If you tell a taxi driver in New York City that you want to go to North latitude of 40 degrees 45 minutes and 21 seconds and West longitude of 73 degrees 59 minutes and 11 seconds, you might expect to be driven to the intersection of Broadway and 42nd Street. Chances of arriving there are better, however, if you instead simply tell the driver the name of the place.

5-39 Amsterdam

This great city began in the Middle Ages as a fishing hamlet on a peat bog at the mouth of the Amstel River. A dam built across the river protected it from flooding while canals served as inland roads. Low-lying lands called polders reclaimed farms with dikes and water-pumping windmills. Trading with a good business sense and staying out of war spawned an economic boom. By 1600, *Amsteldam* (and later Amsterdam) was the "Venice of the North," the most powerful and richest city on Earth with its own canals.

Success heralded a Golden Age of commerce, agriculture, and art. Amsterdam became the center of the shipbuilding industry and shipping in the transoceanic trades. The fishing industry had far-reaching impact owing to know-how in preserving its catch. Amsterdam, too, was a focal point for political sophistication, tolerance of religious diversity, and intellectual growth.

Here in Amsterdam came the sugar, tobacco, and furs from the New World; pepper, cinnamon, cloves, nutmeg, and ginger from the East Indies; and silks and porcelains from China. Trading companies sold many of these goods to other European cities in return for things that the Dutch Republic lacked, for example, timber from Norway. Calling 17th century Amsterdam home were dozens of inventors, scientists, artists, and writers. They designed and made instruments for navigation and science, for engraving maps and making illustrations, and for printing and publishing. They also created works of art and literature. One can justifiably say that the Dutch contributions to world progress in the century was second to none.

5-40 The Fur Trade

In the 17th century, beaver pelts fetched a high price in Europe. Hats and coats made from them were highly fashionable as well as warm. Shoes and slippers made from beaver skins were prescribed for people who suffered from gout.

The biggest marketplace for Dutch ships carrying beaver pelts was in the German states and Russia, where the native furbearers had already been killed off. Of course, it was the wealthy, ruling class who could afford such luxuries.

When beaver garments were worn for a while, the long and lustrous outer "guard" hair was worn away, leaving the thick and plush inner layer. Even this became matted and shabby after long wear. The enterprising Dutch brought them back to the Netherlands to make felt. These were manufactured into broad brimmed hats as seen in Frans Hals's painting, *Laughing Cavalier.* The process involved steaming with a mercury vapor and smoothing it out with a hot flatiron, not the healthiest occupation in the world.

5-41 Scurvy

The scourge of long sea voyages was scurvy. We know it as a disease mainly affecting the formation of collagen in connective tissue. Lack of ascorbic acid or vitamin C in a steady diet of cured and salted foods over many weeks results in bleeding of skin, throat, internal organs, and gums (with loosening of teeth). These signs are often preceded by lethargy and depression, leading to the common notion on tall ships that idleness was the cause of the bleeding. With more prolonged dietary deficiency, death occurs from internal hemorrhage. It can be said that in the age of sail, lack of vitamin C caused more deaths among ocean travelers—officers, crews, passengers, and soldiers—than all the shipwrecks, drownings, battles, injuries, and illness put together.

Mariners blamed scurvy on sea air, cold, constant moisture, lack of washing, laziness, and a myriad of other possibilities. It was long known that sailors with scurvy would recover quickly once landed and provided with fresh food. There were early suggestions that scurvy could be prevented by eating certain foods. These seemingly radical ideas, however, were largely ignored.

In 1536, when Jacques Cartier and his crew were stranded in the frozen St. Lawrence River, they nearly died from scurvy. The shipmaster described the miraculous cure provided by friendly Indians. Their treatment, most likely, was boiled hemlock or spruce needles.

Captain James Cook rediscovered the effect of native curatives for scurvy by reading of Cartier's experience in Canada. On his second voyage into the Pacific Ocean (from 1772 to 1775), he saw to it that his crew received good nutrition and that good hygiene, as understood at the time, was maintained. Not one person aboard his ship died from scurvy. Yet, even this evidence, in addition to a controlled study (the first in medical history!) proving the beneficial effect of lemons in preventing scurvy, did not prompt the Royal Navy to provide citrus fruit for several decades.

5-42 Compass

Surely, the compass is one of the greatest inventions in navigation, going back to the Chinese in the 11th century. Arabian shippers made good use of it. Europeans learned to use it during the Crusades.

The compass is little more than a metal piece suspended in air or on water that points to the magnetic fields in the poles. The first compass may have been a needle magnetized by a lodestone resting on a straw that floated in a wooden bowl of water. The lodestone is a magnet, drawing particles of iron toward it at one end and repelling them at the other. When rubbed over a metal needle, it magnetizes the needle. The free-moving needle then points to an iron-rich North Pole. Columbus found that it pointed not exactly to the North Pole but rather to a constant place somewhat off exact polar north.

To keep level on a rocking ship, the compass sat in an arrangement of rings and pivots called "gimbals." Over time, a brass bowl replaced the wooden bowl. A glass cover prevented spilling. The whole system for housing the compass was known as the "binnacle."

Sailors in the age of sail were mistrustful of anything they could not see, feel, or readily understand. Their skepticism regarding nautical instruments and their suspicions of witchcraft led navigators to keep the compass out of sight.

CHAPTER 6: DRAGON'S BREATH

6-43 Storm at Sea

Ways to predict weather before the science of meteorology were notoriously inaccurate and susceptible to all the folklore of the day. Warning of storms at sea was of most concern and fierce weather could come quickly. When it did, the crew faced one of the greatest of challenges of all.

With a storm of sudden onset, each man had to scramble to some task. Some were high up furling sails in a raging wind and tossing ship. Others closed all portholes and entryways. (The nautical expression of "batten down the hatches" now means for landlubbers, "get ready for trouble".) Anything of substantial weight on deck and below had to be securely tied; a cannon loose in the hull of a tossing ship could soon destroy it. The stress on the boards could separate seams and then lead to leaking that would require continuous working of the bilge pumps.

In heavy weather, it was necessary to prevent the ship from turning sideways into the wind, risking capsize. Steering, then, put great pressure on the rudder and on the whipstaff. Sometimes more than one man was needed in a strong wind to control the whipstaff. When this was the case, the helmsmen were lashed to their post so that a wave breaking onto the ship would not sweep them away. Being "pooped out" refers to spending a stormy night at the helm. (At some point in maritime history the whipstaff was enclosed in a protective housing, thereby reducing the danger to the helmsmen.)

CHAPTER 7: SHIP'S LOG

7-44 Ship's Log

Mariners of old were seldom historians. Yet, the shipmaster's day-by-day account of a voyage is among our most important historical documents. A log kept on every sea-going venture provides us with information concerning ocean currents, the whims of weather, sails set, and estimated speed. It precisely listed the cargo as well as the daily status of expendable provision such as food. Perhaps of most interest to the modern reader are the thoughts of the recording officer and the notable human events going on aboard. Injuries, sickness, and problems requiring disciplinary action were described. The shipmaster also mentioned the sightings of other ships, whales, and other unusual phenomena along the way. Of course, the ship's log was a treasure in geography.

CHAPTER 8: DEVIL'S BITE

8-45 Dutch Luck

The natural resistance against scurvy that Dutch sailors seemed to enjoy might not have had anything to do with genetics. The advantage, in fact, was probably because of something they ate: sauerkraut. Sauerkraut is prepared by pickling shredded cabbage in brine, not by boiling or baking that destroys heat-labile vitamin C. Marinating cabbage in heavily salted water and allowing acid fermentation destroyed some, but not all, of this vitamin.

Dutch sailors readily accepted sauerkraut as a substantial part of their fare. Because cabbage is fed to hogs, English sailors turned up their noses at it. Certainly, this most humble of all foods had no place at the English gentleman's table. Captain Cook, however, appreciated the anti-scorbutic value of fresh cabbage; he attributed the success of his Pacific Ocean voyages in the 1770s partly to his insistence that every crew member eat it.

8-46 Cape Cod

Cape Cod is aptly described as an arm. The long peninsula comes with a bent elbow, a wrist and a hand beyond. Ships heading for New Amsterdam on a latitude-bearing of 40 degrees but off a little to the north may run into the forearm of Cape Cod.

This miscalculation is what happened to our Pilgrim Fathers in 1620 who were on the way to build their "shining city on a hill" somewhere in Virginia. The *Mayflower*, however, arrived in sight of Cape Cod toward nightfall on a cold November day. Shipmaster Christopher Jones encountered a heavy head wind on turning south and worried about the widespread shoals around Chatham, the elbow. He chose instead to go north and around the wrist to find safe harbor for the night. And, as they say, the rest is history.

8-47 Lower New York Bay

The Hudson River pours into the Atlantic Ocean along a deep trench. Ships coming to New Amsterdam from Holland on an accurate north-south track will first see Sandy Hook dead ahead. With its east-west position determined by less accurate measurements of longitude, Sandy Hook is the location where ships and land could meet at night or in dense fog with disastrous results. Shipwrecks here prompted merchants to build an oil-burning lighthouse on the point in 1764. A replacement lighthouse still stands at the site, the oldest in the United States.

The Federal Government eventually assumed responsibility for safety of ships entering New York, building the more substantial lighthouse in 1828. It sat on a high rise in Navisink, behind the barrier reef of Sandy Hook. In 1862, a pair of lighthouse towers replaced it, each having a distinctive look: one square, the other octagonal (to resemble the king and queen of chess). The Twin Lighthouses also had a distinctive night signal, one blinking, one steady. The power from their enormous lenses was amplified with a series of reflectors. Certainly, an approaching ship would clearly identify its position, day or night. The change from oil-burning to electrification came in 1898.

For a long time, the beacons from the twin towers emitted the brightest light in North America, visible up to twenty-two miles out at sea. Today, they no longer guide ships into New York. One of the towers has become a museum, along with the Sandy Hook Lighthouse, hosted by the National Park Service.

8-48 The Narrows

Between Brooklyn on the east and Staten Island on the west, there is a one mile-wide gorge that connects the Lower Bay with the Upper Bay. Giovanni da Verrazzano, an Italian navigator sailing for the French aboard *La Dauphine,* entered the Narrows in 1524, calling it "Santa Margarita." From his brief look at the Upper Bay, Verrazzano concluded that it was a lake.

From the Brooklyn side in 1776, a few cannons fired on an overwhelming British fleet coming to quell an uprising in the Colonies. Across the Narrows on Staten Island, the invading force quickly captured a small stockade set up by rebels. With a history of conflicts, or threats of conflicts, over the years, these two sites morphed into massive fortresses, Fort Hamilton in Brooklyn and Fort Wadsworth on Staten Island.

The forts still stand, but today the Narrows is dominated by the largest suspension bridge in America, completed in 1964. At that time the name of the bridge was incorrectly spelled, showing one *z* instead of two in the name of the Italian navigator. In 2018 the error was corrected, and the name officially became the *Verrazzano-Narrows Bridge.* Of interest also is an engineering fact: the two towers on the bridge are a few inches farther apart at the top than at the bottom; this discrepancy takes into account the curvature of the earth.

One morning each November, about 45,000 people gather to run across the bridge as they begin the New York Marathon. The race covers all five boroughs of New York City in 26.219 miles. It is a time when the least accomplished athletes can compete in the same event as the most accomplished. The winners (who often come from Ethiopia) cross the finish line in Manhattan's Central Park in little more than two hours; others are just puffing across it during the 11 o'clock (p.m.) newscast.

8-49 Upper New York Bay

In the Upper Bay of New York is Liberty Island with its great statue standing tall since 1886. In the words of Emma Lazarus, "I lift my lamp beside the Golden Door," referring to nearby Ellis Island where fifteen million people first set foot as new Americans. Farther east is Governors Island, the first trading post between the Dutch and the Indians. Today, during summertime, the island becomes a visitor's Happy Place with free ferryboat service, a fort museum, arts and crafts, sports, biking, and, arguably, the best views anywhere.

8-50 New Amsterdam

Of course, the most famous of all islands is Manhattan, home of the Manhattoes tribe in the south and the Shorakkopochs in the north. A long Indian pathway that went diagonally along the length of the island's highlands is now Broadway.

8-51 Washington Heights

The highest geographical point on Manhattan Island is Washington Heights. It was here on November 16th, 1776 that General Washington watched helplessly from across the river at Fort Lee as British troops, in their final push to rid the island of revolutionaries, wiped out a large part of his army. Today atop Washington Heights in a more tranquil setting is the Cloisters. Here can be seen the medieval art collection of the Metropolitan Museum of Art.

Fort Lee and Manhattan were connected by the George Washington Bridge in 1931. The little red lighthouse, famous in children's literature, still stands at the foot of the bridge on the New York side. It is a marker of the power of citizen's preservation movements.

Over the years, countless stories on and around the GW have accumulated. One memorable incident occurred in 1960s when the pilot of a light plane, running out of gas over the Hudson River, landed on the upper roadway with only small damage to one wing and none to the bridge or to vehicles trying to cross the bridge at the same time. This incredible feat of airmanship, however, did not please the New York State Bridge Authority or the Federal Aviation Administration.

Another famous incident, later called "Miracle on the Hudson" by the news media, occurred on January 15, 2009. An airplane that had just departed from La Guardia Airport in Queens, N.Y. hit a flock of Canada geese. With damaged engines and loss of power, Captain Chesley Sullenberger and co-pilot Jeffrey Skiles made an emergency landing, gliding the plane to a safe landing on the water. This news-riveting event occurred just south of the George Washington Bridge. Everyone was rescued by nearby boats. The incident was described in the 2016 biographical film *Sully*, starring Tom Hanks.

8-52 Harlem River

Water from Long Island Sound combines with water from the East River to form the Harlem River. It joins the Hudson River at the northern tip of Manhattan Island, entering in or receiving water from the river according to the rising and falling tides. Rapid currents come with this exchange, prompting the name of the outlet of "Spuyten Duyvil Creek" meaning, some say, despite the devil. The river's name, incidentally, is taken from the 1658 village of *Nieuw (New) Haarlem* in New Netherland. It, in turn, was named after Haarlem in the province of Holland.

The Harlem River was once little more than a wandering stream. Crossing at one bend in the stream, where it was possible to wade across at low tide, was a wooden span call Kings Bridge. In the early 1900s, the stream was straightened out and deepened to make way for barges carrying coal from Pennsylvania, loaded at Kingston and then carried down the Hudson River to Long Island Sound.

8-53 Palisades

One of the most awesome sights along the Hudson River is the Palisades. It is a sheer, high wall of bare rock, exposed by an ancient geological fault and by continuous weathering. The rock is basalt, formed in the outer layers of the earth surface through volcanic action. Enormous columns of the rocks lean back. The large vertical cracks between the columns give the appearance of the protective fences of wooden stakes placed around a village or fort; for this reason, they are called "palisades." This enormous wall stretches from Bayonne, New Jersey in the south forty-eight miles north to the Tallman Mountains in Pomona, New York.

Before 1900, many up-scale houses sat at the edge of the Palisades. For a time, there was a massive hotel there by the name of The Palisades Mountain House. In 1900, the states of New Jersey and New York created the Palisades Interstate Park Commission to protect the cliffs from residential and commercial growth. Now it has no houses or hotels and is entirely recreational with some pull-offs along the Palisades Interstate Parkway on the west with terrific views of New York City and farther north.

Because the wind most commonly comes from the southwest, it blows across the Palisades, and is too high to have a predictable effect on a sailing ship. On the other hand, wind from the east blowing toward the cliffs bounces back, causing erratic behavior for the mariner.

CHAPTER 9: THE NORTH RIVER

9-54 Chiprock Reach, Again

A nautical reach is the length a sailing ship can proceed in a river without need to adjust the sails. A reach is determined by the prevailing direction of wind and the width and depth of water. The Hudson River, with its greatly varying topography, deep and shallow places and swooping or sharp curves, had several reaches, perhaps fourteen altogether from the lower river to Albany. The Dutch tended to give them picturesque or at least descriptive names. The "Devil's Horse Ride" and "World's End" give some idea of the respect that the navigators had for the challenge.

In the Hudson River, the first reach area begins just north of the Palisade chain of cliffs. It depends on the usual wind coming from the southwest. This reach extends from the George Washington Bridge to the Governor Mario M. Cuomo Bridge (formerly, the Tappan Zee Bridge). The name "Chiprock" comes from the fragments of basaltic rock that fall from the Palisades. This property made the rock valuable for providing gravel for building roads and almost led to the destruction of The Palisades. It was the visionary effort of woman-activists in 1900 that led New York and New Jersey to establish the Interstate Palisades Commission, preserving this scenic treasure.

9-55 Saw Mill River

This tributary, the Saw Mill River, enters the Hudson River at Yonkers. During the early settlement years it was a vigorous river, cascading over rocks before gushing into the Hudson. It was here in 1646 that Adriaen Cornelissen van der Donck built sawmills. The property, 24,000 acres, some of it overlooking the Spuyten Duyvil Creek, had been a gift from the governor in New Amsterdam for his help with Indian negotiations in Albany. Van der Donck was a lawyer and visionary who appreciated the great resources of his new country beyond a place to get furs. His book, *A Description of New Netherland* reflects the interests and sensitive observations of this "Renaissance man." He wrote of the beauty and grandeur of the diversified land, rich in timber, minerals, farmland, safe harbors, animals, flora, and climate. He knew and admired the Indians and was conversant with their language.

Van der Donck's sawmill and waterpower foreshadowed Yonkers becoming one of the industrial giants in the young country. The name of the city, incidentally, comes from Van der Donck's title of "Jonker" meaning young lord or gentleman. The *J* in Dutch, as in German, is pronounced like an English *Y*.

9-56 Bridges Over the Tappan Zee

The Hudson River, proceeding northward, suddenly widens to almost three miles across, certainly looking like an inland sea to the Dutch mariners. The name *Tappan Zee* means Tappan Sea. The native people living on the west side were the Tappans, speakers of an Algonquian language.

In the 1950s, a bridge called the Tappan Zee spanned South Nyack on the west side and Tarrytown on the east side. In addition to its grandeur and gentle *S*-shaped curve, the bridge was noted for a special feature. Seventy percent of the weight of the center bridge was carried by floatation. Eight city-block sized cement boxes that were filled with air lay on the gravel bottom, providing its buoyancy.

Despite its unique design, the Tappan Zee was not designed to last more than fifty years and, in time, the increasing number of vehicles passing over it daily raised safety concerns. Construction of another bridge began in 2013. The new one, named the Governor Mario M. Cuomo Bridge, is a dual-span twin bridge, one of the widest in the world. The west-bound lanes opened for traffic in August 2017 and the east-bound lanes, in 2018.

9-57 Sing Sing

Sinck Sinck was a rocky hill of granite with a sprinkling of mica. It is an Indian name that refers to a "place of many rocks." Sing Sing prison opened for business there in 1826. It was modeled after a stone-quarrying prison in New Hampshire. The intention was to give inmates a disciplined occupation that would somehow turn them into ideal citizens on the release. A by-product was the sparkling stone that faced many churches and government buildings, both nearby and on Manhattan Island.

9-58 Croton Point

Many Indian tools such as spear points, scraping tools, and stone knives have turned up on this curved peninsula, jutting out into the Hudson River at its widest point. Those skilled at relic hunting still find Indian artifacts on Croton Point. Middens here have oyster shells dating back 7,000 years, the oldest documented Native American site on the North Atlantic seaboard.

Here in 1645, the Dutch signed an "agreement of peace" with the resident Kitchawank tribe, called the "Treaty Oak." By the end of the century, Stephanus van Cortland had purchased the peninsula. Since then, under the Underhill family, it has become a vineyard (establishing the first commercial winery in the United States) and a giant industry in brickmaking. Later, Westchester County developed a modern midden, dumping its garbage here for decades in what was called a "landfill." In the 1990s, the immense mound was finally capped with grass and deep ventilation tubes, leaving a gently sloping, exhaling hill.

Croton Point, today, is a haven for birdwatchers, hikers, historical-archeological museum-goers and those who treasure a quiet scene with wide vistas. In late spring, the stillness is happily interrupted with the "Clearwater's Great Hudson River Revival: A Music and Environmental Festival." The *Clearwater* is a replica of a 17th century Dutch sailing ship designed for easy handling, large carrying capacity, and shallow water.

9-59 Hudson Highlands

Passing northward with Haverstraw on portside and Peekskill on starboard, a ship enters the Hudson Highlands. On portside is a mountain called Dunderberg, a variation of Dutch *Donderberg* or thunder mountain. According to Dutch sailors, goblins created baffling winds with thunder and lightning storms, thereby giving them more work on board. The stories were probably the source of Washington Irving's tall tale, *Rip Van Winkle,* where Rip runs into tiny men bowling and making a drink that cause him to sleep for twenty years.

Anthony's Nose comes up to the right, or starboard. Rising almost straight up from the river, it is blessed or cursed with the strangest name in the world for a mountain.

Back on portside, straight across the river from Anthony's Nose, is Bear Mountain. Connecting the two is the Bear Mountain Bridge which was started in 1924. It is a suspension bridge that accommodates walkers as well as vehicles and the views from it are spectacular! In addition, this area is of historical interest. Two battles in the Revolutionary War were fought here: one at Fort Clinton on Bear Mountain, the other at Fort Montgomery, just north of the Popolopen Creek. Fort Clinton was demolished in order to make room for the new bridge. Fort Montgomery is now a State Historic Site and open to the public. The outcome of the battles? The rebel forces were overpowered by the British troops, resulting in a British victory.

Getting past West Point in the west and Constitution Island on the east requires sailors to make a sharp turn to port and then to starboard. With changeable swift currents and notoriously fickle winds, this place in the river became known as "World's End."

What was once called Turk's Head is now Breakneck Mountain. It presents a face of jagged stone that has become one of the best sites in the United States for hikers wanting a challenging climb and a fantastic view at the top.

In 1846, quarry workers who were mining granite for building blocks, packed the mountainside with too many barrels of gunpowder. A gigantic explosion followed that blasted away the whole southern side. With it, the face of stone came tumbling down.

The Unicorn passed Storm King Mountain on the larboard, where today a road cutting across provides a magnificent view of the river. Seen from the eastern shore, however, the same road appears as a scar on an otherwise pristine natural scene.

Here, the ship emerges from the Hudson Highlands and enters the wide and placid river between Newburgh-Beacon. The chain of mountains continues with Beacon Mountain to the right and extending to the White Mountains in Vermont.

9-60 Leadsman

One arduous task of the common sailor was that of leadsman. When entering a shallow, uncharted water, the leadsman would toss overboard a lead weight attached to a rope. He would next haul it back in as soon as slack in the rope told him that the weight had touched bottom. From the length of rope taken underwater, he could determine (or "sound") the depth. Knots in the rope measured one fathom, equal to six feet. The process, he would repeat non-stop until finding deep water once again.

Some lead weights held animal fat in a hollowed-out end. Gravel, sand or mud adhering to the fat revealed the condition of the riverbed.

9-61 Claverack

On the last long reach on the way to Fort Nassau, sailors could detect the smell of clover (Dutch: *klaver*) wafting across the river. The name "Claverack" stuck even after English displaced Dutch as the language of the traders and settlers.

CHAPTER 10: FORT NASSAU

10-62 Fort Nassau

The Dutch built forts in far-flung areas of the world and named them mostly Fort Nassau. These forts were typically substantial, worthy of the name fortress. Thick, masonry walls had turrets jutting out from each corner, each brimming with cannons. Moats or other barriers may have surrounded the fort. From within, traders enjoyed a high degree of safety as they bartered with small numbers of natives admitted inside at any one time.

History has seen a Fort Nassau in the Caribbean (Bahamas; Curacao), in South America (Guyana), in Africa (Senegal; Ghana), in Asia (Indonesia), and in North America (Delaware River in Gloucester City, New Jersey).

Far different from the imposing Dutch forts elsewhere, however, was Fort Nassau on Castle Island, near present-day Albany, New York. It was a wooden structure of very modest proportions sitting in a partially cleared field. A palisade, two cannons, and some swivel guns may have given some semblance of a fortress. Safe trading meant keeping on friendly terms with the native population. Humble as it was, Fort Nassau on Castle Island was the first Dutch building in what would become the Empire State of New York. Its existence, alas, was brief: from 1614 to 1617, owing to a perfect storm of spring flooding.

CHAPTER 12: MAHICANS

12-63 The Mahicans (Mohicans)

The Dutch paid little mind to the individual groups or tribes of native people who lived along the North River. To the intruders, they were all "River Indians" or "Maaquas." Yet, distinctive tribes did exist, and each tribe had a personality.

The Mohicans, whom the Dutch called "Mahicans," were a population of several tribes, all speaking the language of the Algonquins. Their living space ranged from along both shores of the Hudson River north of the Highlands to Albany and east into Connecticut and Massachusetts. The Wappinger and Housatonic tribes, each with their own chiefs, were Mohicans. What the Dutch called the North River and English called the Hudson River the Mohicans called *Muh-he-akun-nuk.* Their single compound word means "Great River having Mountains" (beyond the falls at Cohoes).

Note is made here of spelling: Mahican or Mohican. Old Dutch charts use the first-named. The people themselves prefer the second. Because the principal figure in this novel is Dutch, the spelling Mahican is used. The stories in the companion books, however, are told through the eyes of Native Americans. In these, the people are referred to as Mohicans.

CHAPTER 14: MOHAWKS

14-64 Mohawks

At the time of the European intrusion, the Mohawks lived mainly along the eastern part of the Mohawk River, what they called *Te-uge-ga, Ga-o,* or "at the Forks." Cohoes Falls was *Ga-ha-oose,* meaning Wrecked Canoe. Their word for the Hudson River was *Co-ha-ta-ted-a* or "Great River in Constant Motion."

A century or more before, the Mohawks pledged to an agreement with other nations along the Mohawk River: the Onondagas, Cayugas, Oneidas and Senecas, all speaking the language of the Iroquois. The purpose was to end wars between the tribes. Hiawatha, the chief of the Onondagas, brokered the deal that became known as the Iroquois Confederation. The inspiration came from Deganawidah, The Great Peacemaker, from the Huron nation along the Saint Lawrence River. Conflicts with tribes outside of the Confederation, however, continued.

The Mohicans negotiated a temporary rite of passage with the Mohawks when their own supply of beavers was exhausted. This truce, it appears, was honored but short-lived.

Regarding the hairstyle: An Indigenous man in the northeast often shaved his head, leaving a "roach," or narrow strip of hair that ran in the middle of his forehead to the nape of his neck. He made the hair stand straight up by applying animal grease. The style is now known as the "Mohawk."

CHAPTER 15: A BRIDGE

15-65 *Sint Nicolaas / Sinterklaas*

A tradition over many centuries in the Low Countries centers on the cult of Saint Nicholas, a bishop in Turkey who lived in the 4th century AD. St. Nick was known for his good deeds (although few have been documented). Over the centuries, the myth of the bishop's goodness grew. Always pictured as old and gaunt, wearing a religious robe and miter (a pointed headdress with fore and aft faces) and carrying a crozier (a curved staff), the bishop lives on in the Dutch mind. December 6 in the Netherlands is the feast (or name day) of Saint Nicholas, or *Sinterklaas.* This date is the anniversary of his death.

On the evening before the feast of *Sinterklaas,* that is, on *Sinterklaasavond,* a man dresses up as the bishop. Before he arrives in his horse-driven wagon, children at home have already prepared for his arrival: they have left some hay or a carrot in a shoe just outside the door for the horse, and have spread out a white sheet, fully anticipating gifts to be there come morning. *Sinterklaas* will leave sweets and fruit for the good children and a birch switch for the bad ones. In addition, a child may find a chocolate letter (the initial of his or her first name). One notes, parenthetically, that this holiday has nothing to do with Christmas and the birth of the Christ child.

The Dutch brought the cultural icon of St. Nick and his feast day to New Amsterdam. The modern image of Santa Claus, however, is very different. It came from the pen of Clement C. Moore in "A Visit from St. Nicholas." On December 23, 1822, the poem appeared anonymously in *The Sentinel*, a newspaper printed in Troy, New York, then a small town just upriver from the first trading post, Fort Nassau. The poem about a "right jolly old elf whose tummy rolled in glee. His eyes —how they twinkled! His dimples how merry!" later became a book, illustrated by Thomas Nash, during the American Civil War. The image of Santa Claus has changed little since that time. The serious and scholarly writings of Moore on religion, philosophy and politics have been overshadowed by the poem that begins "'Twas the Night Before Christmas," which the author termed "a mere trifle."

15-66 Cabin Fever

The curse of isolation in a small enclosure for long periods is known as cabin fever. The fever is a combination of loneliness, boredom, and restriction of body. It has ended in untold disasters in snow-bound people. Alcoholism, depression, carelessness, and lethargy are the symptoms. When more than one person shares the same cramped space for weeks or months, tension can result in quarreling and, sometimes, fighting. Cabin fever is not a condition to be taken lightly.

15-67 Magnifying Glass

Light passing through a pane of glass with parallel surfaces does not change direction. If one makes the glass curve out on one or both surfaces, light will bend toward the center. In a round lens, the waves of light passing through converge onto a point. This is the principle of the convex lens. The greater the curvature of the surface, the closer the point comes to the lens.

The eye has an internal convex lens that adjusts the point of focus according to the distance of an object viewed. The ability of this lens to bring things close, unfortunately, is limited. This ability slowly decreases with aging. Ask anyone in the later years of life who finds reading more difficult without reading glasses or as one says, "needing longer arms." What the magnifying lens does is bring things closer to the eye. In this way, additional details of an object in focus can be observed.

15-68 Firearms

Before the invention of cartridges for firearms, making gunpowder explode in the chamber depended on a spark. The matchlock used a lighted fuse. The flintlock, instead, fired the gunpowder by a friction-made spark caused when a piece of flint in the hammer scraped against a stone or metal surface. Pulling a trigger released the "cocked back" flint. (The word *trekker* in Dutch means a trigger or puller.) This invention provided much more rapid firing. The term "lock," incidentally, comes from earliest development of firearms when a locksmith was the craftsman most familiar with how the mechanism worked.

CHAPTER 18: THE FALLS

18-69 Cohoes Falls

About a mile from where it empties into the Hudson River, the Mohawk River gushes over an immense 1,000-foot ledge of smoothed out rock, creating a waterfall or cascade of about 90 feet. The Mohawks referred to it as *Ga-ha-oose* or a similar name, meaning "Place of the Falling Canoe." It was here that the *Haudenosaunee* or Iroquois Confederacy was created, thanks to efforts of Deganawidah, the "Great Peacemaker," Hiawatha, and Jikonhsaseh (or Jigonhsasee), the "Mother of Nations." (This event is described in Book 2, Chapter 17 of The River Quintet.) Today a plaque commemorating the peace pact can found at Falls View Park on North Mohawk Street, Cohoes.

The builders of the original Erie Canal in 1825 had to make a way around the falls. Later a mill was built, and because it depended on waterpower, it sapped another good portion of the river's flow. Before these diversions, or despite them, Cohoes Falls was a spectacular sight, in fact, the premier tourist attraction in New York. It remained so for decades until the railroads made it easy to get to Niagara Falls. Today most of the river is channeled off to support the New York State Barge Canal, but after a heavy downpour and the melting of Adirondack snow in spring, Cohoes Falls still can put on a pretty good show.

CHAPTER 19: THE TREK

19-70 *Castor Canadensis*

Changing the environment to suit individual needs is not exclusively a human trait. The beaver excels at it. It prefers to live surrounded by water in a self-made lodge having an entrance underwater and a level platform above water. To achieve this safety of design, it exhibits amazing skills of engineering and adaptation.

The beaver first selects a low-lying wetland. It builds a dam across a stream, using logs, branches, rocks, grass, and mud. It also seals off any areas around it where running water is heard. Thus, a pond takes shape. Somewhere in the middle, the beaver deposits a huge mound of wood and mud high enough to protrude several feet above water level. It then chews out an entrance and atrium. Here, tightly knit mates and their kits will live throughout the seasons, well-protected from predators other than humans.

The beaver is admirably equipped for the task of dam and lodge building. Sharp incisor teeth and clawed front feet specialize in cutting and moving trees and branches. Webbed hind feet and a scaly, paddle-like tail make it a superb swimmer, though ungainly on land. A coat of plush fur, waterproofed from an oil-producing gland, and a thick under-layer of fat keep the beaver warm in and out of water. It is the soft fur, in fact, that was the undoing of the beaver. During the heydays of the Dutch colonies in New York, more than 10,000 beaver pelts were shipped to the Dutch Republic every year. Some years, it may have been ten times that many. The beaver is now protected by the State of New York.

A beaver is a strict vegetarian. It eats inner bark, buds, leaves, cattails, apples, and water lilies. Its handiwork provides for others in the food chain: ponds becoming habitats for fish, turtles, birds, insects, and a variety of plants.

19-71 Glen Falls

Most notable in the river's topography at Glens Falls are the rapids and the flat-topped slate "tables." Once a raging torrent punctuated by great islands of limestone, the river at this site was called *Chepontuc,* a Mohawk word meaning a difficult place to get around. Over time, the current carved out narrow and deep caverns in the soft, mid-river rocks.

It was in one of these cavities that James Fenimore Cooper set one of his most memorable scenes. In the *Last of the Mohicans* he writes of two English half-sisters, Cora and Alice Munro, the British army major Duncan Heyward, and frontiersman and scout Hawkeye, along with the Mohican Chingachgook and his son, Uncas. While fleeing from bloodthirsty Hurons, these characters vanish in the cavern behind falling water and remain well-hidden from their pursuers. This story takes place during the third year of the French and Indian War (more properly called the Seven Year French and English War) with each country battling for a lion's share of the continent.

Modernization has tamed the mighty rush at Glens Falls. First came a dam. Sawmills diverted water to power their saws, making boards out of millions of tree trunks that floated downriver from the Adirondacks. Today, National Grid, a multinational utility and gas company, taps into the falls to serve the region with electricity. Yet, the falls, even with the industrial alterations, are still an awesome sight.

One of the stone tables at Glens Falls provides the footing for the bridge that passes over the falls. There is also a place called Cooper's Bridge Overlook where one can get a close view of Hawkeye's secret hiding place. Placards alongside tell something of the story.

19-72 Rockwell Falls

One of the most stunning geographical sites on the Hudson River lies between the towns of Lake Luzerne and Hadley where the downflow gushes into a gorge between bedrock and where a rocky cliff alongside projects over it. The cascade is truly awesome after heavy rains and/or rapid snowmelt from the Adirondack Mountains. Long ago, glacial eddies carved out deep potholes in the bedrock.

A sawmill and a gristmill once made good use of the water spilling over Rockwell Falls. Both structures are gone now. All that is left of a major tannery just upstream is the foundation with a huge, stone chimney. Here, well into the 20th century, bark from hemlock trees that were floated down from the mountains supplied tannic acid for turning cow hides into leather.

Rockwell Falls is easy to see from a narrow bridge that connects the two towns. Locals call their river at this point "The Gateway to the Adirondacks."

19-73 Blue Ledges

When entering Blue Ledges in Minerva, one finds oneself suddenly in an enchanted land. Shallow water rushes over and around boulders that stud the riverbed, throwing up great "rooster tails" with its splash. The roar of tumbling all around stirs the soul.

On one side, toward the north of the now east-west flowing Hudson River, the forest provides a tranquil setting of hardwoods and lichen-covered rocks on a floor of moss. The woodland there rises gently from the shore.

Opposite stands a steep cliff 300 feet high. A few evergreens decorate the wall here and there. A slender waterfall plunges from the top. Across its face, there is a blue cast formed by a thin layer of algae.

19-74 Harmen Meyndertsz van den Bogaert

One of the historical treasures preserved from the Contact Period in North America is a journal by a Dutch barber-surgeon. In it, Harmen van den Bogaert provides a detailed description of observations made during the first recorded extended trip deep into the land of the Iroquois.

In 1634, the supply of pelts brought to Fort Orange dried up. The Dutch suspected it was because the Mohawks were trading instead with the French farther north. The West India Company sent twenty-three-year-old Van den Bogaert along with two others westward to see what was happening. The narrative is mostly devoted to the hardships of slogging afoot in mid-winter along the shores of the Mohawk River. Yet, it provides us with invaluable glimpses of native villages, food, language, burial sites, and rituals, including treatment of the sick. On New Year's Eve, the travelers fired three shots "in honor of the year of our Lord and redeemer JESU CHRISTO." And yes, they did find evidence of Mohawk-French trading, including doors on longhouses with iron hinges.

The journal has survived by a miracle of happenstance, long hidden with the Company's archives in Amsterdam, then passing from hand to hand back in America. Eventually, a collaborative work by a Dutch linguist and an anthropologist translated the journal and provided extensive historical notes, published under the title *A Journey into Mohawk and Oneida Country 1634-1635* (Gehring and Sterna).

CHAPTER 20: THE LOOK-THROUGH STONE

20-75 Chief

The women of an Iroquois clan chose their chief. They also had the power of dismissing him should he prove inept. In this way, the authority of the clan was distributed between genders in an insightful way. The "blue lines" of heredity had no place in the leadership and privileges of clan hierarchy.

Furthermore, the chief had no stronger vote than any of the others in the counsel. Nor did he have veto power. It is clear that the chief exercised his authority through diplomacy, convincing others of the right path to follow in any big decision.

20-76 United Provinces of the Netherlands

The low countries of western Europe emerged from the Middle Ages under rule of the Holy Roman Emperor. German Protestants brought new religious ideas to these mini-states or provinces. In 1579, the northern provinces came together in an agreement known as the Union of Utrecht to defend themselves against the army of Catholic Spain. These seven provinces became a republic, a form of government not known since ancient Greece. After the French invaded the Dutch Republic in 1795, they renamed the nation the Napoleonic Kingdom of Holland. The provinces gained their independence in 1813 and adopted the name United Provinces of the Netherlands. Presently, it is officially called the Kingdom of the Netherlands.

20-77 Dutch Artists

Along with the political revolution in the Netherlands of the 17th century came a revolution in the arts. Painting especially reflected the change, emphasizing the reality of everyday life rather than emotional aspects of religious art. Dutch artists painted not only the wealthy but also the poor, warts and all. They painted children and pets. They painted the working person, a subject ignored by artists since the time of the ancient Egyptians. Dutch painters also delighted in material objects, creating exquisite paintings of pewter jugs, flowers, white pots, and other commonplace things. They created landscapes as well as cityscapes, with scenes of people on ice, on farms and in towns. In their nautical paintings, they showed in detail ship design and rigging, ships at anchor, and ships on calm seas and in storms. They enjoyed trying to reproduce on canvas the texture of cloth, the tone of flesh, and the tricks of light.

The attention of the scientific community also was drawn to the phenomenon of light. The Dutch made major contributions to the field of optics by constructing lenses for improving eyesight and lenses to magnify (the so-called "flea glasses"). It was during this time that they invented the telescope and the microscope and, as asked by Victor Hugo, "Which of the two has a grander view?"

CHAPTER 21: STRAWBERRIES

21-78 Calamity Brook

The mountain stream known as Calamity Brook is one of many that feeds into Hudson River in Tahawus. A small pond lies along the way. It was here in 1845 that an investor and developer of the Adirondack Iron Works, David Henderson, came to look for a source of waterpower that could support the mining industry. During a break in the arduous trek, his pistol discharged accidentally. His death led to the name Calamity Pond and later to that of the stream. Now, identifying the site is an eight-foot-tall stone monument to Henderson; oxen had to haul it there on a sled over the snow.

21-79 Venus

The planet Venus is brightest just before sunrise and just after sunset. The popular names of Morning Star and Evening Star have referred to Venus throughout the world at least since recorded time. Of the heavenly bodies, it is second only to the moon and sun in prominence. It is the only planet named for a female and given unworldly female characteristics. Venus was the Roman goddess of love. She came to symbolize beauty and fertility, as well as love. Folklore and poems through the centuries do not spare the analogies.

Venus and the Earth are similar in size, gravity, and rocky composition. They are both young planets, as suggested by the relatively few hits from meteors, the "impact craters." Science fiction long championed Venus as the place beyond Earth where life existed. This fantasy was squelched in 1962, however, when the United States space probe Mariner 2 (soon after the Soviet Sonet Verera 4) determined that the surface temperature of Venus was extremely hot. We now know that it is about 860 degrees Fahrenheit.

An extremely rare celestial event occurred in June of 2004 and again in June of 2012 with the "Transit of Venus." The planet passed across the sun and became visible as a very sharp dot on the solar face. This phenomenon happens with two transits separated by eight years. More than a century goes by before the pair will recur. Previously seen in 1882, the transit will not happen again until 2117.

CHAPTER 23: THE CHASE

23-80 *Toxicodendron Radicans*

Poison ivy is easily recognizable throughout North America. Its leaves are shiny and almond-shaped, with two of the leaves opposed and the third by itself at the end of the stem, forming its characteristic three-leaf appearance. Some of the leaves may have notches, making them resemble mittens with thumbs. The plant flourishes in poor soil, often where there is little sunlight, filling in the bare spots in the woodlands with light green in spring and turning darker as summer passes.

Some plants are ground-hugging shrubs. Others like to climb, clinging tightly onto the bark of trees with hair-like rootlets until they reach the treetop. In spring, *Toxicodendron* has clusters of delicate yellow-green flowers. These provide protection for butterflies that may seek a haven from predators. Animals, with perhaps the exception of goats, do not eat the leaves. As the first plant to take on autumnal colors, *Toxicodendron* provides brilliant reds, oranges, and yellows in the forest canopy. In winter, its bare stems have waxy, white berries that some birds in a frozen woodland appear to find delicious. Botanically speaking, *Toxicodendron* is a relative of the mango and the cashew nut.

There is another side of the coin. Human contact with any part of the plant will result in a terrible itching rash. More than one camping trip or trek into the woodland or backyard romp has resulted in varying degrees of cutaneous misery. The skin involved may be limited to that making direct contact, often appearing with tell-tale streaks and with tiny to giant blisters. Sensitive persons sometimes develop the rash in more distant areas of the body. Those with exquisite sensitivity wind up with swelling of the neck, ear lobes, and face. Eyelids, in fact, can be so swollen, seeing between them is temporarily impossible.

Poison ivy is stubborn to treat. Limited cases are best soothed with bland creams. The juice expressed from the stems of jewelweed is a time-honored natural remedy. Cortisone-like medications used topically or systemically accelerate healing. In any case, treatment always includes a strong dose of patience. There are several common sayings that offer welcome advice for people on the trail, such as: "Leaves of three, let them be. Leaves of five, let them thrive."

23-81 *Mephitis Mephitis*

We know mephitis as the skunk, a house-cat sized mammal with a very retiring nature. Everybody knows the skunk from its jet-black fur decorated with white streaks. A narrow strip of white begins at the snout and ends at the crown. There, on top of the head, a triangular-shaped patch of white leads to a broad white strip down the back, splitting into two nearing the backside and joining again out into the tail.

A skunk will eat anything that comes its way: insects, reptiles, amphibians, small mammals, berries, nuts, and mushrooms. A mother is highly protective of her kits and an adult male is more threatening. The trait for which this animal is most famous is, of course, its horrendous stink. The spray can be ejected at an adversary as far as ten feet. The odor, from sulfa-containing chemicals, is so strong that a sample diluted one hundred million times can still be detected by the human nose. Predatory animals, including the bear, learn (or are hereditarily programmed) to give the skunk wide berth. The skunk's only serious predator, in fact, is the great horned owl which lacks the sense of smell.

Skunks appear reticent to use this ultimate weapon. When threatened, they may first hiss, stomp feet, arch the back, or turn away. If these warnings are ignored, a squirt of its legendary trademark is likely to come next. The Abenakis named the animal*: seganku.*

23-82 *Impatiens Scapiflora*

Jewelweed grows in wetlands often alongside poison ivy. A tall plant, it is recognized by its yellow or orange horn-shaped flowers. Its seeds mature in small pods that, when ripe, pop open and broadcast the seeds a considerable distance. Just touching the ripened pod will cause it to explode. This feature gives it the common name "touch-me-not."

The extract from the crushed stems of jewelweeds have long been a favorite herbal remedy for poison ivy and insect bites. Here's where tradition and science depart. No benefit from jewelweed rubbings on poison ivy rashes has been documented in credible control studies. Herbalists, on the other hand, profess its healing properties. One can find tinctures and soaps containing jewelweed extracts on the internet.

CHAPTER 24: THE FLOOD

24-83 Spring Floods

Spring is a time that challenges the catchment basin of the northern rivers due to the thawing of snow and ice. When rain accompanies the thaw, the pressure is amplified. In the Adirondack Mountains, the perfect storm of these events is created when a very cold winter is followed by rapid spring warming with heavy rain. These conditions have caused the Mohawk and Hudson Rivers to overflow their banks.

Since recorded history, the region has known severe flooding. When good parts of downtown Albany and Troy came underwater in the 1920s, the State legislators decided to do something about it. They underwrote the making of a dam in the Sacandaga River in Hadley, New York not far from where the river pours into the Hudson River. The dam, completed in 1930, extended the water-holding capacity of the reservoir to 41.7 square miles. Even this enormous project does not always prove secure enough when serious storms appear. For example, Hurricane Irene brought a deluge to the entire watershed in August of 2011. In Troy, a local newspaper reported that the *Dinosaur BBQ* dining deck was flooded up to the windows.

CHAPTER 25: DESTINY

25-84 Aalsmeer

In the Middle Ages, the city of Aalsmeer, not far from Amsterdam, was once a small fishing village. The name, from *aal* (eel) and *meer* (lake), tells the story. Extensive digging up of peat had led to land being replaced by lakes and ponds. A system of dikes and windmill-driven pumps, however, reclaimed most of the below-sea-level city. The polder proved favorable for agriculture, with strawberries the first major crop. The flag of Aalsmeer reflects this history: a red strawberry on a background of green for leaf and black for soil.

Flower-growing soon followed as a thriving industry. Farmers then brought their produce on barges to Amsterdam for sale. Over time, and with the development of greenhouses throughout the countryside, growing flowers changed from a seasonal to year-round industry. Aalsmeer gradually changed into a center for selling and buying produce.

Today, Aalsmeer is known as the Flower Capital of the World. There in one of the world's largest commercial buildings, is a daily purchase by auction of more than 20 million flowers. The number increases around Mother's Day and Valentine's Day. Flowers also come in from South America and Africa and from other European countries for redistribution. Access to the world market is nearby, at the Schiphol Airport.

CHAPTER 26: REFLECTIONS

26-85 The Dream Quest

At an early age, the Iroquois boy had to find his identity and true grit. He was put out in the forest alone for an extended period to survive on his own. During those trying days, he may have had a dream, coming as a visitation from the spirit world. On returning, he told the shaman of the clan all he could about the dream. In turn, the shaman interpreted it. This interpretation helped to explain the boy's basic character and the expectations of him as a man. The dream quest process had an aura of secrecy. Consequently, little is known of the details.

www.ingramcontent.com/pod-product-compliance
Ingram Content Group UK Ltd.
Pitfield, Milton Keynes, MK11 3LW, UK
UKHW041634190726
13854UKWH00006B/2482

9 798989 906321